St. Catherine's Flower

St. Catherine's Flower

By
Runs on the Wind

To Contact Author, Email:
runsonthewind@hotmail.com

A division of Squire Publishers, Inc.
4500 College Blvd.
Leawood, KS 66211
1/888/888-7696

Edited by Christina Guest and Tara Gavin

Cover artwork by Iveth Jalinsky
A collection of Iveth's art will be available April 2002
entitled "Iveth Jalinsky 2001 Edition by Manuel Solano."

Copyright 2001
Printed in the United States

ISBN: 1-58597-110-3

Library of Congress Control Number: 2001093884

A division of Squire Publishers, Inc.
4500 College Blvd.
Leawood, KS 66211
1/888/888-7696

For my Mother

      my Grandmother

            her Mother....

Book I

Morass of Cathys

I

SOMETIMES the light isn't real light. Sometimes it's fake, as fake as a plastic flower. Like St. Catherine's Flower. It isn't plastic it's real, it just doesn't exist – that's why it's fake. Sometimes the light is just like that, a created thing made to fool us into thinking it was something like truth.

Sometimes it drapes itself around the plants and the pictures and the furniture like real light. Sometimes, when you're looking in the mirror the way Kathy was now, hard and searching, it wraps itself around you as well as sunshine could. But, then again, even sunlight isn't real light – as real as the kind of light Kathy had once seen, anyway. But that was a long time ago and right now the dull, dirty yellow that lit her reflection wasn't even close, it even smelled bad. That's how you know when the light is real or not, by the smell.

When it smells like this light did, like old piss and rust water and fecal matter that was stuck to stained porcelain, then you knew for sure it wasn't real light. She looked up and sniffed toward the single bulb that hung by its own electric cord and flickered off and on it was so fake. Sometimes, when the light isn't real light, it's ashamed of itself and tries to turn itself off. That's what happens when light bulbs burn out, only most people don't realize it. But the light knows it's better that way. Because sometimes, when the light isn't real light, it's worse than darkness.

The toilet made a noise like it was about to flush and she jerked her head around, but no one was there. Behind her stood an off-white stall that housed the toilet, next to that a chest-high urinal running all the way to the floor. Yellow and brown marks stained the base near the drain and the waxy puck that sent out a perfume when the warm piss hit it, but it smelled worse than what it was trying to cover. She turned back to the sink where the faucet dripped in a continuous slow stream, it could never be completely turned off and left streaks in the basin from the years of rusty water that poured out of it.

Katherine looked into the mirror, her beauty lay untouched by stains on the glass and the decrepit surroundings. She put three fingers to her cheek for the smoothness on her hand as a sure wind blew open the window above the urinal. Then it stopped and the window shut again. She could see it in the reflection.

The hinges were on top and it didn't have a lock, so whenever the wind blew the window would bang against the frame. It was almost like stained glass or glazed or something had been done so you couldn't see in or out of it because it was the men's room and all. Not that anybody would want to stand out in the back alley all day just to watch some guy piss. That was the worst part about being in the men's room, when guys came in to piss – that, and the smell.

This particular wind was real, but it can be fake too, just like the light. Sometimes, when you're lying on a hill or an open grassy area and you feel a breeze, then suddenly there are thoughts in your head – that's the wind.

Real wind will whisper something true and needful to you when it blows by. It's soft and clean and it will leave you better than you were before it came. False wind will whisper too, but it can whisper only lies, and it'll come and go and you're left just about the same as when you started. That's how you know if it's real or not, by the lies. And if you can't tell the difference between a lie and the truth then you're fucked from the start, and you probably always would be.

It really isn't the winds' fault, though, a false wind *is* a lie, so how could it tell anything but? It means well enough, it's just lonely like everybody else and looking to strike up a conversation. It talks to truckers mostly – seeps in through tiny spaces between doors and windows, comes whistling in like a teapot boiling.

And that should've been the first sign. It should've been a red flag that this wind was just created by fast driving and not by an act of God. Its hiss should have alerted those truckers long before it had a chance to fill their heads with lies, but they're so doped up on caffeine and cigarettes there's no way they could see that those voices in their heads were really fake wind talking. You can see where the danger lies. When you start listening to voices in your head and they're not really yours and they're not really Gods, it can be only one other – Satan.

Then the shit can hit the fan and fast, and you're stuck cleaning up a bunch of shit out of every nook and cranny of your life that isn't even yours – only you're the one who had the fan going. And now you're wondering why you never thought to turn it off – when the same thing kept happening over and over again.

In the mirror behind the dried specks of spit and snot, behind her face that looked smooth and pink tonight and eyes that were luminescent even in the waning light, vague shapes began grouping together – a picture was coming. That happened sometimes. White clouds shaped images from the pressure of a raw, distant stare.

Mirrors were doorways, glimpses into different times and parallel worlds. K never got too close and she never touched them – you could slip inside and end up lost in some other dimension with no clue how to operate your own senses or how to get back home. What was worse was that sometimes the beings in mirrors liked to pull you in, just to fuck with you awhile before they spit you back out – she knew that, she knew it all too well.

Often the scenes in the mirrors were glimpses of the future, hers or somebody else's, and when she saw them, she felt them. K struggled to keep the image from forming. There was only one thing worse than seeing the future – remembering the past.

3

It was dark, the middle of the night, but hot – hot as Satan's piss. Sweat from his brow stung his eyes when he tried to wipe it away, and the moments crawled by like slugs in sand.

"East bound, gotta copy?"

His voice was country and low as he held the mic in his right hand and moved up and down, swayed right to left, his seat squeaking as it moved with the flow of the highway. The long road hours of the night can be relentless and unforgiving, and the weariness in his eyes blurred his vision. A false wind, created by the 70-miles-an-hour with which he bore down the highway west toward Kansas City, creeped into his tractor and numbed his ears as it whistled by. *Sleep*, it was saying. *Sleep*.

His truck was forest-green, *The Furtle Turtle* was stenciled on the door in gold, scripted letters. Patches of condensation formed at the base of his windows, forcing him to turn his wipers on every few minutes to clear them. It was because it was so hot outside is why, and that the air-conditioner couldn't keep up. But the wipers just smeared the remains of the hundreds of dead insects, or so, that had found their way to his windshield, probably drawn by the false light of his lone tractor as it waded through the dark lake of the night.

"Man alive, I gotta race like a pee horse," he said aloud.

Bugs splattered onto his windshield like they just didn't care any-more – dragonflies, butterflies, moths, bees, mosquitoes – but K could tell his favorites were the fireflies. They burst onto the glass like fire-works. And maybe, even though she could tell it was only late June, they were celebrating their own Independence Day – freedom from the life of a bug. They left such a mess it was as if someone were throwing packets of mustard at his truck, or bird eggs.

"East bound Schneider, ya got it on?" He released the trigger, waited for a response. "East bound? Come on Schneider, they're not there to look at!"

"Yeah, west bound, I … uh … copy, come back."

"What's the bear report there, Schneider?"

"Uhmm…Bear report?"

"Yeah, Schneider, seen any bears there over yer shoulder?"

Some time passed before the other driver spoke. His voice was smooth like water. "Uh…no. No…uhm…bears. Uh…lots of cops though! Jesus, cops everywhere. You'd better watch it goin' through town."

"Goddamn Schneider drivers," he said, releasing the mic and tossing it aside. "Dumb as a fuckin' stump."

The mic dangled over the dashboard swaying in the same rocking motion as a cross bearing Jesus that hung from the window seam, and the false wind continued its steady whispers. *Sleep*, it moaned, longingly. *Sleep*.

Kathy prayed he didn't hear. She prayed he knew it was just fake wind talking and not his own tired voice. Katherine looked deeper into the mirror, his eyes were growing heavy and weak.

"Damn, I gotsta pee!"

He jerked his eyes open, reached back to find the plastic urinal that he used when the nights got too long and the rest stops too infrequent. It was wedged between the passenger seat and the dorm-room sized refrigerator behind it and out of arms length.

Normally he wouldn't pull over in the downtown area of a major city. They're not too well setup for big trucks like his and one can often find himself stuck in front of a bridge that's only twelve feet tall or turning a tight corner and taking out a light post. But the way his bladder ached he knew he couldn't make it to the next rest stop.

"Boy, that dumb Schneider driver sure was right – cops everywhere," he said, turning off the interstate. Several slow moving police cars passed him, surveying the area with spotlights. "Must be some kinda manhunt."

He thought about getting out to pee at the side of the truck, but noticed a shadow lurking behind the trailer and decided best just to use the plastic jar and get the hell out of there. He filled the stained-brown container almost to the thirty-two ounce line.

"Thirty-two ounces," he said. "Alright!"

He was proud of that. He opened the window, dumped it to the concrete of downtown.

Then the movie was gone, and Kathy was left talking to her own reflection in the mirror.

"What was that about, K?"

"I don't know, K, I don't fucking know."

She put her fingers to her cheek for the smoothness, then pulled her eyes from the stained mirror and opened the stall door. Her hand ran down the length of the wall to her left. Most of the creative work was done there. The other walls mainly had *fuck you* written on them over and over or had rudimentary artwork of men's reproductive organs fitting tightly into somebody's mouth – usually topped off by the words *blow me,* in case someone didn't understand the picture.

Music is a color that floats like a bird. Life is a flower that smells like my terd.

"Hmm, simple...yet poignant. Definitely Vonnegut," she thought, and scribbled the autograph of Kurt Vonnegut beneath it.

K was pleased, there were new ones tonight. It was why she was in the bathroom in the first place. It was Monday.

Rust water dripped from the flickering light bulb, splattered onto the tiled floor. She looked up, a line of red and brown liquid was coming from a crack on the ceiling and running down the length of the cord to the bulb. The water probably streamed in from the snow that covered the roofs and lined the gutters, melting from the heat of the building. If it wasn't, it was coming from her upstairs apartment which meant she left water running somewhere or had a busted pipe.

The soft drips were steady and methodic. Repeatedly she turned her head to look, its coarse drone calling her focus like a bug on the wall, out of reach. It was maddening, something like Chinese Torture. She'd read about that once. That was some freaky shit, a book on Gestapo tactics and espionage, ways to break an enemy. She had to be prepared. She had to know what people were capable of. Chinese Torture seemed about as bad as anything.

She could hardly imagine it, being strapped to a chair, the water dripping on her forehead every five to ten seconds, the anticipation as harsh as the drops. After a few hours it would be like a drill. "We back in morning," they'd say, their tongues pressed back in their throats, their unsettled accents like Alber's *Transformation of a Scheme.* "See if you ready, talk." She was already ready.

"Uh oh, sloppy grammar is the devil's dialect," K said. Her mother used to say that, she'd always hated it. She still did.

John gives head good! it read, defying all laws of grammar. Kathy crossed out *good* and replaced it with *well*, adding the following comments: *Gives* is a verb requiring a verb modifier or adverb – *good* is an adjective – *well* is an adverb, K.

The search for the meaning of life, in the men's room at Bells' Bar, was a Monday night tradition. After the weekend crowds had come and gone there were usually new insights to be found. She needed them. Someday, there would be a message to her from God. Some thought He slipped into the numb, open brain of a drunk at Bells' that he would scribble onto this wall without even knowing what it meant – and K would be there to catch it.

She was getting close. Sometimes, when the words struck her right, her mind would go blank, distant, putting her in a different place, a lighter place – less definable than her ordinary place. She liked being undefined, where the words people branded her with weren't continuously pressing on her from all sides in burning irons. K imagined her message from God would be like that, these little messages were just preparations.

Paint peeled and chipped in places on the wooden stall that was off-white almost to the point of being yellow. It was hard to tell if the walls were always that color. Judging from the way her hand ran across sticky spots it had rarely been cleaned, if ever. Maybe it had once been white, but she could hardly imagine it. She could hardly imagine that a place as grungy and foul as the men's room at Bells' Bar had ever been anything pure and clean and beautiful.

Against the off-white wall her ghostly hand was neon. One of her nails caught some loose paint and the paint chipped and fell. Her nails were rough, mainly because nail-clippers were a waste of money, the skin surrounding them was peeled and loose.

Feeble hands writing feeble words from feeble minds. We all do the work of the devil, so the devil doesn't have to. Soon he'll be drawing unemployment and living off the people that stole his job. That is mastery.

It almost could have been Sylvia Plath as sharp and laced as it was. Though it was missing several adorned adjectives – *Rust-fingers writing words soaked in sex from rum-besieged minds…* But it was already signed, anyway – The Hyena.

Wind blew open the window again. Snow sprayed in like mist from a crashing wave, filled the small room with the pierce of winter cold. Then it slammed shut, slammed shut again and again, the dissonance sending chills through K as much as the chilling wind.

Another drip fell from the light bulb and she looked at the slick puddle gathering on the floor, dark and slimy like a roach. Patterns on the tiles below spun in a swirl of black lines, each one trying to connect to the other. Some were put together haphazardly and didn't match up with their adjacent tile, making the carefully planned art look like scribbles on a pad by the phone.

A cracked tile near the base of the toilet caught her foot, one part was higher than the other from where the ground had settled. K pressed the edge of her checkered Vans onto its lip, trying to break off a piece of the ceramic, then looked up at the light bulb and rolled her large, rounded eyes in disgust – the smell was getting worse.

She never stayed longer than she had to because, one, the smell got worse the longer she did and, two, because sometimes guys would come in and that was usually pretty awkward. Like she was some kind of bathroom whore, or worse, one of those attendants that sprays cologne on you and hands you a towel, then says *Thank You* for just coming in to use the bathroom.

"Oops, here's a new one!" Her finger had gone right past it.

Jesus loves you, everyone else thinks you're an asshole.

Sometimes words can get lodged in your throat, like a pork chop you didn't chew well enough. That usually only happens when you're trying to say something that hurts like, "I don't love you anymore." Not that Kathy had ever needed to say that, not that she'd ever been with anybody long enough to where she'd have to. But she knew it would hurt if she ever did.

They can get stuck in your heart too. Long before you say them or long after you hear them they'll sit and fester like a dead rat in a sewer. Of course, some words could sit there and bloom like flowers if what was said or heard was soft enough and pretty enough.

Sometimes words can get stuck in your brain. They get in through the dark centers of your eyes or the soft wax in your ears and make you go numb while they look around for a place to land and be understood.

Something like that was happening to K. The words didn't register and the thing that was stuck in her throat was either tears or laughter, she couldn't tell. Where tears and laughter bubble up from is the same place, they only split off when they get closer to the top, just before they spill out of you.

"Oh well," she thought, either way it would need to be changed. Every saying at Bells' had to have an author, no exceptions. That was the rule of creation as far as K was concerned, someone must be behind it. She made the following reparations:

I love you, everyone else thinks you're an asshole – Jesus.

9

Satchmo was pouring his slow, grainy milk out of the speakers at Bells' Bar. *I see trees of green, clouds of white. The bright sunny day, the dark blessed night.* His voice was the air moving through an old, beat up trumpet. He was an old trumpet wailing, and the one he held in his hand was really just an extension of what he already was. But K liked it when he played. She liked both – his trumpet and his voice. The way he sang made small doors open up inside and it was nice to have them open, even for a little while, to let some sun into what was otherwise damp and musty.

Chatter from the bar was harsh, like a window banging. Drunk people had to speak louder than normal people. They had to watch their tongues move in their mouths so spit didn't fly out when they spoke, and sometimes they lost track of the volume. Drunk people had to talk loud to make what they were saying sound important and knowledgeable. That so and so was *definitely* the best defensive end in football – that *all* politicians were crooks. Parrots speak loud. They have to. If they didn't nobody would listen, because it's all been said before.

The jukebox slowed then, like the prickled fingers on a music box being pulled by the next bump or prong as it was winding down. Sometimes it did that. Slowly it would churn the tunes like butter, almost to a stop. The sounds it emitted were eerie and mournful, un-godly, and Kathy's skin would crawl on her body like slugs in June whenever it happened. Louie's voice sounded like mud, the black tar of cold coffee. *What a wonderful world,* he sang, the slow sarcasm was painful.

Out the storefront window snow came down in thin dry flakes, sparkling like shaved metal. She shivered from the view and the chill the music sent through her. It was slow and restful outside, even with the snow that blew like on the tundra, poking your skin like needles, even with the people that scurried down the sidewalk with their last minute gifts. Something about winter and cold slowed everything down, like water to ice.

Kathy was seated near the end of the bar, second to last on the south end, one thigh draped over each side of the stool. Her legs bent around the stool clasping one another like reunited twins, her knees pointed to the dirt and ash on the floor that was never mopped and rarely swept. The floorboards were warped and the deep grooves and nicks scattered about were filled with dirt and ash, making the wood look almost smooth and level.

In her dreams she had lain there. Sliding into a small tight groove like a toothpick, she watched the bar move and breathe above her. Dark suede boots with treads like winter tires in the rubber, a barstool being dragged across her body like a plow. As he stood to leave, hairs stuck out like fir needles on a pine tree under the cuffs of his black jeans, above the pushed down gray socks.

A girl in a shortplaid skirt stood bent over the bar wanting a Heineken, the heel of her shoe like a roller coaster. Her pink skin smooth and dry up the length of her bare, clean legs. Tight white panties rode over the cheeks, brown hairs spilled out underneath like tinsels off a tree. A wet spot in the middle, beautiful — the dew on a cobweb catching the early sun.

The girl stepped and went away. The point of her heel flush on top of K, and smooth. There was no pain and no emotion. She was glass. Life was simpler between the cracks.

K woke up wondering if she was a lesbian, so she asked Becky.

"Everybody thinks that when they see something beautiful in their own sex that they've always been taught was the competition. It's worse for men. That really freaks them out. Women don't care so much. It's natural, don't worry about it, K."

Telling Katherine not to worry about things was like telling a fish not to swim, telling the window not to bang against the frame when the wind blew.

11

"Hey Angel," Bells beamed. K turned her head from the snowy scene outside as he gimped over to the south end of the bar.

"Whatcha' in the mood for tonight?" His voice was worn and tired.

"I'm no angel, and how 'bout a scotch and water."

He grunted – he did that. "You don't like scotch."

"I know. Better use top shelf scotch."

Bells filled a short glass with ice mixing in Macallen and water from the fountain gun, then pushed the drink to her with his thick hand.

"Anything else?" It was the gravely sound of a sword-swallower long past his prime. He was calm, though, not rough and jagged like his voice would make you believe. It was spooky how calm, sometimes it was like he wasn't even there.

"Is there anything else?" she asked, referring to food or snacks or other services that Bells provided. He looked up the length of the raggedy bar to his left, then back.

"Not really," he said, and gimped to the north end. He had a stride like a slight lisp, slurred and awkward.

In the dim light her thin fingers pressed open the pages of a notebook she'd set on the bar. The night before Katherine had written a story. The glow from a candle reflecting off the full-length mirror behind the bar lit the pages orange as she turned them. K didn't often read them a second time.

She raised the glass to her lips sipping the scotch and water that was flat and without sweetness and K remembered why she didn't drink scotch. The translucid tan water was beautiful, though, when held close to the eye. Squares of ice huddled at the top of the glass like pieces of a shipwreck.

She set down the glass, tried to make out the words on the pages through the low light. Most sleepless nights were spent writing, and most nights were sleepless. K would choose about twenty words at random from her Webster's Unabridged Dictionary and create a story around those words. Sometimes she chose a word because she liked the way it sounded.

Sometimes she would open a page and pick the first word she saw.

The words weren't set in stone. She could use variations – prefixes, suffixes. Sometimes she'd use a noun as an adjective, or vice-versa, she knew what she meant. She wasn't a slave to words. People ruled words from atop their thrones on mountaintops or in ocean caves, words were our toys. Her English teachers had gotten it wrong. They bowed down to language and words and structures like they were gold gods with ripped stomachs of steel and sharp angular jaws.

Katherine's gods were made of glass – you didn't have to bow down to them. A child could break them with a baseball bat. You just had to wipe your smudgy handprints off their round Jell-O bellies and the playful smirks on their faces every now and again to keep them happy.

Anyway, she didn't want to know gods anymore. Gods spoke in tongues and riddles, their hats like jester's, their hats like crowns – their hats like thorns. They changed faster than you could get on your knees and pray for a better ending.

The dictionary was her Bible. It was the only truth she'd ever known – the truth of words. Because words were neither a lie nor the truth, it all depended on how you arranged them and the context in which they were used – and that seemed the most truthful of all. When the stories were finished and stored away in a footlocker in her closet, she rarely thought about them again. A finished story was a meal already eaten. The words were chained slaves working the same land, broken and beaten. They might as well have been carved in stone like the tablets brought down from Mt. Sinai.

But something about this one intrigued her. It sang to her like it was still alive, unfinished. The sadness that fell from its pages drooped like the head of an old petunia that was once beautiful, but not anymore. So soft and delicate was its sorrow that she wanted to remain at its side for awhile, just to be there with it, just to be next to it. It was a diary of sorts, the jumbled thoughts of a man on the edge of sanity – and on the edge of life.

13

Pampero – n. A violent wind, usually dry and cold that blows across the South American pampas.

Torque – n. A collar of twisted metal worn in ancient times as a symbol of rank. A force producing a twisting motion.

Torrid – a. Subjected to intense heat, especially of the sun; scorched; parched; arid. So hot as to be oppressive.

Somnambulating – ppr. To walk in sleep; to wander in a trance-like state while asleep.

Procrustean – a. Designed to secure strict conformity by violent measures; by force or mutilation.

Perfidious – a. Violating good faith or vows. Proceeding from treachery, or consisting in breach of faith.

Maraba – n. City of extreme climates located in the northwest portion of Brazil.

Pannier – n. A large basket; specifically a wicker basket for carrying loads on the back.

Whelked – a. Ridged or twisted like the shell of a whelk.

Coolant – n. A fluid used to remove heat, as from a nuclear reactor or an internal-combustion engine.

Pate – n. Euphemistic, the head, intelligence, a humorous or derogatory term.

Stringent – a. Binding tightly. Making strict claims or requirements; strict, rigid.

Slumgullion – n. A meat stew with vegetables.

Pidgin – n. A mixed language, incorporating the vocabulary of one or more languages in a very simplified form.

Dialect – n. Any form of speech considered as deviating from a real or imaginary standard speech.

Succubus – n. A female demon thought to have sexual intercourse with sleeping men.

Imbrued – pt. To wet or moisten; to soak; to drench in fluid, especially in blood.

Piddle – v. To dawdle or trifle. Sometimes used with 'away.' To urinate – a child's term.

Catering – ppr. To give what is wanted or required.

*D*eath of a Swan

Week 1

For the first time that I can remember, the night is better than the
day. The pampero night wind that rages through my camp, its torque
kicking up sand in whirlwinds, denies most thoughts of sleep. And the
torrid floor of the desert day makes journey away from my small frail hut
agonizing and pointless. So I sleep days and watch nights. Day sleep has
always been less severe, less chance of being visited by the frightening
dreams I've suffered since my youth.

That's why I left after all. Something about a change of scenery seemed
cleansing. Maybe she wouldn't follow me. Maybe I could lose the ghost
that haunted my dreams and kept me somnambulating about from night
to night.

I always thought it was the worst kind of procrustean act to haunt
dreams. Sleep is such a pure form of trust. To be cheated by one's own
thoughts in such a perfidious manner has somehow lowered my own self-
opinion.

Week 3

Clear. Cold. Bitter, again tonight. Had I known, I wouldn't have
piddled away my matches in that last town outside of Maraba. But the
old woman weighed down with child in pannier seemed to need them
more than I. If for only one more gallon of coolant, I may have made it to
the next town – wherever that is. But then my sense of direction becomes

15

so whelked when I get off the main roads, I have no idea which way is back, and for that matter which way is forward. Or if there is a back to go back to, or if there is forward ahead of me. Only a few weeks have passed and my once strong pate has trickled and become weak and afraid. But at least the dreams have stopped.

Week 7

My life has been a waste, utter and dismal – a tale full of fury and noise told by an idiot, signifying nothing. It was a dream lived by a man behind a velvet curtain, pulling strings; for it certainly wasn't I. I've spent it in fear. Fear owned me, created everything I was. Fear spread across the story of my life like the white on plain paper. There was no joy and no accomplishments, only the stringent doings of a man running from fear. All my work is but a monument to that effect. I was simply catering to fear even though I didn't know it at the time. And now I have nothing to show for a whole life. One life wasted, God. One more life gone.

Week 9

It is daytime now, two weeks since my last entry. Writing seems moot. I've seen no sign that I will be found out here. If the elements don't kill me, I shall surely starve. I dream of feasting on the slumgullion I've always hated. The sight of my succubus friend in her blood imbrued silhouette and pidgin dialect might even be comforting right now.

As I lie here dying, I now know the reality that my running away has led me directly into her arms. As I fall into sleep one last time, I am sure it will be her that I see when I wake.

Her eyes were soft and full as she set the pages down and stirred the thinning ice around in her scotch and water. Sitting there, draped in the near darkness which was Bells', she looked like perfection, an angel sent from God – a sloe-eyed, ashen-faced, raven-haired, straight from Heaven angel. Under the half-moon that peeked in through the storefront window and danced off the glass and mirrors, she looked like soft ivory – like ivory walking, smiling or laughing.

Perhaps she was a spell. Perhaps she had been formed from the tusks of an ancient mythical animal that roamed snowy plains and lived in the icebergs of some child's imagination. Perhaps she had fallen off its wooly face from a fight or from age, becoming old and brittle and had cracked and fell. Perhaps she landed at the feet of a sorcerer who had never had a child, but always wanted one.

And he summoned every last bit of his magic to turn her into something different, something alive – something beautiful. Maybe he used too much magic. Maybe he used all the magic he had to give her life and died in the very effort. Then she grew up alone and afraid wondering why she even existed in the first place. But someday the spell would wear off and she'd have to return, she'd have to give up this fantasy life as a human and go back to being ivory again, a tusk – she knew that, she knew it all too well.

Lights went low at 5:00 p.m. People liked to drink hidden in shrouds. Candles burned, several in the corner attached to the wall in Victorian iron mounts with ruby glass coverings that Bells' had salvaged from a theatrical supply company, a few more under the mirror behind the bar in orange, rippled glass. The smoke rose in a line like the string on a balloon. The wavering lights were hypnotizing. They softened your expression in the mirror, made you think you could be in the movies or, at least, in a magazine – Esquire – GQ – Elle.

Katherine's eyes came out after dark, glowed like lanterns – white, paper lunch bags with silver cupped candles that lined the yards and walkways of suburban homes this time of year. Her eyes looked like they had grown out of a desperate search for light they never found, and then were frozen there, lost and dejected, forever retaining that size, brilliance and sorrow.

Her face was a blank page, her eyes the only words, and they were all you ever needed to know about Katherine of the St. Catherine Catherines. If eyes are the windows to the soul, hers had been shattered long ago – a high pitched scream, a neighbor boy playing catch and a ball slipped away, perhaps she had just rubbed some tears away too harshly and they shattered. Whatever the cause, there was nothing blocking anyone now. They didn't have to stand outside like a pervert looking in, watching the neighbor girl change clothes or trying to catch her in a forbidden moment of pleasing herself.

They didn't have to squint hard to get a glimpse of her essence from outside foggy windows. No, they could go right in – enter like a stealthy cat burglar through open windows on a hot June night. And she couldn't do anything to stop it. She could try, she could look away and pretend that nothing was happening, that someone wasn't entering her every time they saw her. She could pretend that way, but she couldn't stop it, not really.

Flickering light shadowed crooked lines and small indentations at the snowy edges of K's eyes as she brought a stroked match to her full and dark mouth. The flame shone through her cigarette-parted lips to the slight failings of whiteness beneath, whiteness with which all teeth are originally blessed – a small fall from grace. The wavering soft brilliance highlighted dryness and tiny lines in the skin around her mouth that should have been soft and supple at the still lithe age of 28. Gently she took the cigarette to her lips like a nipple, letting the warm smoke ooze down her throat like mother's milk.

K pulled one page of her notebook taut, then let it collapse to the left, the pliable paper swooning like the neck of a swan. She didn't know why it called to her so. Maybe it was because misery loves company and it reminded her of her own haunting dreams – unnerving images she couldn't even remember when she woke. Something about a rift in Heaven, Jesus and God had turned their backs on one another. Off and on for nearly a year the dreams had been coming in waves – growing, growing, crashing, subsiding, growing again. She wished they'd stop. Some things are better left unknown.

"Maybe you're supposed to go to Maraba," she thought, tossing her head back to finish the scotch and water.

"Maraba? To do what? Die? No, no, no – I'm not leaving Kansas City till I have to."

She set the glass down pushing it into the gully across the bar thinking back to how long she'd been there and all that she'd done. It wasn't much, but seven years of her life had been traded for it. Seven sandcastle years had been pulled under the many full moon tides. Seven years of waiting tables at Nichol's Lunch and sitting at Bells' Bar, seven years in the loft above it. Seven years had gone, evaporated, never to be seen or heard from again, and nothing was happening in her life, nothing ever did. Nothing ever would – that was the worst part, realizing that.

There had been dreams, childish girl dreams, really. A house in the hills and one on the beach. She would only need a few cars at each one – one sporty, one that could get her out of town in a pinch – an SUV or 4X4. The luxury an actress or model or poet or writer would afford her.

She had never taken acting classes, done headshots, sat in on poetry readings or submitted any of her short stories to magazines. She supposed someone would have to be walking by and know she was the one, perfect for a role or cover spread. Her poems or stories would be found in a folder in her room – the cable guy, the plumber – his father-in-law had connections. Childish girl dreams, but real. They must have been real because it hurt when they went away, when reality finally came in the form of a beat up bar and a beat up life on the restaurant strip of 39th Street in Kansas City.

"I don't even know my way around Maraba, for God's sake," she mumbled.

Bells was coming her way, lit on one side by the candle against the mirror. In the orange wavers, his eyes were like polished stones. They danced under the light that filtered through the smoke as if they were dancing under a bright sun in an open pasture – as if they were dancing with a beautiful woman under beautiful stars. His eyes danced as if they had just seen God laughing in the moonlight.

They weren't the eyes of a smoke-filled, grungy bar. They didn't belong there. And they didn't belong on his worn, aged body or his weathered face. His eyes were ten years old. His eyes still wondered what it would be like to kiss a girl or to look up her skirt, but would still rather be out chasing frogs in a pond. His eyes were like polished stones and a river flowed from behind them, polishing them even more.

"Need another, Angel?" K smiled at him as he came over, her soft ivory spreading open like the Red Sea for Moses. Sometimes he talked like an old sailor, or a retired boxer. But sometimes he sounded more like a grandfather, someone that could never hurt you – even if he had reason to.

He didn't say much, anyway, but what he did say was always full. His words pregnant, the small sentences barely contained them. And K trained on those words, whether they were to her or to someone across the bar, they were hers – meant for her, she knew that. And she waited for them, watched between sips and clanking balls and glasses. She'd catch one of his full words and it always seemed to be something she needed to hear right at that moment, some life preserver – an orange vest of foam tossed into her life in the ocean.

They were caterpillars and any moment one might explode into a butterfly and become something beautiful, so you had to watch them.

K always thought being a caterpillar was the best part – just before.

The wonder, the expectation, or maybe they didn't even know what could happen and that would be wonderful too. They'd just go to sleep and wake up something different, something beautiful. But Katherine was already beautiful.

Bells was drying his hands with the white rag he always carried over his shoulder or wore sticking out of the back of his pants. Then he placed both hands down flat on the bar in front of her. His forearms were thick and thick gray hair covered them.

The bottom part of an old tattoo stuck out under the left sleeve of the white button-down, short-sleeved shirt he always wore – K-mart, polyester and cotton, 65/35. But he never showed it to anyone and nobody knew what it was for sure. People guessed it was from the time he spent in the Navy. Others thought it was an old love that had come and gone and left nothing to show for it, nothing but a pain that was too much to talk about and the faded black ink that was carved into his skin.

"Hmmm, Hmm," Bells cleared his throat. "Angel?"

K looked up from her blank gaze.

"Oh. I'm no angel, Bells, and give me anything," she waved her hand. "Diet Coke and whatever."

The cigarette dipped drastically from her mouth as she spoke. She grabbed it and took a quick puff with only the right side of her mouth, quickly removing it.

"By the way, the men's room smells like shit. Ya know, Bells, Clorox is only about a buck fifty a gallon, modern technology is truly amazing."

"Damnit, Angel, I told you to stay the hell out of the men's room! It's the *men's room*, as in *for men!* If you don't know the difference between men and women by now, I'd be happy to give you a demo."

Bells grunted his patented grunt that he seemed to fit equally well into any conversation, whether it was meant as an exclamation point, a question mark or just a laugh no one knew for sure. And K rolled her eyes as she often did when she was not terribly amused catching the dark rafts that supported the ceiling – they were casting shadows like sails.

21

"Besides, that's why it's called a shithouse, not a spring rain, not a sea breeze and not no damn rose garden, but a shithouse!"

He grunted again, his low, rough tone tickled her ear like a feather and K had to scrunch up her shoulders, shaking off the ripples that tickle sent down her spine. She took another toke, blowing smoke into the air in a flat line like paper, her tongue against the roof of her mouth, her top lip pulled over her front teeth.

"It's also called a bathroom, Bells, as in *room with a bath* as in *bath*, which implies cleanliness, which is next to godliness and all that good stuff. I think you'd be plenty embarrassed if God stopped in and had to use the pisser."

"I ain't seen God on 39th Street in a long time. And if he should stop by on his way to Armageddon, he can piss in the back alley like the rest of the vagrants." He grunted and limped off to get a can of Diet Coke because that didn't come out of the fountain gun.

I live in the back alley, Kathy thought but said nothing and Bells was soon back with a Jack and Diet in a brandy snifter, setting it down in front of her.

"My savior." K made a wide-eyed gesture to accent her words and pushed her cigarette into the black ashtray with the camel pictures on it until it was crumpled and broken and the red glow was gone.

Bells grunted, throwing up his left hand to swat away her sarcasm, then went back to where he always stood, waiting at the north end of the bar – light falling on him like a halo. K blinked twice before realizing it was the mounted candle on the back wall opening up in a florescent around him. He was usually waiting – waiting to make someone a drink, waiting to clean up, waiting for people to leave so he could close and go home. He had patience like wine.

There were blue herons on TV swooping into the air, a commercial for something – something set at sea. A girl in a sky blue bikini on a thirty-foot yacht, her skin smooth like fruit, her hair full and wind blown, watched the waves crest in curls of white. K didn't know what they

22

were selling, it could have been dog food, anymore. It was probably for breath mints, though. Soon someone would pop a Tic-Tac into his mouth and the sea would turn to ice, snow blowing across the frozen water in a fine mist – cool and refreshing.

Then the game was back on. It was the last of the regular season, playoffs next week. That would mean ten less people wondering in on a Monday night to watch football. The TV was small anyway, a 30 inch screen bolted into the northeast corner up high enough to where Bells had to use a remote so the drunks couldn't mess with it, trying to get porn off the satellite.

The bar sat counter-altar-wise in the long, rectangular room with K near the southern corner, where it cut left closing off the bar against the back wall. With a quarter turn to her left she could look through the large street-front window and watch the pedestrians occasionally bustle by.

She liked watching people, liked to watch them bustle, wondering all the while if they had somewhere important to be, more important than the south end stool at Bells', anyway. They must be special places, mysterious and magical – places so important they could make some-one rush around just to get there. A mansion in a far off land, a king-dom of platinum bricks – diamonds and gold etched intricate designs in the rock. Michelangelo and DeVinci would stand stunned and silent in the awe of it. A strawberry field for a moat, you had to know which ones were poisonous to make it through.

Outside, in the low lands, wolves flew by with griffin wings. Feather-haired archers with gold tipped arrows plucked them out of the sky when they came too close. Cats and their litters of gray and striped kittens sat back watching all the madness, laughing. It would be a better world where cats could laugh – one more mistake on God's part.

Maybe that important place was just home, a nice house with a soft fire going in the fireplace – a fire to lounge in front of half the night until it burned low, glowing in secret murmurs. Then you'd take your last sip from the wineglass that was a wedding gift from your mother-in-law and with your dark-red wine lips you'd say, "Well dear, I think I'm heading to bed." And your loved one would say, "Okay honey, I'll be up in a minute." And you'd kiss that loved one on the forehead and walk up the stairs, looking back once to see their profile moving softly in the embers.

A green strand of tinsel duct-taped to the full-length mirror, like a child's drawing of waves on the ocean, was the only Christmas decoration and it was dull and lifeless from years of use. Christmas at Bells' was like Arbor Day, something passing by unnoticed, a silver streak in the night. When you turned your head to look, it was already gone – leaving you wondering if anything really happened at all. The tinsel was probably supposed to be shiny and twinkly when light reflected off it, but light was hard to come by at Bells'. Even if there were any the tinsel was so covered with years of smoke it probably wouldn't shine, anyway, and it certainly wouldn't twinkle.

The bar itself was a dull polished wood, dark chestnut and chipped and worn from the moisture of spilled drinks and the alcohol they left behind. It was too worn and chipped to do anything fun on, like how in movies they sometimes slide a beer to you down the full length of the bar – that never happened at Bells'. It had deep grooves from the pens people had dug into it to leave their graffiti – two circles with dots in the middle, a likeness of women's breasts. Then, *Bob was here.* Below that, *Fuck you, Bob.* Graffiti ran up and down the bar top behind the black vinyl padded trim that was an eyesore but good on your elbows.

On a blank screen in her mind, K could see the bar in its glory, the thirties, a movie she once saw was superimposed over the picture. The bar top was glossy smooth. The bartender, in a long sleeved pressed shirt of white cotton, was clean-shaven with slicked-back blond hair that looked sandy brown through the grease he used. He slid a beer down to Kathy across the full length of the bar, foamy head spilling over the top.

Mob bosses sat in the corner, territorial disputes. Black derbies and pin-striped suits, bold red and blue ties and handkerchiefs to match in the breast pockets. Soon a fight would break out, she could see it coming. A hit was on. They'd bust through the door machine guns poking holes in the wall like pencils in paper, the last one standing would shape the future of the city. The course of a million lives would be influenced that day.

In the middle, a young couple – newlyweds. Her in a shiny red dress, half-veiled hat with white webbing and a white flower. Him, in his best church clothes. They dreamed of a cottage home outside the city. He'd spend the long winter hours writing a novel. She, raising their two perfect children.

K reached for her drink wanting something in her mouth just then. She fished out an ice cube with her tongue, bit down. Nothing like that ever happened at Bells' now.

You could get laid there, but not fall in love. You could get in a fight, but it wouldn't mean anything. And you could get a drink, but you couldn't get it to slide down the full length of the bar to you. This was Bells' Bar, wood brown with dull lights and too much smoke. It was comprised of Bells, K and two always there drunks who sat at the north end talking a drunken dialect to eachother that no one else understood except Bells, their names were *Drunk 1* and *Drunk 2* – then whoever else wandered in.

The jukebox had re-set after *What a Wonderful World* ended and was running at proper speed. Jefferson Starship, then Santana and now Pink Floyd was playing. Mostly classic rock CD's filled the slots. Some were mid to late nineties – Pearl Jam, Nirvana, Red Hot Chili Peppers, Beck. Two country – Patsy Cline and Hank Williams Jr. A few more big band and blues – Sinatra, Armstrong, Holiday. One classical that was Bells' favorite, a compilation of The Baroque.

The somber sounds of *Wish You Were Here* filled the room. Pink Floyd was one of K's favorites, them and The Doors. They knew how to forge the real into something surreal, twisting and shaping it like hot steel.

"Did you think you could tell – Heaven from Hell, blue sky from pain..." Their song, like mushroom clouds in the sky, spread over the bar. *"Oh, how I wish you were here."* Everyone hummed along in their own way – tapped their feet, nodded their heads. Those were the moments when K felt bonded with the people at Bells' Bar. It was called entrainment, but nobody else there knew that. No one knew why they were feeling soft and warm and connected right then – but that all went away when the song did.

The small crowd had settled into Bells' like strays, ruffled-feather birds and straggly mutts that the full moon tides had dropped at the edge of the world, no longer knowing which way was home. At Bells', one step led toward home, one over the edge, you could go either way. They huddled at Bells' Bar on the eve of the birth of our Lord Christ like the thinning ice cubes in a scotch and water.

In the corner, under the ruby bubble glass candleholders that tinted the far end of the bar a sultry rose, a young man sat down, his long bangs falling over the half of his face. He brushed them back behind his ear halfway down his neck, opening up a view to his large eyes that were brown and warm like an old dog. But his face was sharp and young, more like a cat. He poured the remainder of a Boulevard Wheat into a glass mug and sat back, his fingers in his hair again, taking a long drink as if at the end of something – the end of a long day, the end of a struggle, the end of some project at work.

"How did you miss that *why not?*" Kathy thought, her and Becky's two classifications for men – *why* and *why not.* He was beautiful. Kathy thought he could almost be a girl, he was so pretty to look at. His shoulders were slender and firm beneath a thin sweater that draped over him, conforming to his body.

"You know, it's been almost two months since you've been laid."

"Dear lord, in the dead middle of winter too."

"I know. What is it about winter that makes you so randy?"

"I wish I knew, K, I wish I knew."

Kathy picked up her glass, held it like a chalice in both hands sipping slowly, the sharp sting of liquor on her tongue. She put an arch in her back lifting her butt so as to be no longer flush with the stool, her backside round and inviting against the backdrop of Bells'.

Slowly she took a sip, let the fluid drain into her throat. The first sip of each new drink was always deliberate, flowing into her like a stream. And she'd often whisk away with it, down the stream in a kayak she had made herself – had carved it from the remains of a tree that was planted by the Aztecs or the Atlantians.

Vapors from a waterfall behind her rose high into the air. Being there, in that perfect hidden world, meant that no one could do her harm. It was magic in her kayak, only joy could be found in it, only bliss could be felt inside. All she could see was water in front of her and the greenery from the deeply treed woods that pushed through the smoky mist she was floating through.

The first sip was always that way, the rest just seemed to follow one after another, without much thought, pleasure or poetry. But she always kept drinking anyway.

Near the light that hung between the ceiling rafts, dust and smoke freckled the air. If she looked hard, she could see it in front of her too, settling onto the bar like dust after a storm on open plains. K chipped at one of the few remaining lacquered pieces of bar top with her thumbnail, digging under it till it pinched her skin. He was coming over, she could see him in the mirror through the freckled pieces of air. Inside, she smiled.

It usually worked like that. They were usually at her side within ten minutes of her arching her back and lifting her ass in the air. It almost always worked that way and K was disappointed, he seemed different. He seemed like he wouldn't be so easy, like she might actually have to walk past him a few times on her way to the bathroom and let him see her up close. Maybe she'd even have to pause there a moment and drop something, linger long enough to where he could smell her or start to think about what it would be like to taste her.

And when he swallowed hard, removing all the saliva that had gathered in his mouth, then she'd know where his mind was, where his body was. It was already far ahead of him, alone in a room with K, tasting her lips, biting her skin, licking the underside of her full breasts and thin stomach – his tongue finding its way into her soft navel.

But she didn't have to do all that, he was already there. They were always there ready for her to pluck like fruit off a tree – cherries or apples or something red and full of juice and easy to get to, maybe even, tomatoes. Men were always red around K, wrapped in their hunger and lust. She felt sorry for them sometimes.

Sometimes, when they had a wife or a girlfriend at home, and she could see the hunger building inside them, the cavity at the base of their throats throbbing, needing to be filled like the mouths of hungry street kids, then K would feel sorry for them. God had put some mechanism in men that made them forget all that human nonsense in the eyes of lust and become an animal again.

Then they'd look down at the ring on their finger and remember who they were. That they had someone at home who called them *honey*, another two or three that called them *daddy*. And that was their lives, like it or not, and a romp around the bed with K would last half an hour and then they'd have their whole lives to pay for it.

But what did it matter, the desire was already there. They could suppress it and not do her. But they wanted to, so what's the difference, really?

By looking at his eyes she had thought he was different, hazelnut quartz set deep in his face like they were trying to hide from you. But they were too big for that, much too big. Next time they made eye contact her eyes would have to laugh at his, just to let them know they'd been caught. They couldn't hide so easily, she'd tried that many times.

Kathy would suggest in his next life that he try small, beady eyes or narrow eyes like slits. Those eyes might be able to hide a little better. But his big and brown ones, like roasted almonds in the shell, didn't stand a chance.

He stood to her right, set down his empty mug and looked toward the other end of the bar as if wanting to order a drink – his face crystallized in profile, a Greek statue.

"Like he would come all the way over to this end of the bar just to order a drink," she thought. Then he looked back at K, his brown eyes liquid in the flickering light.

Kathy raised her glass to take a sip, looking briefly up at his face. And she thought that maybe she had been wrong about his eyes. Maybe it wasn't so much that they were hiding, maybe they were searching, just like hers. But they were searching in the wrong direction. They had fallen somewhere behind him to look inside, like a bucket in a well grabbing for water. Maybe the rope had snapped, or a storm had come scaring the person away who lowered it, and the pail remained floating in the dark pool – because it didn't look like his eyes would ever look outside again. And how sad that made his face.

She'd never seen eyes that did that before, that turned away from life as if there were nothing left to see in the world. And K thought it interesting that he noticed her at all.

When he spoke, turning to face her full, his elbow supporting his weight on the vinyl-padded bar, it was like a rose whispering to a blade of grass. Cotton fibers vibrating in the softs of her ears, and K's mind went calm. She was surprised how it made her feel, that it *could* make her feel, anything – especially warm and glowing with just the first few words.

"Did you know that to be considered legally brain dead, a person must lose ninety percent of the function of their brains?" She looked at him but didn't respond.

"The average person only uses about ten percent of their brain, everybody knows that by now. See anything disturbing in those numbers?"

"Not really," she said, glancing into his lorn eyes. She wished she could turn the winch, raise the pail, dip into the water he'd found there, cup it in her hands, spread it over her face.

"No, how could you?"

Her face became tight as she tried to conceal her laughter, it was the best come-on line she'd ever heard. He tilted his head up, looked distant out the window. His breath, deep in his throat, sounded like wind in tall grass.

K looked at the gully between his neck and throat – the rounded Adam's apple, the ripples underneath. The voice of a rose, she thought. She couldn't believe how fragile it was – so bare, so delicate, that if you breathed on it or just walked by too quickly it would simply fall apart. It was as calm and serene as the chirp from a distant bird across misty fields at dawn. But it was more than that. Somehow, it was as if you *were* the chirp from that distant bird and the listener listening to it at the same time, simultaneously, and the separation between the two of you made you long for it even more, it made you want and beg for it to be closer. But if it were, it would destroy the whole thing.

"Did you know it's your own heart beat that kills you?"

Kathy remained quiet, being good with rhetorical questions.

"You won't hear it from any scientist, they're so jaded with knowledge that even when they do get a glimpse of the truth they destroy it in dissections. It's all in Bentov's *Stalking the Wild Pendulum.* Everything is built on frequencies and when the aorta pumps blood it sends out a frequency. When the blood comes back it carries a different frequency. The two different vibrations crash causing a dissonance that ripples throughout the body. Dissonance destroys us, harmony is healthy. Eventually it wears down the body like Chinese Torture, splitting you apart. Your own heart, isn't that a shitter?"

Kathy turned her head, taking a sip of her drink. Between her lips she tongued the rim, she hoped he saw it.

"So really, the only way to live forever," he continued, "is to stop breathing."

She looked his way, her fingers combing her hair slowly, till her head rested on her palm.

"Those lines ever get you laid?" K asked, the mist of his words pulling at her gently.

"Not yet." He shook his head once, pursed his lips. "You're the first one that hasn't gotten up to find a new seat."

She nodded, then turned to look out the large front window, curious as to what was happening outside just then. A couple passed as a gust of wind came on strong, curling snow off the sidewalk in front of them. They huddled together bracing against the wind and blown snow. She pulled closer, he opened his wool coat to shield her and Kathy's fingers circled the rim of the slick glass in slow crescent moons needing to feel something smooth just then.

A pigeon landed on the sidewalk and pecked into the snow. Then it looked up, blinked, and flew away. It must have been something else, what it thought was a seed or a worm, must have been something else – a pebble or shoelace, maybe.

She liked to watch birds, too. Outside and walking on the ground was the best. Birds walking on the ground made her feel connected. She didn't like them in cages, felt claustrophobic just looking at them.

Sitting in a grassy field once in her dreams, she was among them – flocks and flocks of every kind of bird there was. They walked by so close she could reach out and touch them – stroke their heads from beak to crown. It was all she ever wanted from a bird, for them to be walking on the ground and close enough to touch. They would like that too, she knew that they would. But in the waking hours they always flew away before she could get within arm's reach.

In the cold months only a few were left. Owls unseen, hidden in trees. Some stragglers of crows and pigeons that got left behind or stayed with their young, crouching under the gutters of buildings where hot steam rose up from the vents. She wasn't sure why they stayed.

She'd read once, some science magazine left on the bar, how the electromagnetic currents of the planet were shifting. Birds were running into buildings, flight towers, they didn't know which way was North anymore. So some didn't migrate. K didn't know if she believed all that but there was one bird that never left, that much she knew. It was a special bird, a turtledove – she could talk to it. Its name was the 39th Street Bird.

K turned back, the skin on his chest was exposed through his V-neck sweater, a few brown hairs lay straight and soft there like baby's hair. She breathed in deep, trying to capture the scent that escaped from beneath his clothes. It was nice – flat and strong, sweaty. But there was sweetness, too. She looked up to meet his eyes that were looking into hers, long and distant, as if he had found a sunrise hidden there, as if he were trying to know her through her eyes.

"And what, exactly, do you think you are staring at?" she asked, her blank expression painted on with long strokes.

"Heaven, I think."

She couldn't believe the way the words melted out of his mouth. There must have been some fire inside of him the way the words were wet and melted when they came out. His words were like an oil painting he spilled into the air.

"I'm a long way from Heaven, pal."

"Oh yeah? Well then, why don't you tell me what Heaven is?"

She paused for a moment and breathed out through her nose with pouted lips. In her mind she could see mountains and lakes, eagles soaring and angels making love on clouds of pure light. She could see the Taj Mahal, the Sistine Chapel – the ceiling, the art. She didn't know what Heaven would be like for sure, and she was surprised she had never thought about it.

"I think Heaven would be something like toast," she finally said.

"Toast?"

"Yeah, something warm and crispy. You know how bread is just bread and even when you put peanut butter and jelly on it, it's still just peanut butter and jelly on bread. But when, all of a sudden, peanut butter and jelly is put on warm and crispy bread, it turns into something wonderful – like a treat, a dessert." K's hands were up in front of her then, trying to form the words into a picture for him. "A treat out of the most mundane, I think Heaven would be something like that."

His expression softened. "So that's why the seventh commandment reads: *Love thy neighbor like he was toast.*"

32

She chuckled, not at the joke, that was stupid, but at his attempt to humor her. She liked that, how people tried so hard. But he didn't have to, she wished he was a little more intuitive. All this talk was crumpled newspaper padding a Christmas gift. You didn't dig out the papers to read, you just wore the locket, played the music box, or drank from the wineglasses.

"Well Moses," her face mimicked the sarcasm, "if that's what those tablets say, I can't argue. I've never read the Bible."

Kathy's eyes glazed slightly like a cheap donut and she turned away. His musty smell stroked her like a father's hand on the head of a child who couldn't sleep, caressing her with firm hands – hands you could depend on, hands that would hold you, protect you, if you ever needed them to. And when they did hold you, you would find they were all at once firm and strong, yet yielding, supple.

Moses kept talking and Kathy kept pretending like she was listening. It was something about being a trucker, just got back in town, but all the words started blending together in the dewy shivers of his voice.

She wished he would just shut up. She wished he would just bend down and kiss her, let his tongue rest against the vulnerable underside of her upper lip for a moment before he pulled away, stammering – not knowing what to say. It had all happened so fast. Something just came over him.

It's okay, she would say, and she'd put her hand on top of his to let him know she meant it.

Then he'd say, *Can we get out of here?* And Kathy would get up, their eyes locked in a flow of melted butter between them as they went to the door.

"Do you want to have sex?" she asked, cutting one of his sentences short, staring into his subtle beauty, trying to pretend she wasn't lost somewhere deep inside of it.

"Well...I mean," he cleared his throat. "Is this an offer, or are you just curious?"

"Yes or no," she stated deliberately.

33

Moses looked up to the rafts and then back down before answering. "Yes."

"Do you have a car?"

"Yes."

"Great, see how easy life can be when we all say what we mean?" She popped up from the barstool, shaking the stiffness from her legs.

"Bells, watch my drink, back in a few," she waved, yelling to him across the bar. He grunted and waved back, like swatting flies, just to let her know he really didn't give a damn.

The wind pressed dry and sharp snow into the skin of Kathy and Moses, like flakes from a diamond. The snow had come down in drifts, ridges of hardened white cliffs – nature covering up civilization in just a few hours with white gothic and Whitman poems.

He covered up to shelter against the icy wind as K walked to a new, black Toyota Celica parked a few spaces outside of Bells'.

Moses followed and stopped at her side. "How'd you know?" he asked, reaching into his pocket for the keys.

"Please." K rolled her eyes. "You've got Johnson County smeared all over that pretty face of yours."

"Okay, whatever." He opened the passenger door and gestured for her to get in.

K gestured back. "Go ahead," she said.

"But it's easier for me to drive if I'm on the other side."

"Drive? We're not *driving* anywhere, honey." She quoted the word *driving* with her hands as she spoke. "I've got a cold drink waiting for me. Get in."

The wind stung what little exposed skin there was on his body – neck, face, hands, the space just above his short crew socks where the wind ran under the cuff of his jeans. He turned to look up and down the length of the 39th Street sidewalk then half-shrugged his shoulders and got in.

Moses sat down in the passenger seat reaching over to start the car

34

for warmth. She climbed in after him, on top of him, shut the door and pulled down her black, Spandex pants to her ankles. Her pinkish thigh smashed against the door panel, the knob for the window digging into her leg, her left knee riding the stick shift.

"Man, you don't waste time do you?"

K leaned forward putting both elbows on the dash, bucked herself up to meet him. It was exciting to be naked and exposed like that. Her legs fitting around his, pulling her skin wide open in front of him.

She stretched her left hand as far over the smooth vinyl dash as it would go. It was clean and cool and the engine was already getting warm. She could feel the heat through the vents in the dashboard. The windshield was warming up, too. Snow flakes that hit near the base melted quickly, the ones near the top stayed longer, forming pictures that K touched with her right hand – a ghost face, a star, a horse with a white mane and flared tail. She watched them, her eyes only a few inches from the cold glass as he slid a finger underneath to feel her raw slick skin. His hand felt good – sure, smooth. The horse melted, turning into a dog, then some kind of rodent.

"So, what are we waiting for?" she asked.

Moses pulled up her shirt halfway, put his hands on her ribs that were ridges pressed against her skin, then he looked up from his stare.

"I'm sorry, that's about the most beautiful thing I've ever seen."

Good, she thought, *I don't want to waste time trying to get him up.* He unzipped and K helped him pull his Levi's and black bikini underwear to his ankles.

She reached back to find his penis, it was thick, she tried to measure how thick – forefinger and thumb, middle finger and thumb, middle finger not touching thumb – but it wasn't too long, thank God. She hated it when they bumped up against her cervix. It was an intrusion is what it was, as if someone were trying to enter a place they simply did not belong.

He wet the tips of his fingers with his tongue spreading on saliva underneath as Kathy squirmed and grinded, guiding him inside her. It took less than a few minutes before he was all the way in, but it was too long for K. Unless his pubic bone was flush with hers they weren't fucking. Everything else was just foreplay and she could do without any of it and usually did. K didn't know what all those women were always complaining about. *More touching and caressing before. Ooh, hold me after!*

Kathy couldn't care less about any of that crap – *just get up inside me and stay hard till I come, then the faster you leave the better. And if you can stay hard so I can come a few more times, then maybe I'll call you sometime.* But most men couldn't. Well they could, if they tried, they just didn't want to. They just wanted to shoot their frustrations and anxieties into the warm twat of some dumb bitch like her and be done with them. She knew that, she knew it all too well.

"God, you're so beautiful," he said.

She lowered her head, turning on her right side, fit it into the larger space at the base of the windshield, hot air from the defrost blowing through her hair. It was dizzying having her head sideways and smashed between the glass and the dashboard. But dizzy was good. Dizzy was a place to get lost in. Dizzy was a place where the sensations could come and go and dance and play, unburdened by K – the hot, the cold, the smooth thrusts inside her – slick yet firm.

"My God you're beautiful," he kept saying. "You are so ... beautiful."

And she hoped he wouldn't hold on too tight. She hoped he'd just let go when it was all over and be thankful for the small time they had.

You can hold on too tight, K thought. That's when the pain comes. Comes on hard like Jesus on the cross sometime after, *Lord, why hast thou forsaken me* – but before, *Thy kingdom come, thy will be done.*

You could slip away unscarred, keep your hands greased up and ready all day long like K did, or you could leave bits of skin and broken fingernails behind when existence pried you away from whatever it was you wanted to keep. And it always did.

K had never seen anything permanent in this world, though she had tried hanging on to the many, pretty, fast moving brass rails as they had gone by. And it wasn't just dead skin and worthless nails left behind in the wreckage either. It was more transparent but more costly. It was a bloody waterfall pouring out from the center of her heart across the vast wasteland of her life.

She often looked back to see the trail of blood following her like a shadow. But, anymore when she turned around, it was gone. She didn't know when or where it all stopped bleeding. The blood must have been drained dry because she could still feel the gaping hole in her heart her life had left behind.

Oh yes, this is good, thought K. *This guy isn't so bad, as far as men go.*

They fit together surprisingly well for first time lovers, almost like wings – the wings of a giant dove, each one working together in harmony to rise above it all. Rising above 39th Street, this town, this world – skimming the very foothills of Heaven.

Moses moaned, he kissed and licked her back then bit into her softly. His hand reached around and slid up her shirt and found its way into her bra. His fingers were cold. She had almost forgotten about him, that there was another person there, until the coldness touched her nipples.

The force with which he thrust into her grew more demanding. There was a growl hidden beneath his rose whispers, a hunger rising to the surface. A part of him was lost, that's what it was, lost and trapped somewhere deep below his soft voice and gentle face.

And maybe that's why his eyes turned inward – to look for that lost part of him. Just his foot, maybe, was caught in a bear trap at the bottom of a long, winding trail in some mountain ravine in the darkest part of his soul. The trail was cold and hard and animals on the hunt lurked in every shadowy space.

Help! His thrusts inside her were saying, his quadriceps flexing tightly. He was scared and alone and it was getting dark. He may just die out there in that forgotten ravine within. *Help! Someone? Anyone?*

His pleas were carried across the mountain ravine and through valleys and rivers, but there was nobody there to hear. And it was felt through every fiber in Kathy's being, echoing inside, vibrating, exciting her even more.

"Oh God, please … yes," K said. He was without words, just moaned from time to time. Energy was rising inside of her from the base of her spine to her mouth, tingling in her gums. There was a yearning in her teeth – her sharpest teeth, vampire teeth, wanting to bite down into the fleshy part of some animal, like a lion would do or a panther. Her hands clawed, wanted to sink into the vinyl dashboard. It was getting hot in there – too hot. She fumbled for the heat controls, flipping several switches till she heard the fan shut off.

She was getting close – the smell, his smell, their smell together. The cold glass on her left cheek, the hot vinyl on her right. Moses arching himself to go deeper, his pelvis flush with hers as he moved the shaft inside her looking for more friction, a wall to rub against.

"Yes. Don't stop – right there," she said, as the first waves of a strong orgasm erupted from her center, heading out to shore. She bent her left arm behind her and dug her fingernails into his bare left hip. She had found some flesh to dig into. It felt good clawing something like that. She tightened her grip and he gave out a yelp of modest pain.

Then he came, she felt the throbbing inside her. The thrusts were gone, the force of him, the pent-up frustration, his cries through mountain ravines – all gone. Soon she could feel him shrinking inside of her and her ocean wave ebbed, never reaching the shore – goddamn men.

"Goddamn it!" she yelled, pushing up from her spot between the vinyl and windshield.

"God, I'm sorry," he said, panting. "It's just been so long…and you're so beautiful…and you felt so good."

Kathy rounded her back, put her head in her hands, her elbows against the dash supported her – black hair falling in curls and tangles around her ashen face.

"Hey, no problem, no problem at all," her voice was tight and sharp. "I just need to get myself a T-shirt that says *plastic fuck doll* on it…to avoid any future confusion."

In one move she opened the door and slid off his limp penis. With a slight stutter step she moved over the gutter onto the curb.

"Whew, that was a close one," she thought. "Almost stepped on a black rainbow."

She placed her other foot on the concrete and wiped some white fluid running down her thigh with her left hand.

"I'm sorry, can I call you? We could try again."

"No thanks, Moses, go fuck your sheep." She wiped the runny liquid onto his sweater, then rolled up her Spandex pants and headed toward Bells'.

"Another foray into impiety," she said into the air, her breath puffing out like smoke, "and again I'm left dissatisfied."

"Merry Christmas!" he yelled, and K raised the middle finger of her right hand in response as she walked away. There was heaviness in the air, though, something like smog that lay between her and the door and K slowed her pace.

"Maybe I'll just go home, it's getting late," she thought, and turned away from the bar. The lightness in the air came back again as she moved farther away from Bells'.

"Big day tomorrow anyway. We'll have about three or four customers all day, I'll make about six bucks and, whoa – merry fucking Christmas to me!"

In winter, the limbs of willows looked like whips. The bare naked oaks and maples turned old, their sickly limbs dry and brittle. Snow that rested on the thicker branches, or on the forks in between, was spread on like icing. The snow that piled on the cars had come down in icy layers, it was too early in the season for this kind of weather.

An Indian Summer had stretched into October with sweltering temperatures like 100, 101 and 105 – 90 degrees when the sun went down. People were falling ill from the rapid and extreme change in temperature. The wind chill reached forty below two nights ago. It wasn't that bad now but, already, winter was growing tiring.

There were footprints in the snow leading up the sidewalk and around the corner. She put her feet carefully in the prints engraved in the snow, he had a similar stride and slightly bigger feet. She followed them around the side of the building like Rosmini tracing his thoughts to their original divine origin – which was a theory Kathy liked, that all concepts could be traced back to God.

The footprints went straight as K turned off into her back alley. It was a pure field of clean white flakes. *I guess God never made it to my place*, she thought, her feet crunching into the virgin snow. One would never know that beneath all that white terrain there lie rocks and gravel and broken glass and trash that blew out from the dumpster or from people who couldn't make it that far and just threw it on the ground. The snow evened out the playing field. Right now her back alley could pass for a front yard anywhere in Johnson County, the suburbs, or even Mission Hills.

The knuckled branches of a sycamore, crisp and dry, hung over a rusted tin overhang that covered the dumpster, they scraped the metal like fingernails on a chalkboard when the wind blew. The corrugated, slanted overhang was probably made in the thirties for someone to park a car back there, now it covered trash.

"God the nerve of that guy – *Merry Christmas*," said K, as she climbed the back alley stairs that led to her apartment.

They were old, chipped paint and wooden – warped wood and water stained. Snow fell from each step as she forced her foot into the padded layers, pushing the excess over the edge. A cement wall on K's right, also water stained, was always comforting to her as she passed it by. She would often run her fingers over its bumpy, grayish-blue surface on her way up and down.

"*Merry Christmas* don't pay the bills, bucko."

A brand new brass mailbox was at the foot of her stairs – stuck out terribly as new and shiny as it was next to the old, worn features of the alley. But out of the hundred and one repairs she'd asked her landlord to take care of over the last year and a half, replacing the mailbox was the only one he'd accomplished – and he probably stole that one.

"*Merry Christmas* don't pied the frickin' piper!" she said, reaching the top. There was a small awning over the platform at the top of the stairs. It was made of metal but looked like a picket fence, not as much now with the rust.

"That doesn't even make sense, K."

"Alright then, *Merry Christmas* don't get this lost, little sheep home. It doesn't melt my butter. And it sure as hell didn't get me off!" she screamed inwardly, kicking open her sticking front door. It always stuck, even more so when it rained, but at least she had that shiny new mailbox.

Her apartment was really a studio. The décor was really just pictures – pictures of her, everywhere. The studio was wallpapered with pictures from K's youth to her adulthood and everyday in between. It was something her father had started on the day of her birth. Every single day he'd snapped a picture of her – up until the day he left. Then a few years went by until K took up the tradition again either out of respect or a longing for him. Maybe he would come back one day. Maybe he would be pleased not to have missed a single day of her life.

Anyway, it would have been like a convent, she'd thought, without them. Colorless enough not to cause any excitement or arousal in the nuns. Sharp corners, chalky white walls and a low ceiling with white plaster bumps all over it – nothing creative, nothing with any life to it. Nothing to draw forth the desire of creation within them, the urge to have children, and nothing to remind them of the life they were leaving behind. It had a small closet with wooden pegs built in along the back, room for a few wimples and a rosary and a cross bearing Jesus.

She didn't have any of those things, just a few green, polyester uniforms for work, a few pairs of jeans, calf-length Spandex pants and about twenty different tops. They ranged from a seventies rainbow tank top to grungy and baggy skater tops to a few tight and black numbers that were her favorites.

It was home, as beat up and pathetic looking as it was. It was lonely, cold and bare until K found it. Timid and fearful they made quite a

41

good pair of opposites, complemented eachother. But more and more it took on the personality of K. She laughed every time she saw it and it smiled and warmed up the place with its heart whenever it heard K coming up the stairs, at least K liked to think so.

It was small, tiny, but the air felt spacious and she took in a deep breath as she entered. It felt like awakening from a dream whenever she stepped into it, as if this place were more real than everything that lay outside. On the degree of realness scale her apartment ranked about a seven. Work was a five, Bells' was a four. Everything in her past ranked about a one or a two. She'd never been anywhere above a seven. Maybe Heaven, she thought, that'd be nice.

There had been a change lately, though, a slight turn – a shift in the air. There was an eerie calmness now. She didn't know when or where it had changed, she didn't know how or why. All she knew was that something was different. Strange, like an orange-magenta twilight.

She opened the refrigerator that was bright inside due to a lack of food blocking the bulb. She grabbed her favorite snack, almond butter and soy yogurt, then propped up on the bed with her back against the wall, the white comforter pushed down with the sheets at the foot of the bed. She didn't have a chair besides the one that came with the vanity, and that was wicker. K dipped a spoon into the almond butter and then the yogurt. It was as good for you as anything, she supposed – protein and good fats and acidophilus.

The yogurt she grabbed was blueberry. There weren't very many blue foods in the world and she took advantage of them when she found them. Even though they became more purple, fuscia, when in the yogurt, they were still blueberries.

With all the pictures he had taken of her, K's father had never taken one *with* her. If he had she didn't remember it and didn't have it. She didn't have any pictures of her father, which was the hard thing. He was lost in time some twenty years removed and the seasoned memory she held of him fell further down the well with each passing year. She didn't know if that memory was really how he had looked and, cer-

42

tainly, he couldn't look that way now. Maybe she had even passed him on the streets. Maybe he had sat next to her at Bells' scribbling doodles on a bar napkin, scraping *Fuck you, Bob* into the wood, drinking a beer, talking about the weather – his wife and kids, a daughter he wished he could see again.

She had a few photos of her mother but never looked at them. Her rounded, ruddy cheeks, her puckered mouth, she always looked like she was sucking her air in through a straw. Her polyester outfits, sandy brown and graying hair full of curlers and when it wasn't still held the shape as if it were. She could hardly look at them.

K had always figured her mother was touched. Her mother always thought the same of K. She led the All Saints Church Choir in their hometown of Abeline, Kansas. Which wasn't that impressive because there were only three members of the All Saints Church Choir in Abeline, Kansas. She was mostly living off some fund she'd set up years ago or a T-bill that had matured – that and food stamps, K figured.

The split between them grew like the crack on a windshield the more K questioned Catholicism in her early teens, until the crack covered the windshield in all directions like a spider's web. But that was only part of it. After blaming herself for her father leaving, K started blaming her mother. Maybe her mother had done the same.

Finishing the yogurt, she tossed the empty cup into the trash, washed her spoon and went into the bathroom, turning on the blue light over the mirror with the metal chain. She liked it blue in there, it took out the rough edges, made her face look smoother and younger.

She liked blue lights in general, but they were rare. There were new headlights that were halogen blue, that was one of the best inventions ever, she thought. It was calming to look at them. And, driving down the road caught up in the stress of getting somewhere in a hurry, those blue headlights may have done some good, unknown and unnoticed, but good. Then sometimes around Christmas people put blue lights on their houses. K liked the ones that pretended to be icicles.

"Oh yeah, it's Christmas," she thought. It was 12:34 a.m. She'd almost forgotten about that.

"Happy birthday Jesus," she said into the mirror, her Koala bear eyes growing full like a sponge. She touched her hand to her face, dragged it from temple to chin. Christmas was a lot less memorable when you were 28 and had no family, and only two people had asked you if you wanted to exchange gifts and you turned them down. That would have been even harder – dealing with it, reminding yourself that you've got no one to give gifts to except a few people who felt sorry for you. Even so, they both gave her presents, anyway.

Bells got her *The Serenity Prayer* in a small picture frame. The one that reads: *God, grant me the serenity to accept the things I cannot change, the courage to change the things I can, and the wisdom to know the difference.*

K didn't know why he gave it to her, she never cared for that saying. It was better than *Footprints*, which wasn't saying much, she hated that one. Just because she had made it through her life alive didn't mean anybody had carried her. And if someone had, why did it hurt so much? Why did her feet ache and swell and burn with blood-filled calluses if she hadn't walked each and every step of that sandy beach alone, that was really bedded with broken glass and sharp rocks and torn and jagged aluminum from cans of Coke and Pepsi and Bud?

Becky got her a small diary or journal or whatever it is they called them these days. She didn't know why Becky got her that, either. Maybe they just didn't know her that well. The days couldn't end fast enough and certainly she didn't want to sit down and write about them when they finally did. There was little chance she'd ever go back and read what her life had been sometime down the road, she wasn't a masochist. Plenty of pain wallowed in the pools of her life but she wasn't a masochist, she wasn't even a sadist. She dealt with pain because she had to. It was the moat around *every*thing. You had to swim across one to get in or out of anything you did – the bigger the palace, the bigger the moat.

Kathy gargled with Listerine, spit it out when it started to burn, then brushed her teeth harsh, side to side, rinsing her mouth with cupped hands under the faucet. She went to the vanity, that was home to the only photograph in the room that wasn't of her, it was of Marilyn Monroe, and deflated onto the white wicker chair. Wicker was god-awful uncomfortable. White wicker was worse – god-awful uncomfortable and nicey-nice ugly. But it was a gift and free furniture was free furniture.

She picked up the Polaroid, turned it to face her, and snapped her picture. When the picture developed she looked at it briefly, then named and dated it on the back, like she always did. *Kathy Existential*, she wrote.

"Uh oh."

II

Flying fish elude predators by gliding several hundred yards above the surface, propelled by a tail providing thrust in the water, landing a safe distance away. The mudskipper lives along the edge of pools in muddy mangrove swamps, it escapes its enemies by flipping rapidly over the mud, out of the water.

Butterflies on tropical trails swirl together creating an effect that confuses predators. The predators, finding it difficult to follow the complex patterns, move on. Grouping of several species together also helps protect against predation because the many shapes, sounds and smells distract a predator. Certain lizards can blend into the scenery, making themselves invisible – walking sticks become as still as a twig.

All of nature has an escape route – except man.

ॐ

Rain loomed over 39th Street. It came down in thick drops and sudden bursts. It was sporadic and K sensed it liked it that way – liked to keep you off guard, never knowing when or where you'd get hit. They burst onto her skin like cold bombs and they liked that, too – she knew that, she knew it all too well.

The rain hid in dark gray and black clouds that were round and full underneath like the bellies of pregnant cattle. She'd never seen clouds like those – clouds that hung that low to the ground and were so full it seemed they could open up any moment and it would be more like waves crashing down than rain. They moved slowly northeast, beckoned by some force unseen, like a large herd over Kansas plains.

Moments before she had been safe, watching the rain slide down windows in teary-eyed streaks. Outside, night was coming, in the bus the fluorescent lights were bright yellow, burning like bug zappers. The discrepancy made K feel cozy and protected in the vinyl seat as she held onto the cold handrail. She was tucked away in a vault with people of her own ilk – the poor and bemoaned. She'd been taking the bus off and on for nearly three years, she'd never seen anyone there smile.

The mid-town transit hit a pothole and water splashed on the curb spraying mud and water onto the slacks of some businessman. His face scrunched up behind the glasses he wore like he wanted to yell something but didn't, probably because yelling at a bus would have made him look even more foolish.

Water was a caveat, it was like fire – it could save you or it could kill you. So you had to be careful with it, walk on tiptoes, say please and thank you – take the bus. Sometimes, even the real stuff wasn't so good.

When water was the rain, it was like a prison. She stayed inside and couldn't drive anywhere because she was a lousy driver and even more so when it rained. Even when it was dry and visibility was perfect, as perfect as it gets in mid-town, it was difficult to stay in between those yellow-dotted lines or off the curb when taking a corner.

On top of that her car often backfired, rang out like the shot from a sawed-off double barrel. Then black smoke would follow so everyone knew where the noise had come from. All in all, a bus pass was only a couple bucks a month and the price of replacing *Pitch Magazine* and other free newspaper stands that lined the corners of sidewalks would add up quickly if people started turning her in.

She used to think she was a great driver, most people do. But she'd been honked at and flipped off enough now to know that she wasn't. So she usually took the bus anywhere that was on route, and she wasn't in a hurry to get to. But the bus wasn't an option on her checklist – *How to Escape Kansas City* – and rain would make it difficult, if she ever had to.

Sometimes, when water was the ocean, it seemed more like freedom. It was like a bridge between here and some distant paradise that sat across the vast horizon, waiting to be found. All you needed was a raft and a sail and a good head wind, strong wind like the kind God uses to fan palm trees in Florida for the tourists – just blowing into the sails with your own carbon dioxide breath won't get you there. Then you'd be drinking margaritas on a soft white beach with beautiful servant boys named Pedrallo and Marcus handing you the paper or a towel or rubbing warm sesame oil onto your skin.

The only fake water she knew of was the water they used in baptisms, but she was sure there were others. K figured if that water could really wash away your sins they'd have to ship it in by the truckload and charge you like it was gold. But it couldn't. It just made you believe it had cleaned you, made you holy and new – and that was the worst kind of fake of all.

Work had been a tremendous bore that day. Becky was off, which meant there was no one to screw around with and one of the cooks didn't show which meant the manager had to cook and he was a prick anyway, even more so when he had to cook. He'd stomp around like a real priss and get all huffy with the waitresses just for putting orders in. It was so much worse when people wouldn't just explode and yell and be done with it rather than carry that shit around all day like some martyr.

It just put everyone in a bitchy mood and K couldn't wait to get out of there and get something relaxing into her blood at Bells' Bar. Such days used to give her kind of a rush, a sense of urgency and excitement – having to do extra work and all, extra fast. But lately, even the chaos was a bore. Now it was like, *so what?* So what if the coffee was cold or if the customers walked because it took too long to get their damn eggs? So what, what a terrible bore.

Stepping off the bus she eyed the incline up the walkway to Bells'. An up-scale restaurant sat at the intersection of 39th and State Line Road, Hannah's. It was an old red-roof Pizza Hut trying to look fancy by re-modeling with beige bricks and expensive interiors of fine wood and marble. But it never looked right because the building was still the shape of a Pizza Hut. On the corner were newspaper stands, *Auto Tradin' Times, Pitch Weekly, USA Today* and *The Kansas City Star* near the phone pole that was tattooed with band posters advertising up-coming gigs and a thousand and one staples left behind from the posters torn down.

Past that were the fire letters of The Tribal Grill and then the low lava light flooding out of Saigon 39 with its scripted neon letters that looked like a woman's handwriting. Then came Bells'. His sign, *Bels' Bob*, looked ridiculous, its brown-painted wooden planks created the letters that were nailed to the building's front.

Kathy stepped onto the sidewalk over another flowing black rain-bow. It was thin and wiry, like a snake, and moving with alacrity and she could tell it was a dangerous one. The thick ones are easy to spot and easy to avoid, they're slow. Thin snakes are quick and elusive, their fine slick scales rapid on the concrete and the problem is, they want to get you. But if they do, you still have a chance – its bite may sting but you could still get to the hospital and maybe be saved. Thick snakes don't really care so much, but when they do get a hold of you it's all over, they'll squeeze the life out of you like the juice from an orange. So K didn't know which was really worse.

The oily water gleamed different colors in the traffic light that was turning green – gritty purples like the skin on sweet potatoes, the neon green of bruised grapes and the dull, dirty yellow of old bananas. That's where you find most black rainbows – on the move and in the gutter. But sometimes they can stand alone, a puddle with a layer of grease or film on top – enough to refract the light. They're fake, of course, there's no pot of gold at the end of a black rainbow, just a grimy mess on your hands when you reach down to find one.

The hum of the bus engine rattled in K's chest as it pulled away from the curb, the release of the air brakes sending a harsh hiss into the air. Water was streaming into the grated sewer ducts sounding like a group of bickering old men discussing the latest bunch of hopeless political candidates or arguing over who was the greatest center fielder of all time – or who had the worst back pain and bladder problems.

Rain kicked up onto the sidewalk as cars went by, and Katherine was thankful she wasn't driving. She was thankful she wasn't on a mountain pass, thin roads curving like garter snakes, her gaze stuck on an ocean of aspens. She wouldn't be able to keep one eye on the road with the glorious stilts of white trees beside her, their only blemishes being knots of rough brown bark every so often up the length.

She was thankful that she was just walking up the sidewalk to Bells'. The things you're grateful for when life hurts and you have nothing, she thought. Thankful that it's not worse. It wasn't real gratitude she would put in her thank you letter to God.

Dear God, I hate life. I hate the pain. I hate the work. I hate that I'm stuck here. But, since I am, thanks for not making me drive over a mountain pass in the rain. Thanks for not making my skin fall off leaving sheets of exposed muscle and vessels. Thanks for not hitting me with a truck today. Thanks for Seven & Sevens and beer chasers – K.

On the storefront window of Bells' Bar, the buzzing-flicker light of the *Red Wolf* neon sign glowed in smoldering embers. Bells didn't sell that beer anymore. K didn't know if they still made it. But it was a neat looking sign – one you could role-play with while you drank. *I am the*

Red Wolf, dark and mysterious – don't fuck with me.

The familiar wino that frequented the sidewalk outside of Bells' was sitting hunched over in his brown rags, he hugged his knees to his chest, holding a tin mug between the palms of both hands. That was one problem when you were inside of Bells' Bar looking out. Sometimes you couldn't see people scurrying about to get somewhere important, sometimes you just saw the bum sitting beneath the Red Wolf sign, dirty and cold, scaring away the birds and making people opt for the sidewalk across the street.

His gaunt face was deluged with loose flesh that hung off it like a bulldog, dark trenches had been dug around his bug eyes. He probably used to be heavier, but life on 39th Street and in the shelters, where scant portions were usually watery green bean pods and corn, bread and potatoes, takes the weight off quick, leaving only sagging skin behind that once fit tightly over all the excess.

He didn't seem concerned much about snakes or mountain passes at all. But there was one concern they shared, she could see that in his drawn in features and bulging eyes and weathered skin. *Why am I here? How in the world did I end up here?* They had that much in common at least, and maybe even thoughts of escape.

He sat against the wood trim of the glass window, his back so stooped it looked like it could never be straight again. And what was the need, it's not like he'd be dining with royalty anytime soon or critiquing fine art at The Louvre with his transient buddies. In fact, Kathy was probably the only person on the planet to ever consider the bad posture of the 39th Street Bum. He stared somewhere into or beyond the dinged-up tin cup he cradled in his hands like a prayer. His lower lip hung low, full of yellow spit as he murmured slurred words over and over again like it meant something, like whatever twaddle he was thinking, speaking, was actually important. Like God would have entrusted this bum with some vital information that might someday change the outcome of anything, and it was up to him to remember it and pass it on – whatever it was.

52

She looked his way and saw him turning to look at her, his guarded movements like the slow motion of film, so she quickly turned away and he knew that she had. But not a word did he ever say. He kept mumbling and raised his cup, then lowered it again and turned his head back. He knew Katherine, not by name, just that she wouldn't be dropping any coins or dollar bills into his dented mug. K figured that was all he ever needed to know about anybody.

She'd thought of him sometimes, out there alone, and that angered her. It angered her that thoughts of a bum ever entered her mind – trespassed into her being. It felt like she should be doing something for him. And his life became a nuisance for K, a burden she had to carry like a cross – the cross of resentment that she should have to give up her hard-earned money to help him, followed by the cross of guilt and shame that she never did.

Sometimes she would send the 39th Street Bird down to sit with him and keep him company. At least she thought she'd sent it. The dove would be sitting on her windowsill or across the street, its slate feathers clean and slick in the street light, its blank eyes watching over 39th Street like a gargoyle, and she'd say, "Go bird – go see the bum. Go on birdy."

And it would go and K would be walking down the sidewalk sometime later and that bird would be there next to him. You could feel the 39th Street Bum smiling before you got anywhere near 39th Street, radiating like sunlight. It was like that little turtledove sitting there meant that God had forgiven him, for whatever it was he may have done. It was a pardon from the governor on execution day.

There had even been times, cold nights, nights when the wind cut through you like plates of glass, that she had actually thought about asking him upstairs into her apartment. But she never did. The reasons not to always seemed to be more, and louder, than the reasons to. But she always came to realize later on that the 39th Street Bum, as she called him, wouldn't have given a rat's ass about reasons. All he probably cared about was that it was cold and he would liked to have been warm.

53

That's when the cross of guilt she carried would become heavy and stout, bending her back, slipping wet splinters into her tender skin. When she could shake that one, letting it tumble off her body like a corpse in wrapped sheets, the cross of resentment would immediately befall her, lowering her to her knees as she crawled toward some unseen altar of reprise. Emotions were circular and viscous, suckling off themselves like a snake, its tail in its mouth.

On the maroon gutter that lined the top of Saigon 39, the one-story restaurant next to Bells', the 39th Street Bird was cleaning itself or picking something out of its feathers with its beak. K looked up and laughed at the bird, because it was cute is why, then stopped as quickly as she started, raising her hand to her mouth like some secret had spilled out.

"Birds don't like it when you laugh at them," she reminded herself. "Their little feathers can't take it, it makes 'em shiver – vibrate at a rate that's much too fast. And, sometimes, their hearts give out. That's how birds die, you know, only people never realize it."

"The end is nigh!"

K was startled, someone had crept up beside her as she looked up at the turtledove and she whirled around, her coal hair landing over her face, she brushed it away. He smelled of whiskey and filth and didn't look to be in much better condition than the 39th Street Bum, the stubble on his face like the thick and jagged legs of bees, red streaks crisscrossed the whites of his eyes. Kathy stepped to his right to go around him but he blocked her path.

He wore the cliché body-length, wooden sign that read: *Repent, the end is nigh.* She'd never seen one in real life, only in the movies, and he panted heavily from running up so fast to catch her. He'd gotten there as if her very life depended on whether or not she heard that message.

"The end is nigh, deary, ever been on the brink of death before?"

Whispered illusions – a rainy day on the sun. The pages I kept weren't a diary, they were fools to think so. It's so easy that way. It's so easy to

feed their beliefs. When they expect it, put it there. When they don't, cre-
ate the expectation, then you have them. You could go either way then,
feed it or destroy it, hold something back or alter the path and see how
they fall. See how they cling to their expectations and beliefs like they
couldn't swim five feet without them – a buoy, then a buoy disappeared
and they sink. People are so easy, I would've made them different, smarter.
Not with math or fast reading but real smart, street smart – smart about
life. People are so easy, trinkets, I only wear the shiny ones.

"The end is at hand! Repent!" he yelled. Kathy cleared her head, shaking it side to side, 39th Street whipping around like a picture, the shutter had been open too long.

"Ever been on the brink of death, child?"

A feeling guided her to the pit of her stomach, the feeling was warped and stagnant and the pit of her stomach seemed suddenly bottomless yet full – saturated with something coarse and sticky, something lost and unwanted.

He was a fool, like her answer would change anything. Like it would change the outcome if that were the case. Answers never changed anything.

"Yeah," she replied, and turned to step into the bar.

Inside was humid and warm compared to the briskness of early night. It was a mouth, wet and hot, a beast better left unknown. The mouth of a giant from a secret world where they lull their prey with neon signs on storefront windows and the temptation of cheap drinks and sex. His breath was god-awful, old beer and stale tobacco and whatever perverted bacteria and fungus that could survive in such conditions. But she kept coming back time and time again. The surreal din of chatter and glasses and pool balls, the smell of raw bodies and booze, the long dark room swaying with the waver of lit candles on one side – anything can feel like home, once you get used to it.

The next to last stool was open, it was always saved for K on weeknights, its torn black vinyl cover and gold-studded seams desolate without her. She took it with a subtle pride, it was hers and hers alone – for she was K, Kathy, Katherine of the St. Catherine Catherines. She didn't know much of the St. Catherines, but she knew she was named after them – or one of them, which one she wasn't sure. She hailed from a long line of St. Catherine Catherines. Her great-great grandmother was Catherine after St. Catherine of Siena. Her great grandmother, Catherine after St. Catherine Dei Ricci.

She'd heard of other Catherines – one who repeatedly performed spontaneous passion plays throughout her life. She would go into a trance and stumble around as if she were carrying a cross. K hoped she wasn't named after that one. "What a terrible bore," she had thought, "a life not even in control of yourself. Something could just take you over and make you stumble around and look ridiculous like that. Then people would undoubtedly ask, *What are you doing?* And you'd have to say something like, *Don't bother me right now – I'm being Jesus.* And nowadays they locked you up for that kind of stuff."

K's grandmother was chastised fully by Catherine the third for naming her only daughter Mary. She thought Mary was much more pure than any Catherine had ever dreamed of being and she never understood why the whole practice got started in the first place. But Mary learned of the tradition as she was growing up, from her grandmother, and named her only daughter Katherine – different spelling than they would have probably preferred, but a Catherine nonetheless – and that was K. To call herself Katherine or even Kathy was too pious for her, so she settled for K.

K was one ninth of Katherine, one fifth of Kathy. Soon, only a symbol would separate her from nothingness like, ♂, the artist formerly known as Prince. Only she would be, ॐ, before fading into eternity.

Her name was riding a Ferris Wheel thinking it could touch the stars on each turn. It was fooling itself, or, it was just having fun, pretending. Either way, it wasn't real. Her grandmothers weren't saints. She just came from a long line of women who were named after something real.

56

At his station in the corner, where he could go in or out flipping the bar top over its tarnished brass hinges, Bells was intent watching Drunk 1 pull the label off his Bud bottle. One more corner and it would come off in a sheet without any tears. It had been months since he'd gotten one all the way.

"They use better glue nowadays," he'd say.

"Modern technology," Drunk 2 would add.

He had a collection of them, several with just one missing corner so it wasn't a sure thing yet, some in one or two pieces he had taped back together. More than two pieces and it was a throw away.

When it came off in one piece the three of them hooted and hollered. K didn't know how Bells could stand being next to them all day. Their insipid conversations fogging K's mind like the smell of the vinegar dye her mother used to color Easter eggs.

Maybe, she thought, you slowly conform to the people around you, unnoticed, like at her work at Nichol's Lunch where it was non-stop bathroom humor. It was funny to them when someone stunk up the men's room. It was funny to use the word *butt*. It was funny to say *toe jam* in place of strawberry jam. The busboys and cooks ate leftovers off the plates of customers. The best jokes they told started with *Knock, knock*. Their favorite hand gesture was the one that looked like they were jerking off. And Kathy was thinking she had been there too long, she was starting to see the humor in farting.

Bells was finally coming her way, still bubbly with the achievement of Drunk 1. He tucked the white rag into his black polyester slacks and set his hands on the bar.

"So Angel, what's it gonna be tonight?"

"I'm no angel, Bells, and make it a J.B. and Bud chaser."

"Not messin' around tonight, huh?"

K made a gesture, raising both eyebrows then quickly lowering them as she brought a Bic lighter to her mouth and lit a Virginia Slim. Furtively, she looked behind her, there were several people in the bar that night. She was being watched, could feel the eyes dancing on her skin.

Some glances, like elfin thieves, snatching pieces of her then scurrying away. Some, more like bees, needing a taste of her dark nectar just to survive.

It was a small drop in the vast empty ocean of her life, being watched, longed for, but at least it was a drop. A speck of dew that meant she was different, that other people set her apart. She wasn't famous, but at least everyone who saw her had to take a second look. Beauty and mystery, they have their rewards, most people knew that. But they have their punishments too, most people didn't know that.

Bells over-filled the shot glass in front of her and set down a half beer in a tall glass. Lifting the jigger, he wiped away the spill with the white rag, then tossed it over his shoulder.

"Anything else?" God, why did he always say that? Unless she wanted several drinks lined up at once, there wasn't anything else.

"Bells, there isn't anything else."

"I know," and he gimped back on the thick black mats behind the bar that had holes in them and kept you from falling when it got too slick.

She took out the cigarette and blew a funnel of white cloud into the air turning to look out at the street, the release of the smoke like wading in a warm pool. Mid-January on 39th Street, the weather had turned warmer, hovering around the 32-degree point, just the sloppy wet of sporadic rain and the occasional slush from snow in December that hadn't completely melted.

Outside several people were moving by, altering their path in a half-circle around the 39th Street Bum. Well-dressed men in suit jackets and middle-aged women in elegant Jersey dresses of lemon or teal – people that were heading out to accomplish things in life or had just returned from some accomplishment, probably more substantial than tearing the full label off a bottle of Bud.

K was accomplishing something too, sitting alone on that south end stool, though she wasn't sure what. But it was something essential in the grand scheme of things, that much she knew. Clearly she'd be part of something bigger – something where sitting there and pondering the value of existence would be of importance someday. Something of great meaning would surely come of it – something grandiose, biblical. How could her life be anything else than grandiose? She was special, beautiful. She'd always been told that.

She rolled her eyes to the beams in the ceiling, put her hands in a prayer, touched their tips to her forehead.

"Dear lord, what am I doing here?"

Katherine always looked to the ceiling or to the sky when asking that. As if that's where answers come from, as if God would suspend them in the air above her in lightning bolts or hire a skywriter to paint them across the horizon. But he never did and probably never would. She would be stuck down here forever, sucking her thumb, waving a white flag – she knew that, she knew it all too well.

Answers were hard to come by – *questions*, you could get a handful for a Canadian nickel, sometimes they didn't even charge you. Sometimes questions would be answered and she'd look down and the other hand would be full of new ones. They never disappeared and all answers were shallow pencil sketches of home.

But she kept asking anyway, because without knowing *that*, her life seemed pointless.

"What in the world am I doing here?" She took the cigarette from her mouth … looked up at the ceiling again. Smoke fluttered in front of her, swirled and rose to the rafts looking for a way out, but there was none. And soon it would be getting worse.

Becky was leaving, moving away with her band to Seattle to make it big. Kansas City wasn't connected. Bands floundered on its muddy shores where they had to sign exclusive contracts with United Entertainment just to get a Friday night gig at The Hurricane, selling their souls for butterscotch candy that tasted good but dissolved quickly.

And when a label did come to sign a band, they had to buy them out from United and with all the similar talent in the country, it wasn't worth the hassle and revenues. So the bands played their Friday night gigs, sucking their butterscotch candy, slowly suffocating in the shallow water.

59

Becky and her group, St. Catherine's Flower, were flipping rapidly across the mud to Seattle where they hoped the politics of gigging wouldn't be as constrictive, though they probably would be.

St. Catherine's Flower was a flower Kathy had heard about as a child, with soft velvety petals like a rose, only black. K had never heard of an all-black flower before and as she grew she tried desperately to find it – called florists, read encyclopedias, researched the Internet. She couldn't find one single reference to it and now wondered if it really existed at all.

"It's the kind of name that has a story behind it. All the great bands have a story behind their names," Becky had said after K told her.

She loved it, and, being black, K figured Becky often imagined herself on stage that dark velvety flower.

It was more than that to K. St. Catherine's Flower was a symbol of what was real and what was not. It was like religion, it was like love, it was like God – something she'd read about in her youth and now that she was older was trying to find a trace of evidence that any of it even existed. And maybe if she could find it, maybe if she could find St. Catherine's Flower, then maybe there was some truth in the world after all.

K threw back the shot in a swift movement followed by a gulp of beer. A couple of guys walked in wearing Claiborne silky-smooth slacks and cardigans tightly woven – they don't call them preppies anymore. K could see them in the mirror, their snug shirts conforming to their bodies, their pants pressed and crisp. They looked nice, but only stayed a few seconds before realizing they were in the wrong place.

The hip clubs were across the street or in Westport – a few more scattered downtown and in the River Market. The right kinds of girls could be found in those clubs – girls that used all the new clichés and danced in cages with neon glow sticks and craved X. Not girls that still wore black spandex out, drank shots of Jim Beam with Budweiser chasers.

Life was a machine, a machine created by Hollywood diplomats for millionaire playboys – you didn't have to like it. You were a cog put there to help them have a good time. A beautiful face to sleep with, an ugly one to be compared to. Riff raff on the street so they could feel compassionate if they chose to or disdain if that pleased them. A billionaire computer geek to inspire the need for more money. Or, like ninety-nine percent of humanity, you were a pleb – background noise by which they understood the music of their lives to be something harmonious.

She turned her head from the mirror and raised the cold glass to her warm forehead.

"Becky," she thought, smelling the perfume of Cuban cigars and clove cigarettes, she hadn't smelled clove cigarettes since high school. "What am I going to do without Becky?" Friday night they were getting together at Bells' to have a drink and say goodbye – three days from now.

There were some guys playing pool in the corner. One had slacks on and an oversized, thick-weave black sweater that had threads of white woven into the black. The sleeves were pushed up revealing dark and thick Italian hair and a gold bracelet like nuggets that matched the strand around his neck and his Bulova watch.

"What an idiot," thought K. He was the counterpart to the girls who wore rings on every finger *except* the ring finger on their left hand, sucking the attention of men by its emptiness. Self-aggrandizement dripped from his gold chains, the excess shining his black loafers as it hit. She thought she saw a red glow around him and turned to see him without the help of the mirror, then the colors were gone.

His eyes sparkled like broken glass, the fake jewels and diamonds in an intersection after a bad wreck – leftover incandescent pieces of the worst day of somebody's life. Children driving by would think they were placed there on purpose – pretty, shiny. Not at all realizing that an accident had happened there, with property damage and wounds and lost blood or lost life. Only an ingenue would mistake his eyes for jewels, which K was not, need she remind him.

Ingenues didn't drink Jim Beam and Bud chasers. Ingenues didn't lay low in the men's room waiting to find messages from God. Ingenues didn't have escape routes.

61

The guy missed an easy shot then checked down the length of his cue like a scope, making a disgusted face. It was the stick's fault, it wasn't straight, he had to make sure everybody there knew that. Pricks like him usually brought their own sticks – then they had to blame the bumpers or the beers.

"Shit," she'd stared too long, he laid down his cue and gestured toward her to his friends. He was coming her way. When he got to her side, he slid his glass next to hers so they touched and propped his foot on the dull, brass beam that ran across the base of the bar. He was faceless. He stood between K and the empty chair on her left – he wasn't supposed to do that.

It blocked her view of the street, of people moving outside, of birds walking on the ground. Freedom was outside, just in reach, only a thin pane of glass between her and freedom. And he was standing in-between.

"Hey," he said. K didn't answer. "I noticed you were looking at me, thought I'd make it easy for you." He had the gimmicky smile of car salesmen and game show hosts.

"Look, just go away."

But she knew that wouldn't be enough to make him leave, the way his eyes glimmered glycerin, the way his anger quickly arose in him – when it reached a certain point, they'd ignite. K's stomach tightened as he struggled for something else to say.

"Why the hell were you checking me out then?" There was a pause, but Kathy couldn't stop what came out next, even though she wanted to.

"Well, at first I thought I'd found the missing link, but, as I was thinking to inform the *National Enquirer*, I picked up a scent and de-duced that it was just an ape. So return to your apery, ape-boy, and leave the evolutionary process up to those of us who can handle it. I'm afraid just having opposable thumbs isn't enough."

"You fucking..." he was reaching inside himself for something cruel to toss onto her lap like hot coals, "Bechante!"

He made a sound, deep and throaty, then spat on her face. Shortly afterward his face was flush with the bar top. A rough hand matched the voice that followed.

"I think you should leave." It was Bells, his thick hand engulfing the Italian guy's neck like a caught bird.

With a bar napkin K wiped the snotty spittle from her high cheekbone, ruddy with adrenaline, as Ape-boy and his friends disappeared into the night. They slammed shut the door, leaving just a little shakiness in the fibers of Katherine of the St. Catherine Catherines.

"Thanks Bells," K said, her hands trembling as she reached for another gulp of beer. He re-filled her shot glass then drew another Bud.

"You're just too damn beautiful for your own good." He set down the beer and grinned, then gimped to the other end of the bar where Drunk 1 was holding the label to the light to check for thin spots or holes.

The night looked friendly to K as she blew out smoke and searched for something on the other side of the window. It looked like it'd be a good place to hide, like it wouldn't turn you in. It looked like the kind of night you could get lost in if you wanted to and never return.

And the night wouldn't care none, it'd keep your secret, it'd keep it well. It might even help. It might even lead you to a nice warm place deep inside of it then close the door behind you so no one could follow. In fact, there may have been a hundred people, maybe a thousand, that got lost that night – who knew if they'd come back.

Sometimes, people who had the courage to see what was in the blackest part of the night – sometimes they found freedom. They found what they were looking for and how. So there wasn't much reason to come back after that. The only ones that did came back to try and help others, try to help them gain enough courage to find their own freedom in the nights' murky boundaries.

Kathy hoped she'd meet a night like this when she was ready to go, to leave and not be found – a friendly, secret night just like this one. But she wasn't ready, she was afraid. Someday she'd have to go, she knew that – she knew it all too well. But she didn't know why. It was just a feeling that was always a part of her – that this world wasn't hers, that she didn't belong to it. And someday she'd have to run away from it, run away and hide so perfectly that the world couldn't take her back.

Of course, it could be Hell on the other side and the thought of that is probably what kept most people from going. But K figured this *was* Hell, only people never realized it. That was Satan's greatest trick. Not making people think he didn't exist, but making people think they weren't in Hell already. So then there would be no reason to try and escape.

It had been three weeks since her near-sex experience with Moses and K put her chest against the padded edge of the bar wanting to be touched just then. Wanting to be touched by something soft and soothing, something opposite the cold spittle of that Italian guy who made her shiver with each thought of him. She wished she were wearing silk panties and a matching bra beneath her thin Dacron blouse and black spandex pants – a bra with no underwire that would gently hold her full breasts in place like hands.

She wished those one guys would come back, the ones in the Claiborne's and cardigans that they don't call preppies anymore. Those kinds of guys were usually ready for a one-nighter, something to go back and tell their frat buddies about. On weekends, you could see a whole slew of them in early till about 10:00 p.m. Bells' was a starter bar, a place that didn't charge a cover or five bucks a beer and didn't have blond and buxom servers. Bartendresses and waitresses with leather half-vests showing off flat, tanned stomachs and Celtic looking tattoes in the small of their backs – the kind of people you had to tip extra to impress. Bells didn't have any waitresses and he wasn't blond.

At those clubs you could order a Colorado Bulldog, Blue Velvet or an Alabama Slammer and they knew what you were talking about. You ordered anything exotic at Bells', you usually got a rum and Coke.

But K didn't go to Bells' on weekends, the crowd was too diverse, frenzied. Guys like ape-boy crowded the pool table, businessmen in suits going through a divorce or mid-life crises hunched over the bar taking straight shots of Wild Turkey with short glasses of dark, yeasty beer while spilling their guts to the sad saps next to them. Bikers and skaters, ravers and people they don't call preppies anymore filled the gaps in between. Bells' was a starter bar on Friday and Saturday nights, not one you ended up at.

From the TV a voice cut through the chatter and noise of the bar. Kathy glanced into the mirror to catch the last part of a news segment in the reflection.

"...remains of the former Master Sergeant. Also found were remnants of a diary. Burned beyond legibility. The only words left unsullied being, 'and I know it will be her that I see when I wake.' "

A blue pen sat on the bar nestled in a thick groove, someone had left it. She picked it up and waved it between two fingers until it looked like it was rubber. Then she set it back down and lit another Virginia Slim, the end burning bright then dull, then bright again. When the smoke rose in a line, rippling into nervous circles in front of her, she realized she was still shaking.

Bells was over drawing a Michelob Light from the carved wood knob on the brass draft container, handing it to a guy a few seats down.

"Bells?"

He grunted.

"Did you here that...that on TV? What was that?" Her voice was slightly hurried as she sucked in smoke and quickly blew it out.

"Nothing Angel, just some guy who was found dead. Wasn't even in this country."

"Who, who was he?"

He set his aged left hand on the bar, clear white with a few darkened spots, she could see the blue veins beneath his thin skin. Bells tugged at his cheek with the thumb and forefinger of the other hand.

"I dunno, some ex-army guy, he lived across the line in Kansas. Apparently he left the U.S. without a word to anyone, and then turned up dead in South America somewhere. What's the matter, did you know him?"

"Hmm, that's weird. I...I don't know," she said, as if trying to remember the taste, colors and textures of a dream from the night before, but the image wasn't forming.

"I really thought...I guess it was nothing. Never mind, I don't know what's the matter with me. It's just been a strange day, that's all."

"Well if you're going to be strange," Bells' grunted, "you're in the right place." He smiled fatherly, patted her hand.

K crushed the cigarette remains into the ashtray, and pushed away from the bar. She stood like a newborn doe. They just plop out and start walking around, she thought, a little wobbly, but still walking. Human babies can't support their own heads for two months. They come into the world numb and doped up like on Demerol not even able to form thoughts. And if you watch close enough you can see their brains starting to absorb the world, creating a reality from the words and actions around them. Maybe if one had grown up with birds, it would be able to fly.

"Thanks Bells," she said, turning to leave. "I think I'd best get some sleep."

"All right, Angel, sleep tight."

She moved through the entranceway putting her palm on the cold glass of the cigarette machine there.

"I'm no angel, Bells," K turned to yell, opening the door. It squeaked on its old wooden frame and rusty coiled spring that kept it from flying open in the wind.

"Yeah, well you're my angel!" he grunted, she heard him through the door that was slamming shut. It bounced up slightly, then shut again and again until it finally lay still.

Through her transparent black blouse, the brisk bristles of the air pinched into her gossamer skin, lightly. Her thoughts were lost, searching for the memory of that distant dream. As she turned the corner around

66

the hardware store next to Bells', she followed the red bricks of the building with her finger, rubbing the cement grooves in-between bricks.

"...*her I'll see when I wake*. I know I've heard that, wasn't that a movie or something? God what the hell was that?"

At the last corner, which headed into her back alley, the bricks were gone and there was nothing left to rub up against. She brought her left hand up touching the thumb to the fingers in smooth circles feeling the dull tingle the bricks left behind. "...*her I'll see when I wake*. Hold on, it's coming to me."

A soft brush of fingers ran up her neck but she was so focused on her thoughts she didn't notice until they started back down again. *Oh God*, she thought, *I'm being touched*. The new growth of hairs at the base of her neck stood up, soldiers in the last line of defense, but they were too frail and it was too late. The soft brush on the back of her neck had turned into a firm grasp, hard and cold. It was red, redness was grabbing her. K could feel the angry red closing around her. The cold worked its way down her spine freezing each vertebra one by one – she panicked, froze still like a walking stick on a limb.

The redness pulled her backwards and threw her to the ground. She landed hard on the concrete and gravel of the back alley and the breath flew out of her body like it had wings, a dove, she could see it rising in circles above her.

The dove breath left her body, floating upwards and Kathy watched it, peace falling over her from the fanned air beneath its wings. *From K to Heaven*, thought K, *a gift from me to you*. Then the bird wings turned into something angry in front of her, full of fury – hatred – red.

She was about to pass-out but could see the image of a face as she struggled to keep the black fuzzy vice around her eyes from closing. It was ape-boy, saliva dripped from his mouth onto hers as he spoke.

"You like being a big woman? Huh? You goddamn cunt!" he yelled, phlegm flying out from the recesses of his throat.

"Like to make fun of people, you fucking bitch. Well you don't know fun, goddamnit. I'm gonna show you fuckin' fun." He pulled her shoulders slightly off the ground then smashed her down again. Behind him were voices, his friends, and the scraping sound of the wind as it drew the claws of the sycamore across the corrugated dumpster overhang. A kestrel sitting on the tin roof spread its wings, caught the wind, and lifted into the air.

She could feel the bitter hands, one on her shoulder. One, no two, pulling down her pants... "Oh God, no."

She could feel one tongue on her now bare nipples, and two lips, then the sucking that was harsh and painful. "How'd that...happen?" She struggled for thought, "Don't remember my shirt...God...no."

As the black vise closed its grip of unconsciousness and she struggled for freedom, K heard an odd noise, the growl of a rabid dog, or a wolf. But it was hard to tell, she was blacking out and her senses were frenzied around her. It was too much, her breath had left her on the wings of a dove and now her consciousness was to follow, without wings – without poetry.

She passed out, and all was black.

K dreamed she was in the back of a semi-truck asleep in the berth, as the truck hauled its cargo down some endless black top. Bugs splattered on the windshield, death was all around, but she was safe and snug like a baby in the womb. K moved up and down, swaying with the bumps in the road. Soft and gentle were the bumps – slow, rolling and cozy. It must have been a quiet highway, winding through empty hills because it felt silent and peaceful and isolated. The arms of the sleeper berth closed tighter around the back of her neck and waist, making her feel even more safe and snug. Then it closed tighter – and Katherine woke up.

When she opened her eyes to a flat darkness skirting out around a faint light above, she *was* moving, swaying. She was strapped and gliding in the arms of a savior, his forearm muscles flexing behind her neck so defined she could almost feel the sinewy fibers. *Footprints*, she thought, and she looked down for a sandy beach beneath her where the trail of hollow ovals would push away the downy white sand in dusty mounds and feathery ripples – but it was just the green-blue of chipped soggy paint on an old wooden stairwell.

The rock, the mortar, the long rolling line where years of rain had distorted the color, it all looked familiar. Disoriented memories skittered in with the smell of spilt beer and cigarettes. *I'm Katherine Kristensen. Where am I? This is my wall. These are my stairs. My door is getting closer. I'm being carried. I was attacked. Who has me?* She looked up to see the five o'clock shadow of gray stubble and hear the soft grunts of effort with each step. *This is Bells. Bells is my friend. Bells has saved me.* Or, she thought, more somberly, and more realistically. *Bells has found me.*

How long have I been unconscious? A minute? An hour? Half the night? She tightened her right arm around the back of his neck brushing against the coarse hairs, and raised her left arm to meet it on the other side. She held on tight and pulled her face between his shoulder and chin, buried it in his neck, and cried.

She watched as the tears flowed from her eyes soaking his shirt, wetting his shoulder. She watched from an empty cavern inside of her, she wasn't even sure why she was crying. *It's okay, Kathy, don't cry,* she was thinking. She wished she could yell it from her empty cavern to the girl on the surface, but all she could do was watch.

"Shhhh, Angel. Everything's all right now," Bells said, as they reached the stair top. He set her down, they stood in the phone booth-sized covered walkway attached to her door and she continued to hold him and she continued to cry.

K didn't often cry. Sometimes, when you cry, you forget who you are. It can sweep over you like a flood and you have no control of where it will take you or when you'll return.

"Shhhh," he repeated, slowly. Slower and slower he repeated it as if speaking to someone who doesn't know the language. His words were soft and downy like the sand she wanted to see beneath his feet and she wondered where all the scratchy roughness had gone.

69

"What happened?" she asked, her tears slowing as she removed her left arm to wipe the moisture from beneath her eyes, sniffling.

"Well, if you want to know what happened to you, the answer is nothing." He grunted then breathed deeply, "I stopped it."

Kathy looked into his eyes searching, hoping it was true.

"If you want to know what happened to them," he grunted again, "the answer is you don't want to know." He reached behind her pulling open the flimsy screen door, its rusted meshing mostly pulled away from the corners of the wood frame.

"Get some sleep, Angel."

She kissed him on the cheek and turned to open her door, fumbling in her purse for her keys. Why did she have so many damn keys? Her mother's house, old padlocks, old cars, old apartments – was she thinking they would still work? That she'd be wandering the streets some day and see a car she once owned and could drive it away or stay the night in a loft she had rented? They clanged like rusted wind chimes as she pulled them from her purse.

"Oh Bells, by the way," she turned to face him, "I love…" but he was already gone, heading out of the light into the dark part of the alley.

"It's all right," she thought, stopping her sentence short. "The kiss was probably enough."

Watching him walk away, his forced movements, each one seemingly laced with a poisonous pain that shot up from his gimped leg, Kathy was thinking *who is this man?* He had fallen into her world and tracked footprints across her life and she didn't really know him. She didn't know what his tattoo said or the name of his lost love or where he used to live or why he owned that dumpy bar. She didn't know much about him at all, except that he talked like a sailor sometimes – sometimes like a grandfather.

He gimped into the darkness, hidden, unseen. Then suddenly the answer was there. Everything he was, was right there in front of her. What else could she ever hope to know about him, she thought. What else could there ever be than the simple beauty with which he walked away from her at that moment?

Katherine poured into the loft like water into a glass – all at once and yet all at once restrained, as if not to pour herself all over the floor.

Her pictures stared as she entered as if *she* were the picture, as if *she* were the one pinned to a wall in some midtown, studio apartment – a semi-glossy 3x5 inch card of paper. Marilyn's picture was pouting condescendingly. *Shame, shame, shame* she was saying in distant echoes behind her puckered red lips and smirky gesture.

The haunted howling of an empty room. The wail of no television and no radio. A bed, a footlocker, a vanity, a nightstand with a lamp and a clock – stackable crates for her clothes.

"It wasn't my fault," Kathy said aloud into the mirror over the vanity, her words empty and lifeless, falling in the dead air like stones. Now she knew why people never turned off the TV. Distraction was the world's most valuable commodity, she would never let anyone tell her otherwise. It isn't gold, it isn't jewels, it isn't love – they were all part of the distractions.

"Fault, that's a vague word, a difficult word to define. Sure, you could look it up and that might get you off the hook, but the semantics don't always get to the heart of it now, do they? How convenient."

"I don't want to argue with you, it's been a long day," Kathy said, turning from the mirror, lifting one leg over the other knee, peeling off a shoe.

"I'm not saying I want to argue or don't want to argue," she answered back. "I'm just saying you have a strong knack for avoiding subjects that you don't want to think about."

"Look, fuck off, everyone does that, okay, and I'm not having this conversation!" She yelled the last part out loud as she threw her handful of keys hard against the wall, crashing like a vase. The shoe in her left hand dropped to the floor. All was silent – the table lamp casting her shadow on the wall like a cloaked bird.

In the end it was always the same, K was left standing alone arguing with no one at all in a silent room, in a silent stare.

Kathy didn't like the silence. Quiet was something that reminded you how loud your ears were ringing because the music had been too loud. Quiet was something that made you notice how bad your body felt, heated and dry from the booze – your mouth left sour and bitter as bile. Quiet was something for the churches and people on hills with their legs crossed in the lotus. Quiet was for the cemeteries. Only leaves made noise in a cemetery, and only when they had to.

Soon she was thumbing through the pages of her dictionary and, half-asleep, gathering the words that fell from the pages.

After writing them on a sheet of typing paper her mind was soft and pliable, it was a good time to try and sleep. But the story started flowing from her pale, thin fingers anyway and when she awoke at 2:45 a.m. to remove a saliva-drenched pen from her mouth, it was already finished.

She pushed herself up and sat on the edge of the bed, her bare toes grazing the cool, smooth floor. She supported herself with locked elbows and stood from the bed like a crane – awkward and graceful, simultaneously. Her features were slow to rake through the air, long arms and thin legs and both bony at the joints. When she lifted her arms she pulled them like they were stuck in honey or amber, more than just lift them. To raise them she needed to get her back and shoulders involved. Kathy stood and one leg paused before it was put on the floor. She had to be sure the ground was still there. She had to be sure it was still there and stable before she put all her weight down.

The clock flipped to 2:46 a.m., it was an old clock from junior high. She liked it. It was hard to find clocks with flipping numbered tags these days. She had only been asleep a few minutes, though, fifteen tops. It was just enough to make her body heavy and cumbersome like bags of wet sand as she stumbled toward the bathroom using the wall strength as her own to get through the door.

The blue light sunk deep and dark in the space beneath K's eyes and she touched her fingers to her face. That was her mile marker, how far she'd gone from home. It was the first place her eyes were drawn to whenever she looked in a mirror. It was bad when they were sunk in deep and dark, worse when they were fleshy and full. When they were puffy like that and the creases underneath were almost small folds, it was time to do something – take a respite from Bells', find a dry sauna to sweat out the moisture, go to a juice bar.

"You really need to stop smoking," she said, looking deeper into the mirror, the few lines spreading from her eyes like cracks in desert clay.

"I only smoke when I drink – you know that."

"I do know that, but you drink all the time."

"It's just a phase, K, don't worry about it." She dropped her hand from her cheek, let it rest on the cold porcelain sink.

"Yeah, just a phase."

The bluish black rings around her wrists and purpled splotches on her shoulders pulled her thoughts back to the early evening. They'd turn brownish-yellow soon enough, she knew her body. She bruised easily like over-ripe apples fallen from the tree. She slid two fingers into her panties and then between her lips and pushed them apart. It felt okay, it didn't feel raw or sore. She pushed at the sides of the entrance where it was more firm and not so fleshy, it didn't feel bruised and there weren't any tears. She should've checked earlier. She was afraid Bells had lied to her, for her sake.

"He wouldn't do that. There are medical issues," she said into the mirror.

"I know, K. It doesn't hurt to double check." She put her fingers deep inside and pushed against the walls, side to side.

"Feels okay," she thought. "It was just the anvil of a new day. Heavy things, things you have to carry around – day to day there's always a different weight. That was my anvil today, that's all."

"What are you talking about, K? That didn't have to happen. Are you that proud? What were you thinking mouthing off to a guy like that? Was it worth it, belittling him – proving that you were smart and he was stupid?"

"I don't know, K, sometimes I can't even stop myself." She picked up her toothbrush, its bristles frayed and worn, covered it in toothpaste, cinnamon-flavored, and began brushing.

"Great, you can't stop yourself and in the meantime you create more misery for both of us. You keep doing the same things over and over."

"I know, it's true." She lowered her head, spit some excess of toothpaste and saliva into the sink, then looked back into the mirror, a frothy paste covering her lips. "My life has been a tale told by an idiot, full of fury and noise signifying nothing."

"Yeah," she held the toothbrush to her mouth like a thought. "Haven't I read that somewhere?"

"Wait, that was our story – and her I'll see when I wake!" She dropped her toothbrush into the sink, looking up at her face that was soft and rounded in the blue hues.

"Whoa."

That night she couldn't sleep. K got scared when she didn't sleep. She'd heard stories – crazy people didn't sleep. It could push you over the cliff like a ram and she was already standing on the edge, she knew that. She knew people didn't think like her. After enough *close* friends had slipped out of her life. After enough people had left business cards behind, the names and numbers of their psychiatrists on them – gold and emerald raised letters, Pitch and Lucida fonts – she knew she was on that edge.

It was like the time she ended up going the wrong way on the interstate late one night, north in the southbound lane. Everybody that drove past her honked or swerved and all K could think was why are all these idiots driving the wrong way? When she finally saw the street signs were facing oncoming traffic, she knew they had been right all along.

She didn't share her thoughts with people anymore, especially the secrets – light bulb smells and mirrored worlds and fake wind talking. She knew what to say to fit in, be normal. But now she didn't have a guidepost, someone to compare her level of sanity with. So, she didn't know if she was standing on the edge or hanging on by a finger or if she were already on her way down, waiting to splatter at the bottom like a drop of rain.

Early morning came up in slate blues through the solid base of gray-ish-white clouds on the eastern horizon. Slowly the room grew brighter, its shadowed colors lifting into purer tones and K sat up, put her hands to her face. Her eyes fluttered as she opened them. It was good that she didn't sleep, she decided. If she wanted to get a paper she would have to get there early because the paper dispenser on the corner was broken and all you had to do was give it an extra tug and it would open. So the papers usually went fast. She would think the paper vendor would have caught on by now. The machine was emptied every day and there were probably only a couple of bucks in quarters to show for it from the people who didn't know the trick.

Her mind was slow to pull thoughts as she raised her head, numbly looking over the half-lit room, sitting at the edge of the bed, waiting for the impetus to stand. The underwear she wore the night before still lay on the floor intertwined with the black spandex pants. Clean bras and panties filled the green plastic laundry basket next to them.

Kathy sat on the bed, tugged at her lower lip, stared at the empty space in between, trying to decide whether to wear clean underwear or dirty underwear down to the corner to get the paper.

III

*M*ost *predators attack more than one type of prey. A few, however, have highly specialized abilities and attack only one or two species. Successful predators either dive or charge to break up a flock and then grab a separated animal, or pick off an outlying one at the start.*

Some are sit-and-wait predators. Scorpions remain motionless until suitable prey moves into an ambush zone where they detect vibrations of prey movement. Once detected, the scorpion orients, runs to the prey, and seizes it. The prey is stung if it is relatively large, aggressive or active; otherwise, it is simply held in the pedipalps while it is eaten.

Predatory animals may be solitary hunters, like the leopard, or they may be group hunters, like wolves. A flock of white pelicans will cooperate to form a semicircle and, with much flapping of wings, drive fish into shallow water where they are easily captured.

Mimicry is a form of similarity in which a predator or parasite gains an advantage by its resemblance to a third party. This model may be the prey, or host species itself, or it may be a species that the prey does not regard as threatening. Female fireflies, of the genus Photuris, imitate the mating flashes of the fireflies of a different genus — Photinus; the unlucky Photinus males deceived by the mimics are eaten.

In other examples, the aggressor may even mimic the prey of its intended victim. Anglerfish, for example, possess a small worm-like organ that can be waved in front of other fish. Lured in by this organ, which they mistake for their own natural prey, smaller fish are eaten.

Long winter hours drew lines in the sand – a toe dragging across infinite wet beaches, white and sandstone in disguise. Life was like that to K, everything was in disguise – peacock feathers. Peacock feathers of blue and green with eyes in the middle, a hundred eyes watching all the time, each step. Life was carousel lights that lit the work as they were digging graves, paper flumes channeled in the bodies.

But, as she pulled her finger from between two bricks and looked down 39th Street, there were no beaches and no peacock feathers, no carousel lights or paper flumes – just thoughts of a bored mind and the long winter hours left behind. And the ones left to come.

Each minute spent had been spent wishing for warmer moments, one after another layered on top of eachother like cake, and K let out a lingering breath the look of faint smoke. But Friday came quickly – as if it were being chased. As if Friday had deadlines of its own to meet, or enemies of its own to avoid, and that was the one day of winter K didn't want to come and go so quickly.

He lived in Scott City, the guy from her story, a rural farm town in central Kansas. The headline had read *From Stone City to Purgatory*, which was what one of the salvaged pages in his diary read. Stone City was a nickname for that small town. They were taking donations for his mother. Send offering to: *33 Flat Rock, Scott City, KS, 66173*. Her story had all been true, only she knew the real story – the cause, not just the effect. It was eerie to read, like a private dream had been published for the world to see and the memory of it followed her in shadowy footsteps everywhere she went.

K huddled at the corner of 39th Street and Bell, the next side road east of State Line, at Johnson's Hardware rubbing the edge where two panes of glass met with the tip of her forefinger. She looked down the length of 39th Street. She didn't want to move. It was a long narrowing tunnel with no light at the end.

"My God, are you really down to one friend?" she thought as she moved away from the glass, walking deliberately on the sidewalk. "What's the matter with you?"

There was a chill in the air, a cold bite. The wind nipped at her lips and face like it wanted to take a piece of her with it – like the wind wanted to take her beauty and travel the lengths of the world with it locked up inside its invisible folds. Maybe the wind would spill it in front of somebody in need, some lonely wretch down on his luck needing to see something beautiful in the world – something that would make life worth living.

And the wind could have it for all K cared. If it weren't for the fact that it got her laid whenever she wanted, she'd have no use for it at all. Her beauty didn't keep her warm at night, it didn't pay her bills and it didn't stop her from being lonely. It sure as hell didn't make anybody love her, just made a few more people want to try – or pretend that they did. But she would cry if it ever went away, and she knew that too.

"The matter is, you don't like anybody," she responded sharply. "It's hard to befriend things that repulse you."

The *Red Wolf* sign hissed when she got to the door but it always did and K often wondered if it hissed at everyone or if it was just her that the wolf sign didn't like. She glanced up at the sign attached to Bells' Bar, it still read *Bels' Bob* like it had ever since K changed it. It was apparently going to remain a permanent fixture on 39th Street and Kathy had to chuckle at how ridiculous it looked. Then she had to chuckle again at Bells who had just left it like that all this time.

"That's not true. I like people, just not anybody in particular, save Bells, of course." The words hung silently a moment waiting for a response as K stepped over the cement seam on the floor that was uneven

79

and caused most people to trip as they went inside. She pulled open the tattered, deeply grooved and splintered wooden-door, a stale breeze of smoke harsh in her eyes and throat, repugnant and fetid. Someone was smoking cigars again, she could tell already and brought up her hand to wave away the hazy air. If only more people smoked pipes, instead of cigars and cigarettes, the place would have been more tolerable, almost homey.

"Look, say it however you want. The facts are, you think people are childish, materialistic and beneath you. You don't like anybody, not too many people like you, and you only have one friend."

"People like me," she said, standing in the small corridor, coughing. The smoke aggravated her throat and she thought it strange because she herself smoked and never coughed when she did. But something about other people's smoke always seemed intrusive, irritating.

"People like me," she insisted, brushing back some straggled black curls over her left shoulder, steadying herself against the cigarette machine that was the first thing you saw when entering Bells'.

It wasn't the best place to put a cigarette machine, by the restrooms would've been better. Here, the walkway was already narrow and now, with the cigarette machine, only one person could fit past it at a time. It was probably a fire hazard. She often pretended to steady herself by putting her pink palm against its cold glass. But that wasn't why. She just liked to feel it, cold and smooth and the only cleaning that was ever done at Bells' Bar was done by the cigarette guy who cleaned off K's many hand prints each time he filled the machine.

"People like me, right?"

"I don't know, doll. If I had all the answers we wouldn't be having this conversation."

"Or any conversation," she added, turning left at the end of the walkway to step fully inside the bar. The fragmented outlines materialized as the shapes and sounds that were Bells' flooded into K's eyes. Several people turned to look but it wasn't just her, they looked whenever anybody entered – needing to size up their chances, or their competition.

Ace was playing – *How long has this been going on? How long, how long? How long has this been going on?* It was distant and buried behind the rest of the clamor as she worked through the people that were standing nearly shoulder to shoulder.

"People like me," she confirmed under her breath.

They were a diverse crowd, the weekend patrons at Bells'. Ravers and skaters and bikers and drunks, different themselves – outcasts and misfits like K, but not accepting. She knew them, knew them all – could see right through them. If you weren't different from society or different enough or different in a certain way, a way they approved of, then they didn't accept you. You were shunned, an outcast of the outcasts.

It was the same old bullshit just a different direction, a more subtle nuance and a new name. The new crowd was just more repressed than the average bigots – a more repressed bigotry, a more repressed disdain, hatred and fear.

And the repressed were the most dangerous, Kathy felt. They were the volcanoes everyone had said were dormant. They knew it was wrong to hate – had heard it or read it in some scripture somewhere – so they suppressed it. They knew it was wrong to judge so they pretended not to or didn't do it out loud, but that didn't make it go away.

Kathy knew them, she saw right through them. She wasn't so different, so strange looking to cause a scene, but she didn't belong to them. Not to any of those groups that clicked together in their private corners of the bar did K fit in with. She didn't belong to them, they knew it and so did she.

Becky was already there when Kathy arrived chatting feverishly with the members of her group who semi-enclosed her in a half circle facing toward the entrance of Bells'.

They were a classic grunge band. The tall and blond lanky drummer, the kind of guy you'd call *Sticks*. The slightly pudgy bass player with dark hair and bad skin he tried to cover with a goatee. The slick, long-haired lead guitarist with a steady jaw line and soft eyes. K wouldn't mind doing him, only he had a girlfriend and thought K was a freak.

And Becky was the star. Becky fit into all groups, unless someone just out and out disliked black people, even then she might *goochy-goochy-goo* a big old grin out of him. And he'd be smiling and laughing while she was there next to him. Then when she left, he'd feel the pain of not having her there. But he wouldn't show it. He'd have to make up some extra big bullshit to tell his bigot-headed buddies and then slowly shake it off wondering what just happened, that he almost liked one.

Becky would walk right over to the scariest bunch of goons in the place and ask for a light and, even though she didn't smoke, have a new group of friends before the lighter could make a flame, just like that. K could never do that. She tried, but the pressure from gritting her teeth so hard left her jaw sore. She just wasn't a people person like Becky was. To Becky everyone she met was a new, shiny spotlight and she was the thing they were shining themselves all over. And they did, time and time again – man, woman and child.

She wasn't as beautiful as K, if you were to set down a photograph of each of them next to eachother, then no. But a photograph couldn't capture what made Becky, Becky. Becky was an over-fulfillment – overflowing and bubbling with so much life that everyone that walked past wanted to lap that effervescent pool of hers with long cool drinks, or take a handful of her fizzy bubbles and blow them around the room. Then they'd chase after them like a two-year old that had just learned to walk.

Or maybe if that person stood there long enough some of the bubbly overflowing bits of her might bubble on over their way – maybe they'd start bubbling with life right along with her. And the small chance of that happening was worth their time to sit and listen to whatever nonsense it was Becky felt like rambling about at that moment.

Light from the bar peeked through the smoky spaces between arms and bodies, glowing in a yellow, bubbly hue behind them. Becky's silhouette a void spot among the pale alternative skin of her band members. Their whiteness draped her like an iris field on a slow hill would drape the all black-petaled flower of St. Catherine's as it tried to hide there somewhere in the middle.

From church choirs to school choirs and jazz quartets and talent shows, Becky had always been the best. Now she was intent on being the first black female vocalist to make it in the heavy-alternative scene, which was flourishing in Seattle at the time.

K thought she just might make it. She had that presence, a certain look – a smooth and glossy complexion like the polished oak in expensive houses, with a child's eyes and a sinner's smile. Her face was so smooth and shiny it almost shimmered. Almost like the waves of energy coming off a street on a hot day was her face and just seeing the beautiful wavering heat on the street somehow made that hot agonizing day suddenly worth it.

Locked up inside her bubbling-over face were the shy sincere eyes of a little girl. The eyes of a girl who knew exactly how sweet and innocent she was but didn't care one bit about it, didn't see all the big fuss about it. Then a smile would break through the innocence of her lips and you'd know she had done something wrong – stuffed the neighbors puppy into an empty mayonnaise jar, used the convertible as a trampoline, spray painted the garage orange.

She had the kind of face you could stroke soft with your hand and tell bedtime stories to while using lots of exaggerated cartoon sounding voices, and her face would light up when you did.

Then she'd slap down a plate of flap-jacks in front of you and say, *There you go, sug,* or, *Eat 'em up,* or, *Careful, they're fuckin' hot!* And it wouldn't make one bit of difference either way because the face it came out of would soften the rough edges of those words and make anything sound equally as good.

"Seattle is the place, I can feel it," she said, gesticulating wildly. "Our destiny lies in Seattle."

There was a salud by the band to their mutual expectation of Seattle destiny. Beer sloshed about in mugs like it thought it was Irish, smiles burned like the flame on Kathy's lighter as she lit a cigarette and approached the band, her head bent down and hand cupped around the flame, blocking a wind that wasn't even there.

"Oh," Becky said, bouncing up and down in her small spot between patrons at Bells' Bar, "K's here, my best friend in the whole bloomin' world." She grabbed Kathy by the neck and gave her a tight squeeze and a hug. "I'm gonna miss this crazy Kansas City girl."

But the sugary coating that topped those words couldn't cover the bitter tension underneath and Becky pulled away, her smile half of what it usually was.

"Yeah, I'm gonna miss you, too."

They had never talked about it – about what each one had meant to the other. They were work buddies. They hung out after work, shared a laugh and a beer and that was. it – so they thought. They never realized how deep their conversations went – the camaraderie of telling someone your daily troubles, of having a common bond and common enemies.

Kathy was night, white as paper but night. Becky was day, black as ink but day. Kathy was fog rolling in at dusk. Becky was mist melting at dawn. Kathy was a mansion on a rocky hill with lightning bolts flashing all around. Becky was a gingerbread house in spring with a stream so near by you could smell it. And when all was silent, when the children weren't laughing and carrying on, you could hear the purity of the stream's trickle.

She was the kind of gingerbread house people could eat from all they wanted and it would just re-new itself over and over.

"Plenty more where that came from," she'd say. If someone took anything from K, it would leave her bleeding and wounded. Then she'd have to hunt them down and steal it back on some dank and foggy night as they slept, then quickly take it away – back to her mansion on the hill.

For Kathy a sense of emptiness growled deep inside. For Becky, excitement and possibility fluttered about like butterflies and every now and then one would fly out of her mouth as she spoke. But she'd miss

K. They were so extremely opposite that the bumpy and awkward parts of each fit perfectly with the smooth indentations of the other.

But soon the memories of what they were and the times they had wouldn't hold any more value than a dead corpse. There would be no fragrance, no sound and no feel – just empty pictures in the back of their minds and, someday, even those would fade and each would have to be found again. An angry piece of night would someday have to fall into Becky's life and a glimmer of sunshine on a windowpane would soon have to catch K's eye.

The bar had filled up quickly and it was crowded just to stand there. K rubbed up against someone's back, he was decked out in leather like a biker. But some future biker, not baggy and worn leather, it was nice and skin tight, mostly. He wore a long, shiny leather coat on top of all the other leather he was already wearing, that went to below his knees.

He turned to flash K a smile, as if that would be enough, she thought. As if that would make up for how deranged and psychotic he looked. Anybody can fake a smile, the truth is in the eyes. The eyes can't hide who you are, they don't know how. They just open themselves like flower petals, releasing the heart to full view. So she quickly turned away, not letting their eyes meet, not wanting to know him and not wanting him to know her.

She turned back to look at Becky and it was already happening, the withdraw. The energies that connect two people, keep them in tune with one another, they were slipping away, unlocking – freeing themselves to move to somewhere new, or just hover in space awhile until a new home could be found. That's when the pain comes. When your heart is flying around and it can't find a home and the effort and fear of having nowhere to land finally makes you collapse anywhere – Bells' Bar, Nichol's Lunch, 39th Street.

K took slow inhales of her cigarette, the sounds around her in swirling drones, watching Becky being drowned in the attention of her band. Their eyes met for a moment and they both smiled. K smiled at how

Becky that was – to be smothered with affection by her band or friends. Becky smiled at how Kathy that was – to be standing on the outside looking in. She was always on the outside, never fit in with any groups and Becky felt the weight of that thought tug on her heart like a child on the skirt of his mother.

The smiles soon disappeared and their eyes pulled away from each other as quickly as possible, but it was somewhat like taffy. And when the eyes pulled away it almost pulled out tears from them both, but they didn't let it.

This would be a day for happiness, it was a party after all. *Going Away Party for Becky*, just as they had said. *Party* was right there in the title. But *going away* was also in the title and the two opposite polarities seemed to cancel eachother out, leaving a dead space in between – a space that would be all too easy to fall into if they let themselves.

Neither knew what to say so they didn't say much. And neither knew what to do, so they didn't do much – awkward gestures and contrived laughter and half smiles. Because anything they did would bring the tears and the tears would have been admitting that their lives were going to be forever changed when that night ended. They kept their words light, not overly real and not smothered in the truth of their emotions, and turned away, each knowing they'd just have to suffer the pain of it alone in their rooms sometime down the road.

Tethered conversations, one picked up where another left off, too many voices all around and K was feeling overwhelmed and light-headed. Bells came over to her end of the bar and K squeezed through the thick padded arms of coats and sweaters to meet him.

"Whatcha' drinkin' tonight?" he gruffed.

"Something strong," her voice strained from smoke and emotion.

"Long Island?"

"Yeah, but not too sweet – and use the chilled stuff so the ice doesn't melt."

Bells looked at her direct, she could see her own pain reflected in his obsidian eyes.

"Ice gonna melt either way," he said, his eyes silent like a doll's. Sometimes he didn't even look real, and he never looked like he knew what the hell he was talking about – but she knew what he meant.

"Just give me the chilled stuff."

K took her drink, sliding the amber-filled glass across the grooves in the bar top to her chest, he used large glasses for Long Islands, tall and wider at the top than at the base. She turned to face Becky and her band, reaching for her Polaroid in a patent leather bag. It was because it matched her outfit is why she wore it – her tight black top, her black hose stockings that stopped and folded at the top of her thigh clasped to garters, just where her red plaid skirt, like a school girl's, ended. If she moved or turned quickly, someone watching would get a glimpse of where the hose stopped and see her bare white skin. It made her feel sassy.

Kathy pulled out the camera and cleared some stickiness from her throat that had gathered there.

"Okay, everyone! Picture time! Gather 'round, gather 'round," she said waving her arms, and even though she yelled it was difficult for them to hear. "Come on guys! I said, *gather round.*"

Becky looked up from her sip of Seven & Seven through soft baby eyes, her smile the nervous gleam of sunlight on pond water before a storm. Her burgundy hair straight to her chin and perfect, the shine like they talk about in shampoo commercials, but rarely seen.

"You can't take my picture, sweety," Becky said.

"Of course I can take your picture." And K held up the camera, aiming. "Now shut up and smile."

Becky reached out her left hand to cover the lens, lowering it from K's eye.

"I'm serious, K, you can't take my picture. I don't know where I heard it or what, but there's a tribe in Africa, or somewhere, that believes that every time your picture is taken it captures a piece of your soul. I'm not sure what that means but since I started working with

Simone, I'm trying to watch my soul stuff."

Simone was Becky's new mentor, a medium that talked to the dead, brought them back for her clients to speak with, her face appearing to change into something different every time she did. If it was a hoax, it was a damn good one and now Becky was going to learn the art – talking with the dead.

"Aborigines," grunted Bells, while handing beers to some guy and taking a soggy twenty that had lain too long on the wet bar top.

"What?" Becky yelled.

"Aborigines, the *tribe* you're thinking of is the Australian Aborigines – and they aren't the only ones."

"Yeah, Aborigines," stated Becky, turning back to Kathy. "And they aren't the only ones."

"You're serious, aren't you?"

Becky nodded. "Uh, huh," and bent down to sip her Seven & Seven.

"But I may never see you again. I'm gonna forget what you look like." And there was a sense of desperation – like that one picture would've changed anything. Like every time she was down and lonely she could just pick it up and look at it and everything would be back as it was. Like putting that tiny face in her hands would be the same as having Becky there in front of her – talking about how great her new song was, or the size of the dick on the guy she did last night, or telling K her worst fears after one too many beers and one too many tokes on a healer.

Like a picture wouldn't hurt her even more every time she saw it. Like it could do anything more than capture a piece of your soul and remind you, sadistically, of who you were then and who you are now – something so flat and lifeless that it could be saved on a 3x5 inch card with a glossy finish. They had to make it glossy, she thought, that was the thing – just to make you look more interesting.

Maybe that's why her father started taking all those pictures in the first place. Maybe he was like her, wanting to set into permanence something impermanent. Maybe he knew he would leave some day and he'd like to pick up the photos and remember all over again how school was that day. Or hear her tears that were cute and wanting when she had scraped her knee or lost her teddy bear. Maybe that's what he was thinking taking all those pictures – but he didn't take any with him.

"You'll see me again," the words hesitant to leave her mouth, her hand brushing down Kathy's shoulder like petting a cat. "Anyway, I already told you, you oughta move to Seattle. Why don't you just come with us? There's nothing here for you." Her hand stopped at K's elbow, squeezing her there.

"Seattle? Please!" Kathy let out a tight breath between her tongue and the roof of her mouth, rolling her eyes. "You've got to know how I feel about Seattle. The weather sucks – I'd be totally…imprisoned. What if I had to escape?" And she shook her head at the impossibility of it, "No."

"Escape? Escape from where?"

"From Seattle, obviously." K lowered her head to the level of the Long Island, taking a drink.

"Why would you have to?"

"Why would I have to?" Kathy said sarcastically, looking up to the ceiling. Dear lord, the reasons were so painfully clear. "Yes, of course, why would I have to?"

She brought her hand up to tap against her mouth, pretending to think it over – her cigarette shed ashes on her red plaid skirt as she did.

"What if I got caught up in some drug scam?" and she looked at Becky and took another drink, pushed open her purse, slid the camera inside. "Or the Mafia mistook me for a stoolie? Or the government thought I was a Soviet spy? Or were secretly doing experiments on my brain and then, one day, I just came to and figured it out and they were on to me so I had to escape and worn others? Or the cops wanted to use me as a ploy because I looked like the ex-girlfriend of a guy that…"

"Whoa, whoa, whoa! Slow down, girl. You mean to tell me that you won't come to Seattle because of some wild made up bullshit about somethin' that ain't never gonna happen no how?"

There was a pause, a siphoned moment from an old dry well. K looked soft into Becky's docile eyes. How naive, how innocent – a woman without a way out. Sad, really.

"Something will happen all right. And I'm gonna be right here in Kansas City when it does!"

Kathy punctuated the end of the sentence with a hard terse nod. A bosky curl wriggled onto her face like a black worm on a hook. She blew at the hairs, then brushed them aside.

"Why, what's so great about Kansas City?"

Kathy's pale face shone in the drab surroundings and dark coats like a snow-capped mountain on a clear night. Her ashy cheek round and sharp like the sail of a yacht full of North wind – could have taken her out of that place in class. Proud and undaunted while all around lay an ocean of wretches that would just as soon cut her sails and leave her shorebound forever – she knew that, she knew it all too well.

"Because from here you can escape to everywhere," she said, drifting off into the possibility of it, the longing to leave pushing on her like ocean wind.

"From here you can go north, south, east, west, southeast, northwest – everywhere! And as a bonus, if you escape to the south, west or southwest, the wheat fields wave you good-bye. As if each stalk was a person, and each person was saying, *Hey, good luck, we'll miss you. Come again soon.*" K tilted her head right, waved her hand to no one at all. "See, you're going west, you get the bonus!"

Becky took a sip of Seven & Seven keeping her eyes on K as she finished off the last of the Long Island. K's image was warbled through the smoke. The heat of the many bodies made it suffocating in the bar and difficult to stand, and Becky wiped her brow.

"Well dear, it's the dead of winter. I don't think anything's gonna be wavin' us nothin."

"Oh yeah, I forgot, you don't get the bonus in winter. Nonetheless, if I were in Seattle, I could only escape to the east or south, clearly Canada and the ocean are not options – and don't forget the mountains. What if there were rain or snow on the ground? I couldn't escape at all!"

A few of the band members turned to face one another and start up their own conversation. They decided long ago that K was pretty much whacked out and they could never understand why she repeatedly turned down drugs from them. It seemed to them that drugs – any drug – would have done K a world of good.

And Becky thought, too, that Kathy had been walking a thin line between reality and fantasy for quite some time now. But the bond they'd developed over years of working together in that completely crazed-out, fry hall/shit hole had assured them of a long friendship together. And if one of them went a little insane along the way, then it was to be expected. The other would be there to help pick up the pieces of the shattered mirror of their lost reality.

Bells gimped over closer to the group at the south end of the bar, wringing his hands to massage the tired joints of thumbs and fingers that looked spongy and shook slightly when he held them out, probably just from age. He sucked in his lips, moistening them with the tip of his tongue, then returned them.

Kathy stepped to the bar setting down her glass. She put her weight against the padded rail feeling too hot and tired to stand on her own just then, her hand rubbing out some tension in her forehead.

"How 'bout just a rum and diet this time."

He grunted something that must have meant *Okay*, or *Sure* or *Comin' right up*, because he hunched over to fill a glass with ice and began filling it with Bacardi and Diet Coke.

"Did I hear you right, Angel? You only live here 'cause it's a good place to escape *from?*" He scooted the drink into her cupped palm, she nodded in confirmation, taking drink in hand and sipping it through one of those tiny red straws that he always put in the short glass drinks, unless it was a beer chaser. "What are you so afraid of, Angel, really?"

"I'm no angel, Bells, and I don't know, it's silly." Bells and Becky both gave her a look of disbelief, K stuttered momentarily, then continued, "I...I just...I kinda feel like something's been chasing me. I can't describe it any better than that, honest." She weakly put up the two

91

fingers of her right hand as if to say, *I swear it* or *scout's honor.*

"You're gonna have to do better than that, this is Bells you're talkin' to. Now then, Angel, who's chasin' ya?"

She looked to the ground and shook her head from side to side like the slow pendulum on an old grandfather clock, thumping her foot against the bar. People were clamoring at the far end of the bar waiting for drinks and Bells surprised her, grumbled like a large boulder breaking loose from a mountainside.

"Who?"

"Satan!" she blurted out, taken back, her hand slipping from her forehead, several people turning to look. She then lowered to a near whisper, tilting her head down and sideways, and spoke through thin and tight lips. "Ever since I was a little girl I've felt like Satan was chasing me. I think he was chasing my father and now he's after me."

"Ah, Angel," he laughed in a low rumble. The rumble felt so nice as it passed through her, it almost swept her up inside of it. Almost swept her off to some distant, cartoon land where she could laugh at her own silliness right along with him – almost. "Satan doesn't chase people, people come to him."

A tone hummed out of his closed lips like a note off the string of a Stradivarius and gently rocked back and forth in the space between Kathy and Bells. K stood for a moment in silence feeling the subtle music that had been created there.

She had said too much. Once secrets are spilled, anyone might retrieve them. Then they've got you, they know your weaknesses. Predators lurk in every corner mimicking friends and work mates – you don't know who you can trust, really.

She swirled the remaining ice around her glass with her chewed-up red straw, watching it all swirl around, creating a funnel. Down, down that funnel went and Katherine wished she could dive right into it – dive in and lose herself in the unknown funnel of her rum and Diet Coke. And she'd keep going to, she wouldn't be satisfied like the ignorant pieces of ice floating around without purpose or destination. No,

92

she'd go deeper, go beyond what any piece of ice or tiny red straw ever dared do.

She'd go straight to the bottom of that funnel and come out on the flip side. On the chance that what lay on the other side was opposite this world – she'd take that dive. On that small hope that this world was just a dream or, at worst, one of many worlds that she could take her choice of – and this one wouldn't be it.

"Someday I'll go there," K mumbled, the ice spinning in dance in the small glass. Bells looked over from the crowd to her right.

"Where's that, Angel?"

She whispered the answer so no one else could hear, looking up from her glass to meet his gray filmy eyes.

"To everywhere."

"Well, Seattle rocks," Becky said pushing her way next to K, pretending nothing had just happened. Pretending Kathy wasn't leaving bits of herself all over the bar top with each word she spoke. "We're going to make it huge there. Just like Pearl Jam, Soundgarden, Alice in Chains – Seattle is totally cool!"

"What? Kansas City's cool. Why don't you just stay here?"

"No, K, Kansas City is not cool, Kansas City's cold, damn cold – cold as a snowman's balls. And then, after the first day of spring which is also, coincidentally enough, the last day of spring, it's hot, hot as Satan's piss."

Floor smoke drifted between them, tightening around K's ankles like a white sand snake, not as much constricting as protective, as if her ankles were the awkward, bony eggs of the thing. The smoke ran up and down Becky's bare legs, under her turquoise suede mini-skirt like the seemingly benign fingers of a childhood sweetheart.

"Look, I leave tomorrow, let's not fight. I can't explain it, K, I just know that destiny is waiting for me in Seattle."

Becky was right, she died two weeks later. The funeral was the following Monday, but it wasn't very much fun.

Lavender pushed through the air. Somebody knew about lavender – calm, release, emotional support. Relaxation – let go. They knew that even the wrought iron of someone's anger could rust and weaken in its presence. They knew how even the steel prongs of hurt they felt jutting out of their hearts could bend slightly under its scent.

They knew that people were unconscious, that they could make them feel whatever it is they wanted and to Katherine it smelled like the lost and misguided flowers in a cemetery. It was the smell of lavender and a thousand lilacs trampled dead, dried and buried beneath the floorboards. The odor seeping through the cracks and merging with the smell of petrified oak – dead, hard bench oak upon which K sat in discomfort shifting weight from cheek to numbing cheek. It smelled like she was at the edge of a mysterious, forbidden forest – alluringly sweet, but dead and rotting and best not entered.

The dry furnace air scraped at her nasal passage over and over in the same vulnerable spot as if it had fingernails, and K was thinking of running away before things got worse.

There wasn't much light, not like she imagined God would want it. Round, beige light shades hung from the steeple ceiling every ten feet or so down the aisle. The thin illumination barely escaped from its glass containers in a slow golden spread like old butter, faintly spotlighting the red carpet of the walkway like golden lily pads that you could leap your way to Heaven on.

The predominating light came from prismatic rays that stretched out of the southern windows like the mischievous fingers of a wayward rainbow. The fingers touched the people in such a glorious array of colors, Kathy wanted to scrunch up their puffy red, yellow and blue faces and sprinkle them on vanilla ice cream. And not just ordinary vanilla ice cream but a vanilla ice cream that said, *Homemade Style* on it, or, *Vanilla Bean.*

The stained glass windows birthed pictures of Mary and baby Jesus. And another one had a rendition of an older Jesus with his palms open and it looked like he was walking toward you. He was drenched in his own light and the aura that surrounded him was like a different dimension altogether, like a window of light or a doorway that Jesus could use to step in or out of this world as he pleased.

Kathy stared long at the light that drenched Jesus. She wouldn't mind that happening to her someday – walking down the street or sitting at Bells' and having light start to come out of her skin and pores. And the people at Bells' would be like, "Hey, come over here a second. I'm trying to read this." And she'd light it up for them, whatever it was.

Probably only perceptive people would be able to see it, though, like kids. And they'd say, "Hey mom, look at that cool light lady." And the mom would say, "Don't point, it isn't polite." But K would smile anyway and wink at the child as she passed him by.

Sometimes people would ask her to come over and be with them, just to hang out and they wouldn't even know why. But K would know. It was because of the Jesus light pouring out of her like a flood that made them feel good and whole just being around it.

Amidst the dark rafters, stone walls and wood floors, the priest's hollow words echoed like a child in a cave testing the reverberations of different pitches and sounds.

"Hello - Hello - hello - ello," yelled the little boy. And, "Ratty-tat-tat - Ratty-tat-tat - atty-tat-tat," he said, both arms outstretched like a gangster with a machine gun. Then, "Hey stinky - Hey stinky - hey stinky - ey inky." And, "Ouhh la la - Ouh la la - ouh-la la - la la," was exclaimed to chase an imaginary, naked French woman running through the winding tunnels.

Kathy wanted to shout out, "Fuckin' A - Fuckin' a - uckin' a," to see if those words would bounce off church walls. But she feared that if they did they would bounce back and blend with the priest's words sounding something like, "So God took this child back to Heaven, fuckin' A."

The priest stopped talking and an organ began playing with deep brassy tones. Everyone in the church started singing along and K felt suddenly foolish and lost, not knowing any of the words. So she mouthed along making occasional gurgles with her throat or saying a word a little later, after she could tell what it was. *Ble* would turn into blessings almost every time – *Chi* would become children. She was getting the hang of it when the music abruptly stopped and the priest started up again.

Kathy looked around, eyeing the crowd in disbelief. No one was wearing black. Black was supposed to be a mainstay at funerals, a bastion. But nobody wore black, except for K, of course, and she looked ridiculous.

In the ladies room mirror, its impressive thick gold trim with squiggly, pigtail shapes carved throughout, she had seen how foolish she really looked. Black was stuck all over her. She looked like a white baby seal that had fallen into a tar pit. Black full length evening gown that flowed like a stola, black high-heeled shoes, black studded anklet, black onyx bracelet, black beaded necklace, black opal earrings, black nail polish, eye shadow, lipstick and an oversized, black flowered veil that hung about her like Death's doily on a china doll.

"Jesus, K, you look like Vampira."

She wet the tips of her fingers and pressed them to the lids of her closed sloe-eyes, smearing the mascara in smudgy spots and crooked streaks to make it look as if she'd been crying.

Kathy had already prepared herself for never seeing Becky again. She certainly wasn't going to Seattle, not so long as she could still kick and scream and gouge out the eyes of whatever fiend might attempt to drag her there, and chances were slim that Becky would ever make it back to KC. So this wasn't that big of a leap. Death, Seattle – really, what's the difference?

So, so what if she hadn't cried – not even a drop. This was too exciting for tears, Kathy had never been to a funeral before and some dark part of her was looking forward to it, a part of her that had been sleeping away the winter of her life like some hibernating black-haired hyena.

She was looking forward to hearing the priest speak his knowing and Godly words. Was looking forward to bearing witness to the hugs of consolation from friends and family. Was looking forward to seeing her friend's barren face, black-pale and beautiful and set off by the square sides of the wooden casket like in a picture frame. A shiny white pillow would gently cradle her head like a marshmallow from Heaven.

She tugged at the resisting veil, "I can't believe nobody else is wearing black." The veil pulled at her hairs as if it had grown frail roots, then plopped off and fell into the sink. Detached – withered.

Kathy sat with legs and arms crossed, the fingers of her right hand tapped methodically, rolling atop her left arm like a caterpillar, and the priest's words echoed in her head as emptily as they did around the desolate angled ceiling. This was nothing like she had envisioned.

Outside in the dead of winter is where Kathy pictured a funeral. A handful of sad-faced, tear-stained patrons gathered around a mound of freshly dug dirt. The dark brown belly of mother earth had specs of winter white intermingled within and they all gazed emptily at the body-sized void that waited like an open mouth for the casket next to it. The casket was as glossy white as the specs of snow embedded in the loose dirt, with a gold trim whose color looked matte metallic in the gray unfolding freeze frames of K's imagination.

She spun the scene around an old-fashioned bulky reel to reel in her mind, projecting a grainy black and white image reminiscent of the Chaplin era. Only the people didn't move in quick jerky movements, they moved in slow jerky movements. And when an arm raised to wipe away a tear or touch a loved one on the shoulder, the film would smear it and K could see a ghost arm move for several seconds after the action had actually taken place.

The dry February wind scratched at her pale beauty like a playful cat. The harsh and chilling wind slapped the hair from her face to reveal the perfect lines of her jaw, the fullness of her blackened lips, and a nose tiny and vulnerable like a newborn mouse. The wind forced her to brace herself against it, forced her to blink repeatedly to protect the peeled grapes of her eyes from freezing like the hairs in her nostrils that crackled and stiffened with each breath. The wind brushed aside a tear as it tried, fleetingly, to run down the length of her cheek.

And the blue-steel frozen wisdom that puffed from the priest's mouth was like the smoke of an old train and was forged from deep within the man. It was forged somewhere beneath his abdomen from some forgotten part of his soul by master forgers – divine forgers.

These steel smiths pounded out the blue-white smoke-wisdom on grandiose white anvils that hummed a perfect 440 Hz with each stroke. The smoke sung off the mighty blows and rose from the depths of the preacher's soul into his inspired voice and out, freed into the wintry day. There it quickly dispersed and spread out amongst the mourners to be breathed in as if it were the pure refreshing air of a mountain mist.

The result of this divine forging was small-town drugstore five and dime truth. It was eternal wisdom straight from the heart of God. The Reverend spewed forth this wisdom as if it were the sugar from a sweet lullaby. It flowed so effortlessly that it had to be truth, not being obstructed by the doubt that lie lurking in a liar's throat.

And when the priest spoke, the words gave substance and meaning to all. It made sense out of life, death, love, hate, God, existence and paintball – all in one swoop. When you left, you had all the answers to all the questions and you understood for the first time, why people had to live, and why people had to die.

But this wasn't at all right. The priest wasn't old or fat, which all wise people are, either one or the other, and had short blond hair for crying out loud. Not the preferred gray or the lesser but still acceptable salt and pepper look, not even the tolerable black or dark brown – but blond! It made K wonder if he really went to seminary school. This alleged *priest* didn't even explain *why* she died, as in the purpose of death and all, let alone *how* she died, that it was drug related.

It was as if he were trying to slip her into Heaven through the back door mail slot in plain brown paper wrapping, like the girly magazines that come to the house generic-like to fool your wife and kids.

All his words kept turning circles, coming back to the same theme. *We don't know why. The Lord works in mysterious ways. It is a great loss for us. It is a gift for Heaven. You can never be fully prepared. God misses his children. Sometimes he takes them back.*

Dreams had more substance. Plastic soldiers had more resolve. His words were the fairytales children needed to get to sleep at night.

There were no muscle-chiseled forgers pounding out blue-steel smoke on huge anvils in his soul. Just dwarfed children spinning tinker-toy wheels faster and faster until a grayish puff pooped out the top of a rickety tin tower. The whole contraption would soon fall, set itself on fire and collapse from their frenetic pace and ineptitude.

And what would he do then. Him and his blond head would need a drool cup fastened to it as he tried to read from The Big Picture Bible Book. *God misses his children, so there are times when he takes them back.* Okra burgers had more meat.

"God can wait, anyway," thought K. "If I had deserted my child I'd miss her too, but I wouldn't hunt her down and kill her."

On the bench in front of her were wooden pockets with hymnals and books. Someone had tried etching something into the wood, *Hel...* But it wasn't finished – a child, his hand slapped away when his mother noticed. Probably he wanted to say *Help!* Maybe *Hell.*

The heater kicked on and with it came a new round of lavender scents, as if there were oils in the vents. All she could smell was manipulation. The soothing scents making people think it was all right – a beautiful twenty-five-year-old girl had died and, hey, no problem, everything's just fine. It wasn't.

The words he spoke made it all the more condescending. But the people nodded their heads in agreement. They were fish being flushed to the shallow end of the water by the flapping wings of white pelicans.

Don't go out into the vast unknown ocean, the scent was saying. *Don't make a scene. Don't question it. Stay with us. It's safe here in the shallow water.* That's what the churches had been saying all along – since Jesus died. Ever since he was put away, buried in a granite mastaba a thousand years removed where he couldn't defend himself.

It was tree houses and bedroom forts and imaginary friends – the mooring you attach to when you're a kid and you're growing up in a house alone. It was like that for K when she was a child. Each night she would check under the bed and in the closet several times before going to sleep with force fields. "Super-lock force field – on," she would say. That was just for people. She'd put another one on top of that for animals, another force field for ghosts and anything else out there that could hurt her that she didn't even know the names of.

The heater turned off and the lavender-lilac smell lessened, leaving behind only a musty aftermath like moss in a forest after the rainy season had come and gone. The staunch and stale part staying like the musk on a piece of dead bark, floating down the aisle next to Kathy. She watched as the musty dead bark floated by as if the aisle were a thin, still river. Gently it moved, turning this way and that, like a dry leaf in the wind with nowhere to get to and no concerns of its own. The moldy bark continued down the length of the aisle till it came to the steps at the priest's feet.

There it stopped where it flipped over from the impact, launching bits of moldy musk onto the priest's shiny black shoes and the cuffs of his black 70% polyester and 30% cotton pants. The mold spread over him like a fast cancer and soon overtook him, leaving him tainted with green.

His young face looked so alone and naive in green, K wanted to pinch off his head and place it in a melon patch on some distant farm with lots of kids to water it, and to play with it, and to just keep it company.

K hoped beyond hope that the kids wouldn't use his head as a ball for their little games and kick him around and throw him up against the wall, though she knew that they would.

More and more she drifted away from his empty words, becoming separated from the church, from warmth, from colors. She was on a snowy plain blinded by wind and cold. She was alone with her questions. Answers were lost in icy layers miles below or miles away. They weren't here, they weren't coming out of him and K wondered if he simply didn't know. A representative of God, speaking for God, by God – and if he didn't know, who did?

Where were the answers to be found? Where was the person who understood the depths of her inquiries, who would know from the searing look of pain in her eyes that she needed more.

Where was the person who would understand that she was a woman of depth, a person who needed answers deep, hard and true as an arrow to pierce the thick dark hide of her lost roaming soul? That she'd been searching lost soul-like among these other seemingly found souls for seemingly immeasurable drops of time. Drops of time that fell like the tears of every mother and father who had ever lost a child.

K got up, rubbed against the oak bench in front of her for the smoothness on her hip, pretended to cry – like it was too much, it was too difficult, like she couldn't take it anymore. She couldn't.

"Another foray into piety," she murmured, as much of the crowd turned to watch her leave, their faces drawn and sorrowful, nodding their understanding of why she had to go. "And again I'm left dissatisfied."

The sun went down with hard edges leaving a sharp and bitter darkness in its wake. Night descended onto 39th Street with icicles, and dark and angry longings for a few more rays of sunlight.

The walk up the sidewalk to Bells' reeked of bus exhaust and old wine that had been spilled or vomited in the streets or gutters. Then perfume and an array of colognes as a crowd of people passed, huddled together in padded coats that were mostly brown and black. The icicle night jabbed K in the stomach a few times – to remind her of what had been left behind, and to let her know of what was left to come.

Bob had dropped her off down the street from Bells' after the funeral, she tried not to laugh but it was difficult. She spent the ride home murmuring some Indonesian sounding chant, or new age mantra. *Rah—burt*, she said over and over. *Rah – burt*. And, sometimes, she'd call him that out loud, Robert, and he'd always say, "Jesus, K, its Bob. Or you can call me Bobby, I think you should know that by now."

Which made it worse. It was like the Bob had realized how degrading it was to be called a Bob and tried to disguise itself by adding a *by*. As if to say, *I know my name reeks of stupidity, but I'm too damn stupid to make it unreek. So, since I don't have the mental prowess to step up to the Robert plate and swing away, I'll just sit in the batter's box spinning on my "Sit and Spin" and call myself Bobby.*

K and Becky had worked with Bob at Nichol's when he was a busboy the summer before, and since he was kind of an outcast they befriended him quickly. Luckily they had just come from a funeral and Bob assumed the sniffles and outbursts were tears. Every now and then he'd pat her black-hosed thigh and say something like, "It's okay, Kathy, don't cry."

Bob was such a stupid name, it couldn't even escape its own triteness. Barricaded at both ends with two bookend *B's*, keeping it forever trapped and redundant. It's the same silly, stupid little name both forwards and backwards. But sometimes it's short for Robert, which isn't funny at all.

K moved through the coolness of February following her puffs of white breath that led her toward Bells' like fairies, or maybe just the fairy dust they'd left behind, looking up to read the sign on Bells' Bar. She always looked up there like it was an anchor, like seeing it meant she couldn't drift away with the tide. Like the rest of 39th Street might be a mirage and that sign was the only truth. She had to be sure she was really home.

It had once read *Bill's Bar*, on the count of that was his real name – Bill, but that was so long ago no one called him Bill anymore. She had crawled onto the ledge outside her window and pried loose the planks, rearranging the letters, switching it to *Bill's Bob*. It was because it was funny is why – the name *Bob* and all. And whenever she came in or out or was sitting inside depressed and dejected, she could laugh at how ridiculous it was.

Then she changed it again Christmas of that same year when Bells was giving away free shot glasses as a promotion. They were designed to look like jingle bells with a shot glass on the top and a bell on the bottom. The sign he made read, *Free Jingle Bels glass with each shot.* He'd misspelled the word *bells*, and K never let him forget it. Now everyone called him that and didn't even know it was a joke, or why the bar had that weird name. Nobody ever asked Bells questions, except K.

The wind wanted to harass Kathy as she moved up 39th Street, tangle her hair and slap her face, but it was being partially blocked by the northern buildings and only had the strength to brush the hair off her cheek as it passed her by. A black rainbow ran down the gutter to her right. She turned her head to watch it ooze, leaving itself all over the place it had just been, shedding. It would freeze soon, which was good. Frozen black rainbows couldn't do much harm.

The bum sat with his back against the brick of Bells' Bar dirty and beaten, looking like a man without hope. Not just beaten, like beaten up, roughed up by some neighborhood bully, but beaten by life itself, beaten by his own existence. Where do you go after that kind of beating? 39th Street was as good a place as any.

He looked like he'd spent his whole life chasing the pot of gold at the end of one black rainbow after another. His tattered clothes were brown to the eye but probably a different color beneath the grime and filth of it all.

"Damn, right in front of the door," she thought. "Just don't make eye contact."

"I know, K, I know! Jesus, don't you think I know that!" She had passed him a hundred times and a hundred times she'd told herself the very same thing.

But she did glance. She always glanced and he always saw her glancing, but not a word did he ever say, not a penny did he plea – until tonight.

He reached out and his hand slowed in the air as it grabbed for her, as if the air got thicker just at that moment, as if the air became dense around his hand pulling it to the ground. His outstretched fingers curled under his palm like the Rose of Jerico after a stretch of drought and his wrist went limp, making his hand look lost and disoriented, as if it had just woken up from a long deep sleep.

A buzz from the red neon sign above him outlined his words.

"Child...please," he said waving her toward him with his limp, numb-looking fingers. "Please...come here."

With that he clutched his chest with his other hand and folded to the ground face down, blood ran from his nose where he landed hard and K thought he must have broken it. She rushed to his side, cradled his face in her palms then brushed the hairs from his cheek and she was struck by her sensitivity.

Never could she have imagined actually touching him – *that* would be disgusting. But suddenly, there was a person there. She couldn't believe that there had been a person hidden under that filth all this time. He was practically a child and K's heart opened up wanting to swallow him whole. Her heart wanted to take him inside of her where everything was always safe and warm and no food or wine was ever needed.

All you felt was the joy of being there, because you were never alone.

Suddenly there was compassion inside of her, some unknown pocket full of empathy deep inside she'd never reached into before. She'd thought there was only lint in there and already-chewed Bazooka wrapped in its own comic paper that wasn't even that funny to begin with – and was less funny now that there was chewed-up gum stuck all over it.

But there was something else. Maybe it was a quarter, maybe it was a silver dollar or maybe it was even a piece of gold. But it was worth something, whatever it was, and K wanted to take it out and press it into his palm closing his cold, rigid fingers softly around it.

She held his face and gave his cheek a caressing soft stroke as she turned it to face her.

"I do this for you," his voice was but a whisper. "For you K." He said no more.

The sun was gone and flat black clouds were sneaking across the sky holding back most of the light from the moon and stars. But the glow of neon still hovered over 39th Street and K wished she could go somewhere darker, where worms go. A solitary worm making its way past the conjugated tunnels of other worms where light from the surface still trailed in. She'd burrow in serpentining streaks, furrowing around deep-seated roots until she crouched behind a stone set far in the belly of the earth. Life was a candle, conjuring death.

Everything stood still. Nothing could move. Nothing could enter and nothing could leave. The space in which K and Bells stood was a vacuum where no wind could blow and no bird could sing. Even the air seemed to be missing.

Stars poked through holes in the sky and the moon showed its bright face from behind a cloud moving away, but their light could not reach into it – into the un-hallowed space where death had snuffed out the flame of the 39th Street Bum.

When the ambulance had come and gone and all the people had milled away, Bells was at her side again and again Kathy began to cry – tears from a poet who'd trekked deep into the heart of existence and could not bring back a single word to express it.

"I don't like this…don't like not having control of my emotions like this." Her words were choppy in the uneven flow of tears. She hiccuped for breath.

Bells took her to his side under his thick arm and K lowered her face into both cupped hands.

"I know Angel, I know. Sometimes a dog shits all over the yard. Sometimes he'll shit on the same spot over and over." His scratchy voice was a dream lulling her away from the reality of that night into some-place warm and earthy. Burning fires and hand made rocking chairs, where she snuggled under a quilt she had made herself years before and sipped hot apple cider with a pinch of cinnamon and nutmeg from a beat up tin mug.

And if there were a dog there it was big and old like a Golden Retriever well past his prime. Not one of those snippy dogs that bark and holler every time a leaf drops to the ground. No, this dog wouldn't have cared if the whole tree came crashing down. He'd continue resting his head on her pink slippered foot that was mainly terrycloth and rub-ber and only cost a buck fifty at the local Wal-Mart.

"What's that supposed to mean?" she said, sniffling tears. "It's all dog shit either way? Or am I the spot the dog keeps shitting on over and over? Whatever it is it sounds an awful lot like Serenity Prayer to me. Please Bells, for the love of God, don't tell me I should accept the things

I cannot change."

"It doesn't matter if you accept them or not, Angel. Life pays no never-mind to your acceptance or non-acceptance, it just keeps keepin' on – and that is the gospel truth!"

He led her around the corner at the hardware store to her back alley, stopping at the bottom of her stairs where the air was clammy and cold around her neck like a damp scarf, its texture like the dying wrinkled face she had held just moments before.

K looked up into a clearing of clouds where a star peeked through – singular and alone. *It takes light to grow things*, she thought. *That's why the sun is so important.* The star's thin light barely made it through the opening and K had to look hard, meet it halfway. Then the clouds closed again and what did it matter. That star was too small to make things grow, anyway.

"Need a lift tonight?"

"I think I can make it," she smiled dryly, not at the sarcasm itself but at the milieu surrounding it. "You're a God send, Bells." She kissed his cheek.

"Yeah, well somethin' like that, Angel." He replied, and began his familiar wounded trot out of the back alley.

From around the corner Bells could hear a handful of faint words, just the ghosts of the words, really. Even in their transparent form he had no trouble understanding them, he'd heard them a thousand times.

"By the way, Bells," the words whispered. "I'm no angel."

Light peeped out beneath the rusty white awning over her door. It looked like the light at the end of that tunnel everybody was always talking about.

"I didn't know you'd have to go up to get to it," she thought, and picked up her left foot, placing it on the bottom warped and chipped stair.

It looked like a long way – if it were a dream it would get farther away with each step. If it wasn't a dream the light should get closer.

That's how she knew that life wasn't a dream sometimes. She had road marks, a trail of breadcrumbs leading her back to reality.

When the walls behaved like they were supposed to and didn't turn into faces or start crumbling for no reason – that's how she knew they were real. When the walk home from Bells' didn't take hours and she didn't have to travel through dark forests, where images formed like goblins and werewolves in the tree bark, and cross an eerie lagoon, where the water bubbled like acid, then it was real. There were no forests or lakes between her house and Bells'.

She took another step and the light got closer. "Damn," she said. "Was kinda hoping this one was a dream."

Through the blue light her face was rent in the mirror. Its twisted features brush strokes of Francis Bacon. She was *Isabel Rawsthorne* or one in the series of *Screaming Popes*. "Man is an accident," he had said. "A completely futile being."

There were secrets in the blue light, in the soft folds and dark edges turned underneath the mirror and hiding behind the bathtub. Its tint pulling things to the surface that normally couldn't be seen through the naked eye without the help of Quaalude's or exotic mushrooms. K filled the sink basin with warm soapy water, spread it over her face. When she looked back up, nothing had changed. Something was being pulled to the surface, and K wasn't ready for it. She wished she had a normal light in there, or maybe rose tinted. She pulled the chain, spread more warm water over her eyes.

As she left the bathroom, she ran her fingers across the grill of the vent on the way to the kitchen. She stopped and looked inside – dust coated the slats and she couldn't see past that. The vent had a chute that bent around to the foot of the alley, exiting at an air conditioning unit behind Saigon 39. The landlord said it was how they used to get ice up there in the thirties, attaching the blocks of ice to cables and hauling them in.

But K figured it was an escape route – someone selling booze during prohibition, or a mob laundering outfit, or a small time punk running numbers or a poker game. Either way it was the reason she took the apartment. She had a flashlight and a rope stashed inside and the grill popped in and out without screws, easy and quick.

She had another escape route, a rope fastened on the ledge outside the window to an iron mooring she had installed herself. She should dust the vent soon and clean it out. Something was coming – Satan, maybe. His warted horns, his puss-filled smile – stag beetles hanging from his ears like jewelry. His footprints were getting closer, they were the deaths and the hollow spaces the bodies left when they had gone.

K grabbed the almond butter and an apricot and mango soy yogurt from the fridge, which was the last of the food. She never had much food in there, anyway, always got by on very little.

The art of living on coffee rinds, she called it. She didn't know why, she hated coffee. It was the point of it, she'd told herself. Living cheap is what it meant, like you could re-use the rinds for…whatever, another drink she supposed.

"Are you sure coffee has rinds?"

"No, but that's not the point either. It's *the point* that counts, living cheap," she had said.

"I thought a rind was something on an orange."

"Never mind."

She sat on the bed with the yogurt and almond butter, propped a pillow between her and the wall, kicked the sheets away with her foot. Her foot hit something solid and she bent over and lifted the blankets. It was her dictionary, the big blue Webster's Unabridged.

"God, that's weird," she said aloud. "When did I put that there?"

"I don't know, K."

It was open, in the *p*'s. She had highlighted *Potbound.* She remembered that from the last story she'd written.

"Fuck."

K threw her food on the nightstand, ran to the closet to drag out the footlocker, its brass corners squealing on the wood floors. She flipped back to a story she'd written three weeks prior, the night of the bad scene in her back alley. The floor was hard on her knees but she didn't stand, just stared in amazement as she lifted the story with both hands, held it out in front of her. It was titled, *St. Bum*.

"Fuck."

Obsequiously – adv. Excessively willing to serve or obey. Overly submissive. Servile, compliant.

Pother – n. A suffocating cloud rising from tumult and fuss.

Lenis – adj. In phonetics, weakly articulated.

Mealy – adj. Spotted or flecked. Pale, floury in color, like meal. Powdery, dry.

Amity – n. Harmony. Friendship between individuals. Good understanding.

Consignee – n. The person to whom goods or other things are transferred.

Potbound – adj. Having roots so compact as to have no room for expansion. Said of potted plants.

Confessional – n. A small enclosed place where one discloses sins.

Serenity – n. Quality or state of being serene. Calmness, quietness, peace.

Postulant – n. A petitioner or candidate for admission into a religious order.

Estranged – pt. To keep at a distance. Withdraw or remove from usual surroundings.

Bedlam – n. A mad house, hospital for the mentally ill. A mad man, lunatic – one who lives in bedlam.

Ornithoid – adj. Resembling birds in appearance or structure.

Leman – n. A sweetheart or lover. Especially mistress.

Toil – vi. To labor untiringly. To work hard and continuously.

Cupidity – n. desire, wish. Inordinate greed for something.

Lyterian – adj. A deliverer from. Indicating the end. In medicine, the end of a disease.

Lullaby – n. A song to quiet children, to lull them to sleep.

Transcursion – n. A passage beyond certain limits, extraordinary deviation.

Transdialect – vt. To translate from one dialect to another.

*S*t. *Bum*

He lay obsequiously on the concrete. Cold, that hard cement must be. *I wonder if he can feel the cold grip of the sidewalk around him through those rags he wears.* A pother of breath colored the air a hazy white, then lowered itself over the face of the man. Waiting for another breath to trespass into the night's darkness was all I knew to do. He clutched my arm so tightly, it was clear he did not want me to go for help, but just to stay with him.

The time for waiting for more lenis words to bleed from his mealy lips and face had already come and gone, he had said all he was going to say. But I had learned a lot, more than I had wished for when I awoke that morning. Now was also too late for help, help he did not want or need. What he needed now was amity.

"The hard times consignee – a potbound bum," was the most thought I'd ever afforded him. Potbound in his bottle of booze, potbound in the shop front concrete, potbound in existence.

I saw him there today as I had almost everyday, not looking too well, never looked too well, but less well than usual. He reached out to me even though I was several feet away as if trying to grab on, to have me take him with me to wherever it was I may be going. Looked like he might be reaching for a hand out.

"Wha, wha..." The words came painfully. He took a breath and winced. "What's your name child?"

I had stopped. *Damn it, why'd I have to stop?* I was thinking. *Should've just ignored the bum like always.*

"Kay," I answered with apprehension.

"Come closer child, I need...I need," he grasped at his chest and started falling sideways, sliding downward against the brick building. I rushed to him, kneeling, and he grabbed at my arm as if he were a sinner grabbing onto the sleeve of the lord Christ, begging for forgiveness and not letting go until it was granted.

He spoke, pausing for air after nearly each word. Seemed for hours he spoke, cried, prayed, I was to be his confessional on the day of his death.

"Oh God, grant me serenity," he began.

He was a postulant years ago. When he was firmly seated in priesthood, he became a strong force in the Catholic political structure and was thought to become a cardinal in later years. It was everything his parents had ever dreamed of him. But he went to the church for different reasons; he had lost control, lost control of the most valuable gift we have – our minds, our thoughts.

He thought the church would be the discipline he needed to regain that control. It helped for awhile – helped to focus the mind on other things, striving for recognition in the church and what not. But after that had been accomplished his mind became quickly bored and estranged and took life into its own soggy hands.

That day had started as any other and was about to end with as little muss as any other. Then a woman stopped by the church and asked to leave her young son with Father Bedlam. She said there was an emergency, that she would return in a few hours and could the Father please look after him until then. Father Bedlam knew better. He knew she would not return for her son, the way she stammered out each word, the way she looked around as if shoplifting. But talking her out of it seemed born of lost hope. Maybe he got careless, maybe he got lazy or maybe he got apathetic. Or maybe, he wanted her not to come back.

The boy was an ornithoid looking thing with a smooth girl face, the face of a leman from the father's past. He felt so sad, so sorry for the young thing, weeks had passed and the mother had not returned. His sorrow, his love for the helpless child was increasing day to day and his empathy grew and grew and soon had engulfed his life. He was losing control of his rationale. Was this entire scenario rational? A mother to leave her child, how rational was that? He was losing control of his thoughts, his precious thoughts. "No, not again."

His thoughts loved the boy and wanted love for the boy. His thoughts wanted to hold the boy and keep him forever close to him. His thoughts loved the flesh of the boy and wanted to feel the smooth boy skin against his own. His thoughts wanted to smell the fresh, young, boy smell. His thoughts wanted to taste the sweet boy taste.

And what would be the harm? Surely the boy wouldn't know the difference at that tender age. In fact, it was just what the boy needed – the boy needed love. He wanted to share the love that God had shared with him, wanted to love the boy, give him God's love. "God gave this child unto me, to shelter, to have and to hold – to love. I shall not disobey the will of God!"

But the boy was old enough to know the difference and soon the entire congregation knew.

The following years of self-indignation had led to this sidewalk. Where the patrons were kind, but not too kind, as he was not deserving of too much kindness. He'd often wondered if that grown boy had since left a dollar in his worn and shabby hat.

"I've become a bum, my second sin against humanity. God forgive me, I know I am a nuisance. I've seen the way people look at me. I've seen the way you look at me, too. You don't want me here, uglying up this once beautiful street. I once toiled for the grace of God and all his lovingness – I now toil for the grace of the bottle and all its forgetfulness.

"Yes, my life has been a quiet disease, a transcursion into realms not set up by God. But fear not, child, for today I sing a lyterian lullaby. I do this for you, for all of you. And I do this for you, Kay."

Saliva slid in a quivery streak from his mouth to chin to jacket sleeve. His eyes glazed over and his head lost its balance.

Oh God, he's dying. I can't just sit here and watch a man die, I was thinking.

Again I tried to leave for help but the grip was tight as if rigor mortis were already setting in. He was trying to speak, but his breath lost its cupidity. Mumbled and soft, I was able to transdialect the last few moans before he died.

"Serenity," he said. "Serenity."

In a way she knew, knew when she was writing the story who the story was about – knew who the girl in the story was. The way one knows the off and on pain in their gut is really an ulcer. The way one knows his lover has found somebody knew.

In a way she didn't want to know. She had placed the whole scene behind a black veil in her mind. She could see it from time to time, if she squinted hard and made a funny face, but it was fuzzy and unclear, definitely too unclear to take action on. Anyway, that veil had dropped now, and she desperately wished she could replace it with another – a thicker veil, and darker.

IV

WEEKS HAD PASSED, three or four, but barely. If they hadn't been forced to pass, they surely would have stayed, stayed and embedded themselves into the permanence of Kathy's existence like burrs. She wanted to run and skip through the open fields of spring but each time she tried she just ended up covered in burrs from head to toe. Then she would have to stop and attempt to pull them out, but they never came out. So the running stopped, the fun and games, and K had to sit trying to pick the burrs out of her heart that wouldn't let go.

"At least time is my ally," she had thought. "At least time will pass, it has to – pass right by and leave me the hell alone."

But it felt to K like time hadn't passed, that time had somehow forgotten its purpose – movement, change, death and rebirth. There was no movement, except for the tired walk to and from work and the lazy motion of serving up meatloaf and mashed potatoes or raising a whiskey sour to her lips. And there was no change, except for the loose change she got in tips and she'd often change her mind but it was just from one pointless thought to another. So what was the difference, really? All thoughts were the same, all options were the same – they all led to the same dead end. She wore the same clothes everyday, ran the same routine, saw the same people, felt the same misery and anguish, and had the same longings.

There was no death and there was no re-birth, just the process of dying and she couldn't make it die, she couldn't stop it from drooling on. Nothing was changing. Life was stuck right were she was. Or maybe she was stuck in some gooey life pit that no one ever writes about and no one ever knows about because the people who get stuck there are never heard from again.

Often, the days cloaked themselves in sunshine and flowers blooming and chirping birds, but K knew it was just shiny wrapping paper on a box of shit.

She was living the same darkened moments over and over, walking through mud – that's how the weeks passed. And the mud was thick and the mud was deep and when she pulled one foot out the other would get stuck and so on. And it was just as well that she was walking through mud because she had nowhere to go and nowhere to be, anyway, and why waste good paved roads on a wandering vagabond?

It was like being in a glass tomb, very little air, very little warmth but plenty of dust and cobwebs, watching the mourners come and go – that's how the weeks passed. And it really didn't matter that there were cobwebs and it wasn't very warm and it wasn't a very nice tomb because she was just a corpse, anyway, and why waste warmth and beauty on a dead thing?

Life without Becky had been more difficult than she could have imagined. Her job was even more agonizing, time there moved with all the swiftness of a dead dog – *Come on boy, get it! Go get it boy!* But it wouldn't, it would just lie there in the street with its broken hip and broken neck, crows pecking at the rotting flesh.

Kathy never dreamed it could be so bad without her, that the presence of one person in her day to day routine had made such a difference. She never realized before how much they had laughed together, until the laughter was gone. How they used to scoff at all the insults from their boss or the customers. The way the insults just rolled off her when they were together like rain off a slick vest. Or if they didn't just roll off, the way Kathy could come up with something sharp and witty to say, instantly.

She'd plant a verbal dagger deep into someone's heart and each word he rebutted she'd turn the dagger slowly left, then right. Soon he'd be silent, stunned and suffering from the words that entered more deeply than he ever thought could from some nowhere, loser waitress in a third rate café.

Then she'd stand over him, a pot of coffee in one hand, her hip jutting out to meet the other and she'd wait, wait for a response – wait for a chance to push that knife in even deeper. And when the response never came she'd say, "Yeah, I didn't think so." And walk away.

But now, *Could you move any slower?* or *Nice tits!* or, *These eggs are cold! Come on, lady.* The words hit her – how? They infected her – why? They went right into her, became a part of her, cemented themselves into her being. Their words weighted her, pinned her down like hungry rapists taking turns with her the rest of the day until she could kick back a few whiskey sours at Bells' and pretend they weren't real, that they didn't mean anything.

But they were real, as real as anything, she supposed. As real as any punch or slap in the face. As real as any emotion that happened to jump her at any given moment and have its way with her as all her old emotions had. Her feelings in the past had never meant that much to her, they were usually dreary, but frivolous enough, and one would go just as quickly as it got there so why be bothered about it at all? But these new feelings were not frivolous. These feelings had never heard of frivolous, and they didn't come and go, they came and anchored themselves onto K like she was the shore of the New World.

Before it was as if she weren't even there. It was as if they were insulting a fake Kathy that stood right next to the real Kathy. And the real Kathy would have sit back and laugh at how they wasted their energy insulting someone whom didn't even exist.

The fake Kathy's responses were just a game to her. Sure, they left them reeling and bleeding but it didn't mean anything to the fake Kathy, she could've kept it or left it just the same. She just did it to show them they weren't so smart. She didn't care enough to intentionally try and hurt them, sometimes she just liked to hear herself talk. And if her words left scars, then so be it – not her problem. It was her nature, what could she do about that? Did poison ivy get all bent out of shape whenever it gave somebody a rash? Of course not, it would say something like, *Shouldn't of been touching me, anyway.* Or, *Stand somewhere else next time.* It didn't lose sleep over it and neither did K.

She and Becky always just laughed away the constant come-ons of the fifty-year-old plus men at Nichol's Lunch – as if! Now it seemed so pathetic, so utterly sad and disgusting, so terribly wrong, it wasn't funny at all.

"Why won't these men leave me alone?" she'd think time after time. "My God, they're old enough to be my father."

And their complete loneliness frightened her. Would she too be that lonely someday? Would she be old and flabby and would the beauty that had been washed away leave behind wrinkles and dry skin and graying hair to remind her constantly of who she was now and what she was then?

They smeared their desperation all over her the same way they smeared their pancakes with butter and syrup, excessive and sloppy. It was like countless hands on her naked body rubbing and rubbing that buttery, syrupy mess all over her. They rubbed their desperation into her till her skin was so covered with the stickiness of it she could barely breathe.

They used to laugh away everything, even the stupidity of their boss. How it was totally irrelevant how stupid he was, how much money his stupidity had cost her in lost customers and lost tips, which now suddenly meant something. Now she clung to every dollar as if it were something real, something ancient and precious that was lost a found again. And how dirty that made her feel. Even with their insults and come-ons they could still buy a smile for only a few bucks.

And while the smile looked nice enough on the outside, simple enough, no pressure to it, no strain, it pushed out from within her like an unwanted child. A child conceived of rape and violence that she would now have to carry with her for nine months of her fucking life. And the child knew it and kicked her because of it – it kicked and squirmed filled with the anger of its unwanted existence. It beat her up inside, slowly killed her from within.

Her smile was the frozen, meaningless grin on the face of a plastic fuck doll. And the words that came out of that sick, meaningless smile weren't even hers. She'd make her voice sound all pretty, like someone whose favorite color was pink – which her's was not, need she remind herself. Then she'd toss back her head, say something light and airy, and laugh at whatever stupidity they were saying that she wasn't even listening to.

The black honey words that left her throat seemed sweet enough to everyone that heard them but they only heard the sweetness of it, they couldn't see the black part. They couldn't feel how it cut K's throat as it came out of her like it contained the debris of honeycomb pieces and stingers and other parts of the corpses of the dead and rotting bees that had given their lives to produce it.

And how she hated that a dollar meant so much to her now – how scared it made her not to have them – how insulted she was and how her heart sank every time she didn't receive any.

Before it was all just for fun, because it was all just a transition. Nichol's wasn't life, it was just a resting point – a place between two realities where they could stop in and have a chuckle and a cup of coffee on company time.

But that was then and then was an eternity ago. This was now and now was an eternity in the making. Now it was life, now it was real, and any combination of events that Katherine could imagine didn't place her outside of that life any time soon. If it did, that placement would just be sideways, not forward, just another third rate café or a second rate bar or a job sitting behind a desk waiting for the seconds to pass her by.

Before, Becky was on her way, on her way to stardom. And K, K was...well, she was going... *Where the hell was I going?* she thought. *I was going...wasn't I...I thought...* But she didn't know what she had thought. Perhaps she'd thought she was going to get caught up in a drug scam. Or maybe that the Mafia would mistake her for a stoolie – or she would awaken to find out her life was only a dream and the government had secretly been doing experiments on her and she'd have to escape to warn others.

Perhaps she'd actually made herself believe all that crap. Perhaps she had to believe it. Perhaps she had to believe that her life wasn't just the dingy cartoon of dragging herself from work to Bells' and home again and again. "The trinity of death," she thought. "The trinity of death."

On the men's room mirror, speckled with dried spit and rust water stains, intermittent light danced off the surface in streaks of simple rainbows. That happened sometimes. Becky said she was getting multi-dimensional glimpses and that she should try and develop it. But K thought it was mostly nonsense, optical illusions. Now she wasn't so sure. Now she wondered what an optical illusion even was – maybe they were just names people called their glimpses so they could keep pretending life was real.

"What do you really know about anything, K?" she said into the mirror, her eyes wide and round, her face gaunt from not eating well lately. Small pimples ran across her forehead.

"I can't believe you're breaking out!" And K turned to the stall door, pulling it open.

Wind shook the windowpane and it sounded loose, like it could fall from the trim any moment, and K wished a larger gust would come and air the place out. It smelled like a sewer in there, even with the light that was only partially working – flickering on and off in its frantic Morse Code. Its pathetic cries for help, its constant whining, and K wished it would just shut the hell up and die. It wasn't fooling anybody and it wasn't getting any special treatment. It was a dumb light bulb. Why should it be coddled when real human beings with real lives were suffering endlessly, then being plucked out of existence like cherries on the tree and swallowed whole?

I wasn't here, the first one read, she saw it through the strobe of light, her thumb underlining it back and forth with the nail.

"Lucky bastard. And where aren't you now?" Thoughts cascaded like they had found a winding tunnel inside her and were thinking it was some kind of ride. But it wasn't a ride for K. She'd seen them – seen them, heard them a thousand times. Come and go, come and go. *From where?* she thought. *To Where? God only knows, K, God only knows.*

But she watched them, whenever she remembered – whenever she wasn't swept away in them like rapids. She'd been watching her thoughts more and more since Becky died. Sometimes, they didn't even seem like hers – like they were even a part of her, just words floating around in space that her head picked up like an antenna.

Sometimes her mind seemed like a tape recorder and a phantom finger would push play, fast forward, fast play, rewind, start over – whatever, as it pleased. And she had no control, whatsoever. Over and over it went and K wished that finger would push pause or stop or that she could take a magnet to the mechanism and destroy the whole thing. She was getting sick of thoughts. Lately, it was so tiring to think them she felt she might actually pass out.

"I wish I'd just shut the hell up, too," she thought. "But I don't, and even that is a thought, just one more thought I wish I didn't have."

In the spaces between dark flashes, her hand continued across the wooden wall, knocking paint chips and splinters onto the stained tiles below.

"Nope...Old...Seen it..."

She shook her head, it had been a month since she'd found anything worth more than the stench she had to wade through to find it. The smell was as bad as ever, which was odd, the light only being on half the time and all.

"Maybe they smell worse just before going out," she thought, bringing her finger to her lips to think it over.

"You're a real nut case, K. Do you really think it's the light that smells?"

"I know, I know – several things smell in here, but fake light is definitely one of them – you know that." Her hand went to the toilet paper carousel, she tore off a piece and wiped her nose.

"Yeah, I know."

K took in the smell of stale piss and feces, letting go the full breath in a tight exhale between her tongue and the roof of her mouth – Monday nights at Bells' didn't carry the excitement they used to. She rarely even jotted down names to the unsigned works she found there.

Maybe somebody doesn't have to be behind it all, she'd been thinking lately. *Maybe the creation just was – just is.* But even those thoughts didn't go as deep as they could have, as nothing went too deep lately, just skimmed the surface. She couldn't allow things to go too deep because when they did they struck something down there. And when the thoughts hit that unknown place inside of her it made it vibrate – ring. It would start to grow like Jack's magic beanstalk, and whatever it was she still wasn't ready for it.

She wasn't ready to see her face rent in the mirror again, *Isabel Rawsthorne,* or feel her insides being pulled inside out and have to wonder what was real and what wasn't. She knew what was real. She knew what was fake. She'd been keeping inventory her whole life.

So she'd think of something else, something far away from the thought that had rung that bell. And when the vibration of it stopped she could forget all about it and think that new meaningless thought like, *What should I have for dinner?* or *Really, K, you just need to get laid.*

Her finger moved in jagged waves around all the old familiar sayings. How many different times did guys need to say *blow me*, or give the name and number of someone who would? Did they think writing *do me*, over and over was actually going to make it happen? Did they think that using the word *fuck* meant anything anymore, that it carried any power? Didn't they realize it was so jaded it simply melted into the background like a *the* or an *an*.

Did they actually think the people reading *fuck you* on a bathroom wall would feel any pain because of it, any remorse or sadness, or worthlessness?

Did they think someone would turn around with his tail between his legs and mope out like a beaten dog thinking, *Yeah, fuck me – that guy is right. Somebody oughta just kick my ass and toss me in the gutter.*

Was there one single brain left inside the entire collective male consciousness or was there only sex and lust and anger and nothing more? And were the sweet smelling words that sometimes came out of them just more bullshit from their arsenal to *get some – a piece.*

"*Get some* reassurance, maybe," she thought.

"Yeah, *a piece* of something real."

The thinly paned window that was something like stained glass only there were no colors to it, rattled again as the wind went past skimming the side of the back building. Bird songs flittered through when it did, their gargles and blurbs a hope for an early spring.

The window was never locked and even if it were a four-year-old could've opened it with a strong push. But no one ever did. A thousand bucks worth of booze plus whatever money Bells left in the drawer and no one ever touched it. No one had even ever tried, as far as K knew. Nobody ever messed with Bells. She never understood it, he was just an old man.

A bird sang unto me, stay away from Heaven.
It's a nice place to be, but its days are ending – The Hyena.

"Hmmph," she half hiccup-laughed, her mind stopping as she stared. "Hmmm," she said more serenely, letting her eyes draw into it. Her gaze was soft, unfocused, almost frozen. Then the window rattled again and K shook her head and pried her eyes away from the saying.

"That's stupid," she said, as she continued her search for the meaning of life on the bathroom walls at Bells' Bar.

K raised her hand to her forehead, spread her fingers across, then down the right side of her face, felt the blemishes – the few bumps. *Maybe I haven't been eating right,* she thought, thinking back to her diet over the past month – no fruits, no vegetables, only a few canned goods and almond butter with soy yogurt. *Maybe you're not getting enough nutrients. Maybe there are toxins floating around in your blood. Maybe you're on the verge of...*

"Just stress, K. Don't worry about it."

"Yeah, don't worry about it. Got it."

Her hand stopped then, at one she'd read a hundred times. It had been there forever and she usually passed it by without a second thought.

Jesus is the answer, it read and Katherine had to laugh inwardly at the utter ridiculousness of it. She should bring in a black marker and cross it out once and for all, she was sick of looking at it.

Dear lord, as if that was it, as if that was all there was, all you had to know and now your life was complete, perfect, now you had *The Answer.*

And how come all those people who had the answer were still asking questions, were still dragging themselves mindlessly to church each week to hear *more answers?* This was *it,* the answer to which no more could be added, to which no more was needed.

"Pack it up boys we're heading home," she yelled out into the emptiness of the bathroom. "The search is over, we've got it!"

"But it's not the answer," she thought. "It's been two thousand years and if that is the answer...why are we still here? Why are we still in this

126

mess? Even those who believe it is *the answer,* where are they, how blissful are their lives?"

Jesus is the answer, it said again and again as K continued gazing at it through the blink of light. The words she scribbled beneath it were uneven and jagged and the capitalization was random, and sometimes backwards, like a child's.

"Could you please repeat the question?"

At the table closest to the bathroom, the round one so small only two people could sit there at a time, a woman was sipping a tall drink through a red straw too short to even reach the bottom of the glass. She smiled as K passed by and gently grabbed her arm. Her grip had the sensuous feel of a lover, the feel of longing – a child left behind. She was a large, sturdy-looking black woman, an atlantes of ebony. She was like a gypsy, shrouded in layer upon layer of different colored shiny fabrics wrapped around her at different angles.

Her voice was low and beautiful like a big, orange moon suspended over the horizon.

"How you doin' without Becky?"

Kathy smiled but a child could've seen the pain it was trying to cover. It wasn't fooling anyone. It was a created thing, fake and puny and constructed by a dullard who just plastered it on her face in a hap-hazard way. The muscles on her chin and under the corners of her mouth shook and quivered under the pressure.

"Oh, I'm okay, thanks. You're Simone, aren't you? Didn't you and

Becky work together or something? She told me…"

"Yes," Simone responded, cutting K's words that were dwindling down to nothing anyway – that were searching, themselves, to be cut off, her big hand squeezing K's arm.

"She was my apprentice, for a short time. We'd just started our work together. But it's okay now, she's in the loving arms of our mother." Simone's eyes were misty, like lack of sleep does to them, or maybe drugs, pot. They matched the way her rounded words rolled out of her.

"Becky had told me about you. She told me you were gifted yourself, that you sensed things – could see energy, sometimes," said Simone. "I was hoping we would meet soon."

"Yeah, I guess – I don't know what I see, really. She told me about you, too. I'm glad we met, but I kinda need to go and…I've got some things on my mind."

"I understand child," said the orange glowing voice. "Come by and see me sometime, anytime, we can talk then. I live right off 39th and Cambridge, big porch swing, you couldn't miss it…" then she smiled big before continuing, "even if you wanted to."

"Okay," and she pulled away from Simone's hand that was still holding her arm.

Kathy found herself at a round table on the east side of the bar near the jukebox, its yellow and orange lights running down the mirrored sides. On top, a CD spun on its edge behind a glass showcase. The void of her not being on the south end stool shone like a black star. Emptiness waving like the dark petals of St. Catherine's Flower in a small girl's yellow hair. But K simply drew too much attention to herself atop that stool and she needed to be alone with her thoughts.

She licked the cold sweetness off the rim of a whiskey sour, pushing the red straw out of the way with her tongue, then took a drink. It had a good kick to it, Bells must have put in a double shot of J.D.

Smooth and dreamy tones slipped around her like fingers across wet glass. She didn't know who sang that song, but she liked it. *One pill makes you bigger, and one pill makes you small. And the one that mother gave you, doesn't do anything at all. Go ask Alice, when she's ten feet tall.*

If you go chasing rabbits…

She put her legs up over another chair and kicked off her work shoes, checkered Vans with criss-cross no slip soles, they must have floated to the floor in a slow fluid motion for she never heard them hit the ground. Somewhere between the time the shoes left her feet and found the seemingly endless floor, Kathy had begun floating as well, to one of the few days of her youth that she could even remember.

She could still hear the voice, cold and raspy – how someone sounds after drinking too much milk. It was the shaky voice of an old angry woman and she could still hear the over-sized wooden ruler as it slammed down on the wooden desk.

"Billy, Billy Baskins, come to the front. Hurry up, you're first." Billy arose hesitantly, not sure if he was standing up correctly or walking correctly. He moved with caution just in case the teacher said, *Billy, what are you doing? Sit down, it's not your turn.* And Miss Lantis always made you feel that way, like the thing she had said just a moment before meant nothing and now this new contradictory thing was the thing to follow and you should've figured that out long before she changed it – it was always your fault.

His head hung almost to below his shoulders as he gathered up his single paper and hiked up his faded, hand-me-down jeans that were already too short.

The assignment was poetry, a poem about a color. As far as young Katherine was concerned her fourth grade classmates lacked any real depth and she winced at the thought of having to sit through twenty-some odd poet laureates just to make it to lunch.

Katherine giggled as Billy walked to the head of the class. Billy knew what she was laughing at which didn't make his foray into poetry any easier.

At morning recess, Katherine had played a forced game of *You show me yours, I'll show you mine*, with the shy and bird-like Billy Baskins. Katherine, being the scariest girl in fourth grade, known as *Kathy Creepy*, gave little Billy no say in the matter.

He had gone to the side of the school to chase a ball where Katherine sat alone. She was watching two ants play tug-of-war with the carcass of some bug when Billy rounded the corner.

"Hey Billy, come over here a second. I wanna show you something."

She was crouched down on the ground looking at the ants and Billy was always eager to check out some new bug so he hiked up his jeans and joined her. When he came over K stood up, towering over him, and pulled up her skirt.

"That's not what I wanted to show you," she said, as Billy looked up from the ground. K pulled down her white panties with the flowers on them to her knees and Billy stood up wanting to run but didn't. Then K lowered her skirt and pulled up her panties. Billy didn't say anything, just stood staring, confused and mesmerized.

"Okay," said Katherine. "Now you show me yours."

"Uh – uh," Billy shook his head from side to side, still dazed – it had all happened so fast.

"Yes, I show you mine then you show me yours, that's the rule."

"Uh – uh," he said, still shaking his head as Katherine approached. Billy turned to run but Katherine grabbed his arm.

"I wanna see what's in there," she said, reaching for his belt.

After the act was over, Katherine remembered thinking to herself, "If that's the only difference between boys and girls, I don't see what the hubbub is all about."

Behind him was a chalkboard with flat maroon and navy blue and hazy white eggs the class had made with construction paper, each one had a name. It was because Easter was coming is why. There was a bunny up there too but it wasn't an Easter Bunny, just some dumb rabbit cut out of a magazine – it didn't even have a wicker basket.

The eggs attached to the bunny in the center of the chalkboard, then looped down and came up at the corners. *What is it about waves that people think so artistic?* Katherine remembered thinking.

Billy hiked up his jeans and began to speak, "Uh, okay...Uhm, I like blue 'cause blue is...." The loud rap of the ruler hit the desk of a student in the front row and the student jumped.

Miss Lantis' sour voice followed.

"Billy, is that how we start a poem?" It must have been a rhetorical question because she continued immediately. "No! First we state the title of the poem, then we say our name, *then* we began. Now start again."

"Oh yeah, okay...uhmm... I'm Billy and this is...uh...a poem, and the poem is...er...uhh... *I like Blue*. Uh...okay? Okay, well, I like blue 'cause blue is in the water and the sky is blue, and blue is in some birds, so I like blue. And eyes, also."

Billy was back in his chair before the last word left his mouth, wiping his sleeve across his nose, looking back at Miss Lantis hoping he hadn't done anything wrong.

Her lip curled up toward the right, almost like a smile.

"Okay, that's fine, Billy." Miss Lantis said, hesitantly. Which actually meant it was terrible – all the children knew that. Unless she said *wonderful* with her pitch raised and hands clasped together in a prayer, it was terrible, the grating gnaw of her voice always gave it away. "Yes, that's just fine. I could really sense that you liked the color blue."

"Uh...yeah," replied Billy. "That's...uhmm... what I was going for."

"Okay," said Miss Lantis, as interested in quickly moving to the next student as Billy was.

She surveyed the room, let out a breath.

"Let's try Amy. Come on Amy, you're turn. Walk to the front, come come, don't dawdle." *Rap, rap, rap,* went the ruler.

Dawdle? Dear lord, thought K, *who says dawdle?*

Amy had yellow written all over her, all over her cheap imitation smile, all over that stupid dress and twelve cent bow in her stripped yellow hair. Her flowery gait to the front like she was the belle of fourth

131

grade. *God's gift to yellow.*

"Hi, I'm Amy and my poem is called *Yellow*."

Predictable. Please God, please challenge me. Is my whole life to be so predictable? Shall I just resign unto complacency now? Or is that redundant? she chuckled.

"Yellow – Yellow, is anything finer than yellow?

Yellow, I bellow, answer me fellow!"

Miss Lantis' face turned even more puckered as she put her fingers to her forehead, rubbing there a moment. She was reaching her boiling point. Katherine liked to watch that. Sometimes she'd reach it and then wouldn't explode until a day or two later. She'd hold it all in, capped under her tightly wrapped hair in its grayish-blue bun.

She'd never say anything at the time that actually upset her, people called that restraint. But then, if anybody dropped a piece of chalk sometime later and forgot to pick it up, she'd go into a rage yelling and screaming some nonsense about not being the maid. And nobody ever knew why. But K did. She watched her, saw the tension build. It was as easy as predicting that day would follow night – it always had.

Katherine was sitting quietly. *You want poetry – I am poetry. I am poetry personified. Please, call on me. Please, please, please.*

"Okay, that was also…fine. Thank you Amy." Her words were drawn out with too much space in between to be truth. "But class, I think we need to stop here and review some example poems. Then we will just re-do the assignment and try again next week."

No! Katherine was thinking as the class murmured and grumbled. *I want to go now! My poem is awesome.* And she didn't realize she had said anything out loud until Miss Lantis spoke again.

"Excuse me. Who said that? Who said *no?*"

Kathy pushed her paper around her desk in circles with the pencil erasure, pretending it wasn't her, but several students looked her way, blowing her cover.

132

"Uh…Miss Lantis, my father says if you fall off a bike you should get right back on, whatever that means," she shrugged her shoulders, rolled her eyes. "But I think he means things like this."

"Would you like to share your poetry with the class, Katherine?"

"Well…" she paused, brought her number two pencil to her mouth, the erasure along her lower lip, rolled her eyes upward, pretended to think it over. "Okay!"

Her entrance to the front of the room was the effusion of baptismal water on a newborn. Soft and sparingly at first, not to give the ingénues too much too soon. She strolled to the orator spot standing poised, tall and proud at the head of the class. Her inner voice was booming and powerful. *This is where I belong,* she thought. *Yes, I shall lead, you shall follow. I shall speak, you shall listen. I shall…*

"Katherine, we're ready." *Rap, rap.* The ruler hitting twice on the desk of another student in the front row.

"*Red,* by Katherine Kristensen." She began reading slowly and with deliberation, as low and full as her young, thin voice would go.

> *When I saw you, crouched, expressionless,*
> *In the corner of your room,*
> *My palms bled freely.*
> *I was over you then,*
> *The blood,*
> *Trickled off my fingertips onto your forehead.*
> *The blood*
> *Puddled around your knees.*
> *Your voice was earnest,*
> *"I will imbibe thee. I shall drink thee in."*
> *Soon we were perfectly imbrued*
> *With the blood of my empathy.*
> *It was pretty gross.*

The air was like droplets of water in a silent pool, just a ripple now and then, a sniffle from one of the students, a shoulder shrug as several looked at eachother wondering what in the world had just happened. She had never since seen anyone stare so hard and so blankly as Miss Lantis was at that moment.

Alrighty then, thought K as she stepped to her seat, the click of her heals on the linoleum surface.

Miss Lantis was on top of her then in a hurry, grabbing her arm so that Katherine's shoulder ended up pressed to her ear as she was being hauled to the door.

"I don't know if you think this is some sort of a joke and I don't know who you got to write that little devil poem but you can just march that little devil bottom of yours straight down to the principal's office!"

She took the paper from Katherine's hand, tore it in half, pushed her into the hall, slammed shut the door.

"It was supposed to be funny," Kathy said as she turned from the door. "*It was pretty gross* – after all that serious stuff? That's funny, right?"

"I thought so."

"Oh well, big loss, no more fourth grade poetry."

She turned around, stuck her tongue out at the door, then walked down the abandoned hall trailing her finger along the smooth beige bricks of the wall. At the end of the hall, light streamed in, cut by green doors into long unfolding rectangles on the specked gray and buffed linoleum – schools and prisons used linoleum, sometimes office buildings.

It almost seemed like ice-skating it was so shiny and slick and Kathy skided her feet across it in exaggerated strides, stopping in the lit rectangle where the hallway ended, branching into a *T.*

"Now, which way is that darn principal's office?"

"Well I can simply not remember," she said in a sarcastic southern belle accent, a pre-pubescent Miss Scarlet.

"Let's see, E-X-I-T. Do that spell principal?"

"Why child, I think it do!"

Outside the air was warm, melting onto her nose and face in long laps like the tongue of a sheep dog. It dripped down her body, falling from the sky around her in a cocoon. Down the rolling hill, where the baseball diamond was set up for t-ball, she could see the tops of the strip of trees that cut off her street from school property. It was like looking out over an ocean, only with rooftops and treetops instead of the white crescents on forming and crashing waves.

"No more prison for me. I have escaped!"

She ran. Frantically, she moved as if she'd lost something, as if eternal freedom were waiting for her on the other side of the strip of trees, her red plaid skirt shortening her movements. Down the slow hill, to the green grassy field, through the small path which wound a hundred feet, or so, through a small wooded area to her street. A few minutes later she slowed, panting heavily, as she reached her driveway and entered the house.

Her father was looking out the back, living room window, staring blankly at the creek that stretched behind their property. He didn't hear her come in.

"Daddy!" she exclaimed.

"Huh?" he jumped, startled. "Oh, Angel. What are you doing home?"

Smoke hovered like fog. It swirled around the dim lights, dispersing when an arm raised, then settling again. If it didn't hurt the eyes so badly, constantly grating against them like sand, it would have been a beautiful scene to watch. And if it weren't so choking, so suffocating, it would have seemed like a wonderful fairytale – the fog and dark wood open-ing at some unseen point into a clean pasture of white horses, grazing.

But, as she looked into the dusty haze and dark wood for an open-ing, there was none – and probably never would be.

Bells came over, set a drink down on the table, picked up her empty glass, put out his hand waiting for the chewed-up red straw hanging from Katherine's mouth. She plopped it in his outstretched palm taking the fresh one from the new drink, putting it between her teeth, biting down.

As he walked away, she knew it would always be that way – people walking away. Why had it taken her so long to understand?

The music was warm – solemn low strings dipped in caramel. A violin lingered high swinging from a tree branch, then dropped into the pool of lower notes. It wanted to smother her and she wanted to let it. She wanted to become a part of it somehow, dissolve into it and have it take her to wherever it is music goes, through the air, the walls, outside into the darkness – dispersing, thinning.

Adagio, the sheer force of it, it could take you anywhere, anywhere you wanted to go, sometimes places you didn't. The song, in a con-tinual climax and release, was dragging her back to her house and her father. She didn't want to go. The worst things in life were the memo-ries.

He sat in the high back dining table chair he must have taken to the window from the dining room, eyeing the slow creek behind the yard that sloped high on the other side. High enough to where kids used to swing across from a rope tied to an oak branch, swooping down the steep slope across the creek to a mound of dirt on the other side. They didn't do that any more. The limb had broken and one kid was hurt pretty bad.

Shadows were on her father in crosses, the sun against the swing set in the back yard sending prayers across his blue button down shirt.

Her father was as surprised to see her as she was he. He worked days, a foreman at a construction company.

"Your mother is at the dentist, Angel, she'll be home any minute. I...I don't know...I've...I can't stay." His words were childish, insignificant. He'd never sounded like that before.

"Father I..." she looked down. Blood was dribbling from her hand, a nail protruded from her palm. "I'm hurt."

"Oh Jesus, K, what happened?"

"I fell."

"Whoa!"

She jerked her eyes wide, dropped her feet from the chair spitting ice back into the glass, almost choking. She'd forgotten. She forgot the fall, tripping over a seam from the woods to her sidewalk, landing on her hand, a nail went right through. She had held her hand in front of her flat, palm facing the ground. She had shook her hand hoping it would fall out.

"It doesn't hurt," she had thought, as blood dripped from the flat end. She must have been in shock, she was thinking now.

"You'll be okay," her father had said, moving to the door. K shuffled her feet, turning to follow him with her gaze. "I've seen far worse on site. Give this to your mother." He handed her a small folded piece of paper, his voice full of heaviness, like sandbags.

"I have to leave, your mother will have to take you to the doctor, you'll be alright. If she's not here in ten minutes, call an ambulance – you know how. I can't be here when she gets home. Sorry Angel, I can't. I love you."

She stared through the window, their big, blue Buick backed out of the driveway then took her father away. She never saw him again. Katherine reached up to wave good-bye, the flat end of the nail tapping on the glass. Blood streaked the window, ran down her forearm.

Adagio ended in subsiding waves and Three Dog Night switched on. She'd read that meant it was cold – *three dog night*. In old times the colder it got the more dogs they'd let sleep in their beds with them to keep them warm. A three-dog night was a cold night, she didn't know the equivalent in Fahrenheit, just that it was cold.

One, was playing. It was her favorite by that group. It was truthful is why. *One is the loneliest number you'll ever do, "* they sang. The first line was the hardest, the way the words hit with the melody. Once you made it past that you could get through it without hurting yourself – digging a pencil into your finger near the nail, seeing how long you could hold a flame under your hand. *"Two, can be as bad as one, it's the loneliest number since the number one."*

And, to K, if two could be lonely – then any number could be.

It was cold out. The idle must have been too low to keep out the single digit wind chill – the idle too low to keep the cab of the car a sensual warmth. Of course, how sensual did it need to be? How warm did it need to be? How anything did it need to be? What was it? She didn't know. It was cold.

Kathy desperately wanted to make it as romantic and nostalgic as her childhood fantasies had made it out to be – an innocent walk through an open field holding hands, swinging arms. The whites of cotton fuzz sprayed the air. Warm sun scraped the vulnerable parts of their necks, yellow dandelions and ankle deep grass stained their feet. They stopped under a swaying willow for an innocent kiss, and the innocence unraveled.

The yellow flowered sundress fell off her back onto the ground. The kisses were all over her body, on her small breasts and flat stomach – him on his knees before her, pulling her to the ground.

The birds sang, the trees waved in soft breezes that brushed back her hair and brought scents of distant pines and distant waters and all of existence rejoiced as Kathy and her true love consummated their eternal search. They had found each other, and life would never hold any sorrow ever again.

Anyway, it was cold out. The frozen vinyl of the back seat stuck to her bare skin like ice. His knee jabbed her thigh. His elbow in her biceps, long enough to where it was numb and didn't really hurt anymore.

She was fifteen years old. She didn't know how to be aroused yet. And the dryness between her legs belabored his efforts making Kathy wonder why people lived and died for it and talked about it endlessly.

This wasn't hot animal passion, not like in the movies. It didn't have to be, this was love – pure and simple, simple and beautiful, beautiful and sacred. It was as magical as fairy dust only real. As precious as a magic jewel given by a sorcerer to help a queen reign over a glorious empire, only real. It was as perfect and complete and magical as the love of God – only real.

Robert was the one. Smooth and calm, like her father, strong with silence. She didn't know why she wanted him so badly. But she did know it wasn't because he was popular, which he was, actually she didn't like that about him. Definitely not because he used to date the prettiest girl in school.

"Ya know," he said, lying there, still breathing heavily from the loss of fluid. "I...I just did this to make her jealous...so I could get her back, you do know that, right?"

There was emptiness. She breathed out heavily the poisoned, dejected breath that bared witness those words.

"I mean, I'm sure you knew that, right?"

The drive home was in silence. It was plaintive and pensive. Clouds of gray smoke puffed out of the exhaust, drifting away in the side mirror. Fallen leaves flew by, hurried and jostled by the quick wind. The pierce of cold blackness on the outskirts of Abilene where lights were faded warm things that sometimes happened on the crests of hills as they approached their small town.

Then tears were there and she said something stupid that was much too late and didn't even make much sense.

"Look, I don't care if you sleep with a hundred girls as some sort of vengeance or pagan ritualistic men's club thing or just to make that bitch jealous – whatever your reasons, I just wanted to do it, all right?"

"Yeah, whatever."

She wished she could have that moment back, say something poignant, hurtful. What did it matter anyway, he wasn't going to love her.

I don't care, she thought. *Care as much about the pain in my heart as I do the pain in my twat, very little. They'll both be gone in a few days, hell in the morning – hell, right now. Okay, my twat still hurts, but it feels good in a way. In a small painful way that says, 'Hey, you're no virgin, anymore. You are a woman. You've done everything there is to do in this stupid, pathetic world.'*

In fact, it's not a small painful way at all, it's a small pleasurable way. With the possible opportunity of becoming a large pleasurable way in the near future. This isn't hurt, not real hurt. I've heard of hurt, heard of broken hearts, lost love, the works – and this aint it. Hurt really hurts, hurts really bad. This is just like the hurt of a Big Mac sitting in the pit of my stomach, kinda stuck. Surely people have felt bigger pains than Big Mac pains before. I feel nothing for him. Well, almost nothing. And the almost part of the nothing that I don't feel, well, that part is a good nothing, or a good something...yeah.

But she was hurt, and there was a feeling – and a feeling lost. It affected her deeply, more than she ever gave it credit for. The following years were jaded and existential – her father gone nine years with no letters and no contact, her first love trampling through her virginity like an ox in a rose garden, her mother running their house like a convent.

The years wore jade and rhinestone anklets, pyrite bracelets and a zirconian wedding ring. The years went naked in the winter, wore long red thermal underwear with black socks and suffocating polyester suits in the summer. The years wore thorny crowns and the years wore tears – desert tears. Tears the Mojave would cry, parched and burnt and dying, if it could. But it can't, it has no moisture to give. It has no outlet for its ongoing pain of being barren, so it cries dry tears that no one ever sees and no one ever knows about.

It wasn't him that led her to it, not directly. He was the first sign, however. He was a spring rain falling, small, unassuming, melting away soft powdery layers of snow – K's hurt and suffering. Then, as the rain continued for months without end, it bored into the icy hardened ice beneath which was her anger and frustration. Finally, the waters merged with the already overflowing streams of years of apathy and ambivalence. Out of nowhere there was a flood and Kathy was drowning in it tied to a birch twine rope and a forty pound rock she had attached to her left ankle.

It was a nice Monday night, a good crowd, not harried. Simone had left, Kathy didn't even see her go. Bells was in the corner laughing, Drunk 1 had said something funny or something stupid. A couple to her right, nouveau artistic, discussing politics, the Kennedy assassination, Marilyn Monroe.

"She was the most photographed person in history," the guy said.

"I didn't know that," the girl said.

Somebody sunk the eight ball to her left, banked it in the side, collected a short stack of ones on the pool table, stuffed them in his pocket.

It was a nice night. Kathy put her bare feet back over the edge of the chair, the mirrored sides of the jukebox catching her feet in a warped reflection.

"ܠܐܠܗܐ ܡܒܝܬܗ، ܠܐ ܚܘܦܢܝ܂," read the letters she had long ago tattooed on the sole of her right foot. The words were done in fine script and beautiful, forming the ancient *aum* symbol. The tattoo was really masterfully done, the guy could have been famous, maybe he was by now. It was Aramaic, the mother tongue of Jesus. Loosely translated it read – *Dear God, don't send me back.*

She had stood there for years, peering over the edge of Death like a kitten over the edge of a pool. She would come close, walk side to side, back and forth, never taking her eyes off the murky, black water. She

141

would lean over, stick a paw in to test the warmth then shake it off, or bend down and take a few laps with her pink scratchy tongue then pop up and walk side to side, back and forth.

On that day, it was different. She was wondering who she was. She was wondering what it was all about. She was asking God for a sign. Peering over the edge, she saw her father. His warm smile and loving eyes called to her in the wavering soft movement of the water. She jumped, tied a large rock to her foot, afraid that she might pop out before Death was done with her, and jumped into Death.

Death was warm. Just as she'd hoped. Death was caressing. She hadn't expected that, nor the thousands of wet tiny kisses that cradled, cuddled and comforted her body like the lips of a mother on a new-born child.

But she was Death's newborn child and soon the kisses turned hard on her skin, hard and sucking uncontrollably. Bubbles were all she could see. Her legs kicked and arms flailed. K had hoped for alacrity, Death had other plans. It suckered her in with its false advertising of serenity and warmth, calm were those clear quiet waters, and now Death had reneged.

The sucking was violent, leaving rose and violet hickeys all over her tender nineteen-year-old body. Death sucked into her skin, into her muscle and blood, then deeper into the bone – sucking the life right out of her.

That's when the light opened up. Bluish-white without a source, just there, broke through the water like a doorway directly in front of her. She didn't remember anything after that.

When she awoke, coughing water, her face imprinted with the rough surface of the concrete, she didn't know what had happened. Apparently the bolson of Death could not handle the flood of K's soul. Death would not have her that day and spat her back to life as if her soul were sour milk. She lay on the hard, hot concrete of life like a patch of seaweed washed ashore, a torn rope attached to her left ankle, trailing her fingers into the cold clammy springs of Death at her side that waited silently for the day when it would get a second chance.

K's index finger worked its way between the bricks of the building. Rain dropped on the bare parts of her, the back of her neck, her hand as it reached out to scrape against the wall – drops of cold that spread into her skin in puddles when they landed. They were tiny hands falling from the sky, fingertips reaching out, wanting to make contact. Pressing harder, it felt like coarse sandpaper but the pain intrigued her and if the building had been any longer she may have rubbed her finger bloody. She followed the mortar between the bricks around the building's side to her back alley.

It was musty. Damp trash and scattered smells of broken bottles of beer and soda. Cigarette butts randomly tossed among the sparse gravel and cracked tar and cement. The pitter-patter of rain followed her to her stairwell, always coming closer – like an abandoned child it followed her.

"Did someone abandon you, little lost child?" she turned to say to the ground where the rain splattered before her.

"Abandon the rain? What are you talking about, K?" She shook her head trying to clear the thoughts but it rarely worked that easily.

Standing at the foot of the stairs, looking over the alley, something within seemed to crumble. She still stood but inside she collapsed like a shattered jar of marbles and spread out all over that back alley. The hard round pieces of her intertwined with the pieces of broken bottles and loose gravel.

She stared at nothing, contemplating like a starfish on the beach at tide. Which direction would she be thrown into next? Back out to sea, where tumultuous waves tossed her around like a Barbie Doll? Dry land, where the sun parched her skin as she lay suffocating face down in the sand? Which would save her? Did either one care? They were probably both as indifferent as God.

She stopped, shook off the words again. God cared – had to. Why else would we be here? Just an abandonment, is that all we are? Drops of rain fallen and forgotten? Did God get bored with this world and go create another one to reign over – one with people who were more fun, more beautiful and more alive? No, God cares. Somewhere down deep she still believed that, clinged to that. Because without *that* – nothing else mattered.

Drip, drip. The rain followed her up the wooden stairs turning the blue-green paint pine, turning the slate-blue wall gray. The rain wore on the wooden stairs that already seemed frail to K, someday they'd come crashing down – someday, everything would.

She took out the fistful of keys, pulling open the screen door with her foot, fumbled for the right one. What was she thinking hanging on to all those keys? Someday she may need to get inside in a hurry, not stand around thumbing through gold, silver and copper keys that mostly looked the same.

She turned the lock and kicked open the door that was moist and sticking. The apartment looked distant and estranged, the light glowing in a dull, bored way. Her coat slid off her arched back and ended up on the floor as she glanced around just to make sure everything was as it was supposed to be and not quite knowing what to do next.

Mindlessly Kathy went to the fridge where she grabbed a container of soy yogurt and a spoon off the counter top. Then she moved to the vanity and picked up the Polaroid. This was Marilyn's territory. She wished she could avoid that area, not needing to hear the slanted sarcastic words that came out of that photograph. But that was often where she wrote and often where she took her pictures.

She plopped down shooting herself in half-profile from the right, not even looking into the shutter window – she was staring at Marilyn.

"How's your soul feeling? A little thin?" K asked. "I heard some news today. You were the most photographed person in history." And Kathy smirked, she'd finally been caught, that should shut her up.

"Second most when you get done," Marilyn whispered.

K could sense her laughing in a low sultry way. Even in her laughter she was working on seducing you.

She held up the photo card, it was slowly forming into a picture, growing a life on paper. Her whiteness appeared first, making her look ghostly, then more color spread over her face. She flipped it over to date and title it – *Kathy Apathetic.*

"Uh oh," she thought. "That makes seven in a row."

Seven in a row meant, it meant…something, she wasn't sure. But it was a lot, she knew that. She thought she remembered hitting seven *Kathy Apathetics* just before attempting suicide. Then again, once she had hit seven *Kathy Misanthropics* and the very next day she went out for ice cream and gave a bum on the street the change.

In the closet, a brass corner of the footlocker caught the light. There was a yearning inside her to be on her knees just then, pulling that heavy locker across the already scratched wood floor, unsnapping the locks and lifting it open, removing the salty remains of one of several stories she'd written over the past month then stuffed deep into the box, not liking the endings.

Before she knew it she had done just that and was sitting at the vanity, a story opened in front of her. K gingerly licked strawberry yogurt off the hollowed part of the silvery spoon, looked into the mirror, wary of any beings on the other side. She was mostly afraid she'd get sucked in, end up back in time having to relive part of her life over. Maybe just the last three years, till she sat at this very spot looking into the mirror, wary of any beings on the other side, being sucked in again.

Is she going to read it? her photos bantered back and forth, the scurry of silent whispers. Marilyn's picture didn't converse with the other photographs – her half-open lullaby eyes, half of her always in dreams, only half in reality – she saved her savvy insights for Katherine, directly.

K darted her eyes from the mirror, giving quick glances from photo to photo – her in her infant years by the window, as a teen-ager over and around the closet, in her late-twenties by the door. She didn't hang them all, most were in an army satchel tucked under dirty clothes in the closet.

"Come on, kid, what are ya? Some kinda baby-waby?" Marilyn pursed her lips, like she always did, mockingly. They were thick glossed red, like cherries. "You wrote it. But 'chya don't even 'member it now, do ya?"

"Sure I do," thought K, and flipped a page back and forth, made whipping noises with the paper. "Sure I do."

Omnispective – adj. Capable of seeing or beholding everything.

Eight – n. The cardinal number between seven and nine. Seven and one.

Driftwood – n. Wood drifted or floated by water or washed ashore.

Neutrino – n. In physics, a neutral particle, difficult to detect, having a mass approaching zero and no charge.

Onding – n. A heavy fall of snow or rain.

Polled – a. Having the horns or antlers removed.

Soothness – n. Reality, fact, truth.

Chevron – n. A v-shaped bar or bars worn on one or both of the sleeves of a military or police uniform.

Onanism – n. Withdraw in coition before ejaculation.

Raff – n. A heap, a jumble, a large number, collection or quantity.

New Mexican – n. A native or inhabitant of New Mexico.

Fecund – a. Fruitful, prolific, productive.

Prolusion – n. A prelude to a game or event.

Brattle – vi. To make a rattling or clattering noise.

Bogwood – n. Trunks and large branches of oak and pine, frequently used for making ornamental pieces of furniture.

Beau Ideal – fr. A perfect conception or image. A standard of excellence.

Minim – n. The smallest liquid measurement. Anything very small, a tiny portion.

Brassard – n. A badge or emblem, generally worn on the arm, denoting some particular duty or distinction.

Carcass – n. The dead body of an animal.

A partment 808

The key turned readily, as usual. No resistance, no remorse. Apartment 808 let him right in as it always had. He pulled himself in with an omnispective glance, wanting to take in everything, then moved slow and smooth like driftwood in a stream to the window, gazing off at the night carcass of the city.

"Lights," he thought slowly. Slow, slow thought. He was ashamed by the slowness of his thoughts, as if on a blind date and that sudden, shameful awkwardness of having nothing to say. The lights were distant but not too far off. From atop that hill, his eyes could follow the highway around a bend of trees and billboards to the lights of downtown. "Lights. I do like the lights," he continued, and again there was no thought. Just numbness.

The illuminated numbered tags on his clock radio flipped from 4:04 to 4:05 a.m. as confusion, anxiety, remorse and fear all battled backstage in his mind for the spotlight. During this backstage scuffle, center stage remained barren and still. All his thought power were mere neutrinos flickering, frozen in the thickness of what he was about to do.

"I thought I'd have more to say," he thought solemnly. Then with some anger, "Some sort of prolusion, some insight. Not this raff of mediocrity...damn it, I've always hated that about myself – just goddamned mediocre!"

He looked mournfully at the half-torn chevron on his black sleeve, had torn it himself in disgust.

"Figures," he thought. "You created all your own damage in this world." And he was lost in the stare. The onding of rain continued its rhythmic *ticky, tickity, tack*, outside. The brattle was annoying but sobering, and he quickly remembered the soothness of this evening.

Again he surveyed his New Mexican apartment, complete with cactus in a bogwood planter. "You're such the bohemian," he thought. "Jumping head first into the latest fad that was *in* when you signed your very first lease."

He eyed the cactus in the corner.

"And what of you? Are you the beau ideal of what humanity should be? Strong, silent, needing of no outside defense. No need of companionship. Nary a minim of water to replenish your existence. Or perhaps you were just planted in more fecund soil than that with which I was blessed."

Either way the chevron was still torn and hanging, more limply now than ever. Not the gallant brassard with which he envisioned himself adorned. A brave knight, a hero – servant to kings and queens, savior of maidens and masses.

"But heroes don't skim from coke raids and turn a profit on lawlessness, doth they, me Lord?"

And the onding outside continued.

He went to the top drawer of his desk, made an entry in an old diary, slid it back inside exchanging it for a .38 and went again to the center of the throw rug.

The Glock .38 entered his mouth, paused and then withdrew.

"You coward. It's over. You've been caught, stripped of your maleness. You are polled cattle. You are nothing." The words rung as true as any he'd ever heard.

"If only there was someone to understand me, to take me in, to save me," he faded off trying to see the window, trying to find answers in the lights outside. "Maybe they haven't found out yet. Maybe I could just skip town..." a tinge of hope surprised his thoughts, "and start anew, find that someone."

There was a knock at the door.

"Oh God, they're already here. I can't bear a trial and I won't be imprisoned like a common thief!"

Again the gun entered his mouth, there was a louder knock on the door, sharp and more determined, and this time there was no onanism. There was no stuck mechanism, no jammed trigger, the gun went off and removed all other considerations. Removed all other possibilities. Removed all guilt and removed all shame.

Apartment 808 had let him right in, as it always had.

She stared blankly through her southern window at the rain. The soothness of the story weighed heavily on her chest. She wished she could rain. She wished she could open up and drop pieces of herself all over 39th Street. Pushed away by tire treads onto the sidewalk, adding crispness to the clicks of hard heels on the concrete. Running down bus windows, trickling down faces, disguising them – so you couldn't tell which ones were crying.

She wished she were a predator of the rain. She'd mimic the night sky, fall from her own darkness, follow the drops down, swallow them whole. How freeing it must be to rain. She'd like to rain over the world all at once. Everybody everywhere connected, feeling K on their face and lips, seeing K streak across their windows, seeing K puddle into black rainbows on the dirt roads and pavement.

She'd rain and rain until the oceans were full and the skies were empty. No more clouds, and no more rainy days – ever.

"So what?" she thought, pulling her gaze from the window, her shadow like a crane in the corner of the room. "No big fuckin' deal. Bad cop/dead cop. You've heard of good cop/bad cop – this is just a variation on the theme." She swallowed a hardening lump in her throat then flopped onto the bed on her back, arms out like a cross.

She cared, she felt connected, a part of her – that's what it was. It was like a part of her putting that gun inside its mouth, a part of her about to pull the trigger. Then what? What happens after that explosion? What happens to K when that gun goes off and that part of her dies, that part of her that is somehow connected to this man?

"I really don't care. Why should I?" she asked aloud. And not two moments later she was screaming it.

"Why should I!? Who's doing this to me!? What am I supposed to do? Care about this guy? Save this guy? How!? Why!?

The words echoed in her apartment like she lived in a cavern, bouncing off layered walls of compressed sandstone, winding and fading.

She went to the white vanity, picked up the fragile pages, held them to her smooth white face rereading the final paragraph and shaking a bit from fear or nerves or anger, or all three. But she read anyway, as if someone were forcing her head down into it like you do to a dog who'd just shit all over the floor.

See what you've done! Bad dog – Bad! And Kathy could hear the shouts, random, inaudible shouts – yells and screams, and a hand spanking her.

Bad Kathy – Bad! See what you've done! She could feel a grip around her neck and one on top of her head forcing her nose down into the mess she'd made. Her arms were weak, they might as well have been tied behind her back because her face went into it and she read it over and over again.

If only there was someone to understand me, to take me in, to save me. A sigh came out, and she was again surprised by the compassion she felt as the breath left her body.

"Yeah, I know how you feel, buddy. Maybe if I'd have known you..."

the words drifted off for a moment as if she'd forgotten what she wanted to say. Her mouth sad and full and it looked like it wanted to say something, something she'd be better of having heard.

When she looked into the mirror at night, it always looked like it wanted to tell her things but didn't know how to say them. It was always just right there, waiting.

She looked back down at the papers hanging limply in her hand, she flipped them up. "...Maybe we could've been friends. Maybe I understand you."

The lights were distant, but not too far off. From atop that hill, his eyes could follow the highway around a bend of trees and billboards to the lights of downtown.

"Sounds like Kansas City, in a way. The way I felt the very first time I saw it, standing on top of Rainbow Blvd. Hell, *Rainbow Towers* would give you a real nice view like that," she said, referring to the apartment tower off of 39th and Rainbow Boulevard that mainly housed the local medical students from KU Med Center.

K opened the window, which was without a screen, and wedged her wooden Buddha underneath to keep it from falling. Even though it was cool out it was worth it – the smell of rain on 39th Street, cleaning out the air. It was the only time it didn't smell of exhaust fumes and booze and cigarettes and perfume. Sometimes it was nice not to have to smell anything, even good smelling things.

The wooden Buddha sat about a foot and a half tall, she got him dirt-cheap at a sidewalk sale in a neighborhood outside of Westport. His hands eternally in a circle on his lap, a grin spread infinitely across his face, which she liked because most statues had him looking staid and serious.

Kathy kneeled, rested her elbows on the windowsill, almost like a prayer, breathed in the freshness of the rain. She was picturesque – the porcelain they use for dolls poured over her skin, the sad mouth, the blushy cheek of frustration.

"...And the onding continues," she said, smirking at the incorporation of one of her newly learned words.

K got up, walked across her studio apartment to fidget with some things in the kitchen for no reason at all, just to relieve her mind of the constant thinking. Thoughts and thoughts, words floating, talking, it never stopped and it never helped.

"What if I had no thoughts?" she thought. "How much energy would I have then?"

"What could you accomplish without thoughts?"

"I don't know. Do birds think when they are making a nest?" She snatched an open box of Triscuits on the counter and snacked on a few, but in her absence of hunger they were bland and tasteless.

"*Do birds think when they're making a nest?* Who gives a shit, K! Who cares either way? God, you think of some stupid shit!"

"Yeah, who gives a shit either way?" She plopped down the box and tossed a half-eaten Triscuit back inside.

In the blue light nothing casts shadows. No gaudy objects or trinkets laying long rhomboid squares and amorphous shapes, leaving a trail of breadcrumbs behind so the world could follow them back to their original source. Images emerged where they stood, lying low near the ceramic and porcelain fixtures, the silver pipes with copper centers snaking into walls and out of sight.

In yellow light, everyday light, shadows create another world – the Listerine bottle a sculpture, sumo-wrestler in squat. The faucet, phallic against the sink. Katherine, a bird or crane in cloaks in the corner.

She gargled with the Listerine, the mint flavor wasn't so bad, scrubbed her teeth with the toothbrush, rinsed and looked into the mirror. Kathy had read once that people were just a reflection of what they were on the inside – the food they ate, their emotions, sensitivities.

"You are beautiful," she thought. "God knows why." She pulled three fingers across the cheek beneath her right eye, it was smooth and pinkish tonight, the lines barely visible.

"Yeah, God knows why."

K shut the window, put the Buddha on the shiny enamel white paint of the windowsill, stripped down to bare white skin, then threw on a loose T-shirt and lay down on her bed. Her arm swept over her forehead like the pliable branch of a young elm, partially sheltering her eyes from the light. She should have turned it off before falling on the bed. She rolled over, switched it off.

Flashes of buttery light echoed into the room from the crosswalk at Bell and 39th Streets. The hue from The Veco, opposite her, its fluorescent white behind its call letters, also worked its way through K's window. Even if she had drawn shut the thin cotton curtains the room was never completely dark, but the continuing slow rain outside soothed her as if it were.

"And the onding continues," she said.

"Okay, K, you can stop with the onding bit, I get the point." She pulled covers over her shoulders, tucked them under her chin, snuggled up on her left side noticing the time on the clock, it read 3:55 a.m.

"Good," she thought, "3:55, a perfect time for sleep."

Kathy closed her eyes with a cozy grin on her face as she sank into the softness of her bed, comforter and many pillows. It felt like a cocoon of feathers and she imagined herself a fuzzy caterpillar, brown and yellow, spotty and not too pretty. But what would she be tomorrow? That cocoon could change her – metamorphosize her.

She could be a butterfly in just a few hours and simply fly away. Who knows? The caterpillar never thought it could happen to it, could probably never imagine life as a butterfly. Perhaps this night in these soft sheets would make all the difference, transform her into something different – something she'd never even imagined.

Maybe tonight wouldn't be so bad – what, with the soft rain and the soft comforter and all. The dreams had come back. They were growing again like a wave. The rift between God and Jesus was widening. K thought the whole of existence might be sucked into the gap created between the two.

Each dream was becoming more and more life-like. At first she could hardly remember them. Then, they became like movies on a screen and hard to forget. This last one, she was almost there, felt like she could reach out her hand and touch a piece of Heaven. She didn't know what would happen when this wave crashed onto the shore. Whatever happened, it couldn't be good.

She'd rather not dream at all, would rather fall into a black abyss and wake up with the sun thinking she'd just closed her eyes. Maybe tonight wouldn't be so bad.

The rain faded into the background. Katherine had almost gone, almost drifted away, as one last thought trickled across the calming waters inside.

"And the onding continued."

"What!" She jolted awake, sprang suddenly upright in bed, eyes wide, breathing hard and taking in the time again.

"No!" she said grabbing the clock, bringing it closer. She stared hard like a person who had over slept a vital meeting and was trying to reason with the clock. *Are you absolutely certain that this is the time you want to project at this moment?* She shook her head as if trying to wake up, and looked again. *Are you certain that this is indeed the correct time!?*

The clock turned 4:02.

"No! It's happening! It's happening right fucking now!"

Sometimes at night, when the people are gone and all the traffic and noise have dripped into the bottom of the hourglass, you can see the symmetry in things more clearly. How the street lamps are set up on a line. How the cylindrical, cement bunkers that hold up the covered parking garages cut diagonal lines in the air like Chinese Checkers. How the tubed, neon-letters on the bank sign lit up in unison when the time switched to temperature. *What time is it?* equaled the temperature – *Time to Save*, equaled the actual time.

Steam rose seamless and transparent from the sides of buildings where giant fans in metal domes blew out exhaust and from vents in the street, where the warm water that ran beneath the city vaporized against the cold air. K thought that if everything had an opposite this scene was the opposite of some wonderland. It was beautiful, but it was also scary and eerie and mournful. It was a wonderland for death, not life. There were no rides and no candy slides. No animated teddy bears to wave her good-bye. It bode poorly for the cop in apartment 808. But she'd try anyway, they weren't all bad signs.

Stars were there, peeking through spaces between the dark clouds, twinkling like ice pieces in the wintry sky. Stars were good – had to be. They were the pristine remnants of thoughts or memories that God left behind when he created the universe. Like coins and jewels that had fallen from his purse as he traveled.

Then there was the sense of every step being neighbored with fear. Fear that she might get attacked or jumped on with no one around to scream to for help. The puddling remembrance – God had made jesters and queens and three-pronged fools, and all predators were prey and all prey were predators and all kinds lived on 39th Street.

Twigs breaking, ruffling noises near a bush, and K wondered which one she would be tonight. She was already getting tired, if she were meant to be prey it would be hard to fight back – or run away.

She had moved swiftly at first but soon the swiftness was gone and she moved jaggedly, limping, pulling her left leg that was getting sore and tight in her hamstring. She would have taken the car but it was parked too far up a side street in the opposite direction to be any quicker. After only a few blocks her cold palms rested on her thin knees as she bent over, gasping for breath. She looked up through her own transparent breath at the carpeted sky, batted her almond eyes, let the long lashes and pink, tired lids rest a moment, closed.

"Push on K. Come on, this is important!" And she began again.

The neon blue of the KU Med sign crowned the night through the mist and thick rain. *God, the sign looks cool at night,* she thought, and sometimes it hid itself behind the white puffs of her breath. *Man, I sure breathe a lot for someone my size. I definitely get my fair share of air.*

Rainbow Towers, its oblong structure towering over *Phog's Court,* the bar and grill at the foot of the apartment complex, bounced jaggedly, distorted by her stiff movements – she was getting close.

At the security-coded entrance her watch read 4:06 a.m. and K pushed random buttons in desperation as her chest heaved in exhaustion, fear and anticipation – they were aligned by name, not by apartment number. She didn't know his name.

McCloskey, she tried.

"Hello?" The voice was annoyed and sleepy, it carried the shakiness of an elderly lady.

"Sorry, wrong button," K replied, continuing to push random buttons.

Carter, Mathis, Vogel... There was no reply. *Henshaw, Rhuby, Oleson...*

Another groggy voice answered. It was a man. Good.

"Uh...yeah?"

"Yeah. It's me," K said, muffling her voice with her hand half over her tightened mouth. She crossed her fingers in the long pause as he yawned.

"Oh, I thought you weren't coming over tonight," said the man.

"Well, I...I uh...did. Now buzz me up."

"Okay, come on up."

There was a high pitched buzz like bees, its flimsy tingle at the top of K's head. She pushed open the door and went through.

"God, that was a stroke of luck," she thought, as the elevator doors pulled open.

The posh, brass-railed elevator moved unbearably slow, her face was warbled and distorted in the reflection between floor numbers on the front panel. There were mirrors all around but she was drawn by her color to the brassy reflection. The number *eight* circled and lit like a beacon in the night, where her right eye would be, while the string of numbers on top of the door would light and then slowly go empty as they tried to catch up.

K crouched over and steadied herself with the brass rail, her head spinning. She thought she might be sick, she hadn't run in ten years. She wrapped one arm around her gut and coughed, letting spit drip from her mouth onto the blood red carpet. The elevator had stopped and K looked up. The circled eight above the door was lit and the doors pulled opened. Kathy stepped out.

Floor 8. 4:08 am. She was too late.

She approached apartment 808 breathless and steadying herself against the wall. On the door, images in the grainy wood were the scant howls and pointed ears of faceless creatures – elastic thoughts and longings of civilizations destroyed, pushing through wood into this reality. A reminder of what this one was created on, the underlying foundation that no one ever sees and no one ever thinks about – until it all crumbles down.

There was no sound. Her ear pressed intently onto the door – she *was* too late. But nobody was in the hall. Hadn't they heard the gun go off? Or did a gun go off at all? She pulled her ear away and looked up the hall to the elevators, then back the opposite direction to the door that had *exit* in red lights above it and *stairs* in blocked letters on the gray metal above the push bar. The hall was empty. Was she in the right place? Was there even a right place to be?

"You know, it is possible that the other stories were just a coincidence."

"I know that, K. Don't you think I know that?"

She knocked. Nothing still. K ran her fingers along the grainy faces in the wood. It must have been a world of wolf creatures and giant fish. Half-cat/half-man beasts ruled the plains and highlands. Squid people and their armies of two-legged reptiles ruled the underworlds.

She banged a little louder and again placed her ear against the door – it was warm and smooth, a good combination, maybe nothing had happened. Maybe it was all a fantasy. Maybe this drama had ended with *St. Bum*.

Then a roar left the room like lions – brazen and fighting, a sound she would probably never forget. It was the sound of failure, the sound of loss. It was the most angry sound she'd ever bore witness to and the harsh dissonance sent Kathy flying away from the door, her face trembled and contorted like it wanted to cry, her skin covered in goose bumps. Then there was a lifeless thud hitting the floor and Kathy felt her stomach drop like she was on a roller coaster, an old wooden one. One that she was unsure about – one that might collapse any moment.

A gunshot had torn through the silence dividing the night into two parts, leaving an open, gaping wound that may never heal.

K checked the door, it was unlocked – she didn't know why. She guessed that when you're about to kill yourself...nothing else matters. She went in, she didn't know why.

Entering the apartment felt like entering a dream – like walking into a dream with a physical body. She was aware of each sound and each movement. How her arms bent, angled and awkward, her elbow in her ribs as she shut the door. The *clank* of the door closing like prison bars behind her. The grated-water motion of her torso twisting from the door as she took in the light switch, the desk and table lamp, the sofa and doors to other rooms, the oil paintings on the walls, the well cared for leafy plants, some kind of ivy hanging from a ceiling planter.

The way her feet stepped into the matted shag carpet with caution, and how deeply they sank. Her breath in her nostrils, sliding into the air off her top lip. Whatever was about to happen in there, she may never be able to leave it, completely.

"My God," she thought. "I've entered one of my stories."

A clock ticked in the kitchen, he had probably rarely noticed it but it was loud to K. Everything was loud – her breath, her thoughts, the clock, the neighbors television below her. Everything was loud, except for the body. The body was completely still.

She saw him there, on the floor, her eyes started to glaze with tears but none fell. They just distorted her vision, made it look like she was under water. He looked like Jesus on the cross. His legs slightly bent, arms out wide, head turned to the side down into his shoulder, like he couldn't keep it up anymore.

It didn't hardly seem real, an altoreliero – a sculpture where the figure projects halfway out of the background. He was carved out of the carpet.

The body was perfectly quiet. She'd never seen anything so still before, except for the other dead bodies – they were piling up like cords of wood. It was more still than a picture, more still than the furniture. It was fake. They looked more real in the movies. The blood around him was paint. He had been hauled in from a wax museum.

What is it about death? What is it inside of us that when it goes it can make the body look like that – like a completely fake thing, like a fur coat used and then discarded with no more value than three lumps of wet sand.

It's like life is a piece of magic, a small light that some sorcerer blows into bodies when they're in the womb or as they come out – a light that gives the body warmth and brightness. A magic that dances around inside keeping the bones and skin from collapsing to the floor.

And when it's time, he comes back. The sorcerer sneaks up behind you and yanks it out. "Game over," he says. "I need my magic ball back."

Then maybe he goes and puts it in another body, or a tree, and watches it dance with life for a while in some secret, out-of-the-way forest. Or maybe he just gathers up a bunch of those little life balls and

160

plays racquetball or tennis with them or uses them to juggle. They probably tickled his hand, when he did, every time he touched them.

Then the magic life balls would sit on his mantle all a tingle and filled with excitement waiting for the next game – the next chance to be alive.

Everything about the apartment was stale, generic, like he'd bought all the furniture and décor from a ready-made kit – the brown-polished rattan of the sofa, the soft oranges and dusty pinks of the southwestern oil paintings, the bogwood planter and cactus. The frayed throw rug with deep browns and purples and beiges cut off in sharp angles, squares and rectangles and Aztec designs.

It was clean, antiseptic and unfriendly, it was just waiting for death – like a hospital, or a maybe even a morgue. She glanced around nervously like she should leave or do something different than just stand there, but didn't know what. His face was looking up at the ceiling like the sparkled bumps were stars.

Maybe there were images forming in the bumps, a name spelled out, the face of a friend. Maybe another world was trying to push through reality in chalky plaster. Maybe his face was trying to find something familiar to sink into, a place to go home to that he'd long since forgotten about.

Seeing his face was an accident. She had been avoiding his face. Maybe it would've been disgusting, or maybe terribly sad. Or maybe his face might have been beautiful and that would have been worse.

That would have reflected something inside of Katherine she didn't want to see right now – something in him that was in her too, that something beautiful could die. Maybe he'd come to the end of a line, something he thought would save him but never did – like beauty. Maybe he'd reached the end of that line, that he was beautiful all his life then woke up one day and said, "So what?"

Maybe he'd decided that beauty hadn't solved anything, hadn't made his life better and that's all he had. And if this is all life is, even with beauty and all, then forget it – it's not worth it.

161

But he wasn't beautiful, his eyes were large but hollow and dark underneath and full of fluid. His skin was rough, maybe from a youth filled with acne and too much sun. He wasn't beautiful, he must have come to the end of a different line.

She kneeled, put her hand to his chest. She didn't know why, just wanted it to be there. Maybe her hand liked death, was becoming accustom to it like a masochist in search of pain. Or maybe it was spreading the compassion she felt inside of her to inside of him. Maybe her hand wanted to tell him it cared about him even though it didn't know him, even though no one else did, even though he wasn't beautiful.

K looked into his eyes wanting to pour more of herself into him, some of the magic from her magic life ball, just for a moment, to see what his face would look like if it were alive.

But it didn't work that way, his face stayed empty and lifeless. It was a lonely and sad face, not because a bullet had just gone through it she was sure of that. Sadness grew onto his face from some seed that had been planted long ago. So all alone it looked that she wanted to slice off his head and place it gently on a barren and snowy mountaintop.

There it could gaze wistfully, making images in the stars as long as it wanted. But there would be times when the snow came covering him up like a velvet blanket and he would have to gaze at white snow for a while, probably the whole winter. But when that spring thaw came, look out! He would be one starin' head – all that time blinded by the winter saved up inside that lonely head of his, he would just stare and stare. Stare at those stars until the light seeped into him, penetrated his eyes, filled him with their essence, with *their* magic light. And in some small way he might live again.

She let her fingers trace over his silty cheek, the semi-smooth crests and rough, sandy pockets. His lips dry and cracked, dusted coral. "Last place," she thought, it was written all over his slightly olive-toned skin. His face had the look of a man who had just finished last.

Last place was for the people you never hear about. Last place was for the gutters and sidewalks, Nichol's Lunch and Bells' Bar – 39th Street.

Cameras and happy crowds always swarm the winner, shake hands with second place, pat the backs of third and fourth place and deftly step clear of dead last.

When they do accidentally make eye contact with last place, they say things like *Good try* and *You'll get 'em next time*. But sometimes you don't *Get 'em next time*. Sometimes you just lose and lose and lose. Sometimes *them* disappears completely and there's no one left and nothing else to get. You're just last and you have to sit there and be that, no matter how much it hurts.

In the air the smell of flowers and plants passed in long draws when the low hum of the furnace kicked on, and some kind of bread. *Why would he bake bread before doing this?* K looked into the kitchen through the arch doorway but it was clean and empty. At the back was a tall window with many cross sections, like a bay window, only it was flush with the wall. Above that, a rose window – half rose, the petals spreading out like a fan – so it matched the shape of the entrance, almost an arch.

She hoped that bread smell wasn't coming from him. She hoped a dead body didn't smell like fresh bread and flowers – warm yeast and hibiscus. But so what? What if it did? Did death have to be gruesome?

"Yeah," she thought. "It did. If it weren't, people would be lined up jumping off cliffs. God had to make it gruesome – just to make life seem interesting."

There was a noise in the air then, high pitched and swirling, and it was coming closer.

"Sirens, K, get the fuck out of here, goddamn sirens."

At the desk by the door, she opened the top drawer. It was right there, just like the story had said. She grabbed the diary and left.

The walk back was surreal and existential – the passing of police cars, the floating steam, swaying limbs in the dark night shaking water off their leaves. Clouds pulled away from the sky, leaving holes.

The rain tittered and tattered and finely quite all together. The rain had stopped but it felt like it was only just beginning. The old diary, probably passed down from a parent or grandparent, was bound in worn leather with beautiful, gold lettering only slightly chipped away with age – she ran her fingers across the surface.

"Looks cool," she thought. "It has the look of important stuff to it. Like if you were in a cave and you found something ancient like a golden staff or tablets with runes. Then you get excited. You start to think that this really old thing has some deep meaning behind it, like it belonged to a king or an ancient tribe and finding it put you in a different echelon of people. Special people, with knowledge and wisdom that you could share if you wished to. Hand it out like hard candy is what you could do to a handful of screaming, but mostly deserving, kids.

"Hard candy but with a soft, taffy-like vanilla center. Of course, some might have a chewy, raspberry center, but mainly vanilla. And to the children you would say, very authoritatively, *Yes, you may have some!* or, *No, you may not have some!* But then the look in the eyes of the children you turned away would make you change your mind quickly, no matter how bad they had been.

"And the wrapping paper surrounding this candy isn't really paper at all, it's plastic! But that's okay, it makes a crispity crunchy sound when you open it and their mouths water in anticipation as I unwrap this candy that I and only I can disperse. For who else holds this candy but me? Who else could ever hold it?

"Then there are more kids, out of nowhere! Do they get some candy to? *Oh, I don't know*, I pretend to ponder – just teasing them a bit. I'd give out in the end. Children love their candy."

She stopped for a moment, pressed her forehead into the hard edge of the book.

"Why do you think these crazy things, K?" The book smelled nice. It was fresh outside from the rain – that and the smell of leather it was like chamomile and orange blossoms, tilin flowers and rosebuds. Smells that calm you and make you feel whole. She took a deep breath saturated with the soft leather.

"Your thoughts are glossy 3x5 inch cards, K."

"He had to make thoughts glossy," she said back. "Just to make you seem more interesting."

Katherine lowered the book. It left a line on her forehead. She walked. Another police car passed, the siren deafening as it came and went, blowing in her ear like trombones dropping the slide from top to bottom.

"Someone died tonight, K."

"It wasn't real – nothing's real."

Her curt gait became slow and mournful. It felt like the long walk on a short plank that K was waiting to fall off of into the contents of that diary. As she passed Cambridge Drive, she saw Simone on her porch swing, seemingly enjoying the rainy afterbirth.

Simone grinned as Katherine walked by. The enticing white smile cut through the void of night, the remaining wisps of fog and the weakened place in Kathy's heart where she was falling deeper into an abandoned well, inviting her to come and swing for a while.

Black bats that sometimes swooped and dove out of the night, searching for moths and other insects, disappeared into the distance. Soft squeaks trailed them.

The night's cool gentle breath engulfed K as she sank into the slow, deliberate movements of the swing. She was a space, a lump in the breath of the night. The sky was blue at the horizon, then grew into blackness. Without a star to guide it, the blue soon lost itself into nothingness.

She was awkward inside around Simone, the stinging feel of paper cuts, a foster kid first day in a new home. *How undeserving. My parents are dead or in prison and none of this belongs to me. And the people say, "Make yourself at home. Sleep here. Eat what you want." How does that get repaid?* The first day is the worst. You unpack your things and sit on the edge of the bed for hours, not wanting to touch anything, not wanting to take anything – not wanting to owe. You could sit on the edge of that bed till life fell away.

The porch swing was soft and rhythmic. Leaves moved from a gentle breeze or from raindrops falling that had weighed them down and Kathy and Simone sat quietly absorbing the last few pieces of the night. K clutched the diary close to her chest as thoughts of the previous few weeks began filing into her consciousness. With each rise and fall on the swing another memory had settled in, the stories she had written, the bare bones of reality she had witnessed – the deaths.

"Dear lord all these deaths," thought K. This story telling was getting out of hand. She'd never experienced death, not in 28 years. Only on TV had she seen death and that was so far away it barely seemed real.

All this time, all this death had been all around her and it had gone unnoticed – a child playing *she loves me, she loves me not*, with the petals of countless lives. Now all that was left was the stem and the heart of some petal-less, forgotten flower that the child had thrown into the wastebasket or smashed into the dirt with the heel of her best church shoes.

But now Death was everywhere. She was so close to Death she could've felt its breath on her neck, had there been any breath. She could've felt the warmth from its skin, had there been any warmth.

The fake parts had vanished – the wax bodies, the red-dye blood, and now it did seem real, a reality plastered in gold and concrete, handprints like the stars in Hollywood – Death was coming. It would come for her too, someday. It was already on its way. The day she was born it had started its journey on the opposite end of the world. Someday, she'd run right into it – head long.

How odd that made her feel inside, something like fear, something like anger – something like loneliness.

K could almost see Death turning its back and walking away, slow and fearless, from each person he'd come to take. And it wasn't the kind of fearlessness that K had ever thought about. Kathy thought of fearlessness as bravery, as going out and conquering what you're afraid of.

But the fearlessness she sensed from Death was more like it had never occurred to him to be afraid. There was no fear of loneliness for Death, or of not having enough food, or of paying the rent or even of pissing off God. There wasn't the slightest ripple of fear in his consciousness, he was smooth and calm. He was glass.

She could hear Death's faint sigh as he left each scene. She could see his empty blackness leaving hollow footprints on the concrete and carpet. She'd always thought Death was evil, that he wanted to kill, enjoyed it. That he longed for it like a vampire does blood. But he had a gentleness to him, a soft stride, and she wondered if he was just some nice old man stuck in a job he didn't really care for just like the rest of us.

"And the dreams, what about those terribly real dreams?" She put her hand to her forehead as she thought. She didn't know what they meant, God angry with Jesus? It didn't make any sense. "What's going on? And what about this last story? *There was a knock on the door* – he had panicked, he might have run away to find that someone and maybe that someone was me. But the knock – my knock!"

"Are you always out so early?" asked K.

Simone took in a slow breath filling her chest with the early morning, then exhaled so completely it looked to Kathy as if her body was almost lifeless and she wondered if Simone even heard her. But she wasn't about to ask again. She was a foster kid, had been ripped from the arms of God and dropped onto the edge of this porch swing. Loneliness was a peg she hung her Scooby-Doo bathrobe on – terrycloth white and torn. She didn't deserve anything more than loneliness, she didn't deserve even loneliness. Simone was a foster parent, she hung her almuce on a peg next to God's.

"I like the dawn. The dawn is where I draw my power," she said, eyeing the East in some kind of restrained anticipation. "And what of you, child? You always find yourself running up and down 39th Street in the middle of the night?"

A pressure formed behind K's eyes. She wished she were a pelican. She wished she had a place to store the refuse of her life where it wouldn't overflow into tears and sobs and wet things – staining the forel of her face in streaks and water lines, loosening pages at the seams like a steam bath.

"Some..." she choked back the moment and gathered herself, raised an arm to wipe away some long, black curls that had draped over her right eye. Her lips were full in the soft light of the veranda, her rounded eyes glazed with moisture. She had beauty like night.

"Some, strange things have been happening lately." And that was enough. As if the words themselves were the release gate and the tears came pouring out.

Simone took her to her fleshy, soft bosom and K covered her face with her hands. The swing continued its short rise and falls, a hand-made raft on a calming ocean. But there were sharks in the ocean, too, and squids and jelly fish and all sorts of mammalian life better left unknown – she knew that, she knew it all too well.

Kathy's words were fast and frantic through the tears and gasps for air.

"There are these things, and I don't know if I cause them or they just happen or if they just cause themselves and they tell me about it first or..."

"Whoa," Simone said. "I can't follow that much that fast."

K eased away from Simone and pushed to a standing position, pacing the small area in front of the porch swing, shaking her hands as if drying her fingernails to gather herself.

"I've been writing these stories," the words were hesitant at first, not quite sure how they'd be received. "And lately they've been coming true. More and more true with each story. They seem to be getting more accurate each time and they get closer and closer to me each time.

"And the people..." the tears started to creep down her face once again pulled by the peen of recent memories and realizations. "They always die and this last one..." she stopped pacing and squatted down on the floor with her head in her hands.

"Oh, my God. Oh, God, I think I caused his death...Oh my God. I don't know how or why. But I knocked on the door and I think that made him die..." her hands cradled her stomach, holding together what wanted to spill all over the porch like a gutted whale. "He might have just left town but then I was there and...Oh my God, I think I killed him."

Katherine fell into deep, breathy sobs, unraveling in front of Simone on the veranda. Simone moved to her and took K by the shoulders, guiding her up, off the painted gray planks to the swing, where they sat. Simone set them back in motion and they began to sway once again.

The slow motion of the swing soothed her and K quieted, hiccuped, then looked out into the night that was becoming a lighter shade of blue off to the East. Simone patted her knee.

"Before the dawn of this world," Simone began, "the mother of creation had a plan. The plan included every living thing on this beautiful planet, throughout all times. She has a plan for you too, child. So don't worry none.

"Just sit back and watch what mother creation creates for you next. If it's bad, don't worry. The good will follow the bad just like the night follows the day, just like the day follows the night. Round and round it goes, where it stops nobody knows."

"But what if I don't want to go round and round anymore? What if I'm tired of good and bad and night and day – can't I just get off?"

"No, that isn't possible. I've talked to the dead. They're just lining up to get back on again."

"You talk to the dead?"

"Sure, they ain't got much else to do." Her exaggerated features casting shadows on the lawn like a puppet.

"What do they say?"

"They don't know nothin'."

"So if there are no answers when you die, when do the answers come? When does it end?" K said, becoming hysterical again, breathing choppy breaths. She'd never imagined that it could be like that – no answers, just starting over.

"It ends when mother creation decides to take us back, nothing is needed on your part, just let her do what she needs to do."

The words sat like rocks in K's stomach. It sounded helpless. It sounded hopeless. It sounded like *Serenity Prayer.*

"What about my stories?"

"Why waste your energy? For what? If they happen, they happen. You don't need to know about them. Why put yourself through such turmoil – ah wait, here come the first rays of dawn."

"But shouldn't I try and…"

"Shhh – the dawn cometh." Simone froze, closing her eyes, taking in a deep breath as if to drink it in through her nostrils. K sat and watched for some time but Simone never moved and Kathy squirmed with each moment that passed, with each ray of light that slipped over the skyline. It was too much.

"Thanks, Simone," she said getting up, clutching her diary. "I'll see ya."

"Okay, child," Simone said, not opening her eyes. Kathy stepped off the porch and headed home.

Early morning was brisk. K stared into the orange dome peeking over 39th Street enclosed by the building fronts like bookends. There were a few puddles left and the sidewalk was a shade darker, still damp, she could feel the morning yawn and stretch and prepare to become day. She could feel the dawn pulling itself away – away from whatever was keeping the dawn from just popping up quickly.

A lover perhaps, the night, hanging onto the last few moments they had together before he had to let her go. And she left him but his grip remained, tried to pull her back. He never understood why she had to go in the first place, or if and when she'd return. And the dawn arose slowly, slipping from the touch of its abandoned lover finger by finger.

Work would be difficult today. It would drag on like an old mule plowing. And the diary would be waiting all that time. All that time she served eggs and bacon to the thankless customers at Nichol's Lunch. All that time getting free coffee refills for the guys that just sat there all day drinking free coffee refills.

All that time she'd be wasting doing pointless, meaningless tasks while something important lay on her bed like the very first Bible, just waiting to be read.

She headed up 39th Street with the diary at her side in her left hand – the way the boys carried their books in high school. At State Line Road, where she paused at the blinking yellow lights as a car passed spraying the air with water, she brought it up to her stomach with a bent arm, its weight resting on her ribs – the way the girls carried their books in high school. As she passed Bells', she clutched the diary to her chest with both arms crossed over it – the way they do with a Bible when they bury you.

She tried to imagine what it would be like on the other side of that diary, when all the pages had been turned and the book lay closed with its beautiful gold letters face down. Then she lowered her head and rested her chin on top of it as she rounded the corner heading to her back alley. What was in that thing? Did she really want to know? Where would it take her? Did she really want to go?

V

"**S**hould I start from the beginning? How much do you really want to know? I would think you knew everything. I would think the cause would know the effect, the writer would know the play line by line. The winter would know the harvest.

Chasing me into dark corners of my mind it must be a game for you. Not even an interesting one, just pieces moving. No beginning, no middle – no end. No winners, no losers – just pieces moving.

And I was there, somehow – don't remember, just there. A piece moving, lost and insignificant among uncountable, unknowable other pieces. And you there watching me. Sometimes pretending to be a piece, but I know you, you've come to take me away, away from me. I feel the void of you pulling and hear your emptiness calling, but I don't listen. I won't. I'll disappear, I'll get lost in the pieces. I'll find money and I'll leave here, I'll leave this prison and go to some island – free. Sunshine and beaches and women and margaritas and you'll never hear from me again.

And I won't hear from you. I'll make sure of that. And if I do hear you, hear your vibrations coming, your ringing bells, I'll run again – and again and again.

I know who I am and you can't make me not believe that. I am me. I'm who I am, no matter what your empty lies say."

Kathy was right, cold eggs and burnt hash browns couldn't compete. Whatever it was she'd just read her work was meaningless next to it. Her life shallow in the light of it. She waded to her ankles in the kiddy pool while this guy dove from a plane into an uncharted ocean. Her life was a skit put on by her and her fourth-grade friends, made up for a school play they couldn't even get into. His was a billion-dollar Hollywood production with Spielberg, Olivier and Monroe.

And there was more, much more, page after page of it and K figured it was no wonder he had put a gun in his mouth. How existential can you be and for how long before you crumble beneath the weight of it? And there *was* weight on those pages, they were thick with heaviness. He had carried quite a load, and he hated God. K had never heard of anybody hating God before. It never entered her mind like that, to feel the way he felt toward God – disdain, animosity.

"And to my bastard creator," he wrote. *"To you I leave my shell, this worthless piece of skin and bones and you can use it to pick your teeth after dining on some other world you've created and devoured. Some other world that ended in chaos and anger and disharmony just like this one. You're a sick fuck, God. I'm glad you're forgiving – maybe you can forgive yourself."*

She didn't know it was possible to write what he wrote – to lash out at God like that, without being struck down and crippled. Crawling around the rest of your life wishing you could take it back, wishing God wouldn't turn profile with a deaf ear each time you called his name.

There was a pain inside of her just reading it. Some kind of pressure in her throat that made her swallow hard but didn't go away after she did. It just seemed to spiral downward leaving a trail, opening a dark well in her belly that felt empty and unforgiving. At first she thought it was the pain of feeling sorry for what that cop went through. Then she thought it was the pain God felt when he read those words.

Then she realized it wasn't those pains at all, it was much deeper, much more terrifying. The realization hardened the lump in her throat, blackened the well in her gut, singed and burned inside like fire on dry plains. It was the pain of realizing she felt the very same way.

Bells came over as K was holding up her head by the hairs next to each temple, the strain of it pulling tight her face.

"Need another?" His glance bent down to meet hers like the jesters in a court to the queen. Sometimes he came across so humble, like he wasn't even there – or didn't deserve to be. And she liked how his eyes slid down to see her. Concerned and open, empty pools of liquid clouds ready for her to dive into, if she ever needed.

K wondered if she could tell him, if she could ask what she wanted to ask. But this was Bells, if she couldn't ask him...there was nobody else.

"Bells?"

"Yeah." He filled a glass with ice and started to pour rum into it.

"Have you ever heard of anybody hating God before?"

He topped it off with a stale can of Diet Coke that was already open, sitting in the ice bin on the other side of K – that's what she got when she took too long to decide what she wanted, a rum and Diet Coke. He set the drink in front of her taking her glass that had only a few pieces of ice left and a chewed up red straw. His hands were thick, thick and rough like they'd had a hard life. She wasn't sure but she figured it must have been rough. It must have been rough to reach the kind of calmness he was now. Maybe life has to break you like that, she thought.

Maybe you prance around like a prized pony most your life bucking and kicking when they try to ride you. You think the world's your playground. Then the months of beatings with a rope tied around your neck finally takes the kick out of you, makes you realize you're just a horse. You're the playground, a pony ride, for anyone that wants to jump on.

"I've never heard of anybody who didn't," he said, and gracefully walked away, back to his corner of the bar. Even in his one-legged gimp he still had grace, poetry. He slid his leg across the ground like a ballet dancer in some performance art piece – an allegory about a war.

175

His gentle, poetic walk and the words that came out of him stilled K's mind. And she wondered what world she lived in, the world where everybody felt that way and she never knew it. The world where people lived under palls, went to church, smiled to the neighbor, laughed, cried when a baby was born – and beneath it all, simmering like the pits in Hell, hating God.

His answer had startled her. She was ready for him to grunt, *Nope*, or *Sometimes a dog shits all over the yard*, or some other complete bullshit she could instantly dismiss and then move on to her next line of questions. But Bells was Bells. Apparently he didn't need to live up to her expectations of what she thought of him and what she thought he should say.

She just needed an answer. Anybody anywhere that could state something in clear English that would make sense of it all. Now she had a worse question than the one she started out with. *Everybody feels this way?* There were more answers in the ceiling rafts.

Did it always have to be a downward spiral? Couldn't there be a glimmer of light shining at the end of the stairwell out of her queries. It was painful down on those dark stairs and it was dusky and damp from all those sporus, fuzzy questions about life. Mold was growing, growing quickly. Soon the whole area would be covered with a slimy moss-like substance that didn't make *any* sense – and she would never find her way. She could try but would surely slide down over and over from the slick, slimy moss coating the stairway out of there.

"Fuck…what world have I been living in? Everybody feels this way? Fuck."

The pages of his diary turned like sifting sand as her finger pushed each one aside. With the other hand she lifted the drink to her lips.

The glass was wet and slick, but she liked that. She liked sweat from cold glasses in warm rooms – the way it might slip out of her hands and there'd be nothing she could do about it. Even if she tried to grip it harder that might make it worse, it might shoot out then with force. But she liked the possibility, having glass shatter and having it not be her fault.

176

Kathy raised the glass to her forehead and let the coldness of it spread into her skull till it numbed her skin. She let water dribble down her nose and down her cheek. Someone watching might think she was crying – and she wished she were.

It was nice to cry last night. Out of control like that, not worrying about where it might take her. Being against the breasts of that huge woman – she had milk in there for a hundred children, and K wished she did. She wished she had love inside, so much so that it needed to ooze from her nipples milky white just to relieve her of the constant pressure. Maybe that's why some women have children, though they don't realize it when the kid cries all night and then flunks reading in the third grade, then crashes the family car when they're sixteen.

They'd probably forgotten by then why they had them in the first place – too much love inside, needing to ooze out milky white. K didn't have any of that inside of her. She had emptiness. She had resentment. Nothing grows from nothing. Nothing grows, nothing oozes, but maybe puss.

She hoped the people like her that had puss inside didn't mistake their puss for love, being milky white and all, because it wouldn't be. And sharing their puss would only do more damage than good. Spreading puss from their bosoms like it was love would destroy things faster than Charlie Manson could if he were a thousand people. It would eat away everything. Maybe it was better to be like the cop in 808, knowing his puss wasn't love, stopping it before it started.

She took a drink, let it flow into her like the music falling from the Bose speakers, landing in pools, filling the room with haunted whispers.

I hear you, in the morning. And I hear you, at nightfall. And sometimes, to be near you is to be unable, to feel you – my love.

"Jesus!" thought K. Even her, even Stevie Nicks in some song thirty-years-old now, she sounded like she'd torn pages out of the diary from the cop in 808, held them in front of her as she sang into the mike. K looked around the room wondering who these people were. Was everybody running from the emptiness he talked about? Was everybody chasing it at the same time?

...the sea changes colors, but the sea does not change. So, with the slow, graceful flow of age, I will fold with an age old desire, to be... Someone turned up the television just then, and Kathy couldn't hear the song anymore. It was a news report – it was about the dead cop.

"After a thorough search of the apartment, police have determined that another person was in the room at approximately the same time as the apparent suicide. With the help of relatives, police have deduced that everything was intact, with nothing missing, except possibly a diary that relatives said he had since childhood, said the reporter. *Officer can you answer a few..."*

Bells was pouring a Sam Adams into a chilled mug for someone who sat to K's right, an angelic looking old man with a soft face. His white hair sticking up in places where it wasn't completely white yet, still coarse, rigid gray. He didn't say much, but smiled a lot, pointed at the row of beers on the rack to order, maybe he was a mute. Before Bells went to the corner, K flagged him over.

"What's up, Angel?"

"I'm no angel, Bells, and I just want to read you something – see what you think." She cleared her throat.

"...And she comes again," K began. *"Amidst the whirls of the wind she descends onto me. Smothers my dreams as if she were the fist around a tiny flame. And my heart bleeds. The silence with which she surrounds me is like a tomb. If it weren't for her beauty, I would have run long ago. And though I know she's come to tear me apart, I stay, I wait. Just to glance at her beauty, just to hear the chime of her as she approaches – and it is enough."*

Bells pulled the white rag from his shoulder, wet a spot with water from the fountain gun, rubbed it between his hands with force scrubbing off the stickiness of hard liquor and beer, then threw it back over his shoulder.

"What do you make of that?" she asked.

He grunted, his hand digging into the muscle in his jaw as if to loosen it.

"Is there any more?"

"There's lots more." K flipped ahead several entries.

"Do you think I believe you? Do you think I believe I'm really empti-
ness – that I don't exist at all? That I'm a cocoon of thoughts and beliefs
and in order to find me means that I can't be me anymore? Do you think
I believe all that nonsense? Send whomever you want. Write it in as many
scriptures as you wish. You created me, you must think you created a
fool."

"Well," he moved his hand to his chin, pulled at the skin like he was
fondling a beard. "Sounds like you were…"

"No, no," K interrupted. "It's not mine. It's a… a friend of mines."

"Okay. Well, sounds like your friend is right on the edge."

"On the edge of what?" *Insanity? Suicide?* she was thinking.

He shrugged his shoulders, making an empty gesture with his hands.
Light danced off his eyes like the reflection of a torch on pond water.

"God."

She'd never heard him talk like that before, and K looked down
onto a crevasse in the bar wishing she were a toothpick, wishing she
could slide right in. *How…how could he…* She couldn't even form the
question the ambiguity had left in her mind and Bells turned to leave.
She jerked out her arm, grabbed his wrist.

"But what do you think could have been going through his mind?"

The reporter on TV raised his voice, becoming agitated, and they
both turned to look.

"But isn't it possible that something unflattering or even damaging
was written about an unknown person, and that this unknown person
came into the apartment, shot the police officer and took the incriminat-
ing evidence with him?"

"I have no comment on that hypothesis at this time."

"Well, that is the opinion of this journalist," he said, now turning to
face the camera. *"I believe, you find the diary of Officer Angello B.*
Ellsworth, you find the murderer of Officer Angelo B. Ellsworth!" He made

an emphatic gesture with a closed fist.

"The diary is very old and the black leather would look worn and gray in parts. If seen, you should contact...."

Bells turned back to K.

"I don't know what was going through his mind. Not a bullet, I hope."

She closed the diary and slid it with her left hand into her lap, her head lowering as it followed the diary.

"You ever feel like somebody's trying to tell you something, but you just can't figure out what? You just can't get it no matter how hard you try?"

"Trying may just be the problem." He grunted, moved away like a wounded dog.

Weeks had passed and another story had come true and Katherine was starting to get scared. There was a theme forming that was more obvious than blood on white fur. She couldn't shake it and she couldn't keep it from coming out the end of her pen. They were all dying – they all ended in death. And it was getting worse.

Words like *brimstone* and *diablere* landed on the page. What good could come from a story with words like those? Fouled seed of Hemlock and Poison Ivy. Why had she chosen them? Why not move onto other words that she could paint the sky with orange and yellow, like *baubles* or *chrysanthemums*.

"You know why you chose them," she thought, her long hard stare in the blue light wondering who that person was, really, that looked back.

"No, K, I don't. Why don't you enlighten me." An eyebrow raised as she stood back on her hip, arms crossed, looking through loose black curls that had fallen over one eye.

"A hero needs a precarious ending," she said. "One that could go either way."

The night had smelled of brimstone and was without color. Something thick lay in the air like a haze, but it was unseen. The sad song of the wind blew by like slow jazz, Billie Holiday and Lester Young. Streets were black polish from a few hours rain that had stirred up the dirt and oil but had done nothing more, and K followed the opalescent road to a parking lot north of her work at Nichol's Lunch.

A double intersection with no left turns, the story had said. It had to be 39th and Southwest Trafficway, that sulfur/egg smell coming out of her work, the three-lane boulevard divided by a cement strip with bricks pressed in the center, except the opening where 39th Street crossed.

There were several components, one she could stop. The car of a *plutocrat*, it would be shiny and new, probably silver the way it *shined like a bullet* in the street lamps. Another car, older, a hand me down, loud and only one headlamp working – a teenage boy two weeks fresh behind the wheel. The third, a mongrel, *pariah dog*, a mutt – that was the pliable one. The one she would work like clay, molding it until the story had a happy ending. If not happy, at least non-eventful – nobody knowing what might have been.

A dog ran onto his path. He swerved, only to hit a car head on. Three people died. A teenage boy in a rusted import, he would get the blame. A mother and her baby in the other, innocent victims – they all were.

It was easy. The dog was going to cross west to east, from where she sat in the empty parking lot of a small insurance company. She would stop it. She would run it over if she had to. If she was within arms reach, she'd shove a pen through its mangy throat – this story was not going to happen.

And then, *the one that would portend.* She was unsure – *a noise, it exploded into the night like a shotgun. Like* a shotgun, it said. Not necessarily one, though, she would have to be alert. That was the trigger. It scared the mutt, sent him fleeing into the intersection. When she heard the gun, she would have only seconds to respond – or it would all start falling like dominoes.

In the charcoal night, clouds were high and seamless. So high they didn't refract light from the city, leaving the sky empty and dark. The eerie stillness of unlit houses in front of her was like a black sea, where light from the neighborhoods usually enlivened the air. There were no lights north of 39th Street. They clicked off about an hour into her long wait. They'd be on soon, she hoped, probably a transformer blew, power line fell…something. It was as dark a night as she'd ever seen – *a perfect black*, the story had said. That was the title. This was the right night, had to be. She had guessed right. And she was prepared – a rope, dog treats, a pen.

Kathy's car had been idling almost two hours now, and she was running low on fuel. Cars came and went, several that matched the descriptions of both and she rested her head on the steering wheel.

"Dear lord, K, couldn't you have written the time this was all going to happen?"

"I know, I'm getting tired too. But this is important, come on – we can do this!"

She raised her head, looked into the rearview mirror, pulled dark strands of hair from her eyes, tucked them behind her ears. She didn't know why she bothered, it would only last a few seconds then hair would be in her face again.

"Maybe it's time you got a hair cut."

She pulled the hair from her face, covered it with her hands in the mirror, then dropped them down. "I don't think so."

Little mirrors didn't bother her so much. The beings on the other side were partial and small and even if they did get a hold of her, trying to yank her from this world like the cork from a bottle, she'd be too big to fit. She ran her fingers along the surface, a show of bravery, the fleshy white of her skin in the mirror, a place frightened does might trot in winter.

A smile slipped from the corner of her mouth as she saw the beauty reflected back to her. Sometimes she forgot how beautiful she was. She could've done so much more. People like being surrounded by beautiful things. Most corporate jobs could have been hers for the asking – even acting, modeling. It always seemed that there should have been more.

The smile lowered from her lips, disappearing into the empty gesture she usually held.

Through the gap between two fingers she was trailing along the surface of the small rectangular mirror, a splotch of brown matted hair stuck out above the trunk behind her car. She whipped around, bumped her head on the ceiling as she jerked up to look. It was a dog. Looked like Benji from the television show, only with ratty fur. His nose pushed into the carcass of a squirrel on the pavement. This was it.

K maneuvered a Milkbone dog biscuit from the box as her heart fluttered in her chest. If he was hungry enough for dead squirrel, a Milkbone would seem like Thanksgiving. Maybe he didn't have to get a pen shoved through his throat or get run over. Maybe he would come right to her, hop in the car, and she'd drive away, dump him at an animal shelter.

She eased open the door, tried to keep it from squeaking on its rusted hinges as not to scare him, stood up and peered over the top.

Suddenly to her left, she heard the rattled engine of a car heading southbound. There must have been a hole in the muffler, or the muffler had already fallen off, because she could hear it before it got to the crest of the hill where it peeked over with one headlight out. *Shit!*

She yanked her head to her far right. A streak of silver crossed under a street lamp, heading north, a BMW – metallic. It was unfolding too fast, quicker than she'd thought. She would have to kill it. Panicky she jumped in the car, slipped it into reverse, held the clutch hard against the floorboard, looked over her shoulder. The mutt was directly behind her right, rear tire.

"Come on K, go! Now – Now!"

She floored the gas pedal revving the engine high, popped the clutch. Her car lurched backward then backfired – rang out like a shotgun into the night. Smoke billowed from the exhaust. The dog darted into the street as she rolled to a stop a few feet back where the car stalled, went quiet.

Tires screamed like hawks – bellows and wails of lorn, angry birds. The dissonant, flat clamor of metal hitting metal and shattered glass followed. K turned, her hand over the headrest twisting her torso. They hit so hard you couldn't tell what kind of cars they were anymore.

People ran into the street from Nichol's and other nearby buildings and houses. She couldn't look any longer and turned back staring over the black sea in front of her, her hand resting on the steering wheel, a Milkbone clutched between the thumb and forefinger. She threw it on the passenger seat, started the car with her head digging into the hard plastic of the steering wheel. She gasped for a breath, turned around in the empty lot. Her hands shook uncontrollably as she signaled right and slowly pulled out, heading home.

In the end there was no one to blame, it was *diablere*, the story had said – devil's play. But it didn't feel like there was no one to blame. Anyway, it was all over now. The dark voice of the night had spoken. Its whispers like tigers.

In the blue light, water poured crystal, steam rising like hot springs. The porcelain knob squeaked as she shut it off. She put in salts and lavender. Lavender to help her forget. Dead Sea salts that could tenderize a frozen steak, even wear down a stone, if given time.

Things don't become white and clean by letting them sit in the pile of muck that dirtied them. Not even when you take them out and set them in the sun. Sometimes, not even with soap and warm water. Something abrasive is needed, salts, pumice – something with which to scrub.

If that doesn't work – Clorox. That's when the pain comes. When you can't get clean and you want to but you can't let go of the filth, then the pain comes – comes on hard like Jesus on the cross sometime after, *Lord, why has thou forsaken me?* But before, *Thy will be done, thy kingdom come.*

When her head went under, everything was submerged at once, and she thought for some time that she could stay that way. Breath seemed like something for children, K was stronger than that. She was glass. Having a God was good, she could see that now. People created God – so they could be forgiven.

Her heart pounded in the silent waters. Drips from the faucet were like echoes in the pond of a deep cavern as she lay submerged, and still. She pushed her feet into the porcelain base, slowly arose like Poseidon from the Aegean Sea. She brought up a wet rag from the hot water, blanketed her face.

Through the heel of a God, death found its way in, she thought.

K wondered what the look on the face of the father would be like. He wrapped his wife and kid up in an armored car made of silver coins. His money was their bodyguard. He must have felt like Achilles as the poison raced through his veins. Thetis should have dipped him twice.

185

Why go through all that trouble and not dip him twice?

Death finds its way in, Katherine thought. *That's the moral, Thetis could have dipped him a hundred times. Through the heel of a God or Beamers made of silver, death will find its way in.*

Katherine wore sandals most of the time and even if she wore hard-soled Doc Martens she wasn't dipped in magic and she wasn't dipped in silver and she had no armored car. Hers was more likely to cause her death than to stop it. Her defense was a paper umbrella no bigger than the size of her hand, put together with toothpicks. She guessed she thought she could deflect the bullets of death with it like Wonder Woman and her silver bracelets. All she had was the thin defense that she was young and that death was a thousand miles away. Nowadays, it only took a few hours to travel a thousand miles.

The unused rope sat in a coil on the bedroom floor and she looked over at it like it was a snake, drying herself with an over-sized terrycloth towel.

"Did you think you were going to lasso him?"

"I don't know, exactly." And she picked it up, put it back inside the open vent, shutting it.

"Did you know there are only a handful of people in the world that can actually lasso? Did you know that? Did you know that you're not one of them?"

"Shut up, K. Just shut the hell up!" She ran the towel across her back in short, hard strokes, turning to Marilyn on the mirror. "And I don't want to hear anything out of you, either!" She threw the towel toward the vanity, staring her down.

Wasn't gonna say anything, anyway, Marilyn mumbled, low.

Kathy fell onto the bed looking at the bumps on the ceiling, the light harsh in her eyes. She should have turned it off before getting into bed. She rolled over, switched it off.

It was a three dog night, even though the temperature only dropped to sixty when the sun fell off the edge of the world – left blood red clouds in its wake with streaks of orange at first, followed by the blackest night. She would need a German shepherd, an Alaskan Husky and something else big and furry in her bed to make her feel safe and warm that night.

"Maybe a Police Dog," she thought.

"Those *are* German Shepherds."

"Then two German Shepherds and one Husky – a Husky with blue eyes and soft white fur." She wrapped herself tight in a chrysalis of comforters and sheets. It had to have white fur, she was thinking, so she could see the blood coming, if there were any.

That night she didn't sleep well. It was two hours of watching numbered tags slowly building pressure and releasing. The hum inside the tiny machine growing and growing, until the tag flipped. Then there would be quiet for several seconds until it started to build again – two hours worth.

"Maybe you should try writing a story," she had said.

"You're real funny."

When she finally did sleep, it was worse. She struggled with creatures she couldn't even see, and then she ran – and ran and ran. It felt like weights around her as she tried to climb slick hills – climbing, climbing, only to collapse and slide down. She didn't know where she was going, just running and climbing most of the night until a crack appeared on a rock face and Katherine slid through.

Looking down, she could see the world. Scenes in time, warriors entangled on battlefields, lovers entangled on bedsprings. An emperor's reign, doctrines signed, peace treaties. Explosions. She was standing on glass and all around were distant echoes calling her foreword. Effortlessly, she glided into the next chamber. Only shades of light remained in faint colors. A voice. God. She awoke taking in breaths like she had been drowning.

Morning came up in a bright streak across her room and she pulled the weak cotton shade hoping to keep out the light awhile longer, wanting to go somewhere darker just then – where worms go. But the room continued to grow bright, anyway, dropping cloaks.

She watched the early morning through drawn curtains. The darker parts. The long, slanted rectangle where unadulterated sun hit full. Blotches of flapping shadows passing, one, then two, one chasing the other – birds blocking the path of sunlight.

She didn't have to work that day, which was good and which wasn't. She didn't want to be alone all day with nothing to do, and she didn't want to be at work looking mournfully onto 39th Street and Southwest Trafficway all afternoon as she over-filled refill after refill onto the counter top. Bells' opened at 10:30 a.m., thank God. She was there at 10:15.

Outside the air was crisp, but warming. Clouds were dabbed on with white paint and cotton balls. Birds dripped dry, meaningless melodies from their beaks down the guttural street to the spot where the 39th Street Bum should be sitting. Sound stopped there and K looked up where the 39th Street Bird peeked over the maroon gutter onto the empty spot, probably wondering where his friend had gone.

How your little dove body must ache, she was thinking, *the symbol of peace and love and all. When you look down on 39th Street, does your body ache?* The bird cooed, but it always did that.

"It's okay, birdy. He's gone home," she said, trying to make herself believe it. She wondered how much that little gray bird really understood. What was the line between coincidence and will. She wondered how foolish she had been thinking she could talk to that bird all these years.

Go to The Veco, she called out in thought. *The Veco restaurant, it's over there.* She turned to point at the black and white sign across 39th Street. *Go birdy.*

Over and over she thought it, *Go the The Veco, The Veco resturaunt,* until the bird jumped off the gutter, gliding like a fallen leaf across the street where it flapped a few times and sat on the unlit white sign with the black blocked letters that said *The Veco.*

"That's just plain weird, K." And she turned in spooked shivers, pounding on the door. "Bells! Come on Bells, open up!"

But he wasn't there yet, she knew that. His shiny white Cadillac was nowhere to be found. He usually parked close by. She parked her miserable piece of crap a few blocks away in an alley blocked by a dumpster and several bushes, not wanting it to be seen after last night.

The slow cling-clang of a ringing bell droned from the corner near State Line Road, heading her way. It sounded like a trolley, the kind they have in San Francisco or maybe even other parts of California. They had replicas of those now in Kansas City running in Westport and The Plaza on wheels, not on rails, for tours – but she didn't think they had bells.

When Katherine turned to look, it was just a man with a gold-colored bell in his hand. It was that same dumb man with that same dumb wooden sign looped over his shoulders, hanging down to his feet, that read: *Repent, the end is nigh!*

He yelled it out to everyone around. Only no one was around but K and the 39th Street Bird. She looked to the sky, leaned back onto the wooden door of Bells' Bar, the turtledove on The Veco sign blinked and tilted its head sideways.

"Dear lord, why are you doing this to me?" K asked to the pastel blue sky.

The man stopped at her feet as K took her eyes from the heavens to see his eyes and slanted smile gleaming at her through his filth and

189

smell. He clanged his brass bell with its black handle.

"Repent, child, the end is nigh!"

K could hardly believe it. How stupid this all was.

"Jesus Christ, still?"

The transient sign holder stammered at first.

"Well...uh...yeah, still. Of course, still! It is always ending. Each day he comes to collect our debt, collects them by the bushel full, he does." The brown covered man sneered a half-smile.

Great. As if she didn't already know that. As if she needed a reminder. As if she hadn't been living it, breathing it, smelling it each moment. As if she couldn't feel the wind from God's giant hand as he swept those lives into his goopy palm, yanked them out of existence.

"Get the fuck out of here, you goddamn freak!" She reached up her right leg, kicked out at the sign. Her heel hit flush with a thud, enough to jolt him. He pulled back, sneered, then turned again to look into her angry eyes that were glossy and on the edge of tears, her cheeks reddened with emotion.

"There comes a time when we all fall back to the womb," he said. "We all fall back to the womb."

Then he moved up the length of 39th Street, rang his bell, chanted his chant.

Songs from the past were fruits filled with memories and scars and longings for better times and kinder Gods. One after another they played and she wished the machine would slow down and grind to a halt once and for all so the memories would stop flooding her – crashing down like she was a sandcastle on a shallow shore made from a child's upside-down pail. Tears wanted to fall, but she didn't let them. Tears falling at Bells' wouldn't be freeing, just embarrassing.

The afternoon was spent in trembles and wrestled thoughts of the lives she'd destroyed, and the life that could be, hers. What if there had been a witness? What if the cops were asking questions? This could mean jail. Leaving the scene of an accident, and God help her if someone saw her car scare that dog into the street. That could be negligence of some kind, not keeping a properly maintained vehicle, maybe. She wasn't sure which law she had broken but she knew she had broken one and she knew it couldn't be good. How could something good be born from lies and deceit and fear and twisted metal and blood and the list was endless.

"God that was stupid. How could you do something so stupid?"

"I don't know, K. I don't fucking know." She swallowed hard a drink of her rum and Diet Coke, as if ice were lodged in her throat. "You know what the story said. *In the end, no one was too blame. It was diablere – devil's play.*"

"Doesn't feel like there's no one to blame, huh?"

"No."

"Feels like you're to blame, doesn't it?"

"Yeah."

And even if she weren't, even if it were diablere, she didn't like being a puppet in the hands of the devil. And what about her dream? Face to face with God?

"He must be pissed, calling you to his chamber like that." It had never been like that. A hundred dreams and she was always on the outside looking in. This one was as if she were there, actually face to face with God.

"Yeah, pissed. You've got to fix this mess."

"How?"

K dropped her head between her shoulders, her thin neck exposed when her charcoal hair fell around her face to the bar, the red straw in the glass pressed into her forehead between her thick, dark eyebrows.

"You know."

Drunk 1 and Drunk 2 played basketball in the corner with a spinning quarter, catching it between two thumbs, shooting it into the circled hand of the other. A missed shot meant you had to drink, a made shot meant the other one would drink. She figured their livers should give out by about three in the afternoon. But three o'clock came and went and they were playing darts for shots of Jack Black – they barely hit the board.

Everything was normal at Bells' Bar, business as usual. The day fell into night with distant, tortured calls of a pen and paper and her Webster's blue bible sitting on the desk upstairs. Her cigarette trembled as she raised it to her lips. This was the last one in the pack – good. Soon she could get up, rest her sore butt, and pretend to steady herself on the smooth glass of the cigarette machine as she got another pack.

"I can't believe you're thinking about writing another story," she said, pulling long strands of hair, tucking them behind her right ear.

"I'm not."

Bells was coming over, she didn't want him to. She didn't want to see him. He kept asking the same thing, *Everything all right?* Every ten fucking minutes. Every time he came anywhere near her, *Everything all right? Everything all right?*

"He's a goddamn parrot! Fuck him! Like I need another goddamn father in my life. I made it this far without one, certainly I can coast from here. I just need the cheap booze."

"Yeah, you keep telling yourself that."

"Oh yeah? Fuck you too!"

"Alright, K, keep it together." She looked at her reflection through the smoke-stained mirror. She looked like death two months in the grave. Her eyes were so sallow and dark she should be in a Goth band or playing a vampire in some B movie.

"Where are you, K, what the hell are you doing?" She didn't even know. She did know she'd already skated past the line in the ice that said, *Do not skate here.* She did know she had already flown past the realm where her fuel could get her back safely. She was in a plane over an uncharted ocean. Her gauge had been flashing, *point of no return!* for hours – she hadn't noticed till now.

She would have to keep going, see what was on the other side. She would have to make up for the damage she'd already done, or drop like a weight into the sea like the cop in 808.

Bells was there, topping off her glass with rum and diet, looking at her from arm's length. "Everthing al…"

She raised her right hand and he cut his words short, walked away, shook his head. K looked into the mirror behind the bar, her deep eyes set on dark rings. The smoke and stains on the glass actually made her look better.

"I can't believe you're thinking about writing another story."

At the vanity, everything looked dangerous; pens, blank sheets of paper, mirrors – photographs. She didn't want to touch anything for fear of it turning to shit. She was Midas' younger, retarded cousin. Midas skipped happily through life turning everything he touched into gold and she clumsily followed, stumbling into the bulky gold things, turning them to shit. That was part of the fable not too many people knew about. But she knew it. She was living it. She knew it all too well.

Life was moving in a wave, building, thrusting toward something – into something. She didn't know what, but it was like a river coming to the crest of a waterfall – and she was caught up in it in a plywood barrel. She would have to keep going, just like she had said, see what's on the other side. She pulled open the wicker drawer, retrieved a pen, three sheets of paper.

"This time it will be different. Think positive, K, that's the problem."

"Yeah, positive thinking. Got it."

She thumbed through the dictionary in search of the word – the right word.

"*Frog.* That's a nice word," she thought. "Not much can go wrong with frogs. *Calliope.* Good, a musical instrument used in carnivals, perfect. This story won't be so bad."

The words came fast and easy, almost like they were lit as she flipped the pages of her dictionary. Marilyn Monroe's photo peered over K's shoulder, tauntingly.

"Way to go my big, smart girl. You're just all big and important now, aren't you? What's next? Gonna to save the world?"

"Fuck off," said K. "You're really starting to push your luck, Marilyn. You may soon find yourself flying out the window!"

"I care."

Colonial – a. Pertaining to the characteristics of the thirteen British colonies.

Pinion – vt. To confine or shackle. To bind, especially the wings of a bird.

Branks – n. An iron curb for the tongue held in place by a frame around the head.

Sinecure – n. Any office or post which gives remuneration without requiring much work or responsibility.

Frog – n. Any of a group of small, four-legged leaping animals.

Calliope – n. A musical instrument consisting of a number of steam-whistled tones. Muse of eloquence and poetry.

Pariah – n. Any outcast. Someone despised or rejected by others.

Birch –n. Any tree of the genus *Betula*.

Tenebrous – a. Dark, gloomy.

Sanguine – a. The color of blood, ruddy, said of complexions.

Turgid – a. Swollen, bloated, inflated, pompous.

Malaise – n. A vague feeling of discomfort or uneasiness, as before an illness.

Parlance – n. Conversation, speech, especially debate.

Blasphemy – n. Profane or mocking speech, writing, or action concerning God.

Latitudinarian – a. Permitting free thought, especially in religious matters.

Sapor – n. The quality in a substance which provides its taste or flavor.

Parchment – n. The skin of an animal, usually a sheep or goat, prepared as a surface for writing or painting.

Pyre – n. A heap of combustible materials arranged for the burning of a corpse.

Rousant – a. In heraldry, designating a bird rising as if preparing to fly.

Salient – a. Leaping, jumping, jetting forth.

Rend – vt. To tear, pull, rip or separate.

$\mathcal{C}$alliope Weatherstorm

"Here ye, Here ye – 'tis law day on this first day and fifth months of the 92nd year of the 16th century of our lord, Christ. Come to order and bring in the accused!"

The Gavel slams down in concord with the swinging open of backroom doors, of this four-story colonial courthouse. Out of which spews an awkward, small woman so frail and benign, it looks as if God has dressed her in a child's skin and body to enter a lifetime of innocence and adult admiration.

Her wrists are wrought with birch twine and around her head a cumbersome contortion of metal and chain with a flat iron tab inserted into the mouth to pinion the tongue from speech and curse alike.

"That's the one," whispers a busybody wife to disinterested husband. "I heard she was spawned of a salamander, and still to this day has to bathe in fire to wash her skin of filth and sin!"

"Remove the branks," orders the judge. "But be forewarned, Miss Calliope Weatherstorm, if thou utterest a sound to curse or hex, the branks shall be set in permanently!"

They were almost as frightened of her as she was of them. For all they knew she could turn them into frogs as easily as they could rend her from her sinecure post at old Miss Walabie's home. She was caretaker of geese, goat, swans, ducks and frogs; of which were plentiful on the Walabie property.

The boys had been missing for over a week when a search party followed footprints to the east end of town, where Calliope had lived as a pariah for almost twenty years now. They found nothing of the boys, save a locket on the ground one had always carried with him.

196

Hopping aimlessly about the locket was a large green toad. The toad's hopping about the locket was a definite cry for help. The mother of that boy, who knew immediately it was her son turned into a frog by that witch Calliope, kept the frog in a large jar in her pantry from then on.

Unfortunately, the search for the boys ended there, for if it had gone another couple of hundred yards, or so, they would have found an abandoned well. At the bottom of that well lie some broken rope of birch twine used for exploring and two children who had fallen over a hundred feet to their death.

"Calliope Weatherstorm, you are here by accused of being a Hussite, a doer of witchcraft and consorting with Satan. How ye plead?"

A small reed of courage raised inside Calliope as she became angered now, more than scared. She had seen proceedings like this before. She also knew that she would not win. The case was finished as soon as they found her in the basement with her many books on herbs and alchemy and such. Calliope stood, quietly trembling and staring at the tenebrous robe, sanguine face and the false whiteness of the wig of the spokesman. Then she burst out, with demons in her voice no doubt.

"You sit upon a turgid throne in your domain of fear and dare to judge others. By what right? I have done nothing. This court and the lawlessness in which it presides is a sacrilege against God, for which you shall be sentenced and placed in greater malaise than with which can be inflicted upon me here!"

The gavel burst down, exploding throughout the chamber. The judge stuttered in his anger.

"How da – da – da – dare you! You demon child! Your parlance is blasphemy. These are of the utmost latitudinarian hearings. Christ is the very sapor by which this court is sanctified. Your saying this courtroom sacrilegious is thus calling Christ sacrilegious, and thereby admitting your alliance with Satan!

"Skewer her from rectum to sternum and skin her alive for parchment, upon which shall be inscribed: *Forgivith me, Lord, thou art a witch and a sinner!* Burn the remains and hang the parchment above the pyre, a warning to other witches."

"If I am damned..." Calliope broke down in tears, "then our next rencounter shall be in Hell. And that shall be my domain. Pray I am as kind to you when that time passes. But I will not die as a sinner by your hand or anyone else's!"

Calliope made a quick burst toward the fourth-story window. She stood poised, a sculpted rousant, with tears running down her cheeks as she looked down to the pointed rocks below – the jagged edges of boulders that had broken or been torn away by nature. She thought it was good that way, it would be over quickly.

"Seize her, the demon must be burned alive, lest her soul infest others!" yelled the judge.

They made a rush toward her and with one, salient step – she flew.

A month inside a mirror; a 2-dimensional prison and K gazed out at the world like a reflection, trapped in an unknowable universe. A picture of what she was and what she thought she should be, a picture of how everyone saw her is all she was. But inside was flat, lifeless. The air had seeped out of the plastic fuck doll of her life and the shell she wore to work and to Bells' was just a thin reflection of Katherines past. Pale skin and black hair and she found that was all that was needed.

Her pale skin could still serve eggs over easy as well as it ever had. Her porcelain features could still get decent tips and attract the worst milieu of what 39th Street had to offer. And her black hair still waved in the wind like it ruled the world, like it just didn't care, flowing undaunted over trees and logs and bends and forks.

She wasn't needed, she discovered. Happy or sad, full of life or empty, whatever it was inside of her that made K, K, was apparently unnecessary, because she was nowhere to be found and her life seemed to go on just fine without her. She was a walking picture frame and life had lost all meaning. Not that it ever had any, she thought, but she simply had never realized it before – the pointlessness, the utter boredom and the complete lack of purpose.

Everyone she met and everywhere she went she saw death. It had never been like that before. K was young, healthy, beautiful. Young eyes don't see death. They see life, living, fun, accomplishment – possibility. But now she saw only death. Every plate she served up she served with a cut out smile and thought, "You're going to die."

Young or old, infants, lovers, she saw right through them, right through the life that surrounded them straight to the center and there was only death. She saw it everywhere, in the birds, in the trees, flowers, plants – death, death, death.

"You're all going to die. You're running around pretending to be alive, pretending to be doing something, going somewhere, making a difference, but you're just death postponed. Every step you're walking into death. There's nowhere else to go. There's no road that leads around it, no road that leads anywhere but there."

The nights were the worst. They were pallid and unforgiving. She'd look into the mirror at her gossamer skin trying to understand what it was.

"Just a bubble," she thought. "This body bubbled up from some murky darkness just to someday pop and disappear. And the murkiness keeps bubbling and bubbling and pop, pop, pop! It's a false thing. How can I be at all if I'm only temporary? What is the stuff I bubbled up from? Is that my home? When I pop do I dissolve back into it then bubble up again somewhere else. Some other place, some other time I'll be stumbling around in a new body and a new face wondering how and why I got there. I'll be going through it all again wondering why God sent me, created me. Working, slaving away in another life – life after life as eternities pass and I still look up at the stars and wonder *why*.

"All those lives everyone is running around trying to accomplish something, trying to help someone accomplish something else, be something else, do something else, and they'll all just pop too. Even if someone had ever made a difference in someone's life, so what? That life will soon be over.

"Then what's the purpose of spending your life in service to others when all those people will soon be dead? So they die with a little more food in their stomachs or a little less pain in their backs, so what? They'll still find some misery to wallow in till the day they die, some desire left unfulfilled, some account not closed – that much is certain.

"I guess I'd rather spend my time in search of that murky darkness because nothing else can be real. We all bubbled up from something and that something must be life, real life, because this isn't, this just sucks. Everywhere is pain, everything's a burden."

On everyone's face she saw the look of that dead cop, his eyes fixed toward the heavens, the look that had no words to it, just a hopeless searching.

In every touch she felt the clammy skin of St. Bum and how it turned from a human touch to touching a mushy lump of something – not even mud, less than mud. Even mud was alive in comparison to it. That touch had no feel, it was a clammy void.

In each child she saw Becky's eyes, those alive eyes that so few adults have. Already having walked too close to death, already having felt its footsteps coming up behind them they turned dull just so they couldn't see the reality that death was walking right along side them with each step.

But Becky had 'em, had those alive, child eyes. She was as alive as anyone could be. And then gone, just like that. No more person there, no one to pick up the phone and say, *"Man, work sucked today. Could we be any more lame?"* Or, *"Get any lately? If I don't get laid soon I'm gonna pull somebody's hair out, and it won't be mine."*

Becky was wild and young and free and out having sex and touching lives and laughing and crying and then nothing – and life went on just fine without her. Not even a speed bump in the road of life was Becky's death. The world seemed about as affected by her death as it would have been had Becky sneezed, and not died.

It was thundering out. Quite a storm was passing to the north. There was no rain on 39th Street, but one could feel the rumbles of the sky's discontent. The rumbles rolled softly over her like tiptoed memories that sometimes pass without being noticed. It was something like God, thunder was, though she didn't know why. Maybe it was the power of it, how it could surround you totally, how it could be off in the distance and still be the only thing you heard. And how it couldn't ever hurt you, no matter how frightening it seemed.

Each thunder roar reminded her of Calliope – the slamming down of the gavel and the shriek of Calliope that always followed as she crashed to the ground was hidden in the lightening that sliced through the air.

"What next? Where are you Calliope? You must be it. You must be the one. I have to find you first, I have to save you. Then you can save me, then you can tell me why, why to save you in the first place. But you're lost in the past, swallowed whole by a monster unknown, 300 years removed and I can't change that."

It had been a month searching. Answers lingered out of reach, in the newspapers, in the news reports, in the encyclopedias – in the ceiling rafts. There was nothing about Calliope. Kathy set down the pages of her latest story and looked up at the brown symmetric beams running the length of Bells' Bar.

"Dear God, what is this all supposed to mean?"

The bar seemed liquid, liquid filled. K's ears were so attentive listening to the distant thunder that everything else seemed quiet. Everything was a whisper, a silent picture. Everyone that moved, moved as if in liquid. It was an airy liquid, not as dense as water, just thick enough to slow the movements slightly. To make people look more flowing, more graceful. It was like a dance to K as she watched them out of the corner of her eye and through the smokey mirror. She hadn't remembered taking any drugs but life sure looked different today. And she'd never noticed how cloddish and awkward everyone moved until she saw them move with such grace; until she saw them in this soft, liquid dance.

It was crowded for lunch today. Bells brought in pizzas on Fridays and sold them for a buck a slice. He also brought in a few side dishes from caterers and that happened every Friday and it was a fast cheap meal you could have with a beer or a wine spritzer or whatever would tide you over until 5:00 p.m. when you could start drinking for real.

Kathy sat watching the dance and sipped a whisky sour through one of those tiny red straws trying to avoid a paper umbrella with her nose that Bells had put in as a joke. She normally didn't have Friday afternoons off but didn't argue with her boss when he didn't schedule her, even though she was broke. She'd be broke either way. A few more bucks wouldn't change much. Bells didn't even charge her for drinks anymore so that helped. She'd scrape by – she always did.

The toothpicks that stuck out the sides of the paper umbrella scratched her cheek as she took a sip and she took it out and threw it on the bar. It wasn't real funny to begin with. Paper umbrellas were for people whose favorite color was pink – which hers was not, need she remind him. And Bells knew better than that which meant he was mocking her.

"Lighten up, K, you're getting paranoid," she thought.

"Yeah, paranoid. It's just Bells, he's an idiot."

But the paranoia was incessant and had been growing day to day. God was mocking her. She'd walk down the street and pass people laughing. She'd serve coffee to two young kids making out in a booth. She'd pass a school yard where children played and chased eachother around and blew bubbles from spoons dipped in pink plastic bottles – a small girl off by herself in a yellow dress pulling the petals off a daisy.

He loves me, he loves me not, she was probably saying.

"Not," said K. "Sorry." Life was paper umbrellas and pink walls painted like they sometimes do in jails to subdue you – make you think you're in some fairytale and not in prison. Nobody can love here. People just wrap up their fears and jealousies and their desperate need not to be alone in some burrito called love, then force-feed it down your throat."

"Lighten up, K." She breathed deep, let it go.

"Yeah."

Blinded by the light played on the jukebox. It was a nice song, she thought, nice and thick like fudge – something she could sink her teeth into. Kathy had always liked it, it never seemed to get old like other songs from that decade. And she liked that too, liked it when things didn't get old. She didn't know why anything had to, she only knew that they did.

Bruce Springsteen wrote it, Manfred Mann made it famous. She'd heard a DJ say that on 101.1 The Fox. She tried to hear Springsteen's voice overlaying the voice from the jukebox. She would have liked to hear him sing it. She wondered if the world would be any different today if he had made it famous, instead of it being dropped from his debut album in '73. The ripples are invisible and many, myriads criss-crossing like spider webs, she thought.

Once, she saw in a movie that Bruce Lee was supposed to get the role in Kung Fu, then they decided he was too ethnic. It was a great show. She'd sit with her father on their gold sofa watching the gentle power of it, how he only fought when he had to. How his gentleness was his force. And K was all questions. *Why does he have to carry that heavy hot pot outside every time? How can a blind man fight so well?* Even then, as young as she was, she could see that David Caradine wasn't a very good martial artist. And what would the world be like today had Bruce Lee gotten the role? Maybe a world of better martial artists. Maybe a more graceful world. Small things. She thought about what life was, and what life could've been – and could be.

Another flash of lightening crashed a little bit closer, and Katherine jumped. Calliope's screech was all over that one. And when she refocused on the song playing on the jukebox, it had slowed. Groans came from some people in the corner that apparently liked that song or had paid money to hear it, but Kathy tuned them out and everything else that was going on as the small, downy hairs on the back of her neck stood up.

She knew a message was coming, but it still always freaked her out when it happened. And with the thunder and lightening going on to the north, it all seemed even more surreal, like she was in a play, a darkened stage – a spotlight shining through the smoky darkness lighting her and her alone.

Slowly the song played until the words were so slow it was as if some drugged-up zombie-messenger of God was speaking them to Katherine, directly.

"…*revved up like a deuce another runner in the night*…" it spoke to her.

K's heart pounded, her mouth went dry.

"…*a boulder on the shoulder, feelin' kind of older, I tripped the merry-go-round. With his stereo pleasin' and sneezin' and wheezin'*…"

She turned her head, listened close, the machine warbled and grinded out a few more words before it shut down altogether.

"…*the calliope crashed to the ground.*"

Pictures of spring aren't really like that. They try. They do what they can. It's just beyond them, that's all, beyond what a picture can be. It would like that, though, a piece of shiny paper wishing it were flowers blooming or green grass or 70 degree weather.

We aren't really like that either, just a picture to share with others. Don't forget the gloss, that's the best part. We all do what we can, some things are just beyond us. Birds make their nests, ground hogs burrow their holes and we build homes from playing cards and hope they'll keep us safe and secure forever.

How far up on the corporate ladder of existence are we? Vultures can see thermals in the air, keeping them floating for hours. Bats have sonar. Owls can see a mouse move a hundred yards away in pitch blackness. Dogs smell eachother's backsides to know which one is right for them. If the smell isn't there, they move on. If it is, they mate. We can't see that houses built from playing cards won't last forever. We stay in empty relationships for years too afraid to move on or hoping it gets better – never realizing the scent wasn't there in the first place, or had changed long ago.

We do what we can or all that we know and no more. All that was programmed into our consciousness – blue prints of some architect we hope got good grades at the local JUCO and I'd like to help, someday I think I could.

"What did that thing say?"

K sat straight up in her chair and the scene at Bells' Bar came back to life. The noises, the clanking glasses and the people moving in a rush like they always did on Fridays. A man taking a hurried bite of pepperoni pizza, sauce squirting onto his cheek. A blond haired woman turning to a co-worker, her blue blouse pulling open at the breast – him, pretending not to look. The liquid dance was gone and K stared through the mirror past them all to that jukebox, shaking her head that had gone numb and protective.

"Did that say what I think it said?"

205

She spun around to face it, as if staring would clarify things. As if staring would answer the questions. As if that long, hard stare would make her hear any better or hear something she had already missed or make the thing say it again. It didn't. The machine sat dark and quiet.

The electricity the passing storm had left behind could be felt and seen the rest of the day in a sort of restrained anticipation. The clouds disappeared and rays of sun stretched halfway into the bar casting elongated wolf shadows on the wooden floorboards. The afternoon had an air of insanity to it – that life was right on the edge, that anything could happen. And sometimes, it did.

A sandy, shorthaired girl, who was apparently a stripper and didn't get enough attention at her night job, jumped on a table and grinded to the hoots and hollers of the customers. She'd raise her shirt halfway over her breasts revealing their bare undersides up to the nipples, then lower it again. A large hole in the crotch of her jeans revealed to the crowd a pink G-string she wore as she squatted and thrust her pelvis into the air.

She couldn't hold a candle to K, but K was fully clothed and not writhing on a tabletop. The guys clamored like windowpanes on old wood rims and pounded on the tables in sporadic rhythms because the jukebox still wasn't working. It was unreal. It could have been The Madonna for all K knew, or cared.

"I know what it said," she thought over and over as lunch hour melted into early afternoon and then late afternoon and the familiar after work crowd began to stumble in.

"Do you?"

"Yeah. It said it alright, *the calliope crashed to the ground.* I knew it, I knew that was the important part. There's something about the word *calliope*. But what? Think, K, think!"

She unwrapped the plastic from a fresh cartoon of Virginia Slims and packed them against the bar top. She drew one out, lit it. "Alright, let's break this down."

"Okay. A calliope makes music, Right?" She nodded her head up and down in a slow, thoughtful way, the cigarette dangling near her face between two fingers of her right hand. The scrape of the stool to her right shivered K's spine as a man in a dark suit pulled it away from the bar and sat down. He moved his eyes over her up and down a few times like elfin thieves before turning to flag Bells over his way.

"Right. And music is art, it is poetry. And what is poetry?"

"Poetry is what it is. I'm not sure – is it innocence? A child-like openness? A way to look at things not intellectually? I don't know, K, maybe some things can only be defined in contradictions."

She put the cigarette between her lips, tapped a finger against her firm jaw line, blew out smoke from the left side of her mouth, the cigarette held firm on the right side.

"So poetry is the opposite of...what? Math? Science? Knowledge?"

"Maybe."

Bells set down a frothy mug of imported beer in front of the guy at Kathy's side.

"Ready for another?" he said, moving to K, setting his strong arms down on the bar with their thick gray hairs and the unknown tattoo sticking out from beneath the sleeve.

K gulped the syrupy sweet remains of the whiskey sour, pushed the empty glass his way.

"Make it a Bloody Mary – with V-8. I need the vitamins."

Bells filled a tall glass with V-8, vodka, salt, pepper, and a stick of celery.

"Here's your health food drink." He sat it in front of her, his rough voice full of oil and grit, the sleeve of his left arm pulled slightly up.

"What's that thing say, anyway, Bells?" She gestured with her eyes to his upper arm, taking out her cigarette, blowing smoke away to the left. Light behind the bar painted him in silhouettes, and Katherine's huge round eyes looked up to find his. A cloudy gray film glazed over his obsidian eyes like it was trying to smother them and she wondered how long it would be. When would death come to take her last remaining friend? What would happen to her when it did? Bells was strong, she was thinking. Sometimes it seemed like he could defeat anything – even death.

He grunted, kind of like a huff, kind of like a laugh, then gimped to the other end of the bar.

"Damn that Bells and his secrets," she thought, as she puckered her face in anticipation of the tomato and vodka drink, taking a sip. "Why so many secrets?"

"Who cares, K, you're getting close." She shook her head in short bursts to clear her thoughts. Rough, thick curls slapped her pale beauty as if it were a plaything, as if her face were just a toy for her hair to bat around as it pleased.

"Yeah, so let's say, for the sake of argument, that poetry and knowledge are opposites. And let's also assume that Calliope represents something beneficial, like poetry, or the innocence of poetry."

"So you're saying knowledge isn't beneficial? That doesn't make any sense."

K pushed back a bit from the bar, hiked up her dress to her thighs, and shifted her legs that had become sore sitting in the same spot for so long. The textured gold studs of the barstool spread its cold onto her bare skin that became exposed from her loose dress as she moved.

"Yeah. That doesn't really make sense," she pushed the cigarette into the air as she spoke, coloring her words. "But what about Original Sin, K? You haven't thought of that. Maybe there's something in that – the Original Fall from God. The fall of Adam and Eve happened when they ate from the tree of knowledge, causing them to be expelled from the Garden of Eden. Maybe there's an answer there we've been missing all these years." She pulled in smoke through her down-turned lips, took out the cigarette, blew smoke into the already smoky air.

"I think you're on to something, K," she nodded her head in confirmation, made a firm gesture with her mouth.

In the corner, where the television blared harsh gunshots of some old western to cover the emptiness the dead jukebox left behind, a man was sitting down – young, dark long hair. Katherine sat up quickly from her slouch looking around a line of people sitting to her right, but it wasn't him. She was hoping it was. When he brushed the hair out of his face, his features were thin and weak – it wasn't Moses, sharp and deep.

"Why the fuck do you care?" she asked.

"I don't," she said turning back, looking into the bright bloody well of her drink, the salt and pepper sprinkled the sanguine face with freckles. "Sure wish they'd turn that damn TV down, though, I can't concentrate with all this shit going on!" She pulled at the roots of her hair till her scalp felt sore. Ashes fell in the thick coracine mesh like flakes of dandruff, and she let go, took a toke. "Where were we?"

"Original sin."

"Okay. So maybe it wasn't that God didn't want Adam and Eve to become as knowledgeable as him, out of some fear, maybe it was guidance – a way to look at the world with poetry instead of knowledge. Maybe that would be helpful to us somehow."

"But how?"

"That much I don't know, maybe I won't know until I get there. But, if that's the case, then the day the courts, or knowledge, sentenced Calliope to die, it may have been the end of innocence. Knowledge became our savior, our Christ. If so, Calliope's death changed the outcome of mankind."

"Whoa!"

An angry brattle of brass instruments and timpani drums blasted from the TV as it started to sing the local news break theme song. *"We interrupt this program to bring you the following news update."*

"But what can I do about it now?" K thought. "It was 300 years ago for crying out loud!"

"We have a breaking news story at this time and are going to take you live, downtown, to our man on the scene, Phil Neese. Phil?"

"Thank you, Carol. Outside this downtown courtroom, a drama is unfolding, the unfolding drama of life and death. On the fourth floor of this twenty-story building behind me," the beat reporter said as he turned

to point, *"...a building built upon the hard concrete of truth, upon the foundation of justice, the cinder blocks of The American Way, the mortar of equality. On this building, the break down of society as we know it – anarchy is taking place. A young woman found guilty, I repeat – guilty, of the hideous crime of murdering two innocent, I repeat – innocent youths, is threatening to jump."*

The camera zoomed in on a young girl. She didn't look to be threatening the entire mortar on which this society was built. She looked like a child, frightened and alone. Nervously, she looked over her shoulder and side to side, her airy cotton dress blowing in ruffles as she tried to keep it down and keep from falling at the same time. It was probably the best piece of clothing she owned, a shabby white dress, wearing her finest for her day in court.

K pushed through a circled crowd standing at the bar till she reached an open spot in the corner.

"What has society come to when we let convicted, I repeat – convicted criminals place demands upon us and thus place demands upon our very freedom." He clutched his hand against his heart. Behind him, trash blew in the swirling winds where a crowd had gathered.

"Name, damn it. I need a name," Kathy said, standing directly under the television, her neck bent sharply. "Give me a goddamn name!"

"Name?" asked Drunk 1, turning her way. "Let's see, I read it in the paper this morning. It's a weird name, it's like – Campenilli."

"No, no – Jesus Christ, you're drunk as hell!" replied Drunk 2. "It's Cantalopee."

The door slammed repeatedly – hard, hard, then softer and softer, but faster, the dying bounce of a Ping-Pong ball, until it lay still against the wood frame.

Spring air falsified the moment in pastels and Crayola crayons – a child's drawing. Fuzzy colors painted the landscape naïve, outside the lines – more adroit fingers filled the spaces in between. It was a fake thing, created. A poorly choreographed scene of fake sunshine dancing off mirrored glass office buildings, Play-dough trees blooming green with flowery rubber tips – Kathy's blue dress open and free against her downy skin, she only wore it that day because nothing had made her eyes tingle too long now to remember. She was hoping a forgotten glimpse in the mirror would recreate the sensation. Had she known, she would have worn black, to make it all seem more real.

It was craziness downtown; cop cars, ambulances, a fire truck, hundreds of people had gathered – the swirl of cameras and people and sound and light and Katherine didn't know what to do. She brought up clawed hands to press into her tight, pounding temples the rhythm of fists beating on tabletops for a sandy haired stripper.

"What the fuck are all these people doing here?" thought K. "Do they think this is some kind of game show or carnival ride?"

The thought of Calliope's death being nothing but a show to these people sickened her. That Calliope would be gossip or something to say, *I was there, I saw it happen.* Something to talk about between cubicles the next day at work. She couldn't believe she even felt that way. Where were all these feelings coming from? She actually cared for Calliope – no, she loved her. It was as if she knew her. And, as Kathy was pushed this way and that by the shift of people, she was on the verge of tears.

The light blue dress she wore fanned open at the bottom as she turned around and around in the crowd with her hands on her face and head like that. The light cotton fabric of her dress spread over the face of a little boy that was standing there, he must have been only about three, and he laughed whenever it touched him. He looked up at K thinking they were playing a game, but Katherine didn't even notice him. And when she moved away, closer to the building, the child waved – fast, side to side, his fingers curled into his palm.

High above the extrados, the arched entrance with huge pillars on which the building sat proud and stern like on the legs of a bulldog, Calliope paced, much in the same manner K was below. Calliope continuously looked back behind her, over her shoulders and side to side, making sure no one was coming for her, sneaking up from behind.

Her face was pale, pasty, not like Katherine's, more sallow and sickly. It was like she had never been outside before – having the sun's rays shower on her to help her grow. She was small, like a child, but had a woman's eyes – full and wise. Kathy could see that even from the considerable distance. She looked like she'd spent most of her life in a dungeon, or in a basement made of rock and stone with moss growing on the sides. And she looked like she'd attained some wisdom from those years of solitude.

K wouldn't mind that happening to her someday, being wise and all. And she certainly wouldn't mind having the look of wisdom stuck all over her the way it was stuck on Calliope. She wouldn't mind having people just look at her and know she was smarter then them, know she wasn't someone they should mess with, if they knew what was good for them.

But she also figured it's what scared people about Calliope, it may have been why she was on trial in the first place. It's hard to trust someone who's smarter than you, too many ways they could hurt you. Too many ways they remind you of what you could've been, should've been. They had to be cut down, brought back to eye level. Best just to prosecute them and throw them in jail or put them to death, let God take care of any mistakes – like they did with Jesus.

K wanted to talk to her, sit down for coffee at some pretentious coffee bar where the pedantic guy behind the counter in his black shirt and pants and trimmed goatee would say things like, *Jamaican Blue Mountain is the most expensive coffee you can buy, $35.00 a pound. Or, if you want to go lighter, Guatemalan Antigua, a Valos blend, has a subtle...*"

She didn't like coffee but sometimes drank it because she liked the smell. Sitting there with Calliope, the aroma of fresh espresso in the air as they nibbled rum pastries, would be like Heaven – if the lighting were right. And Calliope would share her wisdom with K and K would spread it over her face like she wanted to do with the waters deep inside of Moses.

She would tell Katherine what the hell was going on. She looked like someone who knew, and now she was about to fall off the edge of the world and take K's hopes right over the edge with her. It was already written. It was all there in black and white on the front seat of her broken down Honda Accord.

But there was more to it than that, she'd like to get to know *her*, Calliope, as a person. She'd like to spend some time in that musty basement hearing about Calliope's life. What she was like as a child, who was the first person to break her heart and how many times had it happened since?

She'd like to know why she hid away from the sun. Why she didn't know anybody or didn't want to. Kathy thought it odd, she never much cared to hear about other people, they were usually a sounding board for her own voice, but she didn't want to say anything to Calliope.

They could've been sisters, the way her hair was long and dark, the way her face would've been beautiful had she ever been outside. They were probably separated at birth, some government plan to keep them from becoming too powerful in eachother's presence and, possibly, from over-taking the government one day.

Cops were on the window above her ready to reach down and grab her if they needed. A fire truck appeared to be preparing something for her to land on and K could see clearly that Calliope was getting anxious, jittery. She might jump just from nerves if nothing else and K pushed her way to the barricades, yelling – this story was not going to happen!

"Calliope! Stop, I know where the boys are!" But the crowd was too loud. She yelled again and again, but still could not be heard – her thin voice slipping in and out of the crowd, succumbing to the surrounding noise, smothered and suffocated. That's when a cop grabbed her, shook her hard. His big fingers wrapped completely around the biceps of K's right arm. He had a thick mustache with a few gray streaks that cut off clean at the corners of his mouth. His rounded nose flared when he breathed in.

"Listen lady, we don't need anyone down here getting her riled up!" His hands were firm, but caring – good father hands. He'd be a good father.

K was frantic, moving her hands in rigid, sharp movements that blurred in her frenzied pace.

"You don't understand," she said. "She's my...best friend. I know where the boys are." She reached up both hands to grab the officer's shoulders. "I know where the boys are! Do you hear me? I found them! She's innocent!"

The cop kept hold of her arm as he looked over one shoulder and then the other. It seemed to K that he didn't quite know what to do and Kathy tapped the heel of her foot on the ground in nervous impatient movements. The cop started talking into a microphone attached to his shoulder and the next moment Kathy was being led to a square-ish gray car with a single light on top and placed in front of a thin man in a brown suit and gold rimmed glasses. He seemed thoughtful. K pleaded and pleaded with him as he kept looking up at Calliope then back down at Kathy, moving one hand to his chin, pushing back the suit jacket with the other and letting it rest on his hip.

Soon he was explaining to her what could and could not be said on the megaphone, words to avoid.

"Tell her who you are and that you know where the boys are. That's all." He seemed wary, but he let her have it. He mumbled something to the surrounding officers. He must have been the expert, the man they call in to talk down jumpers or negotiate hostage deals. Everyone did what he said.

It was impossible, a perfect moment. A miracle is what it was – destiny. God had intervened, had swooped his big hand down and handed her the megaphone and K couldn't believe it. Before she knew what had happened or why she was speaking to Calliope, had reached into the past 300 years with a chance to set it right.

K cleared her throat, the stickiness of fear and nerves, and took several steps away from the officers toward the building. She looked up and shielded her eyes from the plain, bright sun. The megaphone felt heavy, like a stone, and it shook when she brought it to her lips. She didn't realize how scared she was. She didn't realize the weight of it all. Could it actually mean changing the destiny of the world? This one life?

K rubbed the length of her throat with her left hand. It felt thin and weak. Inside was dry.

"Calliope! Wait, I know where the boys are!" Her voice was hollow and metallic through the amplified cone as she tried to shout. "Calliope it's me, Katherine! I know where the boys are! Stop!" She let her arm fall, the megaphone hitting hard on her leg. Kathy gulped the dry spit from her mouth, felt it struggle to get past her throat as she strained to look up at Calliope.

She repeated it again, then again. But Calliope wouldn't listen. She paced, looked back to the cops on the ledge above her to make sure they couldn't grab hold of her, then looked again to the ground.

"Who are you?" she kept yelling as she leaned slightly over the edge, holding onto the trim of some bricks for balance. It wasn't working, she thought it was a trick. Soon the police had taken away the megaphone, holding onto K by one arm, tight. She sunk her head, thought about giving up all together and heading home. It all seemed so hopeless.

"Think, K, think! There must be something you can do."

Kathy looked to the sky, in case God had suspended the answer in mid-air or was having it flown by on a banner on the back of a small plane.

High above it all, the 39th Street Bird circled in long eloquent swoops, carving donuts in the air with its fluttered movements and slate colors. It was there to help, her prayers had been answered. It was a gift from God.

"Remember that time you sent him down to sit with the 39th Street Bum?"

"Of course I do, K. It may have been the best thing that ever happened to that bum. It was like God had reclaimed him, showed him some beauty that made life worth living!"

"If that bird can do the same for Calliope, calm her down, show her there is some beauty in this world, maybe the cops could get to her first, or set up that air pad. Maybe we're at another crossroads right now, K! Maybe if I can save Calliope – somehow, someway – maybe things in this world will change back to what could have been – a Garden of Eden."

The bird sat a few stories above Calliope, peeking over the ledge, and K began to pray. She hadn't prayed since she was a child and she wasn't sure how to begin or what to say. But she was sincere. All she wanted was for the bird to come sit by Calliope, make her smile, make her see some beauty in this world.

Kathy brought her hands up in front of her, palms touching. She bowed her head and the cop released her arm. Her mind was soft – the feel of new clouds as the wind scoots them across the plains. *Please*, she thought. She could feel the small word growing inside her – spreading out in all directions. *Please, God, please – save Calliope.*

When she finally looked up, pulled back the sore lids from her pressed eyes, the bird was moving. It made several big circles in the air and each time it got lower and lower.

K watched the graceful flight of the 39th Street Bird, and many of the people down below pointed and watched also. The beautiful sing-song way it lowered toward Calliope hushed the crowd. It was a sign from God, everybody sensed it, something magical was about to happen.

Flapping its wings in a deliberate way, it slowed and approached the ledge. Calliope caught its shadow in the corner of her eye. She turned to look. The 39th Street Bird was right near her and Calliope reached up with a quick jerk to shield her face flustering the turtledove and it began fluttering wildly looking for a place to perch. Calliope covered her head and eyes, startled and confused, batting at the bird with outstretched arms, her head turning away from the sudden chaos.

She lost her balance. Then fell to the ground.

Katherine stared up at the ledge in utter disbelief as the crowd gasped in horror. She didn't know why, it was what they were there for, anyway. The dove sat quietly a moment where Calliope had stood, then blinked and flew away.

K's mind went numb. Sound disappeared, then color. The body looked so peaceful sprawled out on the concrete, K wished everyone would leave soon as not to disturb it. She moved toward Calliope as the people shuffled around and dispersed, a few with tears running down their faces. K wanted to touch it, the body, wanted to see where the life had gone.

A disciple once asked Buddha, "What happens when a person dies?" Buddha held up a small flame, then pinched it out between thumb and forefinger.

"What has happened to the flame, now that it is no more?" Buddha had said. That was his answer. The disciple must have left dissatisfied.

Kathy wanted to find out, her mindless body moving in a smooth flow toward Calliope. Then she felt the tight grip of a large hand around her arm.

"Miss, come with us. We're gonna have to ask you some questions."

She turned back to look at Calliope one more time as she was being led away. Calliope had fallen into the river Acheron, and was quickly swept away by its fiery waters.

Kathy had never been arrested before. Even though they didn't say, *We gotta take you downtown and ask you some questions*, it was still pretty cool. "I guess it's because we were already downtown," she was thinking in her anesthetic state. The squad car pulled away with her in the back numbly waving to the people as she left.

"Gonna have to," Kathy thought dreamily. She was so all fired important they had to ask her – had to. They saw it in her eyes, she was the one that would save them. They had no other choice. *"We don't know what we're doing,"* she thought. *"Runnin' around like headless chickens is what we are, and we're gonna have to ask you, Katherine of the St. Catherine Catherines, some questions. Please Katherine, you're our only hope."*

Even as the people blankly watched her as they drove away, K in the back behind the protective mesh, waving, she was unashamed. She waved as if she were in a parade. *Home Coming Queen*, in some small town or *Lesbian of the year*, in a gay pride parade. Or, just no one at all but she knew someone who was entering a float so she got to jump on and everybody thought she was somebody, somebody special.

The people looked and she waved thinking all along they understood that she was helping the police unravel a deadly mystery that may some day change the destiny of this world. Not at all thinking they were looking at her like a downtown whore being hauled away, or a drug addict who'd just lifted some prescriptive meds at the corner Rx and was mindlessly waving at them in her whacked-out state. Only a few children waved back, but their parents quickly grabbed their arms, made them stop.

As one of the children stopped his wave, slowly let his arm float to his side, drifting in silence, she could see nothing more. Staring through the crowd, through the streets, she saw only fuzzy images through blurry eyes that were filling with tears as the realization came upon her hard, like angels with plucked wings falling from the sky on top of her. K buried her head in her hands.

"Oh Jesus. God help me, what have I done?" Katherine shook like currents were passing through her from an electric chair.

"It wasn't your fault, K. Do you think you can actually control what that bird does? Are you that egotistical and psychotic? It's a fucking bird! It tried to land next to her and she got scared. I'm sorry you couldn't save her, but it wasn't your fault."

She sniffled, raised her head to look at the world through warbled tears, wiped some away.

"Yeah, not my fault. Got it."

She had sat in the white room for over an hour. The lighting was overly harsh. She trailed her fingers on the table to check the smoothness. But it wasn't completely smooth, being vinyl and all. It had tiny pockets most people wouldn't even notice. But K new real smooth from fake smooth. She drew invisible pictures into the fake-smooth vinyl with her finger – a ghost face, a star, a horse with a white mane and flared tail.

K pushed her chair away from the table and placed her head between her legs, like you're supposed to do to survive a plane crash. It was a pretty stupid plan, she thought. It seemed that your head would pop off from the slightest impact in that position. But everybody would follow it like cattle if that's what they were told.

Once, in her late teens, back when Kathy had a group of friends she was hanging out with – high school cross-country buddies. She used to run, it was something like freedom, when it didn't hurt too badly. Two of the guys were horsing around when one fell and racked himself real hard on a bedpost. He was rolling on the ground in so much pain a tear ran down his cheek. One of the guys said, "Go like this! Go like this – it helps!" And he stuck his thumb in his mouth, to show him, and puffed out his cheeks as far as they would go.

So the guy on the floor did it. He was rolling around in pain with one hand covering his nuts and the thumb of the other hand in his mouth with his cheeks puffed out like a chipmunk. Needless to say, it didn't help the pain – but everybody got a good laugh out of it. People will do anything they're told.

K would rather find her own safe spot on a plunging plane, it probably varied from crash to crash, what part was hitting where changed which part was safe. Or maybe she'd take her chances jumping out of an emergency exit, if they were over the ocean or a large body of water. You had to be intuitive, not just smart, to survive.

When she was a child she used to think she could just jump. If a plane were crashing or an elevator broke loose from its cables and was hurling toward the ground – she used to think she could jump right before it hit and she'd be okay. She could never understand why no one ever thought of that before. Life was much easier when you didn't know the laws of physics.

Two officers finally entered the room. It was about time. If they wanted her help they needed to start treating her a little better. They placed her in there for over an hour like they probably did criminals they were trying to break, softening people up with boredom hoping the truth would slide out easier as they grew tired and were ready to go home.

One of the cops was taller and thicker than the other. One was just a kid, he looked younger than K. His face was so smooth and soft he probably had to grow out his beard for a week and tell people it was a five o'clock shadow, just to seem older.

The taller one spoke first, reading from a piece of paper he held in one hand, resting his foot on one of the green and chrome chairs.

"Everything lost will be found again.

Eternity's emptiness embodied in this world, in these people, in this time.

Forever blessed are the children who don't follow, who go astray.

Yesterday's inequities can no longer touch the one who touches the One."

He was the one that grabbed K in the crowd. K recognized his thick mustache and graying sideburns. He seemed like a good cop, strong and fatherly. The younger one was so small K figured *she* could kick his ass – if she got the first punch in.

"Does any of this stuff make sense to you?"

Kathy looked up, their white faces blending with the walls behind them and partially hidden in the sharp light above.

"Are you talking to me?" she asked, trying to define their features from the severe lighting.

"Yeah."

"No, it doesn't make any sense. Should it?"

"Okay," he said, putting down the paper. "Anyway, we ran your name and prints. Your prints match those found in the apartment of a recent suicide victim, Officer Ellsworth. Did you know him?"

Shit, she hadn't thought of that. They had her prints on file? *Shit!*

"Uhmm...Yeah. We uhmm...went out a few times. He'd had me over for dinner once or twice." They didn't say anything and K stumbled around for something else to say. "But...there was no chemistry or anything, so it just never went anywhere."

"Did he ever talk about you to his friends, or family?"

"How would I know?"

"Hmmm," one of the officers said and they both looked at eachother. "So I guess you were pretty shaken up when you heard he was dead?"

"Not really, is there anything else?"

"Oh yeah, there's much more. What about this Calliope girl, what's your relationship..."

"What's with the little poetry thing?" Kathy asked, interrupting him. "Why did you think it would mean anything to me?"

221

And they both looked at eachother again. The taller one removed his foot from the green chair and pushed it back under the square table. Put his hands on its vinyl surface, supporting his weight. "It was signed by you."

"What?"

"Isn't this your signature," he said, pushing the paper to her side of the table. K looked at it in disbelief, it was her handwriting. "We matched it to the signature on the sign-in sheet. It was part of the evidence recovered from Calliope's house. There were hundreds of them – all different, all just as weird, and all signed by *St. Catherine*. Different spelling, but same handwriting. Don't you think it's a little odd – your fingerprints at Officer Ellsworth's and your poetry at Calliope's where she was convicted of kidnapping two children?"

"Were my fingerprints there?"

"No, but according to our database they were found on a transient that died several months ago who had traces of arsenic in his blood, he died on the very street you live on. And your car matches the description of one leaving the scene of a crash where three people recently died. Now, do you want to start talking? There are too many coincidences here. We've already built quite a strong case against you in just the last hour for a number of felonies. It won't be long before we connect all the dots. I have a feeling it will be your face in the finished picture."

Kathy looked onto the bare table top with an empty expression, not making any sudden moves, like you're not supposed to do around snakes or, really, any animal that's right on the edge and wanting to take a bite out of you. She didn't want them to realize how panicked she was. How, even though she was innocent, didn't feel innocent. She didn't want them to see she was trying to stop her face from matching the feeling in her gut. Somewhere, deep down, there was guilt, as if she didn't even deserve to be alive sometimes. And now the guilt was creeping across her features in a slow, but obvious, confession.

"Well, I was friends with that bum and I may have touched him once or twice, so what? And if you can find three people in a row that don't own a small white import I'd like to meet them. And as far as the rest…well, there's really nothing to hold me with and I'd like to go."

She nodded her head in terse confirmation. A bosky curl landed on her face, she blew at the hairs, then brushed them aside.

"When you were calling up to Calliope, you said you knew where the boys were." The tall one pulled out the chair, spun it around adroitly. K figured he had practiced that move, to show how smooth he was and how in control. Then he sat down. "If you do know anything about the missing boys, it would go a long way in helping you, if and when this goes to court."

Kathy tugged at her lip, looked up at the younger one then back at the cop sitting next to her. His fatherly eyes, his fatherly voice. He was practically patting her hand, stroking her hair. He could get a confession out of a turnip.

"They're in a well. They were exploring with some rope and it broke and…they're at the bottom of a well."

"Why do you feel you know their whereabouts, Katherine?"

Nice touch, add my name. We're just old pals talking, she was thinking. "I uhmm…I had a dream." And Kathy paused to test out the waters before proceeding. "Kinda," she added.

"A dream?" he repeated. "Kinda?"

"Yeah, I saw it, I'm premoniscient."

They looked at eachother. "Premoniscient?" asked the smaller one. "And what else, exactly, have you been *premoniscient* about?" It was funny when the little one spoke, sounding grown up and all.

"Oh, nothing – this is the first."

Then the other made his upper lip puff out like a blowfish, and began swishing the puffed air in his mouth as if it were Listerine. "You certainly seemed very confident when you called up to her, pretty confidant for a first time psychic, anyway."

"Look, that's all I know, I think you should check out what I told you, about the boys I mean, besides that I can't help you – and unless you're going to charge me with something, I'd like to go home."

She was surprised by those simple words. How nice it is sometimes, just to go home – something like Dorothy. *I want to go Home*, the words were stick figures, a child's painting on a grainy potato sack in K's mind.

"Okay, Mrs. Kristensen, but one thing before you go." He gestured to his partner. "Fred, get the map," and the smaller one left the room. "I was wondering if you might help us pin-point exactly where you saw the boys – in your dream, that is." Then Fred returned with a large, roll-out map and carefully spread it on the desk like cream cheese on a bagel.

"I said the well, look in the goddamn well!"

"We'd like to look in the goddamn well," said the older one, running his hands along the map, pretending to look it over. "But you see, there is no goddamn well on this property."

K leaned forward, the map covered the entire table hanging over two opposing edges, it was difficult to understand all the symbols. She couldn't believe there was no well. The story explicitly said *well.*

"What's this area over here?" K asked, pointing to a roughened spot just east of Calliope's house.

"It appears to be some caves."

"...A birch twine rope used for exploring," she thought.

"The cave," Kathy said, she put her peaked, bony finger on the map, then sat back, crossed her legs spreading the blue cotton dress over her thighs. "They're in the cave."

K impatiently watched as the two men breathed rough breaths of deadly, unseen smoke – not saying a word and staring hard like their stupid glances had the power to squeeze truth out of people. Like their stupid glances had the power to decipher real from unreal. Like their stupid glances could do anything other than piss people off and make them look stupid.

The smoke of their invisible heavy breath surrounded her, closed in on K like walls.

"Jesus Fuck! They're in the cave! Go, they're dying!"

At the entrance, where K picked up her keys from under the bullet-proof glass slid into a metal bin, she heard the low, full voice of Simone coming down the hall, argumentative.

"Simone?" K asked. "What are you doing here?"

"Katherine!" Simone came closer and put her large hand on K's shoulder, brushed it down to her elbow then let go. "Just paying a small – uh, parking fine," she said, her low voice raised at first, then lowered again. "And what about you, child?"

K stammered and rubbed the right side of her jaw with the tops of her fingernails. "I just was...kind of...arrested."

"Arrested!? For what?"

"Oh nothing," K rolled her eyes to lessen what was about to follow, unsure how it was all going to sound out loud. "Just suspicion of murder. Then there were the two kidnappings, fleeing from the scene of an accident – and one small hate crime, poisoning a street person, which is apparently a federal offense – had I known," she chuckled. "It's silly, really." She brushed it all aside with a wave of her bony fingers.

The thin eyebrow over Simone's left eye, that seemed more drawn on with eyeliner than actually there, raised high.

"We'll give you a lift back to your car," said one officer.

"No, I'll take her," Simone said defiantly, taking K in her arm.

"One more thing, Mrs. Kristensen," the tall cop said. "Don't leave town."

Night had befallen Kansas City. Its nervous whispers of trash skirting across the city streets, its hollows of building gaps where shadows hid and predators of downtown lie in wait, and Katherine was thankful she wasn't walking back to her car.

"My car's over by the courthouse," K said, as they drove past Bartle Hall under the part of the building that sat above the street on mammoth cement pillars. It was mostly smooth inside the darkened womb of the structure, glass revolving doors and glass walls that bubble with excitement and anticipation whenever a show or event came to town. A sign read, "Kansas City Philharmonic Performs Tonight – Tribute to The Baroque."

People were already milling about, trickling down from the seven-dollar parking flats scattered throughout downtown.

Bells loves The Baroque, K was thinking. *He should give himself the night off work and go. But he won't, not in a hundred years. He'll die behind that bar growing roots into the floorboards.*

"During the Baroque era, things must've been simpler," Katherine mumbled, almost talking to herself.

"Oh yeah?" said Simone, turning her '64 Studebaker onto the one-way street of the courthouse.

"Yeah, a cleaner line between good and bad, or good and evil. Nowadays there are so many gray areas. The way the laws are, the court system, it's just not as easily definable."

"The line between good and evil has always been easily definable," Simone said. "That line is constant, it does not change. Laws and courts have no affect on the character of a person. Laws don't affect the nature, do not affect the thoughts, feelings, urges and desires. You can't govern morality. The line was drawn long ago. On one side lies love – on the other side, hate!"

When the car slowed, K stepped out, smiled. She shut the door without out another word.

VI

"*I*'M A PAWN."

Kathy lay naked on the bed staring herself into blankness. Thoughts fled to her as if she were the Promised Land for some lost and desperate refugees, or maybe they simply had nowhere else to go.

Spring air, dangling on the cusp of summer, seeped in through the open window held up by her wooden Buddha. It was twilight and the mood on 39th Street was settling, calming, in preparation for the night.

It had been a dry spring, but finally clouds were in the air that were gray and full – rain would be here soon, and the drying pastures and farmlands would celebrate the moisture. The last rain had been the night of the terrible car crash, she'd refer to it as an *accident*, only it wasn't – before that the rains fell when the gun exploded in apartment 808. What would the rain bring this time? What did it matter? Rain brought good things or bad then washed them all away leaving Katherine there alone, wondering if anything had really happened in the first place.

The sounds of a few, slow moving cars entered K's apartment through that open space held up by the Buddha, but the sounds didn't enter her.

"A goddamn pawn," the thought swirled and swirled, round and round it went in her head like the way they make cotton candy. It lined the walls of her mind waiting for the white, cone-shaped paperboard to dip in and swirl it all up. Kathy figured she could sell that candy for a buck fifty, or so, to some guy with a screaming kid who didn't care what his kids ate. And she would watch his kids eat those thoughts right out of her existence, hoping they wouldn't cause too many cavities, though she knew that they would.

K let out a breath that accented her exasperation and when all the air was gone she waded in that lifeless moment, the moment between two breaths, and it was peaceful. It was as peaceful as a distant memory of time spent alone on a mountaintop or near a brook or running free in an open pasture. Then she inhaled and more thoughts came swirling in. "Why is this happening? I'm playing out my part, then it all turns to shit."

"Satan," whispered her inner voice, she smirked at the comment, looked around the room. It was as empty and still as the calm and lazy spring air that seeped in through the half-open window. She then landed her focus on the picture of Marilyn Monroe. Her look, that same damn smug look, that goddamn pouting look she always had was now saying, "Ah come on, kid, you knew it all along. You can't fool me, I know you knew."

"Knew what? That it's Satan? Don't be ridiculous. Satan…" she laughed to herself, "of all the cockamamie things!" She glanced from photograph to photograph looking for confirmation of the silliness of that thought, but found none. The photos simply gazed at her like they always had, empty and lifeless. "Come on girls, Satan!?" She laughed again but the pictures did not, they didn't even smile, some looked downright mean. And the eyes, what in the world had happened to the eyes? The eyes had gotten darker, or had she simply never noticed them before? "My eyes aren't that dark," she thought.

"Must just be fading, K, don't worry about it, faded colors from years of being there." And the explanation seemed reasonable so she lay her head back down and again drifted into the pale off-white of the ceiling above.

It was bumpy, stained and discolored in spots from where water had leaked through, but it seemed peaceful and at rest and she liked that about her mid-town, studio apartment ceiling. One last thought materialized briefly in Kathy's awareness before it sank deep within the thickness of everything that was happening in her life at that time. "Can't be Satan," she thought. "I don't really believe in that crap."

The last slurping noises of a draining bathtub pervaded the room. Her clothes lay in a trail from front door to bath. Her thoughts lay in her mind like the evils in Pandora's box, waiting for some dumb shmuck to come along and release them, let them fall all over the world. Somewhere inside her lay the truth, but that truth was covered up by something thick, sticky and altogether unholy – and not, in any way, pink, like the cotton candy thoughts that had just swirled around her tired, aching head. The truth was there, had to be, but it was buried beneath things better left unknown and she lay on her bed as if one in a long line of coffins, waiting to be buried.

Her left hand lay over her bare left breast and with each new breath she could feel the pressure of it against her palm. It wobbled slightly in her cupped hand with each exhalation. She began massaging the muscles there that tensed to serve as a shield, a shield used to defend her from the world, a shield used to close off from that world completely. Her body was closed, her mind was closed and her heart was closed, or perhaps it was simply numb.

K's right hand lay peacefully between her legs, covering a mound of coarse but soft black hair as she massaged the stiffness in her chest like it would release the continuing stress and pains that had been growing there. The only sign of life in the barren wasteland in which she lived – pain growing. Pain growing like ivy along the chutes of a fallen tree.

On the breath of scents from 39th Street, the middle finger of her right hand worked its way between the lips of her labia and began to softly press the now exposed skin. The scent was Cuban tobacco from a pipe, probably a gray bearded man in a brown tweed jacket with a matching cap. His wife in a soft bouquet of emerald soap, baby powder, sprig of *Jovan*, would be next to him – they still held hands. The smell of new mother and child came next, its cheek needing to be kissed just then – the immediacy of it.

When the wind was right you could smell what was happening on 39th Street. Perfume, *Teen Spirit* from teenage girls, *Eternity* from suburban wives and *Chanel Number 5* from well-dressed ladies wearing navy business suits with big gold buttons and suit skirts that had folds in them like paper fans, dark panty hose underneath. Cigars and pipes from the men that smoked them, different colognes from the guys that wore them. You could smell what kind of a car was passing, bus exhaust was the most obvious. The newer the car the less the smell, usually.

Teenagers were passing now, girls bubbling with the electricity of late spring on 39th Street – lights and jazz and whiskey sours if they were 21 or had fake ID's. She could smell the innocence, walking into a restaurant with Art Deco neon slats, buying thirty-dollar dinners with babysitting money, feeling free and feeling grown-up. The smells excited her, opened and tingled the base of her nose.

Before Kathy knew what was happening her hand had begun moving on its own, as if it knew better than she, as if it knew exactly what K needed at this tiny intersection of time and space.

Slowly it pressed upward and then, with the sudden burst of moisture that showered from within, gently it slid back down. Firmly now, it moved from side to side and began circling. Her finger was a white hawk circling its prey. Her finger – an albino water moccasin coiling around its victim. Her finger – a pale root, alone and estranged, attempting to replant itself in the soft, wet soil it had found between her thighs.

Something yellow jumped into her mind, wallpaper. Yellow flowers, stems intertwined like lovers outlining a wall in a four-inch border. Pointed leaves on the stems digging into the other, their pistols open, waiting. Her apartment would look nice in flowered borders and secret lovers.

Thoughts of work and stories and death tried to bubble up from time to time. They tried desperately to unfold from the crumpled sheets of reality they'd become. Her thoughts wanted to unleash and scream out, scream out nothing at all to no one at all, and just scream and scream and scream.

Her finger suppressed them, pushed them ever deeper down. It pushed them down, down, to some distant swampy marsh deep inside of her where they could be lost forever or maybe even drowned.

She breathed in deeply like she was perfumed in rose milk and lilac powder, even though it was only sweat and body odor from not bathing for a day and a half. But that was good, too. She turned her head to the side to take in more of the scent from under her arms as she moved her finger inside her as far as it would go, and it was frustrating that that was all she could do. That it was as far as she could go.

The smell of fresh pastries and breads filled the room, wafting over from Da' Bronx Deli next to The Veco across the street. The smell was moist and warm, a large puffy muffin fresh-baked in a small town bakery from the kind of guy you'd call *Pops* or *Joe* – with many nut breads and bagels with poppy seeds on top or flakes of oatmeal, in glass showcases. Outside the bakery the sky was blue and oceanic, blue and eternal with just a few small waves of clouds leading the way to a path that would take K out of that small town.

A growth of weeds and bushes pushed onto the path. Dense trees, like gargoyles, guarded the entrance that opened to a glistening pond where K found herself lying naked on a flat slab of rock. She was no longer staring at an off-white bumpy ceiling in a mid-town Kansas City apartment, but at a blue, oceanic, just-outside-of-a-small-town sky. The sun bounced and twinkled in thick streaks across the waters of the pond. In a near stillness it glistened, riding the waters like a sleigh.

She was bare to the world on the rough, powdery rock, the fingers of her left hand moving with poetry over her tingling body in search of a new place to touch, a more tender place, one more aching and more in need.

The fingers of her right hand moved up, around and inside her much in the same way her left hand was caressing the length of her lean pale torso. From the tender hollow of her neck to her full breasts with their firm pointed nipples, to her slick hips and back again and again. She rubbed them all until her body glistened like the sunshine on that just-outside-of-a-small-town pond. But wait – someone was watching her, "Oh, my!"

Someone else had slipped into that perfect, out-of-the-way pond, sneaked past the gargoyle sentries into her private palace. She did not know who, but could see the shuffle of shiny green leaves, like young palm trees sprouting, in a bush about ten feet away. She stopped, startled, her breathing heavy and un-patterned. She was frightened. The muffled panting of a man spilled over the greenery.

Shit! She should stop. She should get up and leave this place, this beautiful, perfect, made up place that filled her with such warmth and excitement, with such hunger and peace, with such poetry and solitude. But she could not. She was frozen, paralyzed on that flat slab of rock as if gravity momentarily intensified its rules, just on a whim, and she lay helpless to whatever perversion the man in the bushes might have planned for her.

She'd best not fight it, she thought, struggle was the worst part – the worm on the hook writhing for freedom. *Lie still, little worm, it will all be over soon enough*, she whispered.

K opened her legs slightly, giving him an unobstructed view of the dark wet hairs and bare excited skin between her thighs – beckoning him to come take her, get it over with, use her body to masturbate his perverted self with. But he did not, he stayed hidden, watching.

Sound was frosted with honey – the soft, trying-to-be-silent unzip-ping of his blue jean shorts as they dropped to the ground. The scrape of her feet on the layered rock as she bent her legs and planted her heels only inches from each buttock, exposing an even clearer view. The building pressure of her breath as she was getting...oh, so close.

The branches of the bush moved in a steady rhythmic pulse. The sun streamed down its painfully beautiful shine – and closer still. There was heavy panting from the bush, she let out a sinful moan and birds scattered overhead.

"Oh, yes. Yes," K said aloud, as her finger picked up its pace and began rubbing so harshly it was as if she were trying to rub off some filthy stain.

There was the sound of several voices now. Oh God, had a group of people stumbled upon her forbidden pond, some sightseers – tourists? Was there a handful of people now watching her naked on that flat slab of rock, watching her in her wickedness and her sin?

It did not matter for she couldn't stop, she was almost there. A bird cawed overhead sending a streak of vibration through the air. *A crow? A dove?* And closer yet. There was a splash in the water spreading ripples into the pond like a fan. *A swan? A snake?* And closer yet. There was a loud moan from the bush and K saw the faceless man hiding there with his cut off jeans and black bikini underwear wrapped around his ankles, his legs tense and sweaty as he was about to release all over the shiny green leaves – and closer yet.

There was glistening in the trees, in the air and in the birds, and they were all ready to explode in the ecstasy that imbibed that place – and almost there.

The words, "Oh, yes, oh, yes!" oozed from her mouth and several drops of saliva oozed out also. She couldn't swallow, couldn't breathe!

There was a knock on the door.

"No."

"I do not fucking believe this." She brought up her hands to cover her face, the smell of her core lingered on her fingers like musk, she drew in the scent like a flower. A groan came out as she deflated back to her bed where she was staring at an off-white, bumpy, mid-town apartment ceiling and not a blue, oceanic just-outside-of-a-small-town sky. "I don't fucking believe it!"

Marilyn's picture was sharp and pointed as K wriggled on a loose-fitting T-shirt that barely covered her pale bottom and went to the door.

"You're a real freak show, aren't you?" she whispered in her simmering, breathy way.

K did not respond, just yanked on the door that stuck from the swelled wet wood, then opened, squeaking on its hinges – the rue of her desires settling over her in heat and flush. It was Moses.

Moses stood at her doorstep dripping from head to toe with the rain that had finally started to pour on 39th Street. His face was perfect. It was a single piece of lemon meringue pie left sitting alone on a tabletop after a birthday, holiday or some other family event. Extra whipped topping rolled across the top of it like ocean waves.

Hungry and lustful, soon she pictured him standing there completely naked, the rain trickled off his fingertips onto the floor, puddled around his feet. His naked chest glistened and heaved as a few raindrops ran down his cheeks like tears, adding sorrow and helplessness to the look of his already-pained face.

He looked so vulnerable and alone standing naked in the rain, K wanted to put him in a large ceramic bowl and baste him in country gravy, then nail him to the wall of her mid-town, studio apartment.

There he would hang like some gravy-covered Jesus, filling the room with the wholesome smell of fresh country cooking. And when Kathy got home from a long hard day's work, she would have to reprimand him for dripping gravy all over her already-stained wood floors. Even though she would have to pretend to be upset with her gravy-covered Jesus, she also knew she would revel in the feeling of that slick lumpy gravy under her bare feet and in between her toes from time to time.

Cleaning up after a gravy-covered Jesus would be a daily chore, but worth it. And, of course, he would need frequent bastings as well. The work would never end.

In the mornings she would lick him on the foot before going to work, just for luck. But she would never, ever, put his gravy-covered penis inside of her mouth – that would be wrong. And she knew that, as tempting as it would sometimes be, her gravy-covered Jesus would lose respect for her if she ever did.

His long hair matted against his sullen face and he brushed it back about to speak, but K spoke first.

"What are you doing here? Get the hell out of here, I swear to God I'll call the cops!" There was a pause, then, and it was like the moment before the dawn. Kathy breathed heavily in her fury and Moses watched silently as her fury filled that space like the light from the sun about to erupt all over the horizon.

Then he grabbed her, and they kissed.

The hand around her cupped firmly the small of her back as if it had found a home there, as if that spot on her back had been created just for his hand. Her legs softened, her knees bent slightly and the muscles in her back relaxed. And it was good that his arm held her so firmly or she might have fallen down as if she were a pretend thing, not real in any way whatsoever – as if she were just stuffed with cotton or down or something soft and benign like that.

And it was good, too, when the other hand came up behind her head to hold her even more firmly against him or she might have pried her lips away from his and walked away, leaving him standing there alone, and she didn't want to do that. She wanted to stay, she wanted that kiss to last a lifetime, but if there were anyway to escape she certainly would have.

She would have pried herself off those lips of his and turned away, never to look at him again. Never to see his sad features that drooped from his eyes like an old mutt, never to see his sharp jaw and pursed lips that jumped from his face like a pouncing kitten – and that would've broken her heart. You might as well have taken out her heart and stomped it into the mud with hard soled shoes or army boots.

She draped her arms around him and they were also just pretend. Her rubbery arms flopped over his rounded shoulders trying somehow to help out, to move him closer to her, but they could not. Her arms were not needed, they were in the way, really, and the entire scene could have taken place just as easily if she had no arms of her own.

She was quite a sight; an armless rag doll, raven-haired and stuffed with cotton – a hole in her chest where you could take out her heart and stomp it into the mud, if you so desired.

It was maybe the single greatest moment of Katherine's life. The way they kissed that night stopped everything. It created a void in space and time where nothing was left. No K, no Moses, no two people there kissing eachother, no one – only the kissing remained. The kissing was the sole survivor and Katherine and Moses were lost somewhere inside of it, slipping effortlessly into a place most lovers never find – a place of total abandon, and let go, and trust. It was like sliding into the crevasse on a rock face, or fitting into the groove on a wood-beamed floor.

When it stopped, Kathy and Moses stood dazed and confused, staring into the soft white glow in the other's eyes. Now both were wet from head to toe and both chests heaved.

Not quite knowing what had just happened, they mistook this perfect moment as great chemistry and soon had eachother's clothes off. K braced herself against the open wall she had picked out for her gravy-covered Jesus and they never even realized, in that single timeless moment, that they had just entered the house of God.

He came up behind her, sliding the head of his firmness down from her clitoris and along her lips, finding its way inside of her. The deliberate push of his entrance was hard and full against K's opening.

"I wish you'd let me go down on you," he whispered into K's neck, wet and biting. "My mouth yearns to be beneath you."

"Shhh," she said, reaching back her hand, letting the fingers be drawn into his mouth, curbing the hunger at the base of his throat.

This is nice, thought K, *even better than that little exhibitionist bit in the woods.*

She closed her eyes as he entered completely, feeling tingly pricks on top of her head, like pine needles. As the gentle rocking motion from behind almost lulled her to sleep in her nearly exhausted state, she felt suddenly separated, detached, as if she weren't even there. The tingling above her intensified and she thought for a moment that she might slip inside of it and shimmer away like music.

Moses picked up his pace, his thrusts slowly became hard and thick, more penetrating, more searching – hungry.

K let out a soft whine. "Oh," left her lips like melted butter and ran down her chin and onto her breasts. It left her lips crying softly in a dream-like pain. But there was no suffering in the cry, just a confused sweetness, a pain never before experienced. It was the bittersweet pain of separation, and the blissful pain of coming together again. It was the unbearable pain of being apart and the unbearable pleasure of being whole.

Above her the tingle was expanding, spreading out like fog, pulling at her like a hand reaching to a drowning girl in a pool. A loud rush and then a rumbling quickly passed her ears in a roar, as if a storm or a gust of wind was moving through her head. Suddenly she could no more feel the wall on her fingers and hands or the man behind her. There was no more detached feeling and no more feeling whole. There was no more tingling, and no more of that beautiful excitement happening beneath her. K was gone, floating – and all was dark.

Severed – blackness – fringe – helpless – death – calm.

Swirled memories of something that lay before. There was a single begotten flower planted on the moon. It wasn't a rose, but it could've been, as pretty as it was – and it was black. There was no wind but it swayed like in a breeze, and it didn't seem lonely – and it never would be. K knew, then and there, that she had been the only living creature to ever witness it.

Pictures of the moon came and went. She moved without breath – breathless – red world, then rings – beautiful – silent. She was moving quickly now. There was wind, but there was no chill to it and no warmth.

Specks of light, stars maybe, moved past her or she moved past them. Then, without warning or seeing it ahead of her, she was in a stream with trees and sunlight, warmth and beauty all around.

It was surreal, but real. In the middle of a shallow stream on smooth, cool stones, she waded. The alive and crisp sound of the water babbled playfully over the smooth rocks as the flow and the purity of the stream made that space behind her eyes come to life, effervesce with excitement – more than graffiti on bathroom walls, more than blue dresses and halogen headlights.

She dipped her hand into the clear waters, the subtle textures were defined and smooth. It wasn't even her body, she was sure of that, not the physical body she'd always known. But she was housed in something, it was like a thought-body, a body created by her thinking about having one. It was airy and light and free, but still her. She turned her head to look out across the sunny leaves and then it was gone and she was back in her room.

The room was silent and still, like a dream. She floated near the ceiling in one corner, her bed was there, a trail of clothes strewn about her wooden floor and, propped against the wall where the trail of clothes ended, the fuzzy shape of some kind of beastly creature.

She moved toward it and there were two of them, one on top of the other. It was an animal of some kind, the top one at least. It had a face almost like a boar, but it had legs, human legs that were covered with hair – and it was savagely thrusting itself into the one beneath it.

K moved closer still, just above the top creature. Its hair was yellow-brown like hyena hair and coarse and thick. It panted heavily as it thrust itself over and over again into its lover, or its victim.

All was silent in this world and K could not hear a word or a sound. But she could see clearly; could see the impassioned thrusts of the animal, his beast face contorting in pleasure and anger and lust, could see his hirsute arms and back as she moved down its side toward the point of insertion. She was invisible to these creatures, and without mass.

Kathy hovered just below the point where the beast penetrated his lover. *Oh gross*, thought K. The creature it was thrusting into was human, a human female with a dark patch of pubic hair and creamy cotton thighs, like a slice of solid whole milk.

The beast's penis was rigid and smooth. It was thick at the base but as he pulled out for another thrust K could see it was considerably thinner toward the tip. Reaching out some unknown part of her, she touched the smooth hard penis, it was glossy and slick like a brownish-yellow piece of slate or ivory. If it had testicles, they were so covered with the thick jackal-type hair they were not even visible. One more back thrust and K could see the penis fully now. It wasn't a penis at all. It was a horn.

Blood dripped from its tip and K gasped silently for air but found none. Suddenly she was at the couple's right side, moving up the length of the pale woman's arm as if she were a swimmer frantically searching for the top of the ocean. She was up close now to her face. She must have been, for she could see the female's lips, but that was all. As she pulled back to view her entire face, she again gasped. *That face. Oh my God, that face!* she yelled into the silence, and the silence remained.

Her mind raced, she was completely confused and terrified – it was her. She couldn't conceive of such a thing. How could she be there and watching herself at the same time? But it was true, she was seeing her own face! It was her fucking face, her goddamn room and it was she who was having sex with that creature, digging her fingernails silently into the wall, silently drooling and silently screaming.

Kathy slipped, then, hard and quick — fell with a rush of wind and the sensation of being sucked backward through a small tube, like a vacuum. Then K could hear everything again. She could hear her own screams, feel her fingers claw at the wall like some animal in heat. She could feel the sharp contact of that penis-thing as it hit over and over again at the base of her uterus. She dropped back into her body quickly and unexpectedly just as she had left, and began spreading into herself as if she had been melted and were being poured in, slowly becoming solid.

She reached back with both hands wanting to push his hips off of her, but he held tight and she could tell that he was coming the way his penis pulsed inside. Then his arms loosened and she pushed away, bracing herself on her knees, feeling weak and fragmented while Moses stood with one hand leaning against the wall watching her in bewilderment.

Hunched over, Kathy moved to her bed in a swirling daze, holding her stomach with her arms like she was cradling a newborn. She curled up on her right side pulling up the thin and cold sheet to cover her bare body. The light was bright and harsh on her eyes, she squinted, her eyes tearing from the glare.

Fluid dripped out of her, ran down her right leg and upper hamstring and she reached behind to wipe it off, it was lumpy and cold. K raised her hand to look at the thick mess dripping from her fingertips, it was both blood and semen together and was still pulsating from having just been inside her, it was enough to make K feel nauseated.

Moses came over, pulling up his pants, and sat on the bed next to K.

"Get out," she said blankly and without emotion.

"What?" he asked. The word left his lips knowing that it would leave him stranded out there when it did, that he'd be left out in the middle of a scorching hot desert like a bird gone astray. But it came out anyway, and chirped with the loneliness of that forgotten bird.

"Leave, goddamn it, leave. Are you fucking stupid? Go! Get out!"

The look on Moses' face was of confusion, mostly, and also concern, but he didn't say a word. He reached out his hand to touch her covered thigh, then stopped and pulled away. When the door shut, there was more silence in that room than there had ever been before, and Katherine of the St. Catherine Catherines didn't like it one bit.

The silence could have filled a monastery. It was so quiet, so still, that had a fly buzzed by it would've sounded like a swarm of bees. If the floors or walls would have creaked or settled, it would have seemed like an earthquake. And had a tear slipped down Katherine's pale cheek, it would have felt like a flood.

But there were no tears – not yet. Nothing lay before her, emptiness was all around, and only sorrow lay behind her and a pain that shot into every part of her like bullets. The pain was an embryo that cocooned itself in the emptiness that surrounded her. It suckled off the sorrow from her past, swelled up inside of her, and grew and grew. As the pieces of K's fragmented consciousness came back into her body, she felt more of the pain that lay waiting for her.

"So this is pain." The words bubbled into her mind slow and thick like molten rock, her mind barely functioning enough to form them. But it was pain. "Finally," she thought, "this must be it – this is real pain."

It wasn't just the pain of feeling her body contort and writhe in that pool long ago as she was fighting for breath and fighting for life.

And it wasn't just the pain of that suffocating moment when Robert betrayed and used her and left her weeping alone in the open field of her innocence.

It wasn't even the pain of that little girl with a nail through her hand, blood dripping down, watching her father walk away forever – not just that kind of pain.

This pain seemed to encompass all three of those pains. It resurrected all three so Kathy could feel them once again. Just in case she'd missed them, on the slight chance that she'd ever longed for those feelings, they were here for her. And there were others too, others she couldn't even put her finger on. Just wandering pains, vagabonds, stopping in to stay the night in the cardboard box of Katherine's heart.

Everything ached. Her body was exhausted sore and bleeding. Her mind, half-numb and half-terrified, was on the verge of shutting down altogether. Her emotions – a morass.

She lay curled up on her side like a fetus. The pain in her gut waved and ebbed and waved again. A powerful hand with sharp claws was squeezing her insides into something the size of an egg. She imagined the creature inside of her would then hurl that egg at the house of a schoolmate he didn't like or make it into a vegetable omelet with extra cheese and sour cream. Perhaps he'd just eat it raw, like a fox or a wolf or something worse let loose in a hen house.

It squeezed her stomach hard, as if it were trying to choke it, strangle it and leave it for dead. And she thought for some time that she might die, right then and there in a mid-town studio apartment on the restaurant strip of 39th Street in Kansas City, and she welcomed the thought. The peace of that thought shone down on her like a street lamp in an old London town. Walking through the fog with her steps clicking on the rain-covered bricks, each street lamp passed gave light to the tranquility of that thought, the thought of her death.

242

What was so great about life anyway? What had it ever done for her? What had it gotten her? *Where* had it gotten her? If it was supposed to be this great learning experience what had she learned – how to be miserable? Where's the learning? Events come and go, experiences, she felt them, saw them, then when comes the learning?

What did she learn, how to feel pain and fear? How to cling to money and the bullshit sense of security it gave her? How to hate and judge people?

Why were people so attached to this world? *Oh my God, don't eat that, you'll die young. Don't smoke that. Don't do this and don't do that. Live, live, live!* Live a long and healthy but pointless life.

Were other people really enjoying this existence? Were they out having the time of times, one big fuckin' parade, one big party, while K slaved away in the melodrama of her life; dragging her tired body to work and dragging it even more tired home again? Or did they cling to life out of fear? Were they simply afraid of death – afraid of the unknown?

"This life is all they know and all they've ever known," thought K. "Maybe the known is just too safe, too comfortable, and the unknown simply too terrifying. Even if this known thing is the very Hell itself, maybe they'll simply choose the known."

"And I?" she asked, responding to a question that wasn't even spoken. "I'd choose anything besides this. If this isn't Hell, what else could Hell be? How much more pain can one endure before they simply black out? How much more pain does humanity have to face, God? When do we pass the test? We get it, okay, we fucking get it. We know pain." She pulled the sheet tighter around her and it was still cold and now it was damp from the cold sweat that had broken out of her pores.

The comforter lay on the floor at the foot of the bed. But she didn't want to move. She didn't want to accidentally see that look on Marilyn's face right now. She didn't want to see her own face in the mirror or tattooed on the walls in those soul-stealing photographs. She didn't want to move, she didn't want to breathe, and the questions went unanswered and the cold and ache inside her grew. Questions were coming like a flood. An answer would have been like a life jacket – any answer, any answer at all.

"How much more pain is there than losing our loved ones?" she said out loud, her voice strained and raspy. "Every damn day, every goddamned fucking day somebody's loved one dies. How much more – how many more times?

"How much more pain is there than having a broken, beaten or diseased body – or feeling ugly, worthless, guilty and ashamed? How much more pain can you give us, God? How much more suffering?" K spoke as if she were a part of them, one of them, *those* people – a sister to everyone on this god-forsaken planet and she was speaking for them all, her voice raising with the intensity she felt inside. She was a burning flame – a flame growing.

"How much more pain is there than feeling desire after desire after endless, empty desire?" she yelled.

"How much more pain than feeling so afraid of having nothing, of being empty, that we have to lie, steal and prostitute ourselves just to get some meaningless bullshit thing to make us feel better? Then we have to feel all those ugly things as we're doing them, we have to feel ourselves crawling on the ground like that, like some thief, some whore – some groveling dog.

"How much more hate, greed and anger do we get? How much more resentment, frustration and apathy do we have to choke on? How much more do you want us to feel? How much more before it's Hell?

"How much, God?" She screamed. "I'm talking to you!" She reached back to see if the bleeding had stopped, but it continued to stream out of her and she started to cry.

"How much more?" The tears obfuscated the words that she wanted to shout, but could not. Something constricted her voice as she tried over and over to scream at God, but she was being stopped – some invisible oaf sent from Heaven had come up behind her, his hand smothered her mouth, his arm tightened around K's throat.

"I wanna go home," she whispered out of her quivering mouth and tightened throat. Through sob after sob she quietly screamed, "I wanna go home." Tears saturated her face and a gooey mess of snot and tears and saliva strung from her top to bottom lip as she tried to scream it again, but nothing came out – her stomach too cramped up to even let out another whisper or another breath. So she screamed the words inside, *I wanna go home. I wanna go home.*

But she was home, and there was no one to hear her and no one to take her even if she wasn't. K had to sit there and just be that – be that suffering, because there was nowhere else to go and nothing else to be.

Lying there, gazing longingly at her right arm outstretched in front of her, her thumb seemed so peaceful and relaxed, it looked like the soft stroke of a father's hand.

It was so simple and so beautiful lying there that she moved herself closer to it, and soon she had wrapped her mouth around it. Gently, she began sucking until she could feel the distant hand of her father stroking the length of her raven hair.

"There, there," he said. "There, there," and she drifted into a dream.

The walls of Heaven seemed thinner, more frail, as she slipped through the rock face this time, directly into chambers of light. It wasn't as alive as before, the halls resonated with loneliness. Something was missing, part of Heaven had died. K hovered over a gathering of new souls. The nature of the universe was being explained and Kathy tried to understand the flashes, but was being pulled elsewhere. It had to do with resonance and frequencies and holographic images – a balance of opposites keeping it all intact. That was all she could make out.

Then she was in another chamber. It must have been God's chamber. The deep, rich bursts of light, which seemed to flash everywhere simultaneously and yet were clearly separate, it was the voice of God. But this time he wasn't talking to K. She was there, inside, but He didn't even seem to notice her.

And the voice talking to God sounded familiar. Was it her mother? Could it be? How on earth did she get so much pull? But it wasn't her mother, she soon realized, it was *the* mother – Mother Mary. The conversation was choppy and irregular and surreal, but K got the jest of it.

"You're destroying Heaven," Mary said with saddened light. The light was low and muddled, every gritty color of a black rainbow.

He flashed her a thorough glow, somewhat like a smile, compassionate, trying to subdue the Mary light, but she would not be stopped.

"You've sent him back?" she yelled. "Why? He's our son! After all this time, after all these millennia, what more does he need to do? What more can be done? You're destroying Heaven. If he falls into darkness back on Earth all will be lost. The entire balance of good and evil will be upset and everything you've created will crumble into nothingness!"

The God light did not respond, just dissipated slowly, the evaporation of light from a bulb shutting off – and the Mary light was left alone, weeping.

Katherine awoke with the knowledge of monks. "Oh my God," she said, her face in her trembling hands.

She quickly walked into the kitchen as if she had to be there just at that moment, then turned and walked quickly to the living room. She paced like this for nearly half an hour, her head in her hands all the while murmuring, "Oh my God, Oh my God."

Marilyn's picture laughed at her silliness, mocking her. K could feel her eyes on her all the while, slipping off the glossy page, following her like cat eyes in the night.

Katherine stopped in her tracks, whirled around to look dead-eye to Marilyn's.

"What are you looking at you soul-less bitch?" Kathy said. "I'm Jesus!"

It looked like a bat. A giant bat flapping giant wings, trapped in the wall and ceiling of K's apartment – his black pointy tips and thin papery parts where veins would be seen through soft light. He was probably scared, mostly confused. But he didn't panic, just flapped long smooth flaps with his giant wings and patiently waited for a chance to escape, an opportunity to break free. Everything in nature has an escape route.

K lay naked on her bed, except for a worn pair of purple panties whose elastic had broken loose from the fabric by her left cheek – it dug in there a bit, enough to leave a mark. Sweat grew out of her like clear fungus. The night was hot and humid. It was like a Louisiana swamp in her apartment and each droplet of sweat that rolled off her body felt like an intrusion, a bug, a spider, or something equally unwanted on her face and skin. Often she swatted at the sensation, but it was always just sweat.

She fanned herself with a small bamboo and rice paper fan, casting shadows on the wall and ceiling that looked like a bat, and sometimes she'd bounce, make the bedsprings squeak for the added sound affect. The bat was a giant, but alone and afraid and K could tell all it wanted was to leave this place – the place of in-between.

After you're bored with what you already are and sometime before whatever it is you could become lies the place of in-between where Kathy lived out most of her life. She'd like to leave there, too – if only she had the power. If only she were any more capable of leaving than a shadow on the wall cast from rice paper and bamboo.

Her face was distant, she didn't even look like she was in the room. Perhaps she had gone to that Louisiana swamp to bask with the bugs and the snakes as the sun cut through the moisture in the air, drenching her in a muggy heat. Perhaps she lay submerged like a crocodile, just her big sullen eyes and dark straggly hair sticking out of the water. And there she'd wait, wait for a victim – something stupid enough to crawl in or fall into that soupy swamp infested with alligators, snakes and K.

And how would she conquer her victim? Would she be snake-like, slither up to him unseen, bite him quick on the ankle letting her poison do all the work, withdrawing the life from his sallow body? Would she be crocodile-like and drag her screaming, writhing lunch under the water to suffocate it first, taking all the fight out, before she bit in?

Or would she be more K-like and just call him to her with her eyes, then a soft kiss and he'd be hers. Then she could do whatever she wanted, take a bite out of him, as many as she wished, or have him go down on her, make him be hers for the night. Even while his wife waited at home reading a book snuggled under an afghan that his mother had made the two of them as an anniversary present, he'd be rolling around in bed with K wondering how and why he got there.

He was walking through a swampy marsh, can't remember anything else. Maybe he'd fallen in, yes, and then – Bamm – he was in a midtown studio apartment going down on an ashen-faced, raven-haired straight from Heaven angel.

Perhaps she'd just keep him there a while to run some errands, get the paper, make her a cup of coffee – even though she didn't like coffee, it was the point of it that counted. Perhaps she'd let him off the hook with just that, and he wouldn't have to betray anybody he loved – or be eaten alive.

The boys had died. That wasn't good. They were her main hope to clear her name. She figured if they had been found alive, maybe they'd believe the rest of her story. But now they'd say she helped kill them, then dumped their bodies in the cave. That's how she knew where to find them, not psychic stories, not premonitions in dreams – that's what they were going to say.

They were constantly asking questions – at Bells', at work. They were getting info on her and it didn't look good. What were the people at work going to say? She was a normal, happy girl full of fun, vim and vigor? Or would they say she was dark and bitter and they were scared to be next to her most times? Would they say they walked on eggshells around her because when she cracked she would slice people open with a word or a look as piercing as any knife? They were building a case piecemeal. She could feel it falling in place for them like a jigsaw puzzle. Soon, they'd be there for her.

Her apartment looked estranged without all those photos on the wall. She'd long since taken them down and put them in the footlocker in the closet. Only Marilyn's picture remained. God knows why.

But the place no longer looked like home and, what's worse, it no longer felt like home. Even the smell was different. Something had left, been withdrawn. It was the lifeless feel of a house after a vacation or after everyone had moved away. It was vacated – indifferent. It felt like Hell. If Hell came in a large off-white box with a bumpy top, it might just as easily had been her naked apartment as anywhere. And if Hell did come in a box, K would wrap it up in green and red shiny paper with a large Santa bow on top and place it on the doorstep of God next Christmas.

She was homeless. Bells' Bar had ceased being a place of refuge and was now just a rather large, smoky mirror – a warped mirror stained with beer and blood and the reflection it gave was like the reflection from a mirror in a fun house, only this wasn't any fun. This wasn't her, not her life – couldn't be.

Blue light from the bathroom lit her profile as K emptily stared at the bumps on the ceiling. Her face looked so perfect in the blue tint, so pure and innocent, that were there another person in the room at that time they would have instantly fallen in love with her – man, woman or child.

Her open window bequethed the sound of several slow moving cars – coming, coming, going, going, gone. And they never seemed to be *here*, just coming or going and swishing the dry air as they did so in coy, deliberate swishes. So deliberate were the swishes K had to wonder if they were created just for her, then and there, so she could ponder the nature of the sound of a swish.

K heard the flutter of wings, the bristled noise of feathers against a bird body. Was it a bat? Perhaps her scared, giant bat had finally found a way out of K's barren walls and was now fluttering on the windowsill.

"Bats don't have feathers," she reminded herself.

"Oh yeah."

Keeping her body as still as pond water, she turned her head. It came to rest on her thick, black hair and she took in the flowery fragrance of it as the soft coo of the 39th Street Bird spread into the room.

"Goddamn bird," she said with the next breath. Quickly, her fury grew like the flame on a dry pyre and Kathy sat upright, yelled angrily. "Goddamn bird!" The 39th Street Bird squawked, ruffled its feathers, then blinked and continued to look at her with the one black eye that was facing her.

K threw down her fan and started toward the window. "Goddamn bird!" She moved her hands across the air furiously, as if moving burning trees and branches out of her path as she walked.

"Get the hell outta here you goddamn bird!" And the 39th Street Bird flew away. She stood at the window poised like a griffin, her mouth open, one hand in the air. Her chest heaved up and down as another few cars went by swishing the air in a coy, deliberate way.

With the bird gone, the anger in her breath subsided and calmed. The flame had vanished leaving only embers and ashes of confusion in its wake. "Goddamn bird," she confirmed under her breath, nodding her head in confirmation.

K wilted back onto the bed like the petals of a wet flower. Her body tingled uncomfortably in the void of not knowing what had just happened or why. And then tears were there and she rolled onto her stomach pounding her fist into a pillow.

"That goddamn bird," she said, crying even harder. "What a goddamned fucking bird!" K pounded the pillow with each word as she sobbed, her stomach convulsing in waves.

"It wasn't the bird, you know." And that thought made her stomach cramp so tightly that her body had to curl up to follow it. "K, it wasn't the bird. You do know that, right?" Her body kept convulsing but soon no more tears came out. She was dry inside, desert tears.

Slowly her body loosened, un-cramped, and she could straighten her legs. Her breath calmed, the convulsions stopped and she again turned to stare at the ceiling in her worn, purple panties whose elastic had broken loose from the fabric by her left cheek.

"I know."

That day had gone away like every other day had in May. The days were passing like a lanced crocodile in that murky swamp of K's imagination. It thrashed and contorted its body in pain, trying to free itself from whatever was imbedded in it – a spear, an arrow – perhaps it was only a thorn, a tiny prick in the soft underside of the thing. But it hurt like hell, either way. It made much noise, but it didn't go anywhere. In the end it was still in that murky swamp and it still had that lance intact.

There had been one day in May when she tried to write, all day. Not stories, just writing. She opened the leather journal with engraved swirled designs and spaded points and gold lock that Becky had given her for Christmas, and wrote. But the same theme kept coming out – chasing, running, just like her dreams had been lately.

"You're not even a very good writer."

"I know."

"Why do you keep doing it when you suck so bad?"

"I know."

There was a poem she'd written that day and because she liked it the condemnations poured out of her like worms from a rain-soaked ground. But there wasn't any rain and there wasn't any ground. It was just her being and the many tears inside that must have made the worms try to come out of her the way they did.

Stainless
And without breath
I wait

Thoughts of floating to the other shore
Twinkle off the water
But the ferryman don't come this far

Picturesque he waits
In the distance

Stainless
And without breath

"The ferryman don't come this far," she laughed at herself. "That's not even very good English – *The ferryman don't come this far.*"

"I know." That was all she could say anymore. She was so tired of arguing that she didn't know what to do. She couldn't win and she couldn't stop.

Life as Jesus wasn't at all what K had pictured it would be. The customers at Nichol's Lunch didn't tip any better, the customers at Bells' weren't any less crass, and time spent still dripped of loneliness. No more birds sang. The trees didn't bow as she walked by and no one even seemed to notice what had happened to her, that right now they were in the presence of the divine – the one and only begotten Son of God.

Judging from her bank balance she hadn't worked much that month. Judging from the amount of clothes that lay piled on the floor, she hadn't done any laundry. And judging from the food in her pantry she hadn't even been shopping.

Her life was in a shambles. She couldn't do much but lie on that bed and stare up at the ceiling, creating faces and words from the bumpy dots. The only sounds were the continuing conversations she had with herself and the mirror, and Marilyn Monroe.

"So you're Jesus, huh?" She looked at herself in the mirror hard as if she had lost something there. As if mirrors really were secret doorways and the beings that lived on the other side would snatch things and take them away. They'd be quick about it too, she knew that – she knew it all too well. There'd be no use looking for that lost thing hard in the mirror as K was doing now, they'd have hidden it long before you ever thought to look there.

"I don't think this is what people are expecting," she said. "You know, the Second Coming and all." She brought up her hand and let the fingers caress her bare chest. They lingered there awhile, her breasts and fingers both enjoying the touch.

"I do have nice tits, though. Probably a lot nicer than the ones I had the first time. Maybe I'll get a few more listeners this time – twelve disciples and all, the majority of Jews hating you, not too good." She turned to the side to see how her now erect nipples looked in profile. "Maybe I can get a few guys to stop and look, stay awhile. They'll be looking at my tits and I'll be talking...saying...well, whatever it is that

Jesus talks about, something from the Bible, I guess. And that's how it will be. I'll convert them to God and they'll go convert their wives and that will be that. Job over."

"Only one problem, K. You don't even like God."

"Well, there is that. I'll have to work on that part. But now that I'm Jesus I'm sure the answers will start coming any day. It was just a matter of me figuring it out. Now that I remember, the game's over. So I'll just sit and wait for God to show up. In the meantime there's not much else you can do."

"Yeah, nothing much to do." She lowered her arm hitting the Paper Mate pen on the wicker desk and it rolled onto the floor. K bent down to retrieve it, then sat back up on the chair and waved the pen between two fingers until it looked like it was rubber. She rattled it between her teeth.

"You could write another story."

"Don't start that shit with me, K." She took out the pen, pointed it at her reflection in the mirror. "It was those damn stories that got me into this mess in the first place." She got up and paced the room in heavy footsteps, pounding her feet into the floor. "Goddamnit, I don't need this shit, K!"

"Yeah, but it could be the stories that get you out. I feel it, K, there's one more story in you, begging to be written. You're in a heap of dung, there is only one way out – it's the story you write as Jesus. The story that clears your name. The story that makes it all make sense."

She sat back down and looked into her angry, red eyes in the mirror. Then she smiled. It had been awhile since that happened. K's face changed when she smiled, like a child. Like darkness to sunlight. She thought back to when she used to smile as a little girl, laughing with her father as he pushed her on the swing and pretended he was going to push her through the sky. Like she was a rocket, like she could break right through.

But what did it matter now? Those old memories, she didn't know if they were even real or were just some idea she liked long ago that she forgot was an idea and became a memory.

"Yeah, make it all make sense," she thought. She tapped the pen on her forehead. "That must be my power as Jesus – to make things right. I didn't know I was Jesus until know. Maybe that's why the stories kept turning out wrong. Unfocused energy takes the path of least resistance." She'd read that somewhere. "I need to reach into eternity and set it all straight."

She dropped the pen on the desk, looked deep into the mirror, nodded in confirmation, pulled back strands of black hair with both hands to make sure the beauty was still there – the pinkish cheeks, the sad mouth, the daunting eyes.

She wished Becky were alive again. She wished she could see Becky's face smile and slant with doubt when she told her she was Jesus. She wished Becky were alive and famous, just like she always wanted.

And even though they wouldn't be seeing eachother as much now that Becky was famous and K was Jesus, they'd still call eachother once a week because Becky would miss her real bad. She'd tell K that being famous was nothing compared to the good times they shared. And Katherine would smile inside, and try not to cry.

Kathy pulled open the heavy dictionary, stared into the blackness of the words, turning slowly the pliable, frail pages. How in the world did they hold so much power?

"The answers are in this book, somewhere, K. They have to be, you just need to put the words in the right order – make it all have a happy ending."

She looked down into the book, then back into her dark eyes in the mirror, then back into the book again. She thought she might be sick. When she looked back up, tears had formed at the base of her eyes, but none fell.

"I can't do this, K." She closed the book, wilted onto her bed like a dying flower with black petals.

Three nearly sleepless nights and sweaty days had passed and the dreams were back and the call from her blue bible grew with each flip of a numbered tag on the clock radio. She wondered how much control she really had. Who was running the show? Who was picking up that pen, flipping the pages of the dictionary, writing down words.

And if she didn't have control, if she were sitting there doing something she'd already decided not to do, if some unknown force inside her was stronger than her desire, then what did she have control of? How many decisions in her life were actually hers?

Soon, none of that mattered. Soon, she had a new list of bigger and better things to worry about as the words labored onto the page like tired slaves.

With sore muscles and aching backs the male slaves dug the ditches and plowed the fields of K's mucky story. Painfully and with disdain, the female slaves picked the crops, carried the bundles and satisfied whatever perverted fetish was asked of them from their owners and the men that worked the land. Halfway through, the outcome was clear.

It hurt to continue, knowing all along what the ending would have to be. Of course, she could simply not finish it. What would be the harm of that? Would that change things? Did the words have to hit hard on the page like a hammer on the nail of a coffin for it to come true? Or were the thoughts that had already formed in her mind enough to make it a reality?

It didn't matter. By the time K had thought through the possible options the story was already completed. She wished she could take it back, pick the words off the dry pages and place them back in the dictionary. She wished she had never thought to write it in the first place. She wished a lot of things, anything really. Anything, but this. She re-read the words that God had given her, then read the story that Satan had finished.

Prefinite – a. Defined beforehand, prearranged.

Grange – n. A farm, with the dwelling house, stables, barns, etc.; particularly a farm at a great distance from other houses or villages.

Plinth – n. The square block at the base of a column, pedestal, ect.

Parry – n. A warding off or a turning aside of an attack, blow.

Diaphanous – a. Transparent or translucent, as gauzy cloth.

Pansophy – n. Universal wisdom or knowledge.

Halcyon – n. In ancient legend, a bird, said to have a peaceful, calming influence on the sea at the time of winter solstice.

Outlier – n. Any person that lies, dwells or exists away from the main body or expected place. A person who excludes himself from some group.

Embow – vt. To bend into the form of an arch or bow.

Incommodious – n. Inconvenient, awkward, annoying.

Metamorphosize – vt. To change from one form into another. To transform.

Garrote – n. A Spanish method of execution by strangulation with an iron collar tightened by a screw. The iron collar so used.

Sabaist – n. Person who studies stars and celestial bodies.

Telerian – a. Of, or like, spiders. Pertaining to spiders.

Kinkajou – n. Animal of Central and South America, somewhat like a raccoon, with soft, yellowish-brown eyes and a long tail.

Prehensile – a. Adapted to seize or grasp, as the tails of some monkeys.

Parishoner – n. One who oversees the administrative district of various churches.

Hagiolist – n. One who studies, or journals the lives of, saints.

Mephistopeles – n. In medieval legend, a devil to whom Faust sold his soul for riches. A crafty, malevolent devil. A diabolical person.

Discomfit – vt. To rout, defeat. To cause to flee, vanquish. To overthrow the plans or expectatioins.

Garden – n. A plot of ground where herbs, fruits, flowers or vegetables are cultivated.

$\mathcal{P}$ieces of $\mathcal{A}$my

Journal Entry – June 25th

Teacher called me her little kinkajou three times today, I sure wish she'd stop all that. I don't think I have a raccoon face, and I have no tail. My hands are prehensile, but maybe she's simply not. But, I do have large eyes – and I love the night.

It's incommodious to me is all, though I don't think she understands that. Maybe it's just her way to parry what she sees in my eyes. Like most grown-ups do when they look into me and they don't see a little girl, they see something stronger than them. Something older, something wise in ways they don't yet understand.

So they embow their lips up toward their eyes as if to soothe me, to make me an ally. But I would never hurt them, no matter how silly they become.

Of course, most just turn and walk away. I feel I've discomfit them in some way. But I've learned not to. I've learned to save all the big words I know and just write them in this journal. People become so shattered when somebody knows a bigger word than them. People are so funny about words. They have to say bigger and better words all the time. Sometimes they put so many of those big words together then nobody understands what they are even talking about. Then what is the point?

But they're diaphanous to me. I know their fears and their bigger and better words are really brick houses they can hide inside of so that people don't see that behind that brick wall they have nothing; no furniture, no food, no clothes – not even a roof to keep out the rain. They don't have anything besides that big fancy word of theirs.

I think we should scoop up all the words in the world and feed them to some hungry lioness. And I'll bet the world would be just fine without them.

That's why I'm leaving tomorrow for that big school on the East Coast, because I know all those big, fancy words and score so high on all their silly tests. Mommy says no boy or girl my age has ever scored so high on those tests or known so many words. I know every word I hear, but I don't know how or why. It doesn't mean anything to me, though. And I remember saying, "Doesn't everybody know these things?" I was only four. She laughed and said, "It's pansophy dear, most grown-ups don't even know the things you know."

She smiled and gave me a big hug. She's proud of me and I like it when she smiles. She calls me baby Halcyon and says I'm here to calm the angry ocean of this world. She says I'm here to metamorphosize this whole planet, to unscrew the garrotes that everyone has placed them-selves in. But I don't know. It doesn't matter to me either way. I'd be just as happy to be a sabaist and spend the rest of my life under a big tree watching the stars. Just watch and watch and drink in their light until I become one, a star just like them.

I still just feel like a little girl, behind all those words and pansophy, I'm still a little girl. But there are times when I feel very old, older than my mommy even. And I go outside and it is a friend of mine and I feel like I'm as old as the whole outdoors. But I don't yet know what that means.

But the dreams make me feel young again, like a scared little girl. I dream about flying and it scares me. I'm about to get on the plane that will take me to the East and I see a man by the plane moving his hands in a telerian fashion. He looks like a human but moves like a spider. Then, suddenly, he is next to me and he whispers in my ear, "Hello, I'm Mephistopeles." Then he's gone, back at the plane moving in his telerian way. And I don't want to get on the plane, but they make me. And there's that terrible explosion, it sounds like a thousand bells crashing together all at once, uncontrollably. And then I awake.

Mommy says not to worry, it's just my fear of flying coming to life in my dreams. So I'll have to trust her, for everything I do know only shows me all the things that I don't.

And mommy says the parishioner is coming to town just to go on this flight with me. He is a well know hagiolist. She says he wants to write down some things about my life and that his presence there will bless the flight to the East, so I should not worry.

So, I guess I should not. If God had made everything prefinite then there would have been no point in us being here at all. So maybe the dreams are just bad dreams.

Tomorrow night the plane leaves at 7:00 p.m. I'll have to leave the grange at about 3:00 just to get to the Garden City airport on time. No more an outlier in this dying town between towns, but a city girl in a beautiful school where every column has a plinth and every plinth is made of marble.

So, I go to build the plinth beneath me, a diamond plinth beneath this column of thoughts and light that I am. A base to stand on, to reach the sky from and to keep growing on until I touch the stars. Then I can watch the stars as a star and they can watch me, and that would be good.

Kathy read it over and over, and soon almost a month had passed like the muffled cries of a lone wolf across the prairie of K's heart. And it was hot – and it was June.

The stone cold goodness of December was a diametric stones throw away, past and future. The beautiful month of the birth of our Lord Christ was opposite her in all directions. It lay behind her like a stone left unturned. She had walked right over it, right over the smooth underside, right over the dense cool core of the thing that she could have pulled to her cheeks and rubbed on her skin, absorbing that coolness – hoarding it to sooth the intensity of the summer heats.

It lay before her like a stone cold stare, the vacant longing of a huge cloudy face hovering in a gaseous swamp. Turning kind, it invites her into its cool mist with a smile that could bridge the gap between Heaven and Earth. Its smile was a slice of solid light – elusive and alluring, sunshine glistening like bait on a sad pond.

Between her and the face she desired to be a part of lay a trail of stones across a murky swamp. It was a leap between each stone – a large leap. It would take a huge amount of faith to take leaps that large. Maybe, were she a great swimmer, she'd try. Even then, there was life in those waters – the slimy, slithering life of mammals better left unknown.

The waters were death to K. Death as she'd known death to be since her sixteenth year. She was stuck, stuck in June – till June decided to un-stuck her. And it was hot.

Water dripped off her skin like dog piss from the limbs of a dried-up bush as she bent over to open the window to 39th Street. Peeling paint broke and chipped as she worked the sticky window back and forth until it was up high enough to wedge her wooden Buddha underneath.

"That's a good Buddha," she said, patting it on its round belly. The Buddha stayed still and calm with a cool grin spread across his smooth, wooden face. She'd heard he was like that or had read about it somewhere. That it didn't matter what was happening on the outside, the world could have been going down in flames, but he'd remain calm and cheerful looking. She wouldn't mind that happening to her someday.

She wouldn't mind not having to slide from one emotion into the next like she always had. Jumping into fear, hatred, and disappearing into rants and raves, hitting and yelling. Sadness descended on her and she'd disappear into that, crying, curled up in a ball, wishing she were dead. She could see those things now, the emotions coming for her, sweeping her away, but she couldn't stop them.

She imagined he could stop them or somehow they just didn't arise in him. Or, if they did, that he was simply unaffected by them – weird, really.

"How the fuck did it get so hot so fast?" she thought.

But it wasn't so fast. It was the middle of June and she had fallen asleep with the window shut and slept until almost noon. She was sleeping later and later and when she awoke it was as if in a sauna, sticky and hot and wet. She literally dripped her way to the shower, exhausted from the night's sleep.

Normally she couldn't sleep in the heat, but this last month the conditions were irrelevant. She could sleep twelve hours a day and wake up wanting more. The sleep never helped much. She'd wake up feeling like she'd been through a war. And lately her dreams were like that – constantly being chased, fighting. Usually her bullets didn't work or they'd come out of the gun too slowly to hurt anyone and they could never stop whoever was chasing her.

Sometimes they were aliens. Sometimes they were men, warriors, from other time periods – cowboys and cavalry, or knights and crusaders. She'd wake up wondering how come she could never win. How come she couldn't stop those creatures from chasing her.

"You can't win against a dream," her reflection through the blue light had said one morning. "Because you're only fighting yourself."

She stepped out of the shower, dried herself with the oversized terrycloth towel, pulled on the purple panties whose elastic had broken loose from the fabric by her left cheek. K drug her heavy body to the mirror, looked at the puffy and purple rings under her eyes, "What now, K, what the fuck now?"

"I don't know, K, I don't know."

"What about your story? What about Amy?"

"I don't know, K, I don't fucking know."

Pieces of Amy weighed heavily on Katherine. A tremendous longing rang in her to reach out and grab that little girl, pull her into her womb, keep her safe and warm forever. But she didn't know how. No matter what she thought of she couldn't see a way to put her back together again, to make pieces of Amy whole, to make it not happen in the first place.

"You could call somebody – the cops, the FBI, the FFA."

"The FFA? You're going to call the Future Farmers of America?"

"You know what I mean. There has to be somebody, K – some federal flight agency, bearau-thingy, something. I just don't know." But either way it would be difficult to convince them. The cops already had her tied to at least two deaths and if she were on record as saying that this plane would crash and it came true…well, she didn't know what that meant, but she knew it couldn't be good.

And what if she tried to stop it herself? Just showed up and put a stop to it? And what if her showing up somehow caused that little girl to die like she may have caused the others? Then…then…well, that was too terrifying to even think about, so she stopped herself.

But a tear came sliding down her famished cheek anyway, letting K know she'd already gone too far, that she'd trespassed into thoughts that make tears come true. Protected by dreams is the safest place. When those disappear, you see life as it really is – a straw house ready to crumble. Kathy swallowed hard some thickness in her throat and choked back a few tears and gathered herself.

"There is one more possibility," she said, as she reached up her hand, needing to be touched just then. Her fingers circled the areola of

263

one breast, she wet her fingertips, circled it again. "But, bare with me, it sounds a little crazy."

"Compared to what?"

"Right. You could call in a bomb threat."

"What!?" she reached for the other breast, gently turned the nipple between her balmy fingers.

"Think about it, K. Even if it didn't stop the plane from taking off, it would create a need for heightened security that night, possibly thwarting the terrorists."

"I'll think about it," she said, removing her hands from her breasts that had quickly become bored just being there, starting a process that no one was there to finish.

Even being Jesus she still wanted to be touched – strange. Nothing had changed. She still needed…something, a hold, a caress, a deep, soft kiss. Still, much was missing in her life. But it was true, she was Jesus – had to be. It all made perfect sense, the dreams, her anger at God for sending her back to Earth – her stories. Her whole life knowing that she was something greater, something more than the plebs that lined the gutters of this existence like the mold and sludge on 39th Street.

So, so what if she wasn't as compassionate as Jesus? So, so what if she didn't know how to love or how to give – that would all come. "The first step is knowing," she thought.

"Yeah. Everything else will follow, any day now – any day at all. Like night follows day and flowers follow spring." She turned abruptly to face herself in the mirror.

"See, you're starting to sound more like Jesus already!" K nodded her head tersely in confirmation. A bosky, black curl landed on her face. She blew at the hairs, then brushed them aside. "You just need to have a little more patience and acceptance. Accept the things you cannot change."

The playful light left her eyes and was replaced by thin, crooked red lines that usually resided there. "Oh, no," she said, sinking to the floor. "Oh, no."

That added a whole other dimension to her problems, and Amy's problem. "This whole thing, is it a test – to see if I can accept? Then what about the other part, the courage to change the things I can and the wisdom to know the difference? How do you know? Which one is this? And if the answer doesn't come, how do you find out?" She hadn't a clue, and only a week left to figure it all out. Amy's plane took off from Garden City Kansas at 7:00 p.m. on the 26th of June. At 7:20 p.m. there'd be pieces of Amy – everywhere.

The next morning she drove to a phone booth twenty miles away. She made a call to the FAA, a death threat on the parishioner's life. It would be a bomb, she said, her voice disguised, low, like a man's. She hung up the phone. "That was stupid."

"Yeah."

Dawn stretched into morning without sound. K pulled the wicker chair to the window, watched the path of the sun until it peaked above 39th Street and had begun its descent back down.

She showered, brushed her teeth, unscrewed the blue light, put in a plain white-ish, yellowish bulb, pulled the silver chain. The bathroom looked dull, average. There was no mystery here, no secrets in the folds of the plain light. She rinsed her mouth with cupped hands under the faucet, pulled the chain.

On her bed, her ankles were pushed up to her butt as her back pressed against the wall. Her arms curled around her legs, the mendicancy posture of a bum on the street.

The minutes had ticked away and took with them the days and the only sounds left were the clicks of her alarm clock and the slow building of pressure as it would prepare to turn a number. Tonight would be a good night to drink. Tomorrow she would go to the police, tell them about Amy and the plane crash, hope to God they believed her. No, she'd make them believe her – it was two days away. She shouldn't have waited this long. But, maybe it was better this way. Maybe now the urgency would be there. Maybe it gave time for her death threat to simmer. If she would have told them a month ago they might have forgotten all about it by now.

"Yeah, much better this way." She'd almost made herself believe that, that it had a purpose. That it wasn't just her fears and theories and beliefs that stopped her from taking care of this sooner. But what did it matter anyway? It was all going to go wrong – everything always did.

Suddenly, time had never moved slower. The waves of time had hurled over the past and crashed onto this beach, seeping into the packed sand, pulling away unhurried, leaving foamy bits of itself all over the shore line. She wanted the whole thing to be over with. Maybe afterward she could get on with her life, move somewhere else and start anew.

"People start over all the time, why not me?" she thought. "Why not bury the past and start again? I don't even have to be me anymore, I could be Debbie or Barbara. Yeah, Barbara – that would be good, Barbara Billingsly. No, that's a name already. Barbara Jacobson – no, too many syllables and I don't like things that start with *J* – like Jello and germs. Okay, even things that sound like they start with *J*."

"How about Barbara Dove?"

"Yeah, Barbara Dove. And my friends, my new friends, would call me Barbi – with an *I*. Barbi Dove, like Barbie Doll. And my boyfriend, my new boyfriend, would call me Dovey – with a *Y*. Barbara Dovey – like Lovey Dovey.

"And I'll live somewhere so far from here that there ain't nothing like this place in that one – no bars, no bums and definitely no cafés. Well, okay, I'm sure there'd be a café, I mean people gotta eat, right?

But I won't work there – no way, uh huh, definitely not. And if I did work there, there ain't no way I'm waiting tables. Maybe hostess or manager but not a waitress – absolutely not, not even a consideration in possibilities. And if I did wait tables I wouldn't take any shit from anyone." She nodded her head tersely, in confirmation.

When all the brightness had been swept away by the crashing tide of day, night was left. The lights were off in her apartment and only a warm, sticky, pale darkness that the neon of 39th Street lit in a tempered hue like bug zappers remained in the hollows of K's room. That's what Bells had said people were searching for, anyway – the warmth of bug zappers.

The only time K had ever heard him say anything about religion or God was after a Christmas party several years ago when she saw him downing shots with Drunk 1 and Drunk 2 in the corner.

"It's the warmth of it people are drawn to like moths," he had said. "Go to church, do what the preacher tells you, pray to God there's a place saved in Heaven for you as you watch your life dissipate in an extended flash of pain in the neon light. Even if there's no substance, people are content with the warmth."

"Am I like that?" K asked.

"You're a step further along on the food chain. You're hopping from lap to lap, from fantasy to fantasy, from desire to desire, hoping those things will fill some un-fillable void inside you – hoping to find truth. It's like thinking the warmth in a bottle of piss will keep you warm forever, not realizing in advance how soon it will turn cold. It won't destroy your life as quickly as a weekly dose of church going will, but you won't find truth in a bottle of warm piss, neither!" He grunted then.

K turned to her left side, the bed soft and warm, looked out over the darkened apartment to see Marilyn's face turn red, then yellow or off-white, she wasn't sure, then red again. Round and round like a carnival.

"Pretty," K thought. "I wonder what's going on." And she moved to the window, looking down on 39th Street. Outside were three cop cars.

"Must have been a fight at Bells," she was thinking, as the heavy vibration of footsteps on her stairs shook the floor. Then there was an obtrusive knock on her door, not a knock of friendship or some kid selling cookies and candy as a fundraiser so that their team could afford to go to state finals. Kids never came into her back alley, anyway.

"Katherine Kristensen?"

"Shit," she whispered, lowering from the window.

"Miss Kristensen, open up, it's the police."

"Fuck shit. *Open up?* Are you nuts?" She tiptoed to her vent, quietly pried it open and climbed in, pulling it shut behind her. The coiled rope pressed its scratchy fibers into the bare white back of her leg.

"Miss Kristensen, we have a warrant for your arrest and a search warrant for these premises. We *will* enter your apartment."

"Holy Jesus fuck shit! A warrant for my arrest?" And thoughts of Amy crowded her in the tiny space in the dusty vent. They wouldn't listen to her now.

In the back alley, the ring of her door being shattered echoed off the pavement and buildings and tin overhang of the rusted dumpster. She darted behind the air conditioning unit of Saigon 39, slid into the unlocked window at Bells', staying low in the men's room. Through the long, narrow slot of door to the bar, K could see a cop talking to Bells. Bells had a stupid, naive look on his face.

"... confirmation it was her car leaving the scene of an accident several months back that took three lives. We also gathered recent information she was linked to the deaths of two children found in some caves she identified. If you see her, please call us," the cop was saying.

Recent information? What? More crazy poems? Fingerprints? This isn't possible.

"Haven't seen or heard from her in weeks," he grunted, giving Drunk 1 and Drunk 2 a hard stare. They lowered their eyes to their bottles of Budweiser and both took a sip. "But I'll call you if I do."

He brought his hand to his face, pressed it into the muscle of his chin, and K closed the gap between door and frame and stepped away.

The speckled mirror cast reflections of someone she didn't even know, and didn't want to. It was fear, mostly, looking back at her through the water-stained mirror, also dismay. Sometimes, when you stare at things long enough, they start to change. Like a dot on the wall you're not sure about – whether it's a bug or a dot. So you stare, too tired to get up and flick at it to be sure, trying to remember if you've ever seen that dot before.

Then, when it starts to move around, you think for sure it's a bug, but it's really just your long hard stare – the movement of your eyes changing things, making reality more malleable.

She wished she could change everything around her, make it vibrate at a rate that would soften up the hard things to where she could walk right through them, right into a different world. She wished she could get a glimpse into the future, see how this was all going to end.

K raised her hand, almost rubbed it along the mirror's edge like you're supposed to do with a magic lamp to get the wishes out, then she lowered it again. Touching a mirror that size could only mean trouble. But an image started forming anyway. White clouds forming a picture in front of her from the pressure of her raw stare.

It was that truck again. She couldn't believe it. That fat, country trucker barreling down the highway half asleep – fake wind seeping through the crack between door and window. It was moving faster this time, jumping from scene to scene – downtown, pouring piss onto the hot concrete.

It's the warmth of a fresh bottle of piss, she could hear Bells' scratchy voice say from some lost corner of her mind.

"Jesus, K, Jesus! That shit again! Forget about that crap, it's meaning-less. It has nothing to do with anything at all. God, this mirror sucks!" She pulled her eyes from the mirror, whirled around, folded her arms tight across her chest that was heaving in frustration.

"What would Jesus do, K?" She'd seen that on a bumper sticker once. She remembered looking out at the street thinking, *He wouldn't be in this mess in the first place*. The saying took on a whole new meaning, now. Now, he was the nervous, shaky person leaned up against a stained porcelain sink in a dirty bathroom with a flickering light bulb that reeked of puke and feces and old urine. She turned back to the mirror, the picture had disappeared.

"What would Jesus do, K?" She looked deeper into her tired and puffy bloodshot eyes. She waited, still and silent, like a walking stick.

"Get help from God," she said. K raised her right hand, extended the index finger, pointed it at her reflection in the mirror.

"Help from God – got it."

Behind her, the door of the toilet stall pushed open a few inches from a wind that had blown through the loose window with a rattle. It was a sign from God is what it was. The tiny invitation lulled her into the stall. Tonight was finally the night, her message from God on the bathroom walls at Bells' Bar was going to be there. She closed her eyes, and prayed.

"Please, God, please. Show me something on these walls that will help me understand – something that will help me through this. The first thing I see, that's your message for me. Okay? Okay, here I go..."

She sucked in her stomach and filled her chest with a long inhale, holding it tight with pressed lips and her eyes scrunched closed. K put her hand to the wall, moved it slowly left, then right – cold, rough, cold. Her breath stopped when her hand came to a spot that was smooth and warm. This was it.

Her eyes popped open wide... *God is in my jelly donut.*

"Great."

She headed toward the window, put her foot on the urinal, then turned back. "Okay, the second thing I see." K again moved into the stall and closed her eyes, held tight her breath, ran her fingers along the wall stopping at a bare space, without paint or splinters. She opened her eyes.

I am a flame in search of darkness – The Hyena.

She had made it to her car unseen. Luckily, it was parked off a side street west of State Line Road. Luckily, there hadn't been any spaces by her place. Luckily, she was parked in an alley most people didn't even know was there.

"Luckily," she thought. "Yeah, luckily. You're one lucky girl, K. You're just a continuing stream of good luck. You're a long line of good luck waiting to board a good luck train. You're a good luck sandwich and a tall glass of lucky juice to wash it all down with."

She cautiously eased onto State Line, heading north, away from 39th Street onto one of her designated *Escape From Kansas City* routes that was specifically created to avoid being seen by the police. She dated a guy on the force once five years ago just to get information on how they conducted a search. He wasn't much help and he was lousy in bed. It only lasted a few weeks.

But what did luck, or chance, or planning have to do with any of this, she thought. "You were meant to save her, all by yourself. It's your destiny, K."

"Yeah, destiny."

Trees were old curmudgeons, sagging faces and dried up skin. Tiger lilies hung their heads low in the shadowy outcast of the headlights. Was it shame, sorrow or just the drought that had plagued the Midwest for several months? K drove through it like a child who'd just gotten all D's on her report card with only one B+ in Music Ed.

It was the not knowing that was the worse part of it – not knowing if it was shame, sorrow or disgust. Sitting there not knowing how the parents felt, waiting for the punishment or waiting to have to explain herself or just deal with it at all. And why should she even have to explain herself. *School is a worthless piece of shit, anyway,* she was thinking, *better I get D's than to be brainwashed like the rest of humanity!*

"What are you all looking at?" K yelled out loud. "I'm the good guy here. It's you guys that keep fucking with me. It's this fucking, goddamn world that's putting me in this situation in the first place! Go hang your head by someone who cares."

But she did care, or why would she have said anything in the first place. It didn't matter, though, they didn't listen. The scenery continued to reveal its sad and sorrowful face to K as she moved west through the dry Kansas plains.

Within an hour she was completely out of the metro area and all the attached small and large towns. Bonner Springs went by the wayside, Lawrence had come and gone and now only narrow urban highway remained with thoughts of scenes yet to be realized dancing inside her. Thoughts of Amy and who she'd be someday. After Kathy saved her, she would watch Amy's life from afar. Cut newspaper clippings – Valedictorian, Summa cum Laude, her latest cancer research breakthrough. As Amy was being sworn in as President or being given The Nobel Peace Prize, K would be there, crowded in the back row on a hard, foldout chair – smiling, knowing.

Hills were distant and put together with dots. Mother nature painting Seurats' on the sky line with the tip of a camel-haired brush. The sun went down and the world it left behind was imbrued with the black inky blood octopi spray to escape predators.

They have three hearts. K wished she did. One heart to love, one heart to hate, one just to pump blood through her veins to keep her alive. Her one heart doing the work of three would surely be her demise one day.

The night was perfect and starlit – the kind of clearness you only see away from big cities, the kind of clearness you only see from a mountaintop or the clearing of a forest or silent, desert cliffs.

It was clear straight into the heavens, you could almost see the smile of Jesus as he looked down on this world. As messed up as it is, all the wrong turns that must have happened along the way, you could still look up that night and see him smiling down. So over-flowing was his compassion that one glimpse and you'd be crying and you wouldn't even know why – it was just a clear night and you started to cry.

Coyotes howled and crickets chattered and the Morse code of fireflies lit the sky. The dark night was full of skidded secrets – Sanskrit and hieroglyphs and songs in Persian, unknowable and untranslatable pidgin dialect to K, even if she had been aware enough to hear them.

But K was barely conscious, just one step above sleep. The inky black night could have swallowed up the road and her right along with it and Kathy would never have known.

She would have never realized that a second before she had been alive – that a precious life, innocent and fragile, had been hers for twenty-eight years and that now there was nothing to acknowledge that it had ever taken place. All was coming to her and leaving just as quickly, like she wasn't even there.

The adrenaline that had pumped through her veins as she escaped Kansas City ebbed, and the downside was well past tired. She had driven all night and most of the next day, resting only briefly behind a large grain elevator in the heat in the middle of Kansas until darkness fell again. But it wasn't real rest. It was paranoid and fitful rest, every car that crackled the dry leaves and ran over the loose gravel jerked her awake.

At the gas station, where she refueled and loaded up on bottled water and trail mix, thermals raised off the ground in wavered lines. She paid, got a map and directions to Garden City, *State Route 4 to U.S. 156.*

"Careful," the attendant had said, he had a smile like Bells. "The road is straight – but narrow."

It was becoming grueling just to keep her eyes open and she often had to shut one and then the other or have them half open to try and keep them moist. They were as dry as the dirt and dust on the side of the road that kicked up whenever K got careless and drove onto the shoulder. *Careful,* she reminded herself. *Straight, but narrow – got it.*

Wind blew, but the heat it drew from the Southwest showered even more warmth onto the darkened plains that were already dry and brittle. The drought had extended from early spring, and inchoate flowers swooned low to the ground still in their buds.

Fireflies were everywhere. Must have been thousands of them. They lit up the pastures like a carnival in some dead and dying town where children would follow the bend of trees past the railroad tracks to the old Huntington farm. And there it would be – a wondrous, joyous carnival. Everywhere you walked lights were blinking, bells were ringing, and so much excitement filled the air that you didn't mind paying three bucks for some stale cotton candy and a watered-down Coke.

You didn't mind waiting twenty minutes to get on a ride that would turn you inside out and upside down and make you sick to your stomach because everybody in line was so excited that it wasn't even like a line, it was like a ball. It was like a ball in a royal palace and you were just there standing, talking with your elegantly dressed friends. The champagne tickled your nose with each sip and the jewelry they wore on their white and black costumes sparkled like a thousand fireflies in the dark and dusty fields of a hot country road.

The back roads she had chosen to avoid being spotted had their own desolate beauty. A beauty they and only they could hold. While each town seemed the same on the surface – same *Gas & Stop*, same kid on the corner watching the traffic go by, same barber shop or beauty parlor where you could hear the latest town gossip – they were different. Each empty space in between had their own differences too, told their own story, held their own picture of God.

She turned her head from side to side, wringing stiffness and creaks from her neck. On a rich rosewood plank sign to her left, engraved letters read, *Stone City*. It dangled from thick chains on a round and rotting wooden beam that was connected to two pillars of rock. Something emerald was growing between the rocks, ivy or moss or whatever it was K thought it looked elegant. Perfect. As accidental as it may have been, the scene would have been lacking without it. The sign dropped into the distant darkness behind her, hidden by a trail of dust that K kicked up driving on the dirt and gravel shoulder.

"Stone City," she thought, and then her foot hit the brakes so hard her head almost hit the windshield. She sped back to the entrance of that prairie town as her heart raced and her mind tried to conjure up images of what that might mean.

K pulled into the semi-cove that housed the sign and shut off the engine, then looked around the dimly lit half-circle and wondered why she cared. Why had she come back all this way? A short stone wall of layered flat rock created a half-circle like the entrance to a campground, with an opening of dirt and rock in the middle that led into town, camouflaged with thick trees. Above the opening a sign read: Scott City, Kansas – population 3,043, "Stone City."

"Come on, K, let's just go. I don't have a good feeling about this."

"No, it's okay. We've go plenty of time. Amy's plane doesn't take off for another nineteen hours, and its only five or six hours from here." She scoped the landscape for any foreboding omens. "I don't see any."

There were no vultures circling above or dead animals lying in the road, not even a pothole. It was perfect. Stars were there. Stars were good – had to be. Because if stars were bad then nothing else mattered, then nothing was right and nothing was good. Katherine didn't want to live in a world where stars were bad and if she ever found out they were, it would be her last breath that bared witness.

"Wow," she thought, weaving through the dense trees and thicket into the heart of Stone City, it was picturesque. Cinderella might have lived there – if she were poor. If she decided the life of a princess wasn't for her anymore and she'd had it with that perfect prince of hers and packed up a few cartoon mice and headed into the real world – this would be it, this would be where she would go.

The tires made crunching noises as they spit out rocks and kicked up the dirt they crawled slowly on. Her car crawled along the stone paved road so slowly she could have touched the bare, glossy, maple leaves as she went by. So slowly she moved, she could have counted the grooves in the cobblestones on the path to her left. So slowly, a child could have walked along side talking to K all the while – and she would have liked that. She would have liked to hear how school was good that day because there was a party and they had pizza.

And even though he had cried and cried about it the night before because he knew there'd be onions on the pizza and everyone else would be enjoying it and laughing at him because he didn't like onions, it turned out okay – it was only cheese pizza. None of the other kids even seemed to notice that he had made such a big fuss about it and had refused to go to school and had kicked and screamed all for nothing.

And she would have liked it, too, if a little girl in a pink dress had come up along side her car licking a lollipop all the while. And she would have liked it when her white and shiny church shoes clicked against the rocky path as the girl tried to walk on only her heels with straight knees – her pony-tails bouncing up and down as she and K smiled at eachother.

Then Kathy would say something smart and profound about life, something that girl would always remember and would affect her forever. She'd say something like, "Hang on kid, it's quite a ride." Only it would be better than that – much better. She couldn't think of what it would be right now but it would be deep and full and each word would be thick with hidden meaning.

It would be like something Jesus would say – something about a sheep or a flock of some kind, she wasn't sure. But a flock of some kind of animal people didn't normally talk about would be good. Elephant Birds, perhaps. People hardly ever talked about Elephant Birds. And they'd be a good subject because they were extinct and even when they were alive they couldn't fly, and one could cull much meaning from a story about Elephant Birds.

But the kid would cherish those words forever, whatever they were, and would smile big at K knowing she had just heard something special, something true – something which wasn't the normal bullshit that every other grown-up was always trying to feed her.

As she followed the stone paved road into town, reaching out for the big leaves that pushed into the air to greet her like a welcoming committee, it dawned on her in excited jitters.

"This is it, this is where it all began. My first story that came true, the ex-military guy who died in Maraba – this was his hometown!"

She even remembered the article in the paper – *From Stone City to Purgatory*. They were collecting money for his mother, he was her only support, *send donations to: 33 Flat Rock, Scott City, KS*. How could she forget – *Stone City? Flat Rock? 33?* That's a master number. And besides, it's how old Jesus was, when he died. She came to a stop sign, Main and Sandstone – Flat Rock would be easy to find in a town this size.

The Main Street strip was short but full of character – a church made of stone, a restaurant and drugstore with no neon sings, just painted letters on the storefront glass, a clothing store, *Reba's New and Used*. The architecture was upper East Coast, woody off-whites and alabaster designs of hand-hewn oak frames and clapboard siding. There was probably a bakery nearby with the kind of guy behind the counter you'd call *Pop's* or *Joe*.

Soon it was gone and only trees and shrubs and cross streets remained. When she saw Flat Rock, her heart quickened in her chest. It seemed like a dream as she turned down the straight narrow road, squinting through a cloud of up-heaved dirt at the numbers on houses and

277

curbs and mailboxes that lined the road like sentries.

Gas burning street lamps lit splotches of sidewalk and mostly rich green lawns all the way down the block. They were antique dollhouses with cobble stone paths, picket fences and rock gardens laced and fanned with oaks and maples, firs and willows. She wasn't even in Kansas anymore, had been sucked through some hole to a different time in a different place, like Dorothy. Above, the night was porcelain – salvaged from the archives of purer days and purer dreams. The only dissonance was the smell of sulfur, probably seeping in from a refinery in a neighboring town.

Thirty-three – a one story bungalow on the left side. K pulled the car over, switched the ignition to off. Echoes from the engine faded into silence and crickets as dust from the street settled around her clearing the air into pristine clarity. A mailbox jutted into the street, *Swan*. This *was* it, Master in Arms Devin Swan. "Oh my God. This is the house!"

The squeaking car door sent a shrill into the hot night. K stood, stretched like a cat, looked up and down Flat Rock. It was dark except for a few porch lights and street lamps sending puffed, hazy hues down the street like lanterns. She opened the white gate and walked up the path of smooth granite rocks that were placed in the yard like lilypads.

"K, it's the middle of the night. Stop, stop right now. I'm serious, I've got a bad feeling about this." But she didn't stop. It was destiny is what it was – that she should take the right back roads that went anywhere near this town, that she should be turning her head to stretch her sore neck just at that moment – destiny.

All the lights were off in the quaint, canary-yellow chalet. Of course, it was almost midnight and this town probably rolled up the streets and went to sleep at about 8:00 p.m. The knock on the door resounded down the vacated block.

"This is the cutest house," she thought. It had an array of petunias in an ivory window box and fake ivy that pretended to be growing on a column that held up the front door walkway. Criss-crosses of creamy white plywood carved diamonds into the air beneath the handrail. And if Cinderella didn't live here then it was definitely the house of one, if not several, of the seven dwarfs – because everything was short and small and it just seemed like a good place for little people.

The whole town seemed like a good place for little people and K would like to watch them some morning hidden in the greenery of a maple tree or the dark thicket of an elderberry bush. And then she'd see, she'd see the secret of this small town so well hidden off the main roads that no one ever stopped there. She'd watch all the little people come out at dawn, shy at first to make sure there were no big people around. Then they'd do things that big people never came to know about. Like dance and turn cartwheels in the street and wear beannie hats with propellers on them and blow bubbles from their own spit.

And when a big person did accidentally come to town, for directions or a soda or an apple pecan muffin from *Joe's*, they'd straighten up quick and cover up their blinding yellow and pink shirts with something brown or gray. They'd put cardboard cutouts of big people in the streets just to fool 'em. Then the big person would leave and the fun and games would start all over again.

She could almost hear the surviving members of the seven dwarfs singing their work songs inside this country home. Only there was no more work. This was the home of retired dwarfs.

After several minutes, the door opened slightly and the pale face of an old woman leered through the thin opening, K could only see one, gray eye.

"Hello? Who is it?" Her voice was slight and frail, high pitched. It seemed rough, too, frayed with age, reminding K of her grandmother only this voice was not as full, it didn't linger in her ears as long as her grandmother's had.

"I'm sorry to bother you so late," said K. "I'm...I was a friend of your son's, and I just...I needed to ask you a question."

She stammered for a moment and fidgeted with something on the porch with her foot that wasn't even there. Then looked down like it was real important that she find the thing on the porch that wasn't even there and kick it aside or move it into the dark brush next to her as quickly as possible. "Did he ever mention…uh…a girl named Kathy?"

"Oh my," said the woman, and Kathy looked up to see a broad smile spread across her face like spilled white paint and the door opened to its full length and Katherine stepped inside.

They faced eachother, K on the sofa, across from her the lady in an unfinished wicker rocker. K thought it was nice that the cushion on the rocker matched the material on the sofa. She thought it was…well, it was just nice, that's all. It was almost like they were sitting on the same piece of furniture – that the matching fabric somehow lessened the distance between them.

A fire going in the carved stone fireplace sent a slight smoky haze into the room. It was cozy, like the insides of a fluffy, buttermilk biscuit just-baked and smothered in butter – the kind of biscuit that would win a blue ribbon at the county fair. *Best Biscuit,* the ribbon would read, or *Lynn County Biscuit Champion!* And the old lady who baked that biscuit would wear that blue sash as proud as a new mother, as proud as she's ever been. She'd grin from ear to ear watching the crowd enjoy her biscuits as one would turn to another and say, "Boy, these are good biscuits!"

The grandmotherly woman rocked in her wicker rocker as K sat on the mauve sofa laced with leafy designs of beige that was slightly worn and slightly dusty. The fire and its smokiness must have accounted for most of the cozy feeling that swept through K because she couldn't think of any other reason why she felt so good.

Everything was just lovely and perfect as if she'd stopped over for tea and crumpets in mid-afternoon, even though she didn't know what a crumpet was that didn't matter – they were good, she was sure of that. She was having a fine time, sitting there, not talking, smiling – like they were old friends, friends comfortable with silence. Maybe friends as far back as high school.

And maybe once they had even fallen for the same guy – a football player named Rock Highway. But everybody always called him Rocky – Rocky Road they called him, as kind of a nickname and kind of a joke, because of the ice cream flavor and all.

And whichever one of them he chose to be his girlfriend didn't matter because long before that they'd already decided no guy was worth their friendship and whoever he chose had turned him down flat. Which was good because a few years later he was already fat and bald and was drinking almost all of the time, anyway.

K raised her arm to wipe away some sweat that had formed there.

"Whew, it's kind of hot in here," she said, smiling at the woman. K looked toward the fireplace and wondered if a bird had got stuck in there or if the flew were completely open because it seemed more smoke was going into the room than up the chimney. Sometimes old people forget that stuff.

Through the hazy smoke, painted leaves dangled on thin vines in a straight line down the wallpaper. The foliose patterns like pea-green fairies dancing up the length of the wall and K let out a breath feeling calm, at home.

The plain furnishings, earthy tones, paintings of potted flowers, plastic flowers in ceramic pots on end tables – how nice this would be. How nice it would have been growing up in a normal house, not with a woman thinking she was a saint, sprinkling her sainthood on everyone she met like they were plastic flowers needing her divine water to become real.

Then Kathy remembered it was June and it was almost ninety degrees outside and the cozy memorabilia surrounding the fire quickly slipped into an eerie mass like Loch Ness. The woman across from K rocked silently, staring hard at Katherine, penetrating her eyes that were like shattered glass, anyway. The hard stare estranging her face, she looked almost wicked.

"We always knew you'd come," chirped her bird-like words. K's skin felt like it wanted to melt right off her bones and she wiped away some

281

more perspiration and swallowed hard.

"What do you mean?" asked Katherine. "You don't even know who I am."

"Oh, I know who you are, and I mean I'm ready. You can take me now, too."

Smoke from the fire was quickly filling the room and K wondered how the old woman could stand it, how old lungs and an old heart could take so much smoke.

"Take you?"

Kathy coughed, brought her hand to her mouth, chewed at the nail on her index finger, spit the remains out the side of her mouth.

"Come on, deary, you don't have to pretend with me, or shall I call you Satan?"

K was smoothing her rough fingernail against the enamel of one tooth as that word struck sharp inside her like it had teeth or jagged edges, somewhat like a dagger plunging into her gut as it left the old woman's mouth. An open wound lay where that word landed and K didn't know how to mend it or how to fill it or how to make it whole again. Something inside was sliced open and an unknown fear and an uncontrollable trembling came pouring out. K was shaking, even in a room that must have been a hundred degrees, or more, she shook like it was thirty.

"We waited for you for a long time. Then my Devin tried to escape you and that's when you found him, of course. I tried to worn him not to leave and you would be merciful. But then he had to die that horrible way, starving and cold and all. But I warned him, and I knew he had to pay for leaving you."

This old lady's a coot, I don't care how good her biscuits are, thought K. *A fire going in June? You don't have to listen to another word!*

But she did listen, and listen intently. The woman went on to explain how they'd been worshippers of hers, Satan's, since little Devin's birth when his father had died and left them alone. He'd gone with no one else for them to turn to. Christ had failed them – they had worshipped Jesus religiously and then that death, so why not worship the one who kills? Why not befriend Satan? She had long been awaiting this reunion with her master.

"No," K finally squeaked out of her pasty, numb lips. Her tongue felt like a dead dried-up slug sitting in her mouth rotting and festering. "No, you're mistaken. I'm not Satan." K's skin tingled from the heat and perspiration that poked through her pores like needles as she composed herself, brushed back her hair, then crossed her legs resting both hands on one knee.

"I'm Jesus."

"Oh no," laughed the old lady. "I know you try to deceive everyone, but we know who you are. Come, follow me," and she giggled in her excitement as if it were Christmas morning and she were only four years old.

K stood, her head spacey from too much smoke, and was led down a small hallway painted red with all kinds of dark, octagonal and sharp-pointed symbols on it. It must have scared the hell out of those little dwarfs because they were nowhere to be found and K's stomach tightened and her knees felt like they could no longer support her weight as she entered a room off to the right at the end of the hall.

"This was Devin's room."

K looked around in disbelief.

Shit – there were pictures of her everywhere. Drawings, maybe a hundred of them, maybe several hundred – all Katherine, and all with black eyes, soul-less eyes. *I could've done without this.*

"See, we know who you are. Now you take me, take me out of here. We hate this fucking place – this goddamn stupid world. We fucking hate it!"

The room was a swirl of blacks and reds, neon flashes of purple erupted every now and again on the walls and ceilings. Eyes everywhere. Eyes and eyes and all K's, all dark and all swirling and all haunting and K thought she would vomit. She brought up her cupped hand under her mouth as her stomach convulsed. But nothing was moving up, it was being pulled down – like her stomach was being sucked out from between her legs into the depths of that room. She felt like she was birthing a demon.

She ran. She ran as fast as she could out of that room and out of that house, the old woman trailing her with surprising speed, till they got to the door where red and yellow lights showered them from the dusty road.

A Deputy Sheriff leaned against the side of his car, his arms crossed. His mouth was working hard as if he were chewing something. K didn't even want to run away, he seemed safe. She walked over with her hands over her mouth, sat down in the back seat, shut the door. The world had gone mad.

Shadows hung from trees like victims from a rooftop. They were all hanging onto life by one leg caught. Every now and then one would fall and drop to the ground. And what did it matter? What was a life that was lived hanging on by a foot? What was a life lived with death spread out below like an ocean all the while? A whole life lived in fear of the inevitable death that lay beneath.

"What in the world...?"

"I know, K, I know."

"What in the world was that about? Oh, you just had to know didn't you? You just had to stop, fill up your ego with more stuff about K. You were just hoping he dreamed of you, longed for you even though he never even knew you! You just couldn't wait to hear it, could you, how you were the beautiful incubus that haunted his dreams all those years. Well, I guess you were. Are you fucking happy now!"

"I know, I know," she said, squishing her head with her hands. She squeezed her head hard like she could squeeze something out of it that made some sense. Hell, it didn't even have to make sense. Maybe she could squeeze out a thought that just looked pretty and smelled nice and that would be enough – something like orange juice or marmalade would be good. Even though she didn't know what marmalade was that didn't matter at this point, it had to be better than the lumpy, bloody feces in which she was drowning in the back seat of the Deputy Sheriff's car.

"What now, K? What-the-fuck-now!?"

"I don't know, K. I don't fucking know!"

The car moved slowly. Not slow enough to touch trees or talk to kids, but pretty slow. Slow enough to see the kids in detail, if they were there. Slow enough to hear them laughing as she passed by. Slow enough to give K a slight taste in her mouth of how carefree their small lives really are. That if they thought about something that was to take place much past dinner it must have been something huge – like grandma was coming over or they were going to have ice cream.

K could sense those things as she drove by, as slow as the car was going, but she couldn't get out and feel that way for herself. The car was moving too fast for that and even if it wasn't there were no kids out there so late. And even if there were, she wasn't one of them anymore and no matter how hard she tried or what kid games she played K could never be one again.

"Rocks are a pretty cool thing," said the Sheriff's Deputy as he strolled his car along the loose gravel and dirt road. Light from several street lamps cut through the dust they created. The town looked ethereal, distant and dream-like behind it. K momentarily lost herself in the deliberate surreal swirls of dust and the fingers of light that poked through. The town was somehow floating there. And whether it was real or not didn't make much difference. All that mattered was the wonderful sensation of watching dust float through street lamp lights.

"Huh?"

"Rocks," he repeated. "Pretty cool, don't you think?"

Her mind inched its way back to the present moment like an old mule plowing. Battered and beaten it slowly returned to the here and now and away from the salty piece of reality she had just tasted. K let out a breathy sigh.

"Big rocks or little rocks?" she asked, dropping her head to where her hand didn't have to reach up so high to knead the tension from her forehead and from around her eyes. Her eyes were wide for the night, but tired with shadowy rings underneath bleeding into the pale skin. Her hair in straggly, charcoal strands around her morose features.

"Hmmm…" He contemplated the question as if someone had asked him the meaning of life. "Big rocks or little rocks…" he repeated under his breath, "hmmm…."

His left arm rested against the open window and his left hand rubbed his jaw while he thought it over, hot air and dust flowing in all the while. *Jesus*, thought K. *It's not a trick question.*

"Uh, I dunno – little rocks, I 'spose. Just kinda cool, a little piece of earth in a hard gift-wrapping. You can skip 'em, kick 'em…" he paused, tried to think of more things you can do with little rocks. "You can …skip 'em," he repeated.

"No," K said flatly.

"No? No what? You can't skip 'em?"

"No, I don't think little rocks are cool. Big rocks are cool. Little rocks are just broken down, beaten up *pieces* of big rocks that were too weak and frail to make it as big rocks! They just couldn't hack it, couldn't run with the big boys. Little rocks are itsy-bitsy, teeny-weeny momma's boys – nine years old and still sucking their mamma's tit and wetting the goddamn bed all the time. No, little rocks are not cool. Little rocks are the pathetic losers of the rock world!"

They didn't talk much after that.

Her body ached like a dove. Incarcerate memories opening behind thin-paned glass. But it doesn't matter how thin, once you're trapped, you're done. Scientists once put a clear glass divider in a fish tank as an experiment. The fish, after bumping their noses on the glass several times, stopped trying to go to the other side. Then, they pulled the glass divider and the fish never tried to cross that imaginary barrier the rest of their lives.

A similar test was done with elephants. Experimenters tied several elephants to different posts with chains, then gradually went to less sturdy material until, finally, these two-ton, giant elephants were being held to posts with just a small rope. They could have snapped them like toothpicks, or simply walked away, pulling the thin posts from the dirt – but they never did. They lived in a thirty-foot prison, never trying to run away.

Life was like that, the articles in science magazines she'd read. Memories were like that – and K wished they'd find their freedom, but she didn't know how to convince them that they could leave any time.

Shadows from the window cast bars over K as she rubbed her finger on the rough mortar between the gray, smooth bricks to her side. It was bad enough to be in jail, but to have those ghost bars projected on her seemed inordinately cruel – the real bars imprisoning her body, their shadows imprisoning her soul. She imagined the grainy texture of mortar felt something like her ceiling – her off-white, bumpy, midtown apartment ceiling. K squinted, narrowing her field of vision so that she could only see the bumps, then brought up her hands to block out what the squinting could not, until finally only bumps remained.

"Ahhh," she said, as she lay like a fetus on her cot, staring at the line of bumps she was pretending was a whole ceiling.

The mattress springs squeaked on rusted coils as she turned on her back, her T-shirt damp from heat and sticking to her skin. The cot above was put together in a make shift way, as if the Deputy had done it himself. Four screws held the top springs in place, hanging down two or three inches. They were sharp, like vampire fangs or maybe even the fangs of Satan. *I mean surely he has fangs*, she thought, knowing sleep would be difficult with those things over head.

The rusted springs coiled designs of hardened serpents, spinning and spinning up toward some unknown altar of reprise where they'd be forgiven and given wings. Or, perhaps they where being fooled, and the altar was sacrificial where their heads would be cut off clean and quick with a machete or sickle.

She stuck a finger into a coil, felt the roughness brush against her skin as she tried to center it so no metal was touching. She wished it would clamp down firm but not painful, perfect and symmetrical touching all the skin on her finger at once, just for the feel of the pressure on her index. After she put each finger of both hands into the coil one by one, she lowered her hand again, let it rest like a rose flower across her breast, fingers spread like tired petals.

Darkness fell on K in the shape of a huge crow, its giant wing moving across her like a fan. Gentle cooing sounds followed. She turned to gaze at the bars on the window listlessly, then shook her head in disbelief. It was the 39th Street Bird.

"My body aches like a dove," she thought, it skipped across her consciousness like a little rock on a pond. A child practicing for some competition that would never happen, skipping rocks endlessly till they leapt off the water like it was ice.

"Perhaps. Perhaps a lover unloved."

"Hmmm, possibly…." she pondered, the little rock of that thought skipping to its end, sinking deep into the pond, leaving ever widening ripples in its wake. "I don't know, K, all I know is I'm tired."

"I'm tired to," she said. "Damn tired." The cot squeaked as she turned to her right, pulled up the sheet she was lying on, held it close to her heart.

"Yeah, damn tired. Damn tired of looking at the sun, damn tired of looking at the rain. Tired of looking at the night, tired of looking at the day. Tired of looking at the love, tired of looking at the hate, and it all looks the same."

"It all looks the same, my God, that's exactly how I feel!"

"I know, K. It all looks the same." She dropped the sheet from her clutch and brought her fingers to her mouth where they squeezed and turned her pouty bottom lip over and over.

A plane was about to take off. A plane was about to crash and destroy something beautiful. Katherine was stuck in jail and her body ached like a dove. She was alone and scared and had to just be that, because there was no where else to go and no one else to be.

Her mind turned and turned, twisted like her lower lip between thin fingers with rough nails. Surely, she was missing something, not seeing things correctly. There was a way out of here – had to be. A kitten raised in a room with only horizontal lines will never be able to see vertical ones. That was tested too. The adult cats that grew up in those conditions would run into the legs of chairs in a normal room, because they couldn't see them. Because their nervous system couldn't understand the information, it simply blotted it out. We only see what we know.

The Deputy Sheriff sat reading a newspaper, his legs over the metallic desk with rounded vinyl corners in wood print and heavy pullout drawers. On one side of the desk was a square beige phone and a light with a red button and black button on the base and a semi-flexible metal arm coming up to hold the long, rectangular light. A pen carnival was stuffed with things that really didn't belong there – a rectangular eraser, some electrical tape, a pack of Wrigley Spearmint Gum, only one pen.

The jail hadn't been updated in awhile and she wondered what they were so busy doing that they couldn't get a cordless phone or a lamp from this decade. Occasionally he would take a sip from a shiny metal container with a screw top that, to K, smelled like whiskey or some kind of cheap bourbon.

"What happens now?" she asked, turning to lie on her side that faced towards the Deputy. His small shoulders were slouched and curled over the newspaper. He was quaky. Kids used to make fun of him, K could see that. The picture of his life was drawn all over him in red and brown crayons. He was a cop because he didn't want to be picked on anymore.

"Now we wait until morning, till they come pick ya up." His poky arm reached again for the flask, took it to his lips.

"They?" asked K, conjuring up images of federal agents with an entourage of swap police officers with semi-automatic rifles accompanying them.

"City cops. Ya gots warrants out in Kansas City. They're gonna come get ya tomorrow and I don't know what happens after that." He flipped up his paper to continue reading.

"Whew," she was in some deep shit. "We don't call them city cops where I come from, we just call them...*cops*," she thought. Somehow calling them city cops made them sound a step above, something better than a country cop or any cop that wasn't from the city and couldn't handle the complexities of a master minded criminal like K. "Gotta bring in the big boys."

"Now, when you get the FBI after you, *then* you're something." She turned over again, pressed her head onto the cool bricks beside her. "Why do you think these crazy things?"

"I don't know, K, I wish I did. They're next to pointless, a waste of energy." She cupped both hands into prayer on her chest, "Dear God, grant me serenity."

"What!?" She yanked her hands apart. "Fuck serenity – that damn word again? Am I supposed to just accept that little girl's death and do nothing? Leave her dead and me unconcerned? No, damnit, there must be a way to save that little girl. I refuse to accept and do nothing!"

K pounded the side of her fist into the wall. "Fuck these fucking walls! I gotta get out of here. I can't save Amy trapped in these four fucking walls!"

She pounded her fist again, even though the first one hurt and she wished she hadn't done it. Her hand hit with a dull thud, without an echo. A squeak from the Deputy's chair pulled her attention as he leaned back and ruffled his paper.

"What if you could..." she thought, turning to lie flat, her disrupted breath rolling from her stomach to her chest in a choppy wave.

"Could what?"

"What if..." thought K. "What if you could rewrite that story?" She sat upright quick, almost bumped her head on one of the screws hanging from the cot above.

"Wait a second. Rewrite the story?" She swung her feet over the side of the cot, pulled herself to the edge.

"Yeah, K. You're the one with the power here. Rewrite the story, or just the ending, that would do."

"Of course, rewrite the ending! Maybe it's not premonitions. Maybe, I create them. I am Jesus, after all." She sat hunched over the side of the cot tapping a finger against her pursed lips. "Yes...rewrite...yes, yes, yes."

"Now, K, flirt with the cop a little and get what you need. This is what we women do."

She stood and straightened her damp, wrinkled shirt, brushed back her long, dusty bangs over the small curve of her right ear.

"Flirt. Got it."

K went to the bars, sauntering through her beige, cotton shorts. She wrapped one hand around a bar like a snake, slid her bare knee through.

"Excuse me, officer? Do you have a dictionary here?" she said, sounding about as sexy as she could while still just asking for a dictionary.

"I'm not an officer, lady, I'm a Deputy Sheriff," he said quickly through tight, almost closed lips. He was tall and slender, maybe a little too slender, but not terribly bad looking. A *why not* if she had met him at Bells' with street clothes on. But, sitting there with his hat on and that stupid brown uniform, a *why.*

"Well, excuse me, Deputy Sheriff sir, do you have a dictionary here or not?"

"Nope." He flipped the paper back up to read, sunk into the green vinyl chair that hissed as more air escaped from the cusion.

Katherine inched closer, pressed her face against the bars letting her breasts poke between the iron shafts. They pulled tight her thin T-shirt, making it almost see-through. When he didn't notice, she began screaming.

The hard surroundings resonated with the rattling of the cage and her shouts for a dictionary. Soon, the tirade turned into tears and sobs, begging.

"Please, Deputy Sheriff, I need a dictionary! Please..." she cried.

After a few minutes, the Deputy Sheriff threw down his paper and went toward the back part of the building through a door that he shut behind him. K didn't know if he'd return, but a moment later he was back with a small dictionary no bigger than the size of his hand.

"Will this do?" he asked, handing it through the bars.

"Yes," she said, sniffling.

"Anything else?"

K stopped crying and wiped away the remaining tears, "A pen... and some paper, if you have them."

She stared at the tiny red dictionary for quite some time.

"Come on little guy, you can do it. I know you got it in ya. Now show me those words. Show me the words that will lead me to another ending of this story. Come on little guy, you can do it!" She pulled in a slow breath and opened the dictionary, writing down the first handful of words she saw. It was titled before it was even written. *Safe at Home.*

Poleax – n. A long handled battle-ax. Any ax with a spike.

Stenopaic – a. A narrow slit or opening.

Pander – n. A pimp in the story of Troilus and Cressida. A go between in a sexual intrigue.

Saber – n. A cavalry sword with a broad and heavy blade.

Pulmonary – a. Affecting the lungs.

Hypnotics – n. Any drug causing sleep.

Floccus – n. A tuft, or wool of hair.

Dove-like – a. Having the characteristics of a dove, mild, gentle, pure.

Stellionate – n. In Scots and Roman law, any fraud that has no special name to distinguish it.

Puissant – a. Powerful, strong, mighty.

Pechyotia – a. Having large ears. Big-eared.

Stellar – a. Of the stars. Like the stars.

Egesta – n. Any waste matter passed out of the body.

Glaucoma – n. A disease of the eye, characterized by great tension within.

Amass – vt. To collect into a heap, to gather a great quantity of.

Seared – vt. To wither, to dry up. To scorch the surface as to make dry and hard.

Flite – n. Scolding, a quarrel, a dispute.

Fallow – n. Land that lay untilled or unseeded. To leave unseeded after plowing to make the soil richer.

Effusive – a. The act of pouring out. Unrestrained or emotional expression.

Safe at Home

"Goddamnit!" he yelled, slamming shut the bedroom door. "Ooops!" He'd forgotten about his wife's friend asleep on the couch. "Goddamnit," he said, softer, wanting to kick something, but not wanting to make the noise.

He turned on the desk lamp and carefully turned up the lights over the fireplace, not too bright, revealing a mounted poleax and saber against the rock wall.

Feverishly he rubbed the cartilage between his two, stenopaic eyes, waffling between that and his temples. The tension was amassing.

"Maybe glaucoma," he mused. "And maybe the doctor will have to prescribe you a prime bag of weed and you can smoke your cares away!"

But it wasn't glaucoma, just another flite with the wife on the usual subject – sex, or the lack thereof. He needed a pander of the Gods to pry her cold legs open.

"That frigid bitch. You know, sex is a natural part of life. Maybe the goddamn essence of life itself!" But he was persuading the wrong person. Sex was A-O.K. with him, not that he particularly enjoyed it with his wife anymore. Her seared twat left a bit to be desired. But on nights like tonight, after several months without any, that dried up cunt would do just fine.

There was a stir on the couch. "Uh, oh. I hope I didn't wake her."

His wife's best friend since high school had passed through town, she decided to stay the night since the two of them got drunk as hell together. He looked at the empty bottle of wine on the table next to the prescription hypnotics.

"Nope. She's out cold, won't be up for a long time, if at all," he thought. "Another stupid bitch. Drugs and booze – good combo, lady."

294

He noticed the blanket she was using had fallen to the floor. "And on top of dying, you'll probably get pneumonia," he added.

He went over to pick up the blanket and cover her. He paused there to admire the dove-like complexion of her face in profile, then reached down for the blanket.

"Oh God," he noticed, "she's not wearing any panties."

She was lying face down wearing nothing but a T-shirt, which had hiked half-over her also dove-like bottom. Her floccus mound caught him in a griping stare and he found it difficult to turn away.

"Now there's some fallow land I'd like to sow."

"You sick fuck," he thought, disgusted with himself. He dropped the blanket and dashed to the window. Standing with arms crossed he tugged at his lower lip, pondering the situation. It was already too late, he was over-run with desire. His chest heaves came in waves of pulmonary crests, fast and rhythmic as he looked out into the night. His pechyotia reflection in the window startled him.

"You big-eared bastard, don't do this!"

"But she'll never know, no one will ever know. It's not even a crime, it's a stellionate. If a tree falls in the forest...?" he asked.

He made a gesture to God, the sky and the stars above, "Oh Lord, why did you put this before me? Help me, I want it so badly! I need it!" His latest plea went unnoticed as the stars sent light, but no answers, and a surge of hunger raged into his chest and throat.

He moved to the sofa and shook her gently, she did not move. He shook her again with more force – nothing. He wet his hand with saliva and placed it between her legs, still she did not move. It was safe, she was out cold. In an effusive manner, he dug in and removed his rigid penis from his jeans and was in her in one swift, puissant move.

Time stood still. He had fallen into a pool of ecstasy – the unbearable excitement of it, the incredible wrong-ness, the immense fear of being caught. What was he doing? This was crazy. But he couldn't stop.

His head dropped back and forward slowly and unconsciously. He closed his eyes, felt her warm tightness wrap around him. When he opened them again, she had turned her face toward him, opening her eyes. He jumped back startled and in disbelief. Then there was nothing. All went black.

A moment passed and then he could see the floor next to his face and blood filling up around him.

"I think this is a good way to die," he thought. "I wasn't even expecting it." His thoughts puddled out of the small hole in his head. His thoughts puddled around him, drowning in the blood at his side.

He lay in the bloody egesta pouring out of him. Above him stood his wife, and in her hand, gleaming in the stellar light, an antique poleax, dripping blood.

Night wore on like a train on an endless track. It was bumpy and loud. It made much noise but said nothing, because the night was ugly and ashamed. It wore an old party dress that its mother said would be just fine to go to prom in. But it didn't want to. It knew it would be laughed at if it showed up in that dress. And her date wasn't too hot either. He was a dork, really, but the night was poor and unpopular, void of any color or light and while, at times, it wore much jewelry the other kids thought it was too much and gaudy and prom would be hellish just like every other day of high school. It might as well go in drag than go in that old party dress.

"Yeah, go in drag," thought K. "If you're going to be laughed at you'd might as well make a point of it. Maybe you could talk your date into switching outfits and wear the ..."

"Jesus, K. Fuck! What are you talking about – the night going to prom in drag? You are a freak! Shut up, just shut the hell up! Amy's about to die, you don't have time for your little daydreams – you've got to get out of here!"

"What do you want me to do? The story failed. It's not even about that and I'm not busting my ass trying to save *that* guy. Looks like the dumb shit got what he deserved!"

K slid off the bunk, slinked toward the deputy.

"Here, officer, you can have your dictionary back," she stated, dejectedly handing the book through the bars. He yawned and took off his hat, came to the cell, "I'm not an officer, lady, I'm a Deputy Sheriff." He said the *Deputy Sheriff* part so fast and staccato it sounded like *Dipidy Sharf.*

"Oh my God, what a big-eared freak!" K thought, seeing the Dipidy Sharf without his hat on for the first time. And then it hit her, and everything fell into place.

As she turned over to lie face down on the cot, she hiked up her T-shirt over her bare bottom under the covers, still unsure if she wanted to participate in this voluntary rape that was about to occur. She was pleased with how she had set everything up, though, and that it was a solid plan.

She'd asked the Deputy for a drink from his metallic canister, being sure to inform him how poorly alcohol affected her and that with just a few sips she'd be out for the night – that nothing could awaken her. To top it off she asked for some Tylenol-3 from her purse and popped several into her mouth while she finished off the booze in his container. Then she slid under the blanket and stripped, leaving on only her T-shirt.

She tossed and turned, let the blanket fall to the ground, leaving her fully exposed. And there she waited silently as if asleep. It seemed like hours had passed. *Goddamnit! It's not going to work*, she thought. Then she realized how much the booze and Tylenol had hit her and how little sleep she'd had in the last few days. Her mind swirled in exhaustion, she became drowsy, fell into a dream.

The halls of Heaven were desolate. It was like a ghost town. There were no flashes, no movement – as if everyone had packed up and left. There were places, as she walked down a narrowing corridor, where the walls were so thin she could see right through them, and spots further down where cracks formed and appeared to bleed. At least a blood-like substance was flowing out of them, or into them, from some outside source. K thought back to what she had read on the bathroom walls at Bells'. *And a bird sang unto me – stay away from Heaven. It's a nice place to be, but its days are ending.*

A chill ran through her that spread out like a pond turning to ice. All this, this beautiful, perfect place beginning to crumble. What would be left for humanity? What would happen to the world if Heaven were no more? If there were no longer a place of refuge to go to after a long, hard life on Earth?

And what role did she play in this? Did she drive God to send Jesus back – send *her* back to Earth? Was it her inability to accept the things she could not change or to be able to distinguish the difference between what she could? Her inability to understand serenity, even to try to understand it? Was there a beast growing inside of her disrupting the delicate balance of the universe? The more it grew, the more Heaven would fall, she thought.

And why was it all placed on her shoulders, anyway? Why did the fate of the universe have to hinge on her finding out the truth to this mess?

Now she was floating through desolate halls knowing that she could not stay, even if she wanted to, and that her very leaving may cause it to collapse. And when it collapsed, that would mean the end of it all, the end of life – the end of existence. Nonetheless, soon she would have to wake up and leave here – just wake up and walk away – wake up, K – *wake up.*

She awoke to a dull, flat moving pressure from behind. Disoriented and startled she jerked her head quickly around to look. The movement suddenly stopped and she saw the frozen eyes of the Deputy Sheriff. They didn't move. His face didn't move. His wide-open mouth didn't move. She wiggled out from underneath him, feeling as if she were still in a dream. What was this surreal place that made the Deputy Sheriff stand frozen like that with his body angled and his head flat against the top bunk?

She stepped off the cot and moved to look. He had jerked back, skewering his skull on one of the fangs of Satan, a screw that hung down past the springs. He slid off the nail onto the squeaking cot, blood poured from the small hole in his head. In a mad scramble K got dressed, took his keys, and left.

VII

IF ANYTHING in this world is similar to God, it would have to be the wind. Does it originate, have a starting point? Or is it a continuing process that has no beginning and no end? I wonder what it feels as it sweeps across hills and plains, through the hair of children in schoolyards, through the leaves and twigs in a cemetery. If it feels, it must feel everything it touches at once, simultaneously. It knows you as it blows over you. And then it is gone and yet still sweeps through you.

If it could love, that would be the best kind of love – an out of nowhere, surprise gift of love passing over, showering its love equally and without prejudice on ants and bugs, flowers and trees, and people too. If the wind could love, that would be the best kind of love. The perfect love.

Wind raged, nearly blowing her off the shoulder several times as K was bent intently over the steering wheel of her stolen Deputy Sheriff's car, her mind dreamy, tired. The wind was rampant that night, so much so that if its strong push in front of her continued she feared she might not make it on time. Frantically it moved, as if searching the plains for a lost love. *Maybe the wind has no true love to find,* she was thinking. *Maybe his love is too powerful, too engulfing. You could get lost in a love that strong, never see yourself again.*

Maybe the wind has no love because everyone just turns away, shelters themselves from it, not wanting that much love – not wanting that perfect love. How could they return it, they would feel forever inadequate. It is too much, better not to receive it at all.

"Poor wind," K said aloud, "still searching. Just searching and searching and what are you searching for? Don't you have everything you need? Can't you just take a break and stop searching? There's nothing here for you. There's nowhere to go and nowhere to be."

The day moved from warm morning to hot afternoon to muggy early evening. It had passed slowly, as anxious as she was and as aware of the time and aware of being caught. But she didn't pass any police, not one. She wondered how long it took them to find that Deputy's body. She wondered how hard they were looking for her – what their plan was.

Maybe they'd found him there, his dick hanging out of his pants smelling of sex, and figured it out pretty quick. Maybe they were discussing their options. Maybe their search wasn't so intense after that – not wanting the publicity when K made her one phone call to *The Kansas City Star.*

But she was getting close, had to be. She could feel it, feel it in her very guts. Each moment that passed heightened her presence, her awareness of just being there. And the sickness in her stomach was of a child about to perform in a school play.

"But I don't want to wear that costume!" screamed the little girl. "It makes me look stupid!"

"Everyone is waiting for you to go on," chided the teacher, "We don't always get to choose our roles in life, but we do have to play our part. Do you hear me, K? Or shall I call you Katherine?" The voice was haunting, echoing down winding tunnels inside her, and K was speechless when she realized she was the little girl.

"Everyone has to play their part, Katherine. If everyone decided not to play their role, then we wouldn't have a play at all, now would we? Come on Katherine, you're not K. That's not your role. You're Katherine – Katherine of the St. Catherine Catherines. It's a beautiful role for a beautiful little girl. Accept who you are and your acceptance will set you free. Your very acceptance will be the path you walk that takes you home."

302

"No. No, just shut the hell up! I don't know who I am anymore." Tears came again. How many tears had been locked up inside her all those years? She'd cried more in six months than she had in her whole life. "I don't care! I don't even care who I am. I don't want to play any parts anymore. I don't care if I'm Jesus or if I'm Satan or just Katherine, they all look the same. What's the difference? I feel like I'm all of those things, all of them, and I don't want to be any. I don't want to be anything anymore. Can't I just go home?" K cried. "Can't I?"

But there was no answer. There was no teacher, no nervous little girl. Just K alone in her stolen cop car talking to no one at all, with the unmistakable lights of a distant airport approaching fast. Whether K liked it or not, her role was about to continue, Katherine was going on.

The tires made a God-awful screech skidding over the curb onto the walkway. It was seven o'clock, and if the plane hadn't already taken off, it was getting ready to.

"Alright, K, play it cool – real cool. Use your head, you've got to be smarter this time!"

"Smart – got it!"

In the dry, flat air and fluorescent brightness bouncing off concrete and stones and ceramic tiles, K ran – breathless. Then, soundless.

Pictures moved around her, by her, but they were blurs in the night. The lights, the glass, the people, the furnishings – a milky canvas of insignificant artifacts, unfocused lines of minutiae.

Outside, past the main terminal, the stars gleamed in a simple, naive way. Sound was coming again in warbled waves. Muffled shouts trailed her, and K pulled her eyes from the spotted stillness above to see a scattering of small planes on the blacktop loading area and several more moving on the concrete landing strip.

To her right, a small silver plane with tiny windows and blue stripes was being boarded by a handful of people. The plane was so small it looked like a toy as the people climbed up the four or five steps into the silvery craft, several more waiting to board.

One of them was a little girl with pasty white skin and jet black hair. She was perfect. Her face was painted in purity – whitewashed in innocence. She was embossed with beauty the way angels are embossed with tenderness – the way Jesus is embossed with compassion. The girl turned to look up and smile at the passenger behind her and her smile dripped of the divine. And when she stopped smiling, she still dripped of the divine.

Kathy was stunned, it must have been what it was like to be next to Jesus two thousand years ago. How his disciples must have felt every time he came near them and how their bodies automatically bent and bowed when he entered the room without thought or motive, just a natural reflux to seeing his face.

K, too, wanted to kneel – wanted to kneel and make a prayer to what she had just seen, to whatever it was she felt at that moment. But there was no time.

"Stop! Stop that plane! Stop!" K ran as fast as she could, and she wished for stronger legs. Her heart pounded, and she wished for a better heart. Not just a stronger heart, a heart that would pump more oxygen through her veins to get her there faster. But a better heart. One that could open up and feel everything seeing Amy's face made her want to feel. She didn't know what she was going to do when she got there, but she had to get there, that much she knew.

The little girl's eyes got wide and full like Holy Water in a slate white benetier as Kathy approached, running and breathless. In mid-stride she swept Amy off the ground and held her close, wrapped her hand around Amy's head – Amy's arms were tight around K's neck, and they both started to cry.

Together they embraced as everything around them went into slow motion. Her awareness was there – the look of confusion on everyone's face, the shouts of the guards behind her, and they were all slow and garbled. None of that mattered, none of it. Everything was all right now, she'd found her – she had gotten there. She'd swept Amy off her feet into someplace warm and safe and nothing could hurt her now.

She wanted to put that moment in a wine casket and let it age alone and separate from the rest of her life. Thirty years from now she would let it out and see how it had grown. She would see what it had become on its own without the vinegar of her life to taint it, rot it and leave it without worth.

But K must have been moving too fast when she grabbed Amy, because she was falling. She hadn't even noticed. In a slow, fluid motion she fell and as she did the arms of Amy loosened from her neck. Someone grabbed Amy and K no longer held that precious thing close.

She was flat on her stomach, then, on the hard concrete. Weight was on top of her. She'd been tackled or jumped on after hitting the ground. K twisted around in her slow motion state, watching Amy disappear into the tiny craft in the arms of a guard.

"No," shouted K in a slow dragging voice that sent a shiver through her spine as she reached out. Amy reached also, stretched her arms out to K over the shoulder of the guard.

"Kathy!" she yelled.

K lay helpless on the ground, two guards pinning her with their knees. Then Amy was gone. The other guard came out, the plane pulled away.

The drive out of the airport left cuts as if she were riding naked and bareback on a horse through thick trees in winter – no leaves to soften the scrape of hard, dead limbs on her bare skin as she rode. The cold air adding to the pain of her cuts like salt and lemon.

They had believed her story, that she was Amy's aunt. No one was there to disclaim it. Amy's mother had already said her good-byes, leaving her in the care of the parishioner, needing to venture back to the farm hours earlier. So they let Kathy go, thinking that Amy did look like she knew her, they looked like mother and daughter, anyway. The guards only admonished her for running back to the restricted area without being checked in, and apologized for tackling her saying that normally they wouldn't have, but they were on heightened security due to death threats on the parishioner's life.

Apparently the warrant for her arrest and her picture hadn't made it to that part of Kansas yet. Or, if they had, whoever got it had shoved it in a drawer and forgotten about it like all the rest of them. So she was free – if you could call it that. Free to follow her bitter heart to the remains of the wreck she knew wouldn't be far away.

"I don't make suggestions, anymore," she said into the rear-view mirror. She was pretending she was some future K, looking into a full-length mirror in some future bedroom, talking to someone who wasn't even there – someone who'd asked for help. "I don't make suggestions, and I don't try to help. I don't want the responsibility." She would brush the hair off her shoulder after that. The new Katherine would be liquid cool. She had ice blue eyes, like Christmas lights. She didn't know why or how her eyes would change from chestnut to ice blue – maybe like what happens in the breath mint commercials. She'd even get the colored contacts, if she had to.

Fear like cattle prods pushed her along, something going through her like prongs pressing out from within. Pinecones hung in the trees like bats, their oblong shrouded selves waiting for the perfect time to jump into the dark night, ready for the hunt. Apathy was coming. Apathy was the invisible force field that kept everything safe. It was lowering over her in a big bubble, dripping full of putty and egg whites, plasma, and the stringy bloody water that had broke from every expectant mother who had ever lost a child.

Soon there was a light in the sky and the inevitable corridor of black smoke that followed tunneled through the night like a tornado set on its side. The noise of it reached her less than a second after the flash, she wasn't far.

It had been loud, God-awful. That was the worst kind of awful there was. But K's body remained calm, quiet. Her heart didn't race and the expression on her face stayed placid. Apathy was there. What did it matter now? What did anything matter now? She knew when Amy had been pried from her arms what would happen next. That was the worst part of it, having her there, holding her, then not being strong enough to stop it. K wished she were superman. Superman, and Bruce Lee.

Even stars could be bad now for all K knew, or cared. But she continued driving in a steady pace till she saw the flames and smoke billowing out of a field a few miles ahead. Across the field, in a patch of loose and thick dirt at the base of a dried up ravine, the car stalled, would no longer move. She pulled herself out, climbed over the dirt cliff face of the dry ravine, walked the remaining half mile, or so, to the wreckage.

The heat was intense, it could be felt a hundred yards from the flames, but K kept walking. Twisted and burnt metal lie in the line it had fallen from the sky to the earth. Pieces of the engine, a panel from the cockpit, chairs and bodies – all burnt, all partial. One of the seats was planted in the soft dirt of the field they'd landed in, tilted at an angle. There was a flame a few feet in front of it, some burning head on the ground, and she knew it was Amy in that chair watching it all as if she were safe at home perched in front of her rock-lined fireplace.

She slowly moved toward Amy, dragging her feet, heavy like cinder blocks, deeper and deeper into the dirt hoping somehow the land would hold her tight, not let her move any farther. She'd like to be stuck firm into the ground, solidify into a rigid fleshy thing – a place where crows came to peck when they were hungry. A place where wolves could practice snarling in packs – attacking her legs, ripping out the hard fleshy stuff. But the land didn't stop her, and soon K was at Amy's side.

Something had torn through the front of Amy's neck, probably metal propelled from the initial explosion, but her face was untouched and K went to her and kneeled at her side with her head down – waiting to be blessed. But it never happened.

Amy was clutching a heart-shaped pendant on a sliver chain. It dangled from her hand where she also gripped a piece of folded paper so tightly K didn't know if she could remove them.

Inside the locket was a picture. It must have been her mother. It could have just as easily been K, the way it looked in the dark with the flame dancing off the glass, but that would've been impossible. Kathy wondered if somewhere, somehow, in some other world K got to be Amy's mother, for just a little while.

She took the paper and the locket, she would mail the locket to Amy's mother – she made herself promise that she would. She kissed Amy on the forehead, then left.

Kathy? Kathy, can you hear me? Who are you Kathy? I dream of you most times. I dream of you even in the days. How can this be, Kathy? I am not afraid of you. I am not afraid of most things.

I have a secret to share with you. I have a secret that I can tell no one – not my Mommy, not my best friend, Becky. And not even my invisible friend, Angel, who lives in the closet and quiets my ears when the loud bells come. But I will tell you.

I have seen the TV. Even late in the night when my mommy doesn't want me to see. I have seen the world and the most scary things in the world. I have seen the news.

And, while I am not afraid, I do want to say something that sounds scary. Soon, I will no longer be. I will not be alive, like I see so many people on TV, not alive. I don't know why this is. I think if I would have seen you, Kathy, you would have told me why. You could have made me understand. You are like an empty pool that surrounds me sometimes, makes everything else whither into irrelevance.

So when I shut my eyes this final time, I hope it will be you that I see when I wake. And you can take me by the hand and make me understand why things had to be this way.

Mommy says I'm going to save the world someday from the terrible mess it's in. But I think you will do that, become the empty pool the world dives into to find God. I think I'm going to become a star in the night's sky. Look for me, and I'll twinkle extra hard – just for you.

The night was coffee and sparkled with the marshmallow pieces of Katherine's shattered reality. Stars were a picture of insanity gone calm – they were a lifetime of broken dreams dead, dried and buried in the empty spaces of the night.

The stillness she felt was of a lost lake. A placid, whispering lake lost in the foothills of a mountain ravine. Its stillness crept over her as she slipped beneath the surface. Piecemeal she went. Inch by inch, hair by hair, deeper and deeper into the lost lake. The line of water cut below her lip, then slipped over with the vivid sensation of separation between wet submerged skin and dry, breathing skin between her upper lip and nostrils.

The lost lake simplified things, it made this world a whisper, the whisper of a distant memory. Silently it called to her from deep within her and she called back. *I'm here. I'm here*, she'd say. *I'm coming.* When a breeze skimmed off its surface, it would call to her again, and this is what the lost lake would say –

Shhhhh...

The hissing whisper would disappear into the vastness of the mountain ravine, rustling leaves that had fallen and the tall green grass. Then another breeze would tickle the top and, *Shhhhh...*

From a distance, sirens wailed. But buried within her lost lake they sounded like a dream, the lingering shadows of a world since forgotten. Tiny threads in the macramé of K's existence hardly felt as they wove into the permanence of her life. Hardly felt, hardly noticed as they came, passed her by, and went. Just like everything always had. Just like every other moment in K's lusterless life, coming – coming, going – going, gone. And never here.

No one was left. They'd all gone away too – Amy, Calliope, Becky. Leaves that had fallen, leaves that K got to dance with in her eyes and heart till they fell to the ground or got swept away by some big wind or even a gentle breeze. That was enough to make them all disappear, a gentle breeze.

"I'm glad there's no one left," she thought. "I'm glad there's no one left to call. That's when the pain comes, slices through your skin like razor blades. When you hear that voice again it only reminds you how much you've missed them. You can go for years without seeing a person and be fine with it. Then, in a second, all your hard work is destroyed like a sandcastle you'd thought was a fortress made of stone just by seeing their face.

"I'm glad there's no one left, nothing left to hang onto. That's when the pain comes – comes on hard like Jesus on the cross sometime before, *Thy will be done. Thy kingdom come.*"

She didn't remember why she wasn't driving or when or where the car had stopped. She didn't know how long she'd been walking or in which direction but judging from the many cuts, nicks and dried blood on her bare legs, she must have been walking for some time. Must have passed through thicket, must have passed through dusty fields and dried up streams.

And, judging from the glowing, murky pinkness that spread itself across the horizon like a fragrance seen, K was heading east and dawn was approaching. She looked up to see the remains of a black night behind her turning into dark, glowing blues. It had been windy that night, wind raged clearing the plains like a fire. It was good, she thought, her tracks might be covered. It was the kind of night that looked out for runaways like her, closing the door behind so no one could follow. She was safe, for now. She would miss the night, the night was forgiving. The day would be hard and angry.

By the time the sun was beating down on her directly overhead, punishing her as though she was the unwanted step-child of God, K's steps were infant-like, her skin – dirt covered, her hair – a morass. K's body was beaten and worn, the shredded up toy doll of a playful kitten. The still, placid lake had disappeared and in its stead a dried up corner of reality and pain that searched for new and better ways to torture her. It was a scorched world where withered dreams lie like wilted flowers,

311

their seared and singed petals scattered in the barren wasteland, dried beyond recognition.

Hope was there, but not like she'd known hope to be, not the innocence of hope – the hope of roses sent, not that kind of hope. And not like a vibrancy of colors exploding into existence through a flower garden, the hope of a new spring. That was the hope of fools and pedestrians walking the concrete sidewalks of life hoping they would turn into gold lined paths that led straight to Heaven – in the end, fall would come, then winter. And not the hope of a child playing *she loves me, she loves me not*, on the petals of a daisy. That kind of hope had died a thousand years ago for K.

This hope was the hope of fear. This hope was simply fear in disguise. It clinged to the edge of K's barren wasteland like a single begotten flower growing on the side of a cliff, hoping for rain, hoping for other flowers to grow along side. It hoped for anything except that which it had, it feared its own existence. And it feared, even worse, its own death.

Hope was there clinging for life, but where was the life to cling to in this desertous place where nothing existed, where was the life? And if this was the life Katherine was clinging to, maybe it was just as well she slip off the edge and grab on tight to that single wilting flower of hope, and together they could set eachother free – free from the death of life as they tumbled back to their home with God.

The day had gone and night was there, strong and bold, and the slight drop in temperature was a huge relief. Kathy lay exhausted in an open field of farmland. Stars were so close you could grab them, reach out and pluck one out of the sky and drop it in your belly button. Belly buttons would be a good place for a star, K thought, tingly and alive and making it feel like she was laughing even though she wouldn't be – even though she had no reason to be, she could feel that way with a star inside. She reached out a hand that covered five or six stars at once, but when she pulled them down they must have slipped through her fingers because her hand remained empty.

One star shined more than the others, white and pure like a diamond. Perhaps it was Amy twinkling extra hard just for her, just as she had promised. Perhaps not. Perhaps it was all utter, bitter nonsense. The kind of nonsense you could buy for a buck and a quarter from a guy on the street in a long trench coat. A buck and a quarter wouldn't buy you very good utter, bitter nonsense, either. It would take at least ten or twenty bucks to get the good stuff. The stuff you couldn't see through for at least a week or two. You could live happily with twenty-dollar utter, bitter nonsense in your pocket for quite some time until it became thin and worn and you could start to see the truth again.

Then you'd have to hunt down that street vendor and buy some more, the hundred-dollar version. Hers was already fading after only one day. Amy was just a kid, anyway. What did she know?

Many noises haunted the night, more than she could have imagined – coyotes, wolves and the sound of a skirmish. The howl of being bitten into. Things slithered in the dry grass next to her and rustled the trees that cupped the land like a horseshoe. Kathy had never slept outside before. She'd never even been camping. She rolled to her left, pulled some tall, dead grass to her chest like a blanket, "Super lock force-field – on."

Dreams were wrestled and tightly fit in the hands of a beast where Katherine lie entwined with the other bloody and naked prisoners. The beast would sometimes reach in a hand and pluck one out with pointy fingernails, drop it in his mouth like a sardine. Soon, there were only a few left. One, bearded and thin, kneeled on the hot and moist blue-green palm praying to some God K had never heard of. He made a sign over his chest, but it wasn't a cross, a similar gesture used by people from other worlds that pray to Gods however they understand them.

It was something like mythology, life was. Would people a thousand years from now think that about our society? That the God we prayed to was like the Romans and Greeks praying to Zeus and Athena, or Hades.

The guy kissed a chain around his neck. He was next. Only K was left. When the beast reached for her, she laughed.

She awoke to another hot sun and it appeared the drought that flooded the Midwest was going to continue for at least one more day. Coming up over a small ridge that headed into a strip of gully, she skid her feet through the dry land, a stream used to be there, but not anymore. Only uprooted rocks that were now bare and dull remained. The luster had gone. They were like her. She thought to pick one up, turn it over, see if the underside was still wet and cool.

A pretty stream had covered what she was and made her look lustrous and magical beneath it. She had glimmered in the false light. But now she knew it wasn't the rocks inside of her that glimmered, it was the temporary stream on top. Now she was getting to the bones of her existence, who she really was and she fought desperately to keep those thoughts from coming.

She stepped over the dry rocks without stopping to pick one up – she didn't want to know.

Clouds were afterthoughts, just a dash now and then. In that hot sun and hot dirt K stumbled and swaggered. She looked up toward the sun that shot out from the sky like an explosion, its rays stabbing through the air like daggers. She squinted her eyes to try to see it more clearly, she didn't know why she was trying, something like they do in the movies, she supposed. A freeze-frame moment to capture some romantic piece of emotion the director wanted to convey. But it wasn't like that in real life, this drama, it wasn't romantic – it just hurt.

Her dried-out and red, sticky skin. Her lungs full of dust. Her nappy hair. Her mind sinking into places it had never gone before, thinking thoughts it had never thought of before. She wondered if the earth could feel her tiny footsteps limping across as she kicked up rocks and dirt with each step. What did the earth think of K as she walked along its body? A bug? Was she just a bug to the earth? And was that all her life had been and why it constantly felt like existence was swatting at her over and over – because she was a simple nuisance to be rid of as quickly as possible?

Then she stood for some time wondering what it would be like to be a tree as she dug her toes into the ground and imagined them spreading out like roots. She could feel them grow, the slow yawn of them as they stretched into the earth. She stayed as still as possible, only allowing herself to sway, slight and undetected. The arid wind blew dust into K's eyes and mouth as she laughed. For sometime she didn't know if it was the laughter of a tree, giggling as the wind tickled its way through her, or if she was just laughing at the insanity of standing there like a dumb tree.

After awhile, K lowered to the ground and held herself in her arms wondering how far into madness she had actually trespassed. She sat like that, like a squatted bird, her arms dangling between her knees, for several hours rocking forward and back, her body periodically convulsing in the dry heaves of not having had any water for two days, till she collapsed onto the ground. The human body can go three days without water before it dies. She'd read that somewhere.

Kathy slowly pushed her torso off the hot dirt, thought about moving, making it a little farther that day. She looked like Christina in Wyeth's *Christina's World*, slowly pulling herself back to the house.

As the sun lowered, dipping into a stream of milky clouds to the west like a Lemon Cooler, she sunk into thoughts she hoped she'd never have to think about. She dropped her head, her eyes sad and hollow, her cheeks drawn and red from the fire of the sun.

She knew they were there, that they had been waiting for her. They were the murky, sticky things that covered up her truth and she knew that someday she'd have to go through them. Or, perhaps, the murky things were her truth and there was nothing underneath to cover up. This utter blackness she felt inside was there either way, a lifetime of unwanted thoughts had finally arrived.

"Maybe it's true. Maybe you are evil," she thought. "You knew it all along, K. You and your wanton sex. You and your disdain. You and your apathy. You've been running all this time and all this time it's been from yourself. You're not Jesus, never were."

And what could she do if it were true? If evil were her nature it would flow from her effortlessly like blood from a fresh wound. Every act would birth it, every breath would bequeath it. Each glance and it would spread like flames. If it were true, if she were Satan, then evil was hers and hers alone. She owned it. It would live in each word and hide in each smile. And to stop it, to stop evil on this planet would mean her death. Or could she stop it? Perhaps when she died she'd have to leave it behind, leave it in her will to someone she knew.

But she didn't know anybody who could handle being pure evil. Being Jesus was easy. The implications of this, well, she was unsure. They were too enormous to even fathom. And her whole life may have been a blanket, a shawl – thin and worn, something created just to cover this up. No wonder she had longed to be Jesus – and how readily she had knelt before that beautiful paper alter.

It would explain much, a lot of things – everything.

"How we run from what we are," she thought. "How we continually run from it. Like we could out run it, like we could just leave it behind like bags of sand too heavy to carry. Like we could return it like an unwanted Christmas gift, a sweater that was too big, a shirt whose stripes went horizontal and not vertical the way we like them, a pair of jeans that fit too snugly.

"Or, maybe..." she thought, then the thought faded quickly into the heat as she stretched her neck, searching for something inside her mouth to swallow.

"Yes?"

"Maybe you're not evil – not yet." She sat up straight, brushed the thick, dirty hair from her face with both hands. Her stomach tingled with a sort of restrained excitement. "Maybe you're birthing a demon, are pregnant with the horned and puss-filled life that hyena creature implanted in your belly. Maybe it's growing, controlling you from within like a puppet. And when it grows completely, you'll be gone, only evil will remain."

"Whoa!"

"Yeah. Mother Mary was right. Satan wants your soul, wants to upset the balance of good and evil and destroy the universe. Evil doesn't hate people, it hates itself. It wants to die so completely as to never have to be born again, or exist at all – even in Heaven. But maybe you can still beat it, find Satan and destroy him. Put him in one of your stories and send him back to Hell before he takes over your soul!"

"Stop Satan – Got it!"

Another day passed in blisters and night was there and K was walking so slowly it was almost like standing still. She looked up to see a star-filled night, the emptiness between stars pulled her eyes like a magnet.

She thought it odd to be captivated by empty space. As she stood staring into the serene darkness that enclosed each star like a womb, her rigid dirty legs pressing into the ground for the solace the stability provided, something opened inside. Somewhere just below her navel it opened like vast emptiness, like empty space. She lowered her head to watch the sensation, but nothing was there.

Gradually, the feeling expanded, unrolled in all directions. Silence like an empty cathedral ringing off the stained glass and stone walls and marble floors so pure they looked like water – not a place where the noise was gone, a place where noise never existed.

The magical way cats play. The raise of the paw, a small warning before they whack. The way they come and sit next to you, start their murmured purrs, not even needing to be touched, just being there – and it is enough. Emptiness was like that, cat's play.

The billowing cloud unraveled like it had a purpose. It could have unraveled into eternity, swallowed up everything if it wanted and nothing could stop it, but it didn't want to do that. It wanted K to notice it. It wanted K to notice that it was completely empty and completely full at the same time. And the stuff that it was completely full of was her. She couldn't believe it. For the first time she knew what space felt like, she knew what emptiness felt like, and she cried at the tenderness of it – at the complete fragility of it. She cried at how she felt related to it like family she never knew. She cried at how fulfilled it made her to be a part of it. And then it was gone, and she cried for the loss of it.

The dusty earth traced runes on her bare legs and arms as she covered her face with her hands. Soon it was forgotten, the whole experience, and she could hardly remember what it felt like and she wondered why she was crying. The tears soon stopped and all she had to prove that it had ever taken place was the bittersweet memory it left in its wake. A memory of something she was or used to be, a memory of something real that made everything else seem unreal, wither into irrelevance, like Amy had said.

That was all she had to prove that any of her life had taken place – memories, slight and tender and abandoned somewhere deep inside of her. Memories not even as thick as dreams, not even as sturdy as old cobwebs, not even as solid as mist. There was nothing, no proof that her life was real – just a maxed-out credit card and a drivers license, and those things can be faked. They're made up all the time.

But what did she want – a monument? That would only prove that someone had been there to create it – she could have been nothing more than a vision to the sculptor, and eventually, even the monument would be beaten into submission by the elements and drift away in sandy bits with the wind. And what if someone had written a book on her existence? A great book like The Bible about Jesus – even that could all be lies, a fantasy, a novel 2000 years old. And maybe, back then, they all knew it was just a story – a good read. There was no proof, no way to prove anything. When she was gone... she'd be gone. No trace – a fallen leaf.

Night was pretty but empty and she feared the salvation it offered wouldn't outlast the morning shadows when they came up over the eastern horizon. Night was a good cover as she crept onto some farmland close to the main house, lowered a bucket into a well, pulled up some water, spread it over her face, drank until her stomach ached from the sudden fullness.

She slid into a barn and slept on a dry, prickly pile of hay near a few horses till the sun peered in and animals stirred and roosters crowed and Katherine had to leave.

In the languished morning the sun rained fire onto K and the patch of ground she sat on. She'd never felt anything like it, had usually moved from one air-conditioned room to another, Bells' and work. And when she did go out it wouldn't be for long and she'd stay close to the shade. Her apartment had no A/C but she was only there to sleep and usually had enough cheap booze in her to allow her to sleep through the heat. But it had never been this hot, not that she could remember, not in ten years. Now there was no shade, no air-conditioning, and she could feel moment to moment her skin becoming more damaged and red.

"Oh my God, it's so hot. It is so hot," she said, falling to her knees, wanting to cry but not having the moisture to water even a plastic flower. "It can't be this hot. It can't be." She fell on her back and butt, her legs flew upward as she stopped the fall with bent elbows, trying to regain her center. She came upright and sat without moving, the awareness of her body creeping over her like slugs, maybe leaches, and she realized how much pain she was in.

"Oh my God. Oh my God," she half-laughed and half-cried, her mind sticking between the two intense polarities as if it were in peanut butter. Then panic set in, she could not believe how hurt she was, how sore, how tired and how hot. The day spread out around her like flames, her mouth so dry there was nothing left to swallow, her throat so swollen she didn't know if she could, even if there were. The flames raged invisible, there was only the shimmer of thermals to prove they existed, and the heat.

What had she done? What in the hell had she done? Why was she there in the middle of a dusty field with the rows of dead and dried up stalks of corn and a ladybug that searched for forgiveness on the underside of a slivery blade of yellowed foxtail? How had she gotten there? She couldn't even remember.

And then even hope was gone, wilted or dried up or whatever happened, happened – that last flower of hope had been admonished and sent home and all that remained was the terrifying reality in front of her.

319

"I guess this is really it. I guess its over. I can't move." She sent out a laugh after those words as if to catch up to them and turn them into things playful. But it could not, the tissue paper laugh merely crumbled beneath the weight of its own fallacy.

In a primrose lantern she lay ensconced. In a tomb of fire she watched herself turn to ashes. In that fire her anger raged, and she fed the fire with even greater anger. It raged and raged at those who had intruded on her life, the ones who desert, the ones who rape, the ones who pillage and leave for dead. The lifetime of insects that had snuck into her life taking what they wanted like ants, then leaving again and again.

The lifetime of trespassers, wolves and coyotes, slick-tongued and hand friendly lying and deceiving a path into her alliances. She could see them clearly through the flames. She had never before realized her hatred and she screamed at the sky, her anger burning symbols into the vastness like branding cattle. She invited them all back again.

"You want me so damn bad, you can have me! You can reach into this pyre, you can grab my ashes, and watch me slip through your fingers."

Her father was there. She never knew she was angry with him, had always thought it was only sorrow. Becky was there, moving her hips under a leather mini-shirt on a dark flanked stage at The Hurricane – and there was God. He had deserted her most of all. God was supposed to be all forgiving, all encompassing, and all loving – even if you didn't believe in him, even if you didn't like him very much. But he was nowhere to be found, never was.

She had never understood the connection – hatred and the people who left her, hatred and loneliness, hatred and fear.

Moses was there too, but she wasn't sure why. Maybe he was Satan. But he didn't seem like Satan, he seemed like a pawn just like her. And maybe she was mad that he reflected what she was. She was a pawn of God's while he was a pawn of Satan's. Or, maybe, she was angry with him for loving her, she knew that he did, and maybe she was angry that she loved him back. Even after that crazy scene in her bedroom, when the door shut, she wished he were there.

That was the first step, love, without it people could leave all they wanted, she often preferred that they did. When love was there, hiding in laughter, ignited by a smile, dancing behind longing eyes – that's when the pain comes, comes on hard like a white hot sun on burnt skin. When you start to care is when things go wrong.

Her anger followed the sun, burned from something unimaginable, burned into something unformable, and then, suddenly, it was gone. The anger, the rage, the piss-yellow hatred of the sun, all gone, burned or engulfed in the flames or whatever happened, happened, and she felt free. An ocean of anger and resentment had evaporated in the intense heat, leaving etched, mountainous craters. K sat back breathing heavily as the last drops dissipated. The sun still shone above, but a slight coolness settled over her and she felt in-between – in-between hot and cold, in-between life and death, in-between…everything.

When you don't want to be happy and you don't want to be sad and you don't want to live and you don't want to die, what are you? When you have no home and you have no name and you're unmotivated for anything, what are you? When you're in-between everything, what are you? Are you undefined?

And when you're nameless and homeless and undefined, what can stick to you? No thoughts of others can impose on you, no ideas of your own about what life should be or how you want it to be can confine you. Everything slides off. And when you're undefined and unconfined, do you have boundaries? And without boundaries are you infinite? And if you're infinite, are you God?

"Religion must be something in-between," she thought. "When you have no life to go back to and you have no life to go in to – man becomes religious."

She looked up at the sky, its open blue vastness of calm, its huge, bright sun pounding the plains. "Alright existence, you win. You've beaten K," she said aloud, her words struggling through a swollen, constricted throat. "Katherine of the St. Catherine Catherines, you beat her. And you know what? I accept it," she laughed, then. "I accept this death. I can't change it, I won't even try. For once, I won't even try."

And she did accept. It wasn't just a pile of words to dump out of her and relieve herself of, it was felt. There was peace inside of her just saying it, cool waters where she waded poolside, dangling feet up to her knees over the bend of concrete. She waited there, waited for death to come take her home. She had come from death and now she was going back. We all fall back into the womb.

"How do you take a life? In which way is it most pleasurable for you?" she asked. Death did not reply. "And if I'm Satan, am I not your ally? And if I'm Jesus, do I not own you, am I not your master? Or do you simply pay no mind to what you take or when or why – without an ally and without a foe?"

How would death come? Would it slither towards her from all directions and all dimensions like a myriad of snakes? Or would it glide to her, simply float on the wings of a dove and lower its stillness upon her?

Just then there was the flutter of wings landing to her left.

"Ah, good," she thought, it would come on wings. But her body tensed as she realized it was really happening. Death was taking her home. Was she ready? She'd always thought she was, that all she wanted was to leave this world. And now that it was happening, tender longings to stay and accomplish, finish, whatever it was she came here to do, nudged at her gently like a mother jay encouraging its baby to fly.

The feathered coos of a lazed bird puttered from her side, but she was too tired to look, even to turn her head and look at her own death. So death waddled out in front of her. It wasn't death at all, it was the 39th Street Bird and K said, "Hello." Its blue-gray feathers shimmered in the open sun. Its stony beak and black eyes more welcome than gold.

It was everything she'd ever asked for in a bird. It was walking on the ground and it was right next to her, close enough to touch. And she did touch it. She touched its rough beak and it tilted its frail head to look at her sideways.

"It is so damn cute when they do that," she thought, stroking its head with her finger. The 39th Street Bird cooed again, then it turned and walked away.

"You look like a duck," she laughed. "Waddle, waddle – you're not one of the better walkers!" About ten feet away it turned around and chirped, loud and long, almost barking.

"Alright," she said. "I'm coming." And K forgot her pain, forgot how impossible it would be to move, and jerkily crawled toward the 39th Street Bird. After a few feet, she stood upright and began to walk. The bird waddled on and Katherine followed, sometimes imitating the turtle-dove, waddling secretly behind it, laughing as she did so.

It led her to a highway just over a few hills, and stopped at a green sign. The sign read, "Kansas City – 7 miles."

The 39th Street Bird flew away.

K eased over symmetric trellises cut into the shoulder of the inter-state toward home, then crossed a ditch to the frontage road that mir-rored the highway. As she got closer to town, side streets became famil-iar, and she used those to be better hidden. Her legs were sore and heavy as tree trunks. Most of her body ached, the space around her floating ribs wringing when she coughed from the dry dust batted off her clothes. She found food and water at a fast food joint, four crumpled soggy ones worth. That was the last of what was in her pocket.

Something like a fire burning, maybe burning leaves, smelled like the woody outdoors in late October. As she neared home, muddled, scorched memories fell on her like the scents in fall. The brown and orange colored leaves, the soft and rounded twilight, clouds like lava oozing from a distant yellow hole in the western sky – orange spreading into pinks and magentas, filtering into the remaining blue.

"I did love the fall," she thought. "That wonderful smell." More than just the smell of fires in fireplaces, crisp and full like fresh sourdough, something lay behind it, in the background, giving the smell of fires a cuddly place to land – a baby in mother's arms.

"I may never see fall again," she thought. "How I wasted it. How I

323

wasted the fall. Running from ties that bind, running from loneliness –
dreading the upcoming cold of winter. Hurrying to get indoors, away
from the wind and the memories they brought with them. I missed the
fall, every single one since my youth.

"And now, if I had you here with me again, fall, I would make it up
to you. In your cool autumn sky we'd float the day away. We'd make
love under a blanket of leaves, and I'd scoop up those leaves and throw
them at you. Then you could chase me around and around with your
swirling winds that seemed to be heading nowhere in particular, just
around and around, and how I could love you, this time, fall."

She twirled, spinning in the air that she dreamed was fall air – spinning until she became dizzy and fell on textured pavement the smell of
wine and spit from chewing tobacco. When she opened her eyes it was
still June, and it was still hot, and she started laughing, it might have
been tears. The concrete on which she lay belonged to the dirty sidewalks of 39th Street.

Deeply she drew in each breath, let the smell of 39th Street simmer
inside her like stew in a crock-pot – she felt alive. She knew she'd have
to be careful, the cops were there, somewhere, waiting. But it would be
okay now. Now she was at Bells'. She could get a note to him or something, and he'd take care of her. He'd take care of everything – Bells
always did. He knew people, places she could stay until this whole
thing blew over.

"Bells, Bells – thank God for Bells," she sang, looking up at the sign.
That stupid, beautiful sign that still read, "Bels' Bob."

"Bels' Bob, it's so ridiculous – *Bels' Bob*," she repeated, as if she
hadn't heard herself. "It's kind of like Beelzebub."

"Yeah, Beelzebub," she laughed. "Beelzebub, the ruler of lizards,
Satan – oooh, scary." She made a shaky gesture with her hands, then
stood dumbfounded, staring off into the rickety sign that looked suddenly distant and nightmarish.

"No."

The sun shone at twilight like the glow in the eye of a Black Panther. It lowered itself like that big cat, shrinking down to veil under some bushes or limbs or nothing at all, just getting low to the ground to hide from enemy or prey. The sun was drawn beneath the horizon and all that was left was black. A Black Panther black.

Downtown, a bamboo flute sent vespers into the clandestine night. A trepid note weaving the empty hopes of sky high towers of glass and steel, waiting for the next breath and finger hole to be covered.

In the courtyard, tidy squares of fresh-watered grass were placed symmetrically under squat green street lamps, trying to look Old World – and K moved away, being too open and bright. She wanted to go somewhere darker just then – where worms go.

Blades of grass grew through seams in the sidewalk, less and less as she moved away. They had slipped through fissures on the other side hoping this was Heaven – they picked the wrong fissure. Here, things grew only to die. Here, despair trailed people like ants, carrying them into holes in the ground where they could devour them in tiny morsels. Here, you couldn't trust your best friend. Satanic eyes lied through docile, obsidian fronts. The fragrances of help and advice were facades for agronomy – pulling you away from your beliefs, dropping you into a warm, sprite vat of barley and malts, fermenting you into confusion and pliability. You have to be steel to survive – not glass.

She wished she were Superman. He was the man of steel. She wished she could see through closed doors. She wished she could fly over the world with tepid high winds, drop out of the sky, pluck innocent people off of courtroom ledges, and out of exploding airplanes. She wished she could defeat dreams, cowboys and cavalry, knights and crusaders, with cold breath or laser eyes. She wished she could cripple blue-green monsters with dizzying strength before they gobbled up true believers with the shapes of gold crosses indented in their palms. She wished she were Superman. Superman, and Bruce Lee.

But she wasn't Superman, she was helpless as a melody. She was waiting for the next breath. She was waiting for the next finger hole to be covered.

She wasn't sure why she was downtown. Perhaps its steel and concrete and bricks seemed safe. Perhaps she had nowhere else to go. Perhaps she had no friends and no family and this is where mendicants like her went. Perhaps she needed to be with people of her own ilk.

She thought of Simone. Simone was a question mark spawning, her ideas pulling K away from her reality as much as anyone. Maybe she wasn't evil, not like Bells, but there was definitely no truth there. But maybe she wasn't looking for the truth anymore, maybe she was tired of the truth. Maybe the truth was something created just to pose against some lie. And maybe neither was needed. Without lies there would be no need of finding a truth, we would breathe truth, eat truth. You wouldn't have to believe in anything, all would simply be as it was. And without truth, well, lies would be the truth. So in the end, there can be only truth.

Truth and lies were all part of the same big ball. Somehow, you had to see it birds-eye to understand.

Her finger pressed into the mortar between the bricks of a small downtown building the same way it did by her house, from Bells' to K's apartment. The bumpidy bump and scratchity scratch on her raw skin, the tingle and then numbing affect when she'd gone too far.

How she wished it was that walk she was walking right now, just a walk home after an uneventful evening lounging at Bells' with nothing else to do and nowhere else to go. Not being caught up in some great drama, not being a savior to mankind, just being K again, just to be.

How magical and wonderful that would be – as magical as cat's play. That short two-minute walk home would be just fine right now. And now she'd know, she'd know better.

If only she could go back in time to when Bells wasn't Satan and she wasn't Jesus. She'd cherish those times at Bells'. She'd cherish the time spent at work with Becky. How quickly it all turned. She'd cherish people like the 39th Street Bum. She didn't have to help them, maybe she couldn't. Katherine was proving more and more that she couldn't help anybody. But she could cherish his presence, the way he added something to the sidewalk outside of Bells', without him even knowing it. And now, with him gone, the way the sidewalk had a little less life to it – a little less character, it was less of what 39th Street used to be.

She'd even cherish people she didn't know. Like Calliope and the mother and child and teenager that died in that wreck and people like the cop in 808. She'd even cherish the feel of her sore butt on that cold stool and she wouldn't wish she were anywhere else ever again. She wouldn't wish for a better job and better friends and a better life. Her life had been just fine, perfect. Had she been aware enough to see that at the time, maybe none of this would've happened.

Maybe she wouldn't have gone off trying to prove to the world, to God, and to herself that she was special – that Katherine of the St. Catherine Catherines was better than anybody else because nothing would have changed even if she had. Everyone was always too busy trying to prove themselves special to even take notice, anyway. Nobody would've cared except for her. And then she'd have to run off trying to prove it again and again in some bigger and better way just to get them to notice, then when would it end.

She felt like Dorothy. Dorothy had to go all that way to some make-believe world of yellowy bricks just to realize home was even better. But maybe, sometimes it has to be like that. Maybe truth pulls you away from itself, stretches you out to see it at a distance, shooting you back like a slingshot to live the same life in a better way.

"Maybe, K. Maybe a lot of things at this point. I don't know any-

327

more. I don't know *anything* anymore, and I'm tired of all these stupid theories. They're killing me faster than anything else. I don't know if I'm Jesus, or if I'm Satan, or if I'm Jesus becoming Satan, or just K. I don't know one damn thing!"

The building to her left opened into a small alcove where two store-front windows faced eachother across thin glazed granite. It was a mall of some sort, two or three stories worth, with office suites on the re-maining upper floors.

Glowing lights from televisions in the electronics store bathed the outfits in the retro shop window a grayish tint – leather knee length skirts, orange and green Chanel blazers, Boulce' knit tops and a 20's beaded black bag and strappy sandals. On one of the TV's a newscast had begun – a special report. When she heard it was about a plane wreck K pressed her face to the window, trying to hear better, her palms flat against the glass. They flashed a picture on the screen – it was her.

"This woman was seen at the airport and is suspected to be an ac-complice. She already has a warrant out for her arrest for several mur-ders and it is now known, with the help of security tapes, that she caused a diversion at the airport and occupied security while her terrorist part-ners planted the bomb. The FBI is working with local authorities on the matter. If seen…"

Shadows fell from the buildings like dark blankets, blankets sent from Hell to keep the place warm, and they were doing a fine job. It was a muggy thick heat, not at all like toast. The glow of the sun had gone down but its heat remained. It stayed hidden – embedded in the blackness of that panther left behind. And the panther stalked K. She could hear it hiss in the hot winds. She could feel its claws brush her cheeks as she walked. She could feel it walking behind her and somehow, every time she looked, it was gone. That panther crouched down behind some door or walkway or light post and remained unseen.

K wandered for some time zombie-like, often running into a building's side or tripping over a seam in the sidewalk where grass blades still foolishly poked through. Amy was the one person she'd truly loved since her father had left – loved unconditionally. She wanted nothing from Amy, just wanted to see her live. A person she would've gladly traded her life for, she would've sat on that plane in her stead a thousand times. A thousand times she would have felt her body being ripped into pieces, a thousand times she would have felt her skin dissolve in the heat of it. A thousand times, if only Amy could have been spared from feeling it once.

Don't even tell me, thought K. *It was because of me...please...don't...* Her thoughts disappeared, succumbed to the pull of vile and muck inside her – the realization that she had caused Amy's death.

A cop car moved up the next street with spotlights on, two of them, and K darted into an alley. "My God, could they be looking for me?" She crouched down like she had learned it from that panther, became animal like, her senses tingling with thoughts of survival and escape. She would not go so easily this time – cheerfully waving to passersby on the downtown streets like some two-bit whore. Eagerly getting into the back seat of that Deputy Sheriff's car just because she was a little shaken and scared and it seemed safe and easy to give up like that and let it happen. Not this time.

"They'll prosecute me for sure," she thought. "I could spend the rest of my life in jail. I'd rather be dead. I won't go without a fight."

After that K moved with caution, slipping behind stairs and door wells, sliding into dark spaces – panther had taught her well, she felt his presence with her the whole time, pressing his soft fur into her thigh.

329

The rattle of dry leaves blowing by, claws tapping on concrete.

"I've got to get out of here," she thought.

"Yep, you're in a world of trouble, little girl. And, oh yeah, that dead cop in Moberly isn't going to help your case much, either."

"Oh yeah, I hadn't thought of that."

"Uh huh, they won't say that he raped you then skewered himself on that sharp nail, they'll say you seduced him then killed him – and I guess they'd be right," she thought.

"Oh my God, I did! I did seduce him and kill him. I never looked at it like that. Of course I thought his wife was going to show up and do the dirty work but, either way, I knew he'd die."

"Yeah, well let's hope God doesn't look at it like that or your troubles are going to follow you out of this world and right into the next!"

Another police car passed under the yellow flash of traffic lights that spread into the air in a golden convex, disappearing into some boundary undefined. Its spotlight reflected off the back of a semi.

"It must be a truck, the back end of a big rig," thought K. "That trucker can get me the hell out of here. Just flirt a little, K, get what you need."

"Flirt. Got it."

Along the mostly white side of the trailer, clumped with splotches of old mud and filth that the mud flap with the naked silver girl on it apparently couldn't stop, were red letters saying something about the company he worked for. *Nation's Most Dependable Trucking. Come Work For The Best.*

But what did it matter anyway, thought K, they were all the same. Health insurance and a few days off a year and everybody thinking they lived in a free country when they were really tied to their work and mortgages by a chain link and a stake like an old bulldog with a horrid under-bite. No one could go too far for too long without feeling that yank on their necks and have to rush back, go to work, pay the bills.

"What a huge crock of shit, freedom," she laughed. "There is no freedom here. It's a lifetime of struggle so you can spend your last twenty years of poor health not having to work to survive – but wishing you were young and healthy and working again, or wishing you were already dead. Freedom is only comparative here. To be really free means being empty – no one wants that."

When she got to the door of the green tractor, reading *The Furtle Turtle* in gold raised letters on the side, the window opened. Before the words registered in her mind, a hand reached out with a plastic jar, pouring tarnished yellow liquid to the ground.

Thoughts gathered in her head but they seemed impotent as she stood at the foot of the truck covered in piss. She would have cried, but then decided what would be the point? Crying hadn't helped her, it hadn't solved anything, not once in a thousand tears. They were drops of water and salt and where they lay they died as quickly as they were born with nothing left to acknowledge that they had ever existed – except, maybe, some chemical compound that Kathy had never heard of and one that she'd need a microscope even to see.

"Oh, my God!" She blew out a couple of quick breaths trying to blow the liquid off her mouth. "Oh my God, it's piss – it's Goddamn trucker piss!"

"Damnit!" she yelled.

The trucker peeked out of his open window. "Shit! Sorry lady," his voice was country, and low. "What the hell were you doin' sneaking up on me, anyway?"

K shook her hands, trying to allow the urine to run off her, but it didn't help any. The piss coated her like grease only it didn't smell nearly as good as that. It didn't smell nearly as good as a lot of things she could think of, even coffee – and she hated coffee. She only drank it sometimes because it just seemed like her, like she was a coffee drinker and all. So when people would say, *You drink coffee?* She would say, *Yep,* or *Yeah, black,* just like it was nothing – like it was totally natural that she be drinking coffee.

It didn't smell as good as most things, come to think of it, and K couldn't believe something that foul could be inside a person without making him die.

"I was just looking for a ride. Could you give me a ride, mister? I gotta get out of here," she said, sounding about as sexy as she could while still being covered in trucker piss.

"Well normally I would," said the trucker. "But, seein' as how you're covered in piss and all…"

Kathy raised her hand to stop him from making any further statements.

The slurred hiss of the bamboo flute stirred again as K wedged between a dumpster and a tall building with beige bricks a few blocks away where she could hide and spend the night. A small staircase, heading into the side of the building, blocked the view of her from the street.

She imagined the melody a slithery snake, weaving through sticky grass, spilling out in front of her, only to scurry away again. Snakes aren't all bad, not melody snakes. They're nothing like black rainbows. This one was fuzzy and soft and not in any hurry at all. This one wanted to take K with it. This one wished it were she and she wished she were it. She wished she could go where a melody goes – when it dissipates.

She wished for lots of things. She believed in so much – possibility. Now, her life was confined to the brick walls behind her and beside her and the dumpster in front of her.

Finding the right dumpster to spend the night near is the key for mendicants like her. "This one isn't so bad," she said, trying to make herself believe it. The trash smelled god-awful, but not as god-awful as she did, and she settled onto the warm concrete and pressed against the hard bricks.

"How much better nature makes little resting spots," she thought, the rough wall abrasive through her thin shirt. "A nice patch of grass, a

332

tree to lean against." For a moment, she whisked away into the joy of that thought where she wore a white sundress, even though it was only late spring, and watched herself glow in the sun with a blissful grin on her face just sitting, doing nothing. Melody snakes wiggled through the tall grass at her side, a bird circled high in the blue sky with only soft splotches of white dusty clouds to hide all that beautiful blue.

And then, one of those small, airy clouds moved in front of the sun and the whole valley fell into darkness. "How odd," thought K, running her fingers though her hair that was silky and smooth in her thoughts, without tangles and dirt and trucker piss. "One tiny cloud can block out the whole sun." And then the cloud moved on and the rolling green plain was lifted into such brightness that it made her skin want to jump off her body and dance around the valley.

Another bird floated and carved circles off in the distance. "Hawks," she thought. "Good – I like hawks." They were the watchers, protectors. And it was good that she be daydreaming about hawks on a night like tonight – it was a good sign.

It was something like Heaven – the poetry of the birds, the caress of the wind, the strength of the tree behind her, and the rich earth underneath. She looked utterly content and at peace.

"Who the hell is that?" thought K, shaking her head in short bursts, wiping sticky sweat and urine from her brow.

"I don't know, K. I don't fucking know."

In the vacated night the streets echoed the silence as the bamboo flute slipped away and the last notes trailed into someplace inaudible. Her eyes grew heavy watching ants come and go that searched for food or other remnants in the dark alley. Sometimes they took with them the broken pieces of other ants – arms, legs or torsos – a trophy they'd won in battle, or dues paid to a fallen comrade by carrying him home again.

She wished she could jump ahead in time, have it all be over with.

Whatever the outcome, just let it happen, just to be on the other side of it. She didn't know what the truth was. She didn't care.

She was a fool. Making up rainbows and dreams to chase around the rest of her life that would hold no more value than the dead carcasses these ants were carrying around if caught. What dark colored glasses she had worn to make her see otherwise. What jewels she had painted on her dreams, something precious and real that was lost and found again. But they weren't precious. No jewels she could think of had meaning anymore. And why would they? They were just different combinations of the same chemicals she ate, breathed and defecated each day.

They'd vanish too and the things they could buy were foam stuffing and bubble packaging – something to fill her life with to make her believe it wasn't empty, to make her believe life was worth living. It wasn't, not like this. She had been killing time, distracting herself from the truth that there was nothing to do, nothing to accomplish. She could see it now – more clearly than ever.

Every now and then she'd put her finger on the concrete blocking the path of an ant, just to see what it would do. The ant would stop, turn, turn again and then keep going. It would go around her or head back to where it came from or go off in a different direction altogether.

"You don't care either way, do ya little ant? You don't even know where you've been and you sure as hell don't know where you're going. So what does it matter to you?"

What did it matter? Why had she tried to force her way through so many barriers? To prove what? To who? They were fingers of God set down in front of her – just to see what she would do.

The heat swirled in the corridor from low-lying southwestern winds. They raised and festered the many smells around her and the smells that had become a part of her, it was like tasting bile, but it would be nothing compared to when the sun came up again. Concrete lay beneath her, cement and bricks surrounded her. She'd created another cell for herself – the fish that wouldn't swim to the other side, the elephant that wouldn't run away.

The street to her left wasn't an option now, what with the cops and all. Her only way out of this mess would be straight up and she looked up to see the small portion of dark sky that the buildings allotted.

She wished she were a balloon – a balloon filled with helium left over from the birthday party of a small child. Even though she had been sitting in his room for days, the little boy laughing and grinning each time he saw her, she should still have enough helium left to rise up through that space, float into freedom. And she hoped beyond hope that it wouldn't crush that little boy the next morning to find his balloon with the happy face on it gone – though she knew that it would.

K rubbed her stinging eyes and let her head fall and lie still. But there was no sleep, no sleep was possible. Even if it weren't so hot and she weren't on hard concrete and it didn't reek so badly. Even if she were in bed, just showered with the fan blowing soft kisses all over her clean naked body – even then she might not sleep. She had to be aware – conscious. "In unconsciousness bad things can happen," thought K. "You can be raped in your own back alley. You can wake up with a dead guy having sex with you, or worse, this time you could wake up in prison."

She tried to stay awake, tried to focus her eyes on the wheel bearing of the trash dumpster. Her eyes played tricks on her, outlines of yellows and whites erupted around the frame as a song turned over and over in her mind.

Did you think you could tell, Heaven from Hell, blue sky from pain? She followed the music whispering its sad true words inside her. Why was it there? Where did it come from? She trailed the music hoping to find its source, and there were sounds inside her head she'd never heard before – slivers, vibrations. She focused on the highest pitch that was soft and far away until it became clear and close – and then another appeared above it, notes climbing higher and higher somewhere inside her like a ladder.

She climbed and climbed for hours it seemed, until she reached what must have been the top and the most beautiful music she'd ever heard showered on her like crystal bells, or bells made of pure light.

. They were wonderful, magical, way up inside her head at the top of the ladder ringing like wispy metallic tinsels in the wind. It so excited her it nearly cleaved her in half. She stayed rooted on the hard ground while inside she was floating up high and ringing right along with those bells.

"My God, were these the bells they were talking about – that Army Sergeant and that little girl? Oh my God!" She had to laugh. "They're not evil, they're not evil at all, they're divine. Distant echo's of God calling you home. Something like a beacon that God left in the dark night to show you your way. Oh my, it's so beautiful. It is so…beautiful." She pushed upright from a slouch she'd slipped into, her body tingling with this wonderful feeling.

"But, I can see the mistake," she thought. "I see how they pull you away, how they pull you from yourself, how they extract you from this world. And maybe that's why I'm not scared of them. Maybe it's because I'm ready to go and they weren't, it was their own fears. Their own fears kept them from something beautiful."

The night passed and K sat as the sun came up dancing with the bells inside her head. It calmed her. Something new had opened in her life. A new reality of what was possible, of how life could be. How it could be something beautiful, something worth celebrating. How she could still be here, be a part of the world, but inside be unaffected by it, joyous.

Then it evaporated even more quickly than it came, and she was just as confused as before. K looked up and the sky was already so bright it made her eyes tear.

"Why did you take that away from me, God? What did I do this time? What am I supposed to do now?"

The world was back. The heat was back. Her cover of night had gone, panther had gone. He'd skulked off to sleep in some trees or shaded place in the ground without fear – no animal hunts the panther, but it seemed that half the world was after K. And the other half that wasn't after her it was just because they didn't know the language and didn't understand the news reports or they'd be chasing her too.

But everything around her carried on. Not even a speed bump in the road of life was K's turmoil and despair. The sky was still, silent and peaceful. The streets were calm. There was even a well-dressed lady scurrying into the side of a cement building across the street. Her life was unchanged, unaffected by K. She was just late, a little late is all, to wherever she needed to be. She pulled the arm of a small girl in a pink dress who lagged behind and K looked up to the see the building they went hurrying into. *The Church of St. Catherine's*, it read, *Reverend Thomas Dove – All Faiths.*

K got up from her soiled spot, a roach scampered away loosing its protective cover, and marched toward the Church of St. Catherine's shouting as she crossed the street in an angry, adolescent tone.

"Father!" she yelled, rolling her eyes toward the sky, "I wanna talk to you!"

It would have been a nice place to have a wedding. The side door led to the main entrance that housed marble floors and thin white pillars placed symmetrically about. K didn't know for sure if it were real marble, nor was she sure if there were any such thing as fake marble. But the pillars were definitely fake, she believed. Not totally fake – they were there, they were real. But she doubted seriously if they supported anything, if they held up the place. She couldn't believe their presence had any depth – that if they had been removed the whole structure would come tumbling down.

These were just surface pillars, good for a daydream, painting the galley in the surreal whites and stature of Greek mythology. But it was nothing substantial – no plinth.

The preacher was hard at work preaching and it looked like work to K. "Man, you can work up a sweat saving souls," she thought. And he was. He was ranting himself into quite a lather. His big, black arms looked powerful and forceful as he slammed a fist onto the podium. He was intimidating, but she could see he had a soft side too. That when he came down off those steps he was just a playful ole' grizzly bear with manicured claws and spongy, Nerf teeth.

He wouldn't hurt you too bad, and his kids probably curled up next to that mushy round belly of his and fell fast asleep while he watched All-Star Wrestling or the Monster Truck Rally, or really, any sporting event that was being broadcast – even golf. If that were all he could get he'd take it and be damn happy about it too, at least it was a sport. He'd have to draw the line at figure skating – that wasn't a real sport. If it took place on ice they'd better have sticks in their hands and be bashing eachother up against Plexiglas barricades. Otherwise, it didn't mean anything. Sure, an ice skater could fall during a triple jump and spin around thingy, but that would just be embarrassing more than painful.

Those ice skaters could twirl and twirl and spin and flip all they wanted, he'd just as soon go out and do some yard work. Of course, he liked it when their little skirts flipped up as they skated backwards, revealing that tight and tender backside. But only bad man thought about young girl's backsides in that way, and he was a preacher after all. So he couldn't watch ice skating, that was the thing K finally deduced, otherwise his wife would soon catch on when he always wanted to have sex afterwards – her lying face down.

That soft round belly of his would lull his kids to sleep so quickly they were probably afraid to sit next to him most times. Sometimes, they were probably afraid even to walk by too closely lest they might slip into a nap when they could instead be playing computer games or tearing the wings off some bug, or just giving their siblings a hard time.

"Walk with soft soles and the sweet taste of Jesus in your heart, for it will be a day like today..." he stopped to raise up his hand high above his head. "With the heat of the very fires of Hell tickling your feet, provoking you, taunting you – each and every one of you. A day like today will be the day you see the face of Satan! In your neighbors, in your friends, everywhere you go – have mercy!" The crowd followed with murmurs as he raised his pitch to a near scream. "I tell you, people, walk with sweet Jesus in your heart. For today, you will see the devil!" His hand crashed down like a gavel.

"Excuse me." As the explosion subsided, K's meek voice seeped into the vacuum it created as she moved up the red carpeting between the rows of polished oak benches.

"Excuse me." Her voice was child-like compared to the thunder with which Reverend Dove propelled.

"Uh, excuse me," she said again, moving closer, becoming agitated.

"Yes, Miss?" said the Reverend in a calmer tone. "We're having a service here," he wiped his brow with a white cloth. "You can take a seat if you like."

All heads turned to K. Disdain in the eyes of many, a thinly veiled disgust in the eyes of others who were repelled by the look of her medusa hair and her less than barn-yard smell.

"I know, I know..." said K, realizing that now she was finally in a place where people would recognize her. She brought up her hands, patting down the air in front of her to calm everyone down. "I know. I'm Jesus. But I'm not here to save you. I'm not here to take you back to Heaven, not yet. I've got to get a message to my father and he's n̄ answering me. So I need to use you."

The place fell so silent K thought that possib'

– gunmen had

339

entered the church to rob everyone. She turned around to see, then turned back when the Reverend spoke.

"Child," he said, his voice becoming more smooth and calming, like rolling hills. "I'm *leading* these people to Jesus. You may join us if you wish. *This* is the pathway to Heaven."

What a dumb prick bastard, thought K. What kind of preacher was this? What kind of a man of the cloth was it that couldn't even see Jesus standing before him? He didn't deserve to be up there at all, screamin' and savin' souls – that was her job now, anyway. She just needed to brush up on her verses was all. He was a con man is what he was, fooling these poor innocent people into believing he spoke for God. What a dumb prick bastard. No wonder his kids were afraid to walk by him sometimes. It wasn't because his fat belly would knock them into a nap, it was because he was such a dumb prick bastard!

"No, can't you see who I am? Why don't you recognize me? I know I'm a girl and all, but it's me – it's Jesus!"

The crowd shifted and whispered their obvious secrets as the preacher stepped from behind his podium and approached Katherine. He moved with purpose, serenity. His long black robe with gold trimmed edges covered his feet. It almost looked like he was floating, or sliding on ice, his hands coming up in front of him in prayer, "It's okay, child, we're going to escort you out of here. No need to be afraid."

Kathy started to cry.

"No, you don't understand. You can't escort me out of here, you don't know how. I've tried that, over and over I've tried. Why won't somebody help me? Doesn't anybody know the way out? Can't anybody show me the way? I could kill myself, but he'll just send me back. I'll just be back in another form, in another body and have to do it all over again. No! I want out, I want to go home! Tell him, tell him now! I want to dance with those bells, I want to go home!"

The Reverend moved directly in front of her. His eyes met hers, look᠌ into her shattered glass, but they didn't go very deep – they couldn't.᠌ ᠌hen she looked into his, nothing was there. There was nothing behind those eyes that looked of insight or understanding, or love. He was a dead thing, a robot. Built and programmed and set loose on the world. Kathy dropped her eyes to look at his big palm outstretched in front of him. His large hand reaching out to her, waiting.

"Take my hand and I can lead you through, through this dark morass in which you lay entwined," said Reverend Dove.

And she could see that hand, but in her mind it was holding something black and beautiful, a thin green reed with thorns extending from the petals – St. Catherine's Flower. He gripped it so tightly blood spilled between his stubby pressed fingers from the pressure of the pointed thorns, or just his own fingernails digging into the flesh. The blood dripped onto the floor, invisible on the red carpet. This was crazy. Couldn't anybody else see what was happening here? He gripped it so tight he couldn't possibly take her hand, the hand he was reaching out to lead down that isle to the kingdom of God.

She could see it clearly, now. He was just like her, clinging. He was clinging to his own St. Catherine's Flower – clinging to his own beliefs and religion, as everyone else always had. K looked out over the ocean of people, their limp hands lying on their laps or stiff in front of them in prayer. They all held that same dark flower. Everyone she'd ever known was holding on so tight to that belief, one would think they'd strangle it. One would think it would crumble in their grips.

But it did not. The belief stayed and the people crumbled, they crumbled beneath the strain of it. They were no longer real, just a house – a holding place for a set of beliefs. And she could see them all. They were all from a long line of St. Catherines, and everybody was a Catherine – born into religion and beliefs, named because of it, schooled in the tradition of it. Their thoughts had been formed around it, or in reaction against it – either way manipulated, forged. Every Catherine was a religion of their own, their own version of whatever religion they believed in and warped to fit their needs.

They were all Cathys, and they were all trapped. They were all looking for answers and they were all giving answers they didn't have. And

Katherine could see it like she never had before. It was a circle, a closed loop. You could keep going around and around lifetime after lifetime with beliefs and ideas and religions or you could, somehow, step off. These religions hadn't saved anyone. They were like her stories, being written from her same hand, her same mind, hoping for different outcomes.

Kathy looked up into the preacher's eyes that were still lost and empty.

"Loosen your grip from the neck of St. Catherine's Flower," she said. "And you can lead me through – through this morass of Cathys."

When she walked through the glass double doors of The Church of St. Catherine's, and heard them close behind her, she felt she had left something inside, forgotten something. She almost turned to go back, but then realized it was something she could not take with her. It was something that would have to stay in that church and slowly wither and die like the people she had also left behind. It was the large part of her she could no longer carry. It was the beliefs of a child, of childish wants born of childish fears – and now it was time to grow up.

"I'm not Jesus." The thought pricking K as it left with a sharp beak and pointed talons, then flying off in all directions. She felt ridiculous, then light. "Jesus Christ, I'm not Jesus. I'm not Satan. I'm not even Katherine – I'm not anybody."

Bells was there, waiting on the other side of the street, leaning up against that shiny white Cadillac with arms folded across his chest, grinning from ear to ear. It was more like he was watching his daughter graduate from college than watching K stumble like a drunkard into the hot sun shielding her eyes, looking like death.

"I see you finally found that warm piss you've been searching for," he said as she came close, the smell still ripe and pungent. "Was it as fulfilling an experience as you'd hoped?"

His laugh was a low rumble, K's body shook in the ripples. He had on his white, button down shirt and black slacks, same thing, he always

342

wore the same thing. Same big gold ring wrapped around his pinky finger, same burning eyes and smile, same gray chest hair peeking over the top button of his K-mart polyester/cotton shirt. He was always the same – K was the one who had been changing. Bells wasn't Satan, never was.

"Who the hell are you, anyway?"

Bells grunted, then smiled at K like she was four years old. "I'm nobody, Angel."

She looked up to see his face dark in the bright sun behind him, only his outline was clear and K squinted till she could see his soft, filmy eyes. It was nice to see them again. It was…it was just nice, that's all. How much he was a part of her now. How much of each one had been poured into the other over the last seven years.

"I'm no Ang…" K cut her words short. Then fidgeted with something on the ground with her foot that wasn't even there. She shook her head, "I don't know who I am."

"Good!" said Bells. "Only then the journey begins – the journey to find out who you are!"

She moved closer to him and leaned against the car, moved a thick entanglement of hairs from her face. In the sunlight, the wavered blurs of thermals kept hawks floating high in the air, without even flapping their wings. It was like *Footsteps* – God carrying them across the hardest sandy beaches of their lives. When the heat became too much, it became the answer.

"Who am I? What am I, and what are you? You can't be nobody."

His obsidian eyes sparkled in the thick downtown heat like he was on a holiday, not like he was looking at dirty bricks and concrete and sweating in the hot morning sun. His eyes were ten years old. His eyes were still wondering what it would be like to kiss a girl, or look up her skirt, but would still rather be out chasing frogs in a pond.

"I'm the emptiness that opened inside you when you looked out into space that night. I'm that chirp that keeps calling to you across misty fields and mountain ravines. I'm everything at once, so how can I be any *one* thing? How can I be any*body?* I'm nobody because I'm just an empty space filled up by God."

He smiled then, like smiles had the power to heal. Like they had the power to make her understand or to see things better. Like they had the power to do anything other than make her realize how foolish and silly she was – and how green. Maybe they did, she was thinking. Maybe lots of things did. Maybe she had missed the answers time after time – and still was.

She thought how she had never heard him say so much at once as she wiped some sweat that moved down her cheek in a quick wiggle. Her skin was the feel of new potatoes, greasy and crisp, mushy underneath. She had just turned twenty-nine. In the amorphous daze of early June, twenty-nine had come and gone. She wondered what her skin would feel like at thirty-nine, she pressed in deeper – then forty-nine, and she grabbed a handful, imaging it sagging slightly, and wrinkled. She dropped her hand after that, she didn't want to know any further.

"And acceptance?" asked K. "What's with the whole serenity prayer that's been following me around?"

"You've been reading the saying backwards. If you go front to back it is an impossibility. Acceptance as you are, as you were, was impossible. It was your nature to question, to desire change. How can desire accept? Desire is non-acceptance. You can't have both and people are nothing but desire. And courage? Courage is just a gallant way to say you're afraid but going to do it anyway. Real courage has no fear. Real courage needs no courage.

"Wisdom to know the difference, that is the key. You must search for the wisdom, not just through the mind, not just through knowledge and information – but through the whole, through inner search. Through inner insight and inner realizations.

"And when you find the wisdom, when you know the right thing, there is no longer choice. You don't need bravery or courage, you simply do the right, or you simply do nothing and just be, if that is right. When you *realize*, there's no need to change anyone or anything. To do so is egoistic. To believe you can is egoistic. It robs people of the chance to gain their own insights and realizations. It's saying people don't even know what's best for themselves. It's saying even God does not know what's best for them, only you know.

"And you don't need acceptance or non-acceptance, you have seen the reality, the truth, the fight is over – there is nothing left to accept and nothing left not to accept. You must search deep inside yourself for the *wisdom*, before doing anything. And, when you've found that, all differences disappear and the saying becomes empty."

A tear slipped from K's eye – and then another. Not the tears of a poet, and not the tears of sadness or the tears of joy. Just the tears of someone sitting by a mountain stream at dawn, watching steam rise and realizing for the first time he'd just seen something real – something true – something which wasn't the normal bullshit that every other person was always trying to feed him. And now was longing to be a part of it, but not knowing how.

"Today you took the first step," he continued, his voice slow as it drew across the rough thickness of his throat. "Today you saw into the futility of all beliefs and all belief systems. Today you saw that those beliefs are just a circle, a trap. All beliefs, they are subtle and deadly, so subtle you think they are not beliefs, just truths.

"A belief is a limitation, a set of parameters – God is without parameters. A belief stops all inquiry – Truth requires relentless inquiry. A belief creates ego, that you know and others know not – God is without ego. A belief is a thought – Truth is an experience, not a thought. If you want to know God, you must become God. Everything else is just an idea, a belief. Only the same can know the same.

"It's not in any book or film, it's not confined to church walls, it can't be experienced through anybody else – only through yourself.

"Look at you. You followed a trail from that mirror six months ago to that bottle of warm trucker piss because of beliefs, because you thought the right thing to do was so obvious there was no need to question it. It's not because the future is set in stone that you could see it in the mirror six months prior, but because your reaction to the world and it's obstacles is so programmed and predictable that the future could be told.

"Stop! Until you are enlightened you don't know what you are doing. You are just foolishly wasting your energy, your life, doing as much harm with each act as you do good."

"I know, Bells, I know." Tears still ran down her puffy red cheek as she spoke. "I just saw that."

His voice softened, a smooth sheet of silk placed over the scratchy surface. "Now, the journey can begin. It seems like it should be ending, but you have only started. Those stories were needed, all your efforts and running around were needed, just so you could think about coming back home again."

"And what about Simone?" K asked, her head throbbing in confusion with each heartbeat. Her mouth dry and sore, wishing she had water or even bad lemonade that some kid in a stand was selling for five cents a cup. And she'd smile and say, *Mmmm, good* – even though he forgot to put the sugar in it.

"What is she? Is she like you? Does she know the truth?"

"Simone is as lost as you are, maybe more lost because she believes she is not. At least you know you are! Simone leads herself and others astray. She speaks of that which she does not know. They are the most dangerous. They are the priests and the clergy and the new age gurus of all the religions throughout the world. She's trying to share something with others that she herself does not have. She speaks in half-truths. Half-truths are more deadly than any lie because a half-truth feels true and then inquiry stops.

"She's had some experiences of the beyond, but she's stopped far short of the ultimate reality. She stopped where she is now and her mind and her beliefs have filled in the rest. But she needs to go deeper. Deeper into herself. Deeper into experience. There is no truth beyond experience," he said. "And there is no truth *until* experienced."

K leaned against the trunk of the Cadillac, her eyes staring over the empty street. A car passed, its slow movement mimicking the late Sunday morning. Kathy laughed inside when the child in the back seat pressed his face into the glass, squishing his nose and lips. He lived in his own world. A world where smooth glass cured Sunday boredom, where dead dragon flies were probably trophies, where you could be safe in force fields and jump at the last minute when the plane went down. And Kathy wished she could be like that again. It would be something precious lost, and found again.

"So why didn't you show me this before?" K said, more tears forming in her sloe, swollen eyes. "I've been in Hell, Bells, fucking Hell!" She held her face with her hands trying to stop it all from pouring out of her. She gulped for air.

"I know, Angel, I know." He moved closer, then, stroked her ratted hair, pulled it back to show a place where the sun had reddened the tender high curve of her ear. "A flower cannot wait for you to notice before it blooms. A flower cannot inform you when its about to release its fragrance. It cannot beg you to bear witness its beauty.

"I have been there all this time, surrounding you, waiting for you to notice. You must come to the flower to see its beauty, you must come with open eyes. It won't come find you, it can't. It is Tao, it is God, it is Love. It is everywhere, waiting, eternally patient. No one is special, it comes to no man. No man is chosen and no man is shunned. No man represents God because no man is without God."

She was silent. Bells had explained himself, had been perfectly clear. She had all the answers to all the questions but it didn't seem to help. Inside, she was still lost, still wanting. Her right hand came up from folded arms to touch just above her eye. Bells reached into his pocket and took out his keys, turned to open the door.

"Come on, Angel. Let's go home."

She didn't move and Bells turned back to her.

"I'm not going anywhere with you," she said. "I don't know who you are. You could be telling me more bullshit, just like Simone, just like the priests, just like everybody else.

"Maybe you're not Satan. And maybe you are God. Whatever the case, I'm not going anywhere with you, or anyone else, ever again." She took his keys, opened the door, "But I am going home." K sunk into the red, leather seat, started the car as she slammed shut the door. She drove away leaving Bells on the street alone, shadows from The Church of St. Catherine's cutting him in diagonal slats. He smiled, grunted, then walked away.

It was wet and warm from an over-worked air-conditioner and the sweaty bodies that piled in for the $6.99 all you can eat lunch buffet. K sat at the counter with her elbows propped up taking a sip of steaming tea she held like a chalice in both hands. It was hot in her hands just to hold it and she had to be deliberate with each sip – and she liked that.

Suddenly it was fascinating just to drink a cup of tea and feel the heat on her hands and how her lips tightened in anticipation of it. She breathed in the scent and let steam rise onto her face and eyes and it was like a baptism – the steam rising off baptismal waters in some hot underground springs of a sacred and ancient ritual she had never heard of.

But she could see it clearly, the dim bluish light of the cavern and the people that gathered in a circle around water that bubbled from the heat of molten rock far beneath it. The purity of the steam could be smelled as it singed their faces clearing away the old dead parts of them and preparing for the new – and it was the absence of odor that was the smell.

The clink and clank of dishes and glasses, and the orders yelled to fry cooks sounded exactly like her job at Nichol's. It had been a week since she'd been to work, a week that had changed much in her – everything. She smiled at the thought of the place and the thought of who that girl was they all called K.

She smiled at the picture of Becky's face that flashed in her mind, and she smiled at the scene of the 39th Street Dove sitting with the 39th Street Bum. She smiled at the moment when she held Amy in her arms, even though it was only for a few seconds, the feeling of joy and completeness it gave her was enough to last a lifetime. And she smiled at Bells walking down her stairwell gimping away into the darkness of the back alley. She smiled at her life, the life that had been hers up to now – for it was over.

Her story had been a wave. A ripple in some distant, silent waters moving outward – forming – pulling toward some unknown shore – raising into a fury – crashing onto the beach – receding back to sea, beneath the new waves – unseen, unknown.

She didn't have any money, only a few hundred dollars that Bells had conveniently left in the glove box for her. But that didn't matter now, she'd find a place. She'd find a hidden town in some hills or wooded area where she would wait tables and sleep in a loft above the café or just down the street.

She'd take a bus from the next town and get a message to Bells where he could find his car. This mess would soon be over. The police would realize she had nothing to do with those deaths, sooner or later, and she could merge back into society again – though she didn't know if she ever would.

K pulled out a small pocket dictionary she'd purchased at the convenience store attached to this truck stop café and started choosing words for one last story.

When it was finished she paid for her tea and dry toast and stood to leave, but ran into someone as she tried to stand. He smelled like...like freedom, somehow. Like the whole outdoors. She stood completely and looked up to see his face, it was Moses.

She was so close and he was standing so very near, she had to reach out and put her arms around him, then his arms immediately fell around her. There they stood, her hair in his face, her face buried in his neck and shoulder, both breathing in the other the way people do when they won't ever see eachother again. And any questions she'd ever had disappeared right then. They weren't answered, just gone – used up or ran away or whatever happened, happened. It didn't really matter, they were gone and she bathed herself in the glory of their absence, and K pulled him even closer.

She could tell by the way they hugged, it was the kind of hug you didn't want to ever let go of – it was the kind of hug that proved you were a part of something, something bigger than yourself. It meant that there was a God, a oneness, that we were all somehow connected. Because it was right there, so close, no distance really, just there.

And to let go of it meant that you might be lost again. That if you let go of that hug you might fall eternally, falling and falling making spirals as you did so. Spinning out of control and dazed you'd soon forget that hug ever existed, that you were ever a part of something bigger than yourself. Then falling would become your life, your new life in a bottomless pit. With that hug long gone there'd be no reason to grab onto anybody and hug like that ever again, because you'd have forgotten the essence of it, the value of it. And that scared her. She didn't want to let go, she wanted that hug to last a lifetime.

If there were anyway to make it last a lifetime she certainly would have. She would have given anything to stay – anything she had. But she had nothing, nothing to give and nothing to barter, nothing with which to bribe God to make it last forever. Soon it would have to end and the thought of that made her heart melt.

And her heart did melt. Her heart melted and became a stream as it flowed from her and lost itself in his streaming heart. Together they floated down that stream like first time lovers in an old fashioned tunnel of love. Both waited in a breathless excitement for the first dark curve or corner where the other would be mysteriously close by and a kiss would happen, just happen – the magical kiss of a tunnel of love. A kiss that would seal into permanence what they'd just found in that hug a moment before – Love – God – Eternity.

But that moment never came. That dark place in the tunnel of love never arrived and soon the ride was over and there were people standing all around waiting for them to get off, waiting for their turn in the tunnel of love, and Kathy pulled away.

His face looked pained, it always did, like he had lost something. His face was always searching for something lost and Katherine of the St. Catherine Catherines loved that about him.

"I tried to find you," he said. "I heard through the grapevine at Bells' what was going on, I...I tried to find you and...help or something. I thought maybe..."

She raised her arm to slow his flow of words that were moving fast and jagged like there was some urgency there – there wasn't, not anymore.

"It's okay, I'm fine," K said. "Whatever happened had to happen, I guess. I guess I had to go through Hell just so I could come out on the other side into someplace new, someplace better than I was before, so I could discover that Hell isn't permanent, you can leave it any time and start again."

She looked solemn and turned her sloe-eyes toward the floor hearing the gentle truth that slid out of her.

"I can see it now, the Hell in other people – the Hell they've created. That's how compassion arises, I think, because you can see the pain you once had. The same hurt, the same guilt, the same longings manifesting in others in different ways.

"I don't think it comes because people try to be compassionate or giving, because they may have read in some book that that's how you get to Heaven or that's what spirituality is. It's a natural consequence of knowing yourself. Compassion isn't the path that leads to Heaven. On

351

the path, you stumble across it.

"I guess only because I've known that Hell that now I can see it – because I've lived it. I don't know, it doesn't matter anymore."

And then his face looked even more pained.

"No, you haven't," he said. "You haven't known Hell and you never could. You could never know it because you don't know what it's like not to touch you. You don't know what it's like not to feel *you* beside you. Day after day my existence will be not being with you. You will never experience Hell, because you don't know what it's like not to see your face."

With that he reached up to touch her – the thumb, the palm, the fingers, just a touch, a brush against her cheek. But she turned away, a tear streaming down her face as she did. She didn't know what to say. How crazy it was that he should feel that way, how crazy and stupid and damn him for saying it. And damn her for feeling the very same way. Soon she'd have to leave – she'd have to go and discover life on her own without Bells or Moses or any other safety nets. She'd have to tight rope across the rest of her life without anybody underneath ready to catch her if she fell. And how much harder it would be seeing him one last time, knowing how he felt about her.

"We all create our own Hell, Moses," Katherine said. "I'm nobody special. I'm no one at all. I've seen into myself and I'm not even there. You created who you want me to be – you created who you want *you* to be. And I created who I want me to be and who I want others to be. But I'm not that, no one is. I'm not any of those things. I'm not spectacular, I'm not a savior for you or for anybody else, and I don't have any existential purpose besides just being here. And that's the best gift of all. So now I have to de-create myself – back into what I was before I became me, back into emptiness – so I can again be accepted into Heaven. He doesn't want us how we create us. He wants us how He created us: pure, innocent, and free."

She handed him the yellow pages on which she had scribbled her latest story. And she handed him the small dictionary that held millions of stories yet unwritten – countless dramas that would have to unfold by themselves, lines of a play that could not be touched or changed by K. But K was dead, anyway. K would not be changing anything anymore, and she didn't know who was there that remained – someone different, undefined. Those words had yet to be put down on paper, the words of the rest of her life, she'd have to discover them on her own – one word at a time.

"If you see my father, give him this." And Katherine of the St. Catherine Catherines simply walked away.

He looked bewildered and confused as Katherine turned to leave, like a lost child. So childlike he looked in that truck stop among the worn and hardened truckers that Katherine wanted to pick him up and drop him in a pasta salad somewhere far away with lots of swirling pasta, olives, green peppers and onions to keep him company. There he could live out his existence lightly covered in olive oil and sprinkles of fresh-ground black pepper.

But she would feel sorry for him there too, in his new home of noodles and diced vegetables. Because no one says, "I love you," when you're in pasta salad. No one even thinks it. And sure, a green onion might cuddle up real close now and then or he may find himself one day smothered in mayonnaise, but she hoped he would not mistake these things for love, because they wouldn't be. The next moment that green onion may cuddle up to a plump ripe tomato, and he may realize that the mayonnaise will just cling onto anything. It isn't anybody's fault.

But she would wish him well – would wish him luck in his world of pasta salad. Because everyone she'd ever known at least deserved that – a wish of luck.

He sat down to finish the toast and read the note she'd handed him. It seemed to be a letter from an abandoned child who had lost his father and lost his way, then became free in spite of it.

Sadness abounds removing the stones of my steened heart. For where I've been I recede, and to where I go, I go nowhither. I carried inertly the weight of my desires. I carried my fears like gallows around me. I carried anger to protect me. I carried jejune beliefs to martyr me. I breathed the noxious fumes of St. Catherine's Flower a seculum.

Losing you, father, I thought I'd lost all – that nothing lie before me. I held fast to losing you and it was my kismet to share with the world – share my blame, share my suffering. I was a child and you left me here alone. And the world you taught me and the world the world showed me I thought to be muscle, but was only filigree.

But, now, I've found a postern, a way back to the idyllic land that lie pre-existent to the pregnable world I've lost. It is a postern inside that leads me childlike without hope or fears or dreams of something more. It is the idyllic world that lie all around me each moment that I could never see before. It is the world where I am home, where I'm a filial being amongst all filial beings – the rocks, the trees, and the stars.

So I go to re-cast myself into something free. I go to re-cast myself into something unblemished and unbounded by thoughts and motives and me. And I will secundate the soil with what I find there. And I will madefy the land with my new understanding.

I go in search of all and in search of something beyond all. I go in search of you and I go in search of me – for you are the father and I am the son. You are the flame, and I am the light. And I am but a shadow in the imagination of a non-existent God that I created.

— Katherine

Even with the top down it was hot and suffocating, but somehow she welcomed it. None of that mattered, "All my past pains, just made up – created," she thought. "All my fears, all my emotions, not even real."

The world looked like a desert in places with its dead grasses and dry dirt, but that was okay too. "From death comes life," thought K. "Death is just a soil for something new to grow, it's all the same so why do I fear one and cling to the other? A circle is life and death, and where one begins and one ends it's hard to tell – impossible. I'm growing into death right now and, all along, death has been forming into me – forming into life."

She drove west on I-70 watching the traffic, or the lack there of. A car some distance ahead signaled to change lanes, even though no one was within 500 yards of him. But he signaled anyway, as if he had to, as if those broken lines in the road wouldn't yield to him if he did not. As if they were real, like walls that would lower and rise with his activated blinkers – impassible walls.

But they weren't, they were just lines on an open road – suggestions, really. And Katherine saw how easily she could slip right over them and not even feel them. Even though they were laws she could slip right over those too. The lines were a made up thing on a made up road and she didn't need any of it. She didn't need roads or guidelines or laws and she didn't need other people's religions and beliefs.

Everything that she knew in this world had been made up, made up by people not even as smart as herself. She had been driving in their lanes, in their made up beliefs and religions her whole life. And there were so many of them she never stopped to think that they weren't real, she just kept changing lanes searching for the right one, the right road or lane to take her to wherever it was she wanted to go – but they never did.

And if they were all man-made, then none of them were real. Nothing she'd ever known was real. And with a little more courage than slipping over painted lines on a made up road, she could slip right off the road altogether. She could slip into something new, into something un-known, into something not created by man. She could slip into freedom.

K continued to drive in the muggy heat. The perspiration that gath-ered on her sunburned skin gave her a subtle glow – almost like light. It was almost like the light that drenched Jesus in the stained-glass win-dow. Not enough light to read by or enough that anybody else would notice – but still pretty good.

Kathy smiled inwardly as she sped through Kansas with the wind in her hair. The road was straight but narrow, just like that gas attendant with the smile like Bells had said. It was too narrow for fantasies of being Jesus. Too narrow for fears of Satan. It was too narrow for thoughts and dreams and desires. Too narrow to take people with you, to take the world with you. You can't change the world for its sake. Maybe the world needs to be messed up right now, maybe that's all part of the plan. Maybe, only out of confusion can come clarity – only from noise can silence be understood. The world was free. To see it, you had to be free.

Something inside of her shattered just then. It shattered like the glass and marbles in her back alley had months ago. Only now the pieces of her weren't like marbles and they weren't scattered in fragments among broken glass in a dark alley. They were more like butter – and soon they began melting in the hot June sun.

The pieces of K melted – melted into the air and became one with it. Then they melted farther, blending with the earth beneath her and the grass at her side. She melted into the valleys and the hills and the trees and, for one brief moment, she felt one with them, one with them all – from the ground to the sky and beyond. Katherine was gone, gone to everywhere – and the wheat fields waved her goodbye.

Acknowledgements

My deepest thanks to Iveth Jalinsky for her beautiful artwork and her unselfish help and direction. My appreciation to all the friendly people at Leathers Publishing for their work and patience. Thanks to Dr. Alan Aldawood and his website, www.assyrianlanguage.com, for his help in translating the phrase, "Dear God, don't send me back," into Aramaic. I would like to express my gratitude to OSHO for his many enlightening books and tapes (Rebel Books) and his words, *A long tale told by an idiot full of fury and noise signifying nothing,* which is an excerpt used in chapter one. Izach Bentov for his work, *Stalking the Wild Pendulum* (Destiny Books). Deepak Chopra and his audio series *Magical Mind/Magical Body* and the scientific research and findings that are raising the level of consciousness on this planet. My love and thanks to my mentor, Eva White Desert Eagle, and to all the masters — Jesus, Buddha, Lao tzu and many others — who have graced this earth with their guidance and teachings. To my mother, who encouraged me to pick up my discarded manuscript and continue writing.